"But just so ___ ___ ___ business with ___

He hadn't asked h___

She shot him a fiery look. "I may be a woman, but I can do my job."

"I never said you couldn't," Justin said.

"Good, I'm glad we got that out of the way."

He had to admit he was intrigued by her spunk. Obviously she'd battled her way up against men in her field who probably thought she was incompetent based on her sex.

Either that or they were sidetracked by her good looks.

He wouldn't make that mistake.

And he certainly couldn't or wouldn't allow her pretty little face to distract him. He was here to solve the case of the missing girls.

Nothing else mattered.

Especially the little zing of lightning that had sizzled between them when he'd brushed her hand earlier.

COLD CASE AT CARLTON'S CANYON

BY
RITA HERRON

MILLS & BOON

Published in Great Britain 2014
by Mills & Boon, an imprint of Harlequin (UK) Limited,
Eton House, 18-24 Paradise Road, Richmond, Surrey, TW9 1SR

© 2014 Rita B. Herron

ISBN: 978 0 263 91345 3

46-0114

Harlequin (UK) Limited's policy is to use papers that are natural, renewable and recyclable products and made from wood grown in sustainable forests. The logging and manufacturing processes conform to the legal environmental regulations of the country of origin.

Award-winning author **Rita Herron** wrote her first book when she was twelve, but didn't think real people grew up to be writers. Now she writes so she doesn't have to get a *real* job. A former kindergarten teacher and workshop leader, she traded storytelling to kids for writing romance, and now she writes romantic comedies and romantic suspense. She lives in Georgia with her own romance hero and three kids. She loves to hear from readers, so please write her at PO Box 921225, Norcross, GA 30092-1225, USA, or visit her website, www.ritaherron.com.

To my own hero, Lee—love you always,
Rita

Prologue

Kelly Lambert did not want to die.

But the kind person who'd offered to give her a ride when her car broke down outside Sunset Mesa, the person she'd thought had saved her from walking late at night on a deserted road, had turned into a maniac.

A rancid breath bathed Kelly's cheek, and her stomach roiled.

"Please…" she begged.

Her words died as fingers tightened the belt around her throat. Rocks skittered beneath her feet as her attacker dragged her nearer the edge of the canyon and forced her to look at the rocky terrain below.

Hundreds of feet loomed between her and the ground. Even if she managed to land on the level part between the jagged rocks, the impact of the fall would kill her.

"That's where you belong," the crazed voice murmured. "Mean girls like you deserve to die."

"No, please stop," she gasped. "Why are you doing this to me?"

A pair of rage-filled eyes glittered back at her. "You know why."

Kelly's lungs strained for air as the leather dug into her throat.

But she didn't know. Didn't know why this person wanted her dead. Why anyone would want her dead.

Her attacker shoved her closer to the edge. Kelly's legs dangled over the canyon like a rag doll's.

She struggled again, desperate to escape, but whatever drug she'd been given had made her too weak. Fighting back was impossible. She couldn't move her hands, couldn't lift her arms, couldn't kick at all.

Tears streamed down her cheeks as the fingers dug deeper into her throat.

"No…"

Her attacker's bitter laugh echoed through the canyon, and Kelly gagged.

Her life flashed in front of her like a series of movie clips. Her mother braiding her hair before she'd died. Easter egg hunts, Christmases, proms and dance lessons.

High school boyfriends and college parties and…her upcoming wedding…

She had her dress picked out. The flowers…roses…the bridal shower she was supposed to have today.

And the honeymoon…a honeymoon she would never get to have.

Panic seized her, and pain knifed through her chest as the belt crushed her windpipe. Nausea mingled with terror and her head spun.

Then the lush green of spring faded into black as death came for her.

Chapter One

Sergeant Justin Thorpe was a loner. Always had been. Always would be.

It was the very reason he was good at his job. No entanglements to tie him down or distract him.

He stared at the decomposed body of the girl floating in Camden Creek, trepidation knotting his gut.

He had a hunch this was one of the girls who'd disappeared from Sunset Mesa, although the medical examiner would have his work cut out to identify what was left of her. Other girls who'd gone missing from various counties across Texas were possibly connected, as well.

Too many girls.

At first no one had connected the disappearances, but Justin had noted that the women went missing in the spring, and that one fact had raised a red flag in his mind.

So far though he hadn't found any other connection. But he would. He just needed time.

Dr. Sagebrush, the ME who'd also worked a case in Camden Creek involving a serious bus crash that had killed several teenagers a few years back, stooped down to study the body as two crime techs eased it onto the creek bank.

Thick trees shaded the area so the ME shone a flashlight over the corpse while crime techs searched the water and embankment with their own.

A tangled web of hair floated around the young woman's

mud-streaked face, bones poked through the already decaying skin and there were bruises, scratches and teeth marks from animals that had picked at her marred body.

She was still clothed, her thin T-shirt torn and tattered, her jeans full of holes and layered in dirt.

The CSU team snapped pictures while Dr. Sagebrush adjusted his glasses and examined her.

"How long do you think she's been dead?" Justin asked.

"Hard to say yet," Dr. Sagebrush replied. "The temperature of the water could have slowed down decomp, but I'd guess a while. Maybe a couple of months."

Two young women had disappeared within that time frame.

Justin eyed the creek, scanning the terrain up and downstream with his flashlight. "You think she was dumped in the creek or floated in from the river?"

"Don't know." Dr. Sagebrush shrugged, his eyes narrowed as he pushed strands of wet hair away from the girl's face. "Look at this." The ME pointed to the bruises on her neck.

"She was strangled," Justin said, frowning at the angry, inch-wide red lines cutting into the woman's throat. "Looks like the killer used a belt."

Dr. Sagebrush nodded. "Probably the cause of death, but I can't say for sure till I get her on the table. If there's water in her lungs, she might have been alive when she was dumped."

Justin's stomach knotted as an image of the girl fighting for her last breath flashed in his eyes. The current in this part of the creek was strong, the rocks jagged. Kayakers and raft guides trained on the wider, rougher sections as practice for the river. If she was alive, she'd probably been too weak to fight the current and save herself.

But the doctor lifted the girl's eyelids, and Justin saw petechial hemorrhaging and guessed she'd died of strangulation.

One of the crime techs dragged a tennis shoe from the muddy bank, then compared it to the girl's foot. "Could have belonged to her. We'll bag it and see if we find anything on it."

Justin nodded. "I'll look around for forensics although, like you say, she probably wasn't killed here."

Justin knew the drill. He'd been working homicide cases, hunting serial killers and the most wanted, for ten years now. Nothing surprised him.

Yet a young woman's senseless murder still made sorrow fill his chest.

He walked over to the edge of the river and studied the foliage, then dipped deeper into the woods to search for any sign that the girl had lost her life nearby.

If they found hair or clothing, even a footprint, it might help track down the killer.

Anxiety twitched at his insides. Only two of the girls who'd gone missing in the past few years had been found. One dead; the other had run away.

But there was no sign of the others. No notes goodbye. No phone calls or ransom requests.

No bodies, making the police wonder if the girls were alive or dead.

So why had this woman's body been dumped where it could be found?

Were the cases connected? And if so, were any of the other young women still alive?

SHERIFF AMANDA BLAIR sipped her umpteenth cup of coffee for the day while she skimmed the mail on her desk. An envelope stamped with the high school's emblem and a sketch of the canyon for which the school had been named, Canyon High, caught her eye, and she ripped it open.

The invitation to her high school class reunion filled her with a mixture of dread and wariness.

She'd moved away from Sunset Mesa after her senior year when her father had been transferred. Having grown up with a Texas Ranger for a father, she'd known she'd wanted to follow in his footsteps and work in law enforcement. And there had been nothing for her in Sunset Mesa. No best friend. No boyfriend.

No one who'd missed her or written her love letters or even asked what her plans were for the future.

Truthfully she'd been glad to move. She'd always been a loner, a tomboy, more interested in her father's cases than joining the girly girls at school with their silly obsessions with makeup, fashion and boys.

She'd chosen softball and the swim team over cheerleading and dance competitions and had felt more comfortable hanging out with guys at sports events than having sleepovers or going shopping with her female peers.

The one event that had colored her entire high school experience was her classmate Carlton Butts's death.

Juniors in high school were not supposed to die. They especially weren't supposed to commit suicide.

Regret, that she hadn't been a better friend to him and sensed how deep his depression ran, taunted her. She'd had nightmares about him plunging to the bottom of the canyon for years. In fact, most people in town now referred to the canyon as Carlton's Canyon—some even called the high school Carlton Canyon High.

Occasionally she even thought she heard Carlton whispering her voice in the night. Calling to her for help.

Begging her to save him from himself.

Only she'd missed the signs.

Guilt had driven her to search for answers, only none had ever come. Then young women had started disappearing across Texas, two from Sunset Mesa, and she'd felt her heart tugging at her to return to the town. To find out what was happening to them because she'd failed to help her own friend.

When the deputy position had come available in Sunset Mesa, she'd requested it. Sheriff Lager had been a friend of her father's and had handpicked her for the job.

Then she'd realized that he was suffering from dementia. He eventually admitted he knew he had issues and told her his plans to retire.

Sighing, she stuffed the invitation to the reunion back in the envelope, doubting that she would attend. There was no one from her class she particularly wanted to see.

But what if one of them knew something about one of the missing women? It was her job to find the answers.

What better way to get the scoop than at an informal gathering where everyone was supposed to be friends?

Intrigued by the idea, she tucked the invitation into the calendar on her desk, then added the date to her phone calendar. Plans that week included a family picnic on Friday, then a cocktail party and dance on Saturday night.

No family or husband for her.

Memories of watching Julie Kane and Thurston Howard sharing the prom king and queen dance drifted back, reminding her how much of a wallflower she'd been.

You're not an eighteen-year-old geeky kid anymore, Amanda. You're sheriff.

And a stupid high school reunion was not going to turn her back into the shy awkward girl she'd once been.

The door to the front of the sheriff's office suddenly burst open, and Amanda looked up.

Larry Lambert, the manager at the local bank, rushed in, his normally friendly face strained with worry. A younger man, probably in his late twenties, stood beside him, his hair spiked as if he'd run his hands through it a dozen times. Tension vibrated between the men, a chill in the air.

Amanda stepped from behind her desk. "Mr. Lambert—"

"You have to help us, Sheriff Blair," Mr. Lambert said. "My daughter Kelly…" The six-foot-tall man broke down, tears streaming from his eyes. "She didn't come home last night."

Amanda's heart clenched. Spring was supposed to be a time of renewed life. Instead, a woman had gone missing just as one had every spring the past few years. A woman she'd gone to high school with. A woman close to her own age.

Which broke the pattern. Kelly was older than the teens who'd disappeared.

Still, could she have met foul play?

Was Kelly dead or could she still be alive?

JUSTIN WAS ANXIOUS for the results of the autopsy and crime scene findings, but his early-morning phone call had gone unanswered. Suspicious that the girl was one of the missing ones from Sunset Mesa, he decided to visit the sheriff and give her a heads-up.

He'd spoken to her after Sheriff Camden from Camden Crossing had conferred with her about the disappearance of his own sister and Peyton Boulder, two girls who'd disappeared after a fatal bus crash seven years ago. At first they'd thought the cold case might be related to the string of missing persons from Sunset Mesa, but they'd discovered it wasn't.

Dry farmland and terrain passed by him as he veered onto the highway toward Sunset Mesa. He'd heard that the town had gotten its name because of the beautiful colors of the sunset.

Radiant oranges, reds and yellows streaked the sky, painting a rainbow effect over the canyon that was so beautiful it made him wish he was here on vacation, not hunting down a killer. But he never stayed in one place more than a few days and wouldn't get attached to this town either.

He navigated the road leading into Sunset Mesa, wondering about the new sheriff in town.

He'd met her once and she seemed okay, but he hoped to hell she wasn't some flake, that she had a head on her shoulders and would cooperate with him. Police work was his life, and he couldn't tolerate a law officer who wasn't committed to the job.

A small ranch pointed to the north; then the sign for Sunset Mesa popped into view. Like every other small town he'd been in, the town was built on a square. The buildings looked aged, a Western flair to the outsides, a park in the middle of town with small local businesses surrounding it.

The sheriff's office/jail/courthouse was housed at the far right, an adobe structure painted the same orange that he'd noted in the sunset.

Early-evening shadows flickered along the pavement as he parked in front of the building, climbed out, adjusted his Stetson and strode to the front door. When he'd first spoken to Sheriff Blair, he'd formed an image of her in his mind.

Her voice had held a husky note, a sign she was probably mannish. Then he'd met her briefly once and realized she was nothing like he'd pictured.

Even the sheriff's uniform hadn't disguised her curves and beauty. Not that it mattered what she looked like. He was here to do a job and nothing else.

The dead girl's face taunted him, and he straightened and opened the door. Getting justice for that victim was his priority.

Once he'd failed at his job and it had cost another young girl her life. He wouldn't fail this time.

No one would stop him from finding answers.

Wood floors creaked with his boots as he entered, the pale yellow walls and artwork reminiscent of days gone by. A row of black and white photographs of the town and the canyon lined one wall, rugged landscapes on another.

A noise echoed from the back and he frowned. Heated voices. A man's.

No, two men's.

He rapped on the wall by the door leading to the back. A minute later, a woman appeared wearing the sheriff's uniform.

A petite woman with lush curves and hair the reddish-brown color of autumn leaves. Amanda Blair. Rather—Sheriff Amanda Blair.

Her looks sucker punched him again.

Eyes the color of a copper penny stared up at him, a strained look on her pretty face.

"Hello, ma'am." He tipped his Stetson. "I don't know if you remember me, but I'm Sergeant Justin Thorpe with the Texas Rangers."

She looked him up and down, and for the first time in his life, he wondered if he came up lacking. Not that he usually cared about a coworker's opinion of him, but something about her made him want her admiration.

But her look gave nothing away. "Yes, I remember."

He couldn't tell from her tone how she meant the comment. But it didn't sound good.

"Did someone call you about coming here today?"

He frowned, confused. Maybe she'd already heard about the body they found. "No, I needed to talk to you about the missing-persons cases."

"You heard about Kelly Lambert?"

"Kelly Lambert?" Justin tried to remember the names of all the women on the list so far, but hers didn't ring a bell. Had she received word about the identification of the body before he did?

Her expression clouded. "The girl who just disappeared last night. Her father and fiancé are in my office now."

Justin's gut clenched. That explained the raised voices. But Kelly Lambert wasn't the woman they'd found in the creek because that woman had been there for months.

Which meant Kelly Lambert might still be alive.

Dammit, he and Sheriff Blair needed to find her before she ended up dead like the poor woman they'd just dragged from the water.

Chapter Two

Amanda fought the fluttering of awareness that rippled through her at the sight of the tall, dark handsome Texas Ranger. She'd met him briefly once when Sheriff Camden from Camden Crossing had asked them to confer on the case involving his sister, and had finally managed to get his sexy image out of her head.

Now he was here. Back. Planning to work with her.

And dammit, she needed his help.

She couldn't help but stare at him. He towered over her, his massive shoulders stretching taut against his Western shirt, his green eyes a surprise with his dark coloring and black hair.

She sized up his other features—a chiseled jaw, a crooked nose that had probably been broken and a cleft in his chin. By themselves his features didn't stand out, but the combination made him look tough, rugged, a man not to be messed with.

But that silver star of Texas shining on his shirt reminded her that he was here on business.

Amanda never mixed business with pleasure.

She'd worked too hard to overcome the stigma of being a female in a man's world and couldn't backtrack by getting involved with a coworker.

No one would respect her then.

"I think we'd better start over," Sgt. Thorpe said. "You said that another woman has gone missing?"

Amanda nodded. "Kelly Lambert. She didn't make it home last night and her father and fiancé haven't heard from her."

"So it's been less than twenty-four hours," Justin said. "Too early to file a report."

Amanda shrugged. "Actually it has been over twenty-four hours. They haven't heard from her since early yesterday morning. She's been planning her wedding, and she never made it to her bridal shower this afternoon. A shower she was supposedly excited about."

"Maybe she got cold feet and ran off."

"It's possible, but I didn't get the impression that she was that kind of girl from her father and the groom-to-be." Amanda folded her arms. "Wait a minute. If you didn't know about Kelly, why are you here?"

The Ranger's mouth twitched. "Because the body of a young woman was discovered in Camden Creek earlier."

Amanda's chest started to ache. "You think it's Kelly?"

Suddenly a choked sound echoed from behind her, and Amanda spun around to see Mr. Lambert and Kelly's fiancé standing at the doorway.

"You found her?" Mr. Lambert asked in a broken voice.

Kelly's fiancé, Raymond Fisher, paled. "Please, God, no…"

Amanda tensed and glanced at Sergeant Thorpe. "Mr. Lambert, Mr. Fisher, this is Sergeant Thorpe with the Texas Rangers. Sergeant Thorpe?"

Justin motioned with his hands as if to calm the panic in the men's eyes. "We haven't identified the young woman yet, but it's not Kelly. The ME thinks this woman has been dead a couple of months."

Relief mingled with horror on the father's face. "But you think this woman's death is related to Kelly's disappearance?"

The fiancé stumbled forward and sank into a wooden

chair near the desk. He leaned his head on his hands, a sob escaping. "You think she's dead, don't you?"

Amanda's mind raced to the missing-persons file on her desk. Carly Edgewater and Tina Grimes were recent names on the list. It could be one of them.

But compassion for the fiancé and Kelly's father forced her to keep her thoughts to herself. She was a professional. Her job was to find answers.

She also needed to keep these men calm. If Kelly had been abducted, they might know something to help track down the kidnapper.

"It's too early to tell that," Amanda said as she patted Fisher's shoulder. "Right now all we know is that Kelly didn't show up for her bridal shower and hasn't contacted you. Maybe Sergeant Thorpe is right and Kelly just needed some time alone. She could have ducked out to think things over before the wedding."

"No," Fisher said with a firm shake of his head. "Kelly wouldn't run out on me. She loved me, and I loved her. She was excited about the wedding."

"He's right," Lambert said. "Kelly wasn't the kind of girl to run out on anyone. She was dependable, smart, had a good head on her shoulders." He fumbled with his phone and angled it toward Amanda. "Even if she did want some time, she would have told one of us. I've called her at least fifty times in the last few hours, and she hasn't answered or returned my calls."

"I've called her, too," Fisher said, pulling out his phone. "I've sent dozens of texts, too, but she hasn't responded. I even drove by her place, but her car wasn't there and neither was she."

"What kind of car does she drive?" Amanda asked.

"A red Toyota."

"Do you know the license plate?"

He jotted it on a sticky note from her desk.

Sergeant Thorpe exhaled. "I understand your concern,"

he said in a gruff voice. "Sheriff Blair and I will do everything we can to find your daughter."

Amanda's lungs squeezed for air as she stepped aside to call her deputy, Joe Morgan. She quickly explained the situation.

"Drive around and see if you can find Kelly's car. She drives a red Toyota." She gave him the license plate and hung up. Maybe if they located Kelly's car, they'd find a clue as to what had happened to her.

She just hoped they found her alive.

JUSTIN CONSIDERED THE circumstances and knew he had to remain objective and treat this woman's disappearance like he would any other case. To assume Kelly had been abducted by the same person who'd killed the woman in the creek—and possibly a half dozen others who still hadn't been located—was too presumptuous.

Making assumptions was dangerous. It could lead him to miss important details and send him on a wild goose chase.

After all, it was possible that Kelly's fiancé was lying. He and Kelly could have had a major blow-up and she could have run off. She might need time to compose herself before contacting her father. Or hell, she might be off planning some sort of surprise for her fiancé.

But his gut instincts told him they were dealing with a serial criminal who'd been kidnapping female victims for nearly a decade and would continue until he was stopped.

But he wouldn't be doing his job if he didn't explore every option. With the publicity surrounding the ongoing missing-persons case, someone could use the disappearances as a smoke screen to cover up a more personal murder.

Like a fiancé getting rid of his girlfriend if she decided to call off the wedding…

"Sheriff, why don't you take Mr. Lambert back for coffee while I talk to Mr. Fisher for a few minutes?"

Amanda's gaze met his, questions looming, but separating victims or suspects was customary, so she nodded.

"Come on, Mr. Lambert. I'll start the paperwork for the missing-persons report." She glanced at Justin and Fisher. "Would you guys like coffee?"

Fisher shook his head no. "I don't think my stomach could handle it right now."

"Coffee would be good," Justin said. "Black."

Her brows rose a second as if to say that she wasn't his maid, and his mouth quirked. After all, she had offered.

She led Lambert back through the door to the back and returned a moment later with a bottle of water for Fisher and a cup of coffee for him.

"Thanks," he said with a small smile.

A zing of something like attraction hit him when her hand brushed his as she gave him the mug. Her mouth twisted into a frown as if she'd noticed it, too, and she jerked her hand away and rushed back to talk to Lambert.

Sweat trickled down Fisher's forehead. Was he simply upset about Kelly's disappearance or was he nervous because he was hiding something?

Justin took a sip of coffee, surprised at the taste. Most law enforcement workers could handle a gun but didn't know a flying fig about how to brew decent coffee.

Amanda Blair could do both. Intriguing.

"Mr. Fisher, how long have you and Kelly been together?" Justin asked.

Fisher gripped the water bottle with white-knuckled hands. "We knew each other in high school but didn't date until our senior year. We got engaged last Christmas. Kelly took some time after high school to do some mission trips, then decided to get her teaching degree. She just graduated with a masters in education and is looking for a teaching job."

"What do you do?"

Fisher shrugged. "I'm a financial consultant. I just started with a new company in Austin. We were moving there after the wedding."

"Any problems between you and Kelly lately?"

Fisher shook his head, his leg bouncing up and down. "No."

"No recent fights? Arguments over where you'd live? Money?"

"Not really. We get along great."

"Do you and Kelly live together?"

Fisher nodded. "We moved in together our senior year of college."

"What did her father think about that?"

"At first he wasn't too happy," Fisher admitted. "But eventually he realized it made sense. And when a student was raped on campus, he said he was actually relieved she was living with me." Emotions made his voice warble. "He felt like she was…safe."

Justin heard the guilt in Fisher's tone. He understood that kind of guilt. "Do Kelly and her father get along?"

Fisher frowned up at him. "Yeah, why?"

"Anything you tell us about Kelly might help us find her," Justin hedged. "So they get along?"

Fisher nodded. "Kelly's mother died a while back and they went through a rough patch. That was before we started dating. But they were both grieving and adjusting. She said the last two years they've been close."

"How did her mother die?"

"Cancer. She was sick a long time."

So no skeletons that might suggest Lambert had hurt her. "What did Mr. Lambert think about the upcoming marriage?"

Fisher sipped his water again. "He was cool with it."

"But?"

Fisher shifted in the seat. "At first he wanted her to wait until we saved more money. But Kelly assured him we'd be okay."

"You have money?" Justin asked.

Fisher shrugged. "A little. I had scholarships for college, so I saved over the summers, enough to get us by until we both started getting paid."

"So Mr. Lambert gave you his approval?"

"Yes," Fisher said a little curtly. "Now why all these questions? Shouldn't you be doing something to find Kelly?"

"We will do everything possible, Mr. Fisher. But like I said earlier, we need to know everything about Kelly to help us." He hesitated and decided to take another tactic. "You said Lambert wanted you to wait until you were more financially sound. Did he offer to help out financially?"

Fisher shook his head. "He was paying for the wedding, but not our rent or bills. I saved the money for a down payment on a house."

Admirable of the young man. Maybe he had nothing to do with Kelly's disappearance.

If not, he'd have to look at the father.

And the serial killer they had nothing on yet…

"How are Lambert's finances?" Justin asked.

"He owns the bank in town. How do you think?"

"Being a smart ass won't help you," Justin said, his voice sharp with warning.

The young man shoved his hands through his hair. "Sorry, I'm just nervous and worried." He gripped the edges of the seat. "I feel like I need to be out looking for Kelly."

He'd check Lambert's financials just to verify Fisher's statement. If Lambert needed money and had an insurance policy on his daughter, that would provide motive. Although, the man appeared visibly distraught.

If he had money and had nothing to do with her disappearance, and this case wasn't related to the serial kidnapper, Lambert might receive a ransom call.

Fisher unscrewed the lid of the water bottle and swallowed a huge gulp.

"What about arguments between the two of you?"

A slight hesitation. "We disagreed over seating my uncle Jim next to her cousin Monique 'cause Monique will talk your head off. But that was small stuff. Nothing she'd leave me over."

"How about exes?"

His lips tightened, and he glanced to the doorway. "Her old boyfriend, Terry, called her a couple of weeks ago. Said he heard she was getting married and wanted to talk to her before we tied the knot."

"Talk to her about what?" Justin asked.

Fisher shrugged, dropped the water bottle cap, then bent over and picked it up.

"She didn't tell you?" Justin pushed.

"No," Fisher said. "I asked her if she still had feelings for him, but she laughed it off."

"Did *he* still have feelings for her?"

Fisher toyed with the bottle cap, rolling it between his fingers. "She said he didn't."

"But?"

Fisher scowled. "But I saw a text he sent her and it sure as hell sounded like he did."

The anger in the man's tone raised Justin's suspicions. "Did she agree to see him?"

Fisher squeezed his eyes shut for a moment, then opened them and took another sip of water. "I don't know. When she didn't come last night, I thought…maybe she'd met up with him."

Justin pushed a pad in front of Fisher. "I'll need his name and any information you have on him."

"I don't know his number, but his name is Terry Sumter."

"When was the last time you saw or spoke with Kelly?" Justin asked.

Kelly's fiancé dropped his head into his hands with a pained sigh. "Yesterday morning for breakfast," Fisher said. "We had waffles, then she said she had a million things to do—a dress fitting, shopping for bridesmaids' gifts…. The list went on and on." Regret flickered in his eyes. "I was only half listening. I had no idea it might be the last time I ever saw her."

Justin gritted his teeth. The man's fear sounded sincere. So did his guilt.

But were his guilt and fear real because he was afraid of getting caught?

"She was supposed to come home last night?"

He nodded, rubbing at his eyes. "I called and called and finally I received a text saying she was going to spend the night with one of her girlfriends."

"Which one?"

"Betty Jacobs," he said. "But when I called Kelly this morning and she didn't answer, I tried Betty and she said Kelly hadn't been there."

Justin would pull everything he could find on the ex-boyfriend as well as Kelly's phone records and Fisher's.

Three different scenarios skittered through his head.

Kelly could have met with the old boyfriend, decided she'd made a mistake in agreeing to marry Fisher and run off with him.

Or Sumter could have tried to convince her to leave with him and either kidnapped or killed her when she'd refused.

Or Fisher could have discovered Kelly had feelings for her ex, and fought with her about it and killed her…either accidentally or in a fit of rage.

THE PHOTOGRAPH OF Kelly Lambert went up on the wall beside the other girls'.

All such pretty young women with their glossy hair, perfect lips and orthodontist-enhanced smiles.

All girls who were ugly on the inside and deserved to die.

One by one they would leave this world.

And everyone at Canyon High would know the reason why.

Chapter Three

Amanda knew dividing Lambert from Fisher was the best police approach. If one of them was lying or hiding something, separating them was the best way to get the truth. But she didn't intend to let the Texas Ranger run her investigation or tell her what to do.

Lambert glanced back at the door, a nervous twitch to his eye. "What's that Ranger talking to Raymond about?"

"Just asking routine questions, finding out background information," Amanda said. "It helps us to get a full picture of Kelly. He'll want to know who her girlfriends are, when Raymond last saw her, anything that might help us figure out what happened to her."

"We have to find her," Lambert said. "I lost my wife... I can't lose Kelly. She's everything to me."

Sympathy for the man made Amanda squeeze his shoulder. "I promise you, Mr. Lambert, that Sergeant Thorpe and I will do everything we can to find Kelly and bring her back home to you."

He glanced down and studied his knuckles. Amanda narrowed her eyes. He had scrapes on his left hand. A gash on his right.

She casually poured them both coffee, an image of Kelly at eighteen, when she'd won an award for most congenial, flitting through her head. "What happened to your hands?" she asked, sliding a cup of coffee in front of him.

He twisted his fingers in front of him, his expression odd as if he didn't remember. "I...was nervous when Kelly didn't call me back. Went outside and cut some wood. Guess I scraped my knuckles."

His explanation was feasible. Still...his daughter was missing.

"We'll need a current photograph of Kelly for the media and to spread around to other law enforcement agencies."

Lambert reached inside his back pocket, removed his wallet and pulled out a picture of her. Amanda's heart tugged. Kelly had always been pretty and had grown more so. She was dressed in a print dress, her long hair sweeping her shoulders.

"That was a couple of months ago," Lambert said. "I took her to the club to discuss the wedding plans."

Amanda studied the photo, thinking of her own father and how special their father/daughter dates had been.

Worry gnawed at her for Kelly's sake.

If Kelly had been kidnapped by the same person who'd abducted the other girls, they might never find her.

Kelly could already be dead.

Or...she could be suffering now.

Which meant every minute counted.

Amanda claimed the chair across from Lambert. "You say your daughter was excited about the wedding. Does she have any enemies that you know of?"

Another wave of sadness washed over the man's face. "No. Everyone loves her. In high school she was voted most congenial and most likely to succeed."

Amanda had forgotten about the most-likely-to-succeed award.

"In college, she worked on the school newspaper," her father continued, "then earned her degree in English and planned to teach high school. She's been applying for jobs and hopes to start in the fall."

Amanda cradled her own coffee cup, aiming for a casual tone. "You and Kelly get along?"

"Oh, yes," he said. "Kelly means everything to me." He coughed. "When we lost her mother, she was depressed, and at first I thought what the hell am I going to do with a teenage girl? But then...we both missed Janelle and..." His eyes flooded with tears as he looked up at her. "She's a good girl, Sheriff. A good girl."

"I know she is," Amanda said, battling to keep her compassion at bay so she could ask the tough questions that needed to be asked. The first rule of police work was not to let your emotions get involved. Her father had taught her that, God rest his soul.

"How about her and Raymond?" she asked. "Do they have any problems?"

"Not that I know of," Lambert said. "She adores him. I wanted them to take it slower, not marry till they had more money in the bank, but they insisted on going ahead, said they'd survive on love."

Amanda grimaced. She'd never been that naive. Maybe because she didn't believe in love. Her mother and father sure as hell hadn't loved each other.

"Mr. Lambert, what about you? Do *you* have any enemies?"

His eyes widened. "You think this might be about me?"

"I don't know, but we have to look at all the possibilities."

He stood and paced across the room. "No, I mean I own the bank and a few people got angry at me because I turned down loans. Filed a couple of foreclosures. But that's business."

Money was a powerful motivator. "I'll need their names."

He paused in his pacing, smoothing his hands down his suit jacket. "All right."

"Tell me about your financial situation," she said. "Do you have a large portfolio of investments? A big savings account?"

"You mean in case we receive a ransom call?"

"Yes," Amanda said. "That's a possibility." In fact, it would be preferable to the alternative. If someone called with a ransom request, they might have a chance of saving Kelly and catching the kidnapper.

"I have some money," he admitted. "Enough."

"Enough that someone might take your daughter to force you to pay them off?"

He paled. "If this is about money, I'll pay whatever they ask."

"Just make me a list of all of the people who might have a grievance against you," Amanda said. "We'll also need a list of all of Kelly's friends so we can talk to them."

"Of course."

He headed back to the chair but paused by the whiteboard in the corner. Amanda tensed. On the back of that board she'd tacked photos of all the missing women from the past ten years. She didn't want him to see them. "Mr. Lambert, sit down and—"

But a strangled sound escaped Lambert as he flipped it over. He staggered back, shaking his head in denial.

Anger hardened his voice when he spoke. "You haven't found any of those girls, have you? And you're not going to find my Kelly either."

Fear mingled with anger in Amanda's chest. She'd inherited the ongoing case from Sheriff Lager, but Kelly had gone missing on her watch. An image of the pretty woman's face taunted her. Kelly was her age, vibrant, planning her wedding. Looking forward to having a family and a long life ahead of her.

But her life might already have been cut off because some crazy maniac had targeted her.

And Amanda didn't have a clue as to who it was.

What if Lambert was right? What if she couldn't save Kelly in time?

JUSTIN TAPPED THE notepad in front of Fisher. "Make a list of the groomsmen in the wedding and their contact information for me."

Anger blazed in Fisher's eyes as he realized the implication. "What the hell? Kelly's father and I came here for help, and now you're treating me like a suspect. You think I had something to do with Kelly's disappearance?"

Justin forced his voice to remain level. The majority of missing-persons cases wound back to the family members or close friends. The fact that a string of females around the same age had gone missing was suspicious, but he couldn't discount anything at this point.

"I didn't say that. But it's important for us to talk to everyone who knew Kelly," Justin said. "Female and male friends included. Maybe one of them saw or heard something that could be helpful."

Fisher shot up, glaring at Justin. "That's bull. You want to ask them how Kelly and I got along. If I was jealous enough of an old boyfriend to hurt her."

"I will ask that, but it's routine," Justin said. "The first thing we do in an investigation is to clear family members and friends. Oftentimes, someone may tell us some detail to help us—it might be something small that you don't even think is important."

He motioned to the chair. "Now, if you want us to find Kelly, sit down and make that list. You're wasting valuable time."

Fisher's gaze met his, his eyes stormy with emotions and red rimmed from crying or lack of sleep. Maybe both.

Finally he released a heavy sigh and dropped back into the chair. "All right. But I love Kelly, and I'd never do anything to hurt her."

Justin studied him, wondering how he'd react if he was in this man's shoes. He'd be tearing apart the office, demanding answers, pushing for the police to comb the streets.

Ready to kill the person who'd stolen his fiancé.

That is, if that was what had happened.

Fisher took the pen and began to scribble names and phone numbers.

Sheriff Blair and Lambert appeared in the doorway, Lambert's face ashen.

"Mr. Lambert, Mr. Fisher, I'd like your permission to put a trace on your phones," Sheriff Blair said. "Just in case Kelly calls, or you receive a ransom call. We'll also need to look at Kelly's computer and phone records."

"Of course, whatever you need," Fisher said.

"Yes, check the phone records and computer." Lambert's eyes cut toward her. "Do whatever you have to do. Just find my daughter."

Sheriff Blair nodded, but she looked worried. "I'll get Kelly's picture in the missing-persons database and on the news right away. Hopefully someone saw something and we'll get a lead."

Fisher shoved the paper into Justin's hands. "Call us if you find her."

Fisher huffed, then strode out the door. Lambert glanced at Justin. "I saw the pictures of those other young women back there. I don't want Kelly's picture up there. I want you to find this bastard."

Justin shook the man's hand. "Yes, sir. We'll do everything we can."

"Do more than that," Lambert said sharply. Heaving a labored breath, he followed Fisher out the door.

Justin couldn't blame the man for being angry and frustrated. He didn't even know Kelly Lambert, and he felt like kicking something.

"I didn't mean for him to see the wall of photos," Sheriff Blair said.

"He's scared," Justin said. "Do you believe him?"

Sheriff Blair winced and gestured toward the notepad in her hand. "I think he loves her. I want to look at his financials. He turned down some folks for loans this year, had to foreclose on a couple of people."

Justin arched a brow. "So this could be about money?"

"We'll see if he receives a ransom call," Sheriff Blair said. "Maybe someone he angered decided to get their loan money from him after all."

"Revenge is a powerful motivator," Justin agreed.

"What about the fiancé?" she asked.

"He seems sincerely distraught, but it could be an act. Apparently a former boyfriend contacted Kelly recently and wanted to see her before the wedding. He or Fisher could have had a jealous streak."

Sheriff Blair nodded. "I'll have my deputy pull financials and talk to the folks at the bank." She made the call while he finished his coffee.

"I have a list of Fisher's friends and the ex's name and phone number," he said as she turned back to him. "I'll request Kelly's phone records and access to her computer as well as Fisher's and the ex's."

"Sounds like a plan," Sheriff Blair said. "At least a beginning."

"Maybe we'll find something at Kelly's place."

"Let's go," Sheriff Blair said. "You can make the phone calls in the car."

Justin followed her outside, then climbed in the passenger seat as he removed his phone from the clip on his belt. "Sheriff, if we're going to work together on this case, let's start by getting on a first-name basis."

An almost panicked look flickered in her eyes, making him wonder why she was so wary. Was it him personally or his badge that she didn't like?

"All right," she said tightly. "But just so you know, I don't mix business with pleasure."

He hadn't asked her to.

She shot him a fiery look. "I may be a woman, but I can do my job."

"I never said you couldn't," Justin said. Although her statement told him far more about her and her past than she probably realized.

Amanda chewed her bottom lip as she started the engine. "Good, I'm glad we got that out of the way."

He had to admit he was intrigued at her spunk. Obviously she'd battled her way up against men in her field who probably thought she was incompetent based on her sex.

Either that or they were sidetracked by her good looks.

He wouldn't make that mistake.

And he certainly couldn't or *wouldn't* allow her pretty little face to distract him. He was here to find Kelly Lambert and to solve the case of the missing girls.

Nothing else mattered.

Especially the little zing of lightning that had sizzled between them when he'd brushed her hand earlier.

THE DATES FOR the tenth reunion had been posted on the marquis in front of the high school. The members of that graduating class were returning to town to celebrate their accomplishments.

They would be partying and drinking and rehashing their fun times. The pep rallies. The football game wins. The dances. The bonfires by the canyon.

Graduation night.

They'd all be happy and laughing, bragging about their accomplishments and careers and awards. Showing off their wives and husbands, and their children.

Back together for the first time in years.

Which would make it easier to find the next ones who had to die.

Chapter Four

Amanda silently chided herself. She shouldn't have blurted out that comment about being able to do her job.

But Sergeant Thorpe's—*Justin's*—suggestion that they use first names felt somehow intimate. Friendly.

Tempting.

Because he was the first man she'd met in years that made her want to forget her vow to not get involved with a coworker.

But doing so would mean losing his respect.

And holding on to her respect was all she had. She'd had her heart broken too many times to trust it to someone again.

Her own mother had left her father because she'd said he was married to the job.

Amanda was like her father—married to the job, too.

Justin phoned his superior to request phone records for Kelly, her father, her fiancé and her ex-boyfriend, then disconnected.

"Your father was a Texas Ranger, wasn't he?"

His question took her by surprise. "How did you know?" Had he researched her?

"I saw his photo on the wall at the central office. He was a hero."

She focused back on the road to keep her emotions at bay. He'd been gone for five years, but his death had left a hole in her heart. "Yeah, he was."

"He died saving a little boy?"

She nodded, proud of her dad. Yet his death had left her alone.

Still, she had to understand his devotion. She was just as dedicated to the job as he had been. In fact, she'd always wanted to be just like him.

But she didn't want to talk about personal things, especially her own life, with Justin. So she remained silent as she turned onto the highway leading to Kelly Lambert's apartment.

She parked in front of the complex and searched the numbers. Then she and Justin walked up to the door together. Fisher had already arrived, and he let them in, his expression guarded.

"I don't know what you think you'll find here," he said. "But go ahead and look around."

Amanda noticed boxes stacked everywhere. "You were moving?"

Fisher nodded. "We bought a house near my new job. The movers were supposed to come tomorrow." His voice cracked. "We wanted to get moved in before the wedding. I was supposed to start work the day after we returned from the honeymoon."

He ran his hand over one of the unclosed boxes, which held kitchenware, looking lost for a moment as if he didn't know what to do.

Justin cleared his throat. "Where's Kelly's computer?"

Fisher gestured toward an oak desk in the corner, and Justin addressed Amanda. "I'll take a look at it if you want to search the place."

She agreed and started in the kitchen while he slid onto the desk chair and booted up Kelly's laptop.

Fisher paced for a minute, then seemed startled when his phone jangled. "It's my new boss," he said before stepping onto the back patio to take the call.

Amanda opened kitchen cabinet doors, noting they were

empty, then checked the drawers. Kelly must have already packed up all the silverware and kitchen supplies. She scanned the counters, finding a bottle opener and a basket with a couple of envelopes inside.

A power bill and a bank statement. She pulled out the statement and skimmed the summary of transactions. The grocery store, household bills, a payment to the florist and wedding caterer made two days before, all signs Kelly had planned to go through with the wedding.

Her account still held five thousand dollars, not enough money to warrant anyone kidnapping her for it. Then again, Kelly's father was the one with the big bucks.

Satisfied the kitchen held no answers, she headed toward the couple's bedroom, but the refrigerator caught her eye. A magnet held Kelly's wedding invitation. Beside it, she noticed the invitation to the high school reunion.

The reunion was the week before Kelly's wedding. The timing meant that a lot of Kelly's friends would be in town. That is, if she still kept up with them.

Unlike her, Kelly had been a popular girl.

Moving on, she stepped into the bedroom. An eight-by-ten of Kelly and Fisher sat atop the dresser, the couple embracing for a romantic kiss. Both looked completely happy and in love.

More boxes were stacked on the floor. Most of the dresser drawers were empty, but when she opened the closet door, she found a long white satin wedding gown hanging inside. Pearl buttons ran down the back to the waist, where the gown flared with yards of organza and lace.

It was a beautiful dress; Kelly would have been a beautiful bride.

Had her life been cut short?

So far, her fiancé and father's stories held up. She wanted to talk to Kelly's girlfriends next. They might be able to shed some light on whether or not Fisher or Kelly's father should be considered suspects.

If they were innocent, she couldn't afford to waste too much time on them. Every minute she did meant whoever had taken Kelly was getting away.

If the same person who'd abducted the other missing girls had abducted Kelly, what was the reason? How was he choosing his victims?

Studying victimology could help her find answers.

Her cell phone buzzed, and she saw it was her deputy, Joe Morgan, so she snatched it up. "Hey, Joe, what's up?"

"I got your message and will look into the bank angle. But I found Kelly Lambert's car."

"Where?"

"Off of Old River Mill Road."

Amanda held her breath. "Was Kelly in it?"

"No," Deputy Morgan said. "The car had nosedived into a ditch. There are skid marks on the road as if another car ran her off the road."

Possibly a hit and run? "I'll call a crime unit to lift the tire prints."

"I'll wait here for them. By the way, Kelly's car is red, but I noticed pewter gray paint on the side. I'll have them take samples of the paint, too."

"Good work, Deputy. Did you search the area for Kelly? Maybe it was a hit and run and she's lying hurt nearby?"

"I already looked. She's not here, Sheriff. But I found a blood trail leading from Kelly's car to the edge of the road."

Amanda's lungs constricted. So Kelly was hurt.

If the driver had forced Kelly to go with him, where was she now?

JUSTIN SEARCHED KELLY'S computer, first skimming her emails, but nothing stuck out. Some were personal correspondence with friends, excited chatter about the upcoming wedding, which confirmed Fisher's story that Kelly still planned to marry him. Other notes were to vendors finalizing arrangements for the ceremony and reception. The emails were dated the day before Kelly disappeared, also confirming that she didn't have plans to run away or cancel the wedding.

A note from someone named Eleanor Goggins asked if she was going to attend their high school reunion. Two others girls, Anise Linton and Mona Pratt, had joined that discussion, all commenting on how much fun it would be to get the old crowd back together again.

He checked Kelly's financial records. Her account was stable, most transactions relating to household bills and payments to vendors. A large deposit had been added a week before from her father, which was probably meant to cover wedding costs. But nothing out of the ordinary.

He checked her browser history and found wedding decoration and planning sites, then noted she'd researched teaching positions and had sent applications to three different schools in Austin.

All confirmed Fisher's story.

Next he examined her social media sites. She was on Twitter, Facebook, Goodreads and Pinterest. He took a few minutes to skim her posts and discovered she liked mystery books and classics, and she tweeted and wrote Facebook posts about her job search and upcoming nuptials. Photos of her and Raymond filled her Facebook page: shots of them at college football games, hiking and sipping drinks on a beach vacation trip and engagement pictures taken at a mountain cabin.

Nothing suspicious. In fact, everything supported Fisher's and Lambert's story.

Amanda appeared from the bedroom, her expression troubled.

"What?" he asked.

She glanced at the patio and seemed to be relieved that Fisher was outside. "My deputy called. He found Kelly's car."

Justin arched a brow. "Where?"

"Out on Old River Mill Road." She lowered her voice.

"It appears someone ran her off the road. Deputy Morgan found blood on Kelly's seat and paint from another car on her Toyota."

Justin's jaw tightened. "Someone intentionally ran her off the road, then abducted her?"

"That's what it looks like. I'd like to go out to the site and see for myself."

"Do you know what kind of car hit her?"

She shook her head. "No idea of the make and model yet, but it was pewter gray. Hopefully the crime team can tell us more from the paint sample."

"What kind of car does Fisher drive?"

"A black Lexus. There was a picture of him and Kelly washing it." Amanda's expression softened. "They were laughing, covered in soap bubbles."

He closed the laptop. "I didn't find anything out of the ordinary. Let's go see her car, then we'll question the ex-boyfriend. If he drives a gray car, he might be our perp."

Justin's nerves jangled. He hoped to hell the ex was the man they were looking for. They might have a chance of getting Kelly back.

If not, she might disappear for months or years...or forever...like some of the other victims. And her father and fiancé might never know what happened to her.

AMANDA AND JUSTIN left with a word to Fisher that they'd keep him updated. Without even discussing the situation, they silently agreed not to tell him about finding Kelly's car.

"What kind of car does Mr. Lambert drive?" Justin asked as Amanda drove toward Old River Mill Road.

"A silver Mercedes."

"So far, Fisher and Lambert's stories hold up."

A sense of trepidation overcame Amanda. The image of Kelly's wedding dress hanging in the closet taunted her. Poor Kelly...she had been excited about her wedding.

And now it may never happen....

Night shadows hovered along the road, a breeze stirring the dead leaves and blowing them across the road like tumbleweed. Everything was dry this time of year, the temperature chilly.

Deserted land and cacti sprang up, making her wonder why Kelly would have been driving out on Old Mill River Road. Where had she been going?

Had she been planning to meet someone? If so, whom? And why out here in the middle of nowhere?

Amanda wound down the road, noting signs for rental cabins along the creek a few miles to the north, but spotted her deputy's car ahead and pulled over.

"Why was she out here?" Justin asked as he climbed out.

She grabbed two flashlights, tossed him one, then retrieved her camera and a crime kit. "I was thinking the same thing." She spotted the red Toyota down in the ditch. Her deputy walked toward them along the side of the road. "How did you find the car?" she asked.

"Tracked her cell phone." Deputy Morgan held it up in his gloved hand. "Battery was low but it was still on."

"Did you check her call history?" Amanda asked.

Deputy Morgan glanced at the Ranger, then at her, and Amanda realized she hadn't introduced them. She quickly covered the bases and tugged on gloves

"Did you get anything from the phone?" Justin asked.

"Her last call was to a girl named Anise yesterday about ten a.m. After that, there were dozens of messages from the father and fiancé."

Amanda took the phone and clicked to listen to a couple. Each message sounded more frantic and panicked. "Fisher and Lambert both sound worried," she said.

"What about texts?" Justin asked.

Amanda checked the text log. "There's a couple from Fisher. He sounds more and more anxious as the night wore on."

"Fits with what they told us," Justin commented.

She continued to scroll backward. "Wait a minute. There's one here that came in yesterday about nine a.m. It's from someone named Hailey. She asked Kelly to meet her at the cabins I saw on that rental sign. Something about a surprise for her fiancé."

"We need talk to her. She may have had the last communication with Kelly."

Amanda handed him the phone. "You want to call the tech team and have them trace that text?"

"Sure." He glanced at the deputy. "Did you call a crime team in?"

The deputy nodded. "They should be here any minute."

Amanda tried to recall if there had been a girl named Hailey in their graduating class, but couldn't remember one. Maybe Kelly had met her at college instead of in Sunset Mesa. Or maybe she was a real-estate developer or event planner.

She shone her flashlight along the road as she followed the deputy, her heart hammering when he pointed out the blood trail near the car. Determined not to miss anything, she snapped photos of the car and surrounding area.

The driver's door was open, the front window and bumper smashed, the weeds and brush crushed from the weight of footsteps—or a body.

Blood dotted the front seat and was splattered against the steering wheel.

But there was no sign of Kelly anywhere.

Except for her purse. It had fallen onto the floor, probably from the impact. Kelly's lipstick, wallet and compact, along with other miscellaneous items, had spilled across the mat.

Amanda picked up the wallet and looked inside. Driver's license and credit cards intact. Fifty dollars.

Not a robbery.

A cold chill swept over Amanda.

Judging from the blood on the seat, Kelly *was* injured. Although the amount of blood didn't suggest there was enough blood loss to kill her.

But since had been injured, she'd been easy prey, too weak to fight off a kidnapper or escape.

Chapter Five

Justin looked up and down the road while he waited on tech to check the phone records. The tire marks needed to be photographed and studied—maybe they could discern the make of the car from the prints.

They might even get lucky and find some forensics evidence to help them.

The tech cleared his throat into the phone. "Okay, the text from Hailey came from a burner phone. There's no way to trace it or find out who bought the phone."

Dammit. "What about the fiancé's phone records? He said he received a text from Kelly saying she was going to spend the night with a friend named Betty Jacobs. But Betty said she didn't come over. Did Kelly call the Jacobs girl?"

A slight hesitation, and Justin heard computer keys tapping, then the tech's voice again. "There's a minute-long call to Betty Jacobs yesterday morning about eight o'clock but nothing afterward."

Justin headed down the hill to examine the car, noting the blood splatters on the car door. "Check Fisher's records."

Another moment passed and Justin reached Amanda. She and the deputy were searching the trees surrounding the car crash.

He shone a flashlight and caught sight of a partial footprint to the left, then noticed a stiletto heel stuck in a patch of weeds.

"Sergeant Thorpe," the crime tech said. "I just examined Fisher's phone and you won't believe this, but the text that Kelly received from the burner phone—well, that came from the same phone that sent the message to Fisher saying Kelly wouldn't be home that night."

"So Kelly didn't send that text to Fisher. The kidnapper did."

"I'm surprised Fisher didn't notice that the number was different."

"There are a lot of their friends in town for the reunion. Maybe he thought she was using one of their phones."

The facts clicked together in Justin's mind, giving him a good idea of what had happened. He told the tech to keep looking at all the phone records from Lambert, Fisher and Kelly, then hung up and called out to Amanda.

"Did you find something?" Amanda asked.

"A shoe." He pointed to the foliage and Amanda raced over, then knelt to examine it. Her gaze shot back and forth from the car door to the wooded area and the trail leading back up to the road. "The driver hit Kelly's car, then dragged her from the crash and forced her into his vehicle."

Justin nodded. "That's how it appears." He sighed. "I just talked to tech. The text Kelly received asking her to meet this person Hailey was sent from a burner phone."

"So Hailey could be a fake name?"

"Probably. The text Kelly supposedly sent Fisher saying she was going to her friend Betty's house for the night—that was a fake. It came from the same burner phone."

Amanda ran a hand through her hair. "I assume there's no way to trace the number?"

"Afraid not. The texts were obviously a setup."

Amanda winced. "Someone lured her out here with the intention of kidnapping her and doing God knows what else." She gestured toward a shoe in the bushes. "The question is why? And if he went to all that trouble to lure her out here, then our unsub targeted her specifically."

He admired her logical mind. "That's true. Up until now, we wondered if the victims were chosen randomly. Now we know that someone specifically wanted Kelly Lambert."

"But who?" Amanda asked. "So far Mr. Lambert and Fisher seem to be telling the truth."

"Let's talk to Kelly's ex-boyfriend," Justin said. "Maybe he wanted her back badly enough to kidnap her."

AMANDA CONSIDERED HIS comment. It was a very likely scenario. Especially if Terry Sumter was obsessed with Kelly and was desperate to win her back.

Although they had to look at all angles.

"That's a possibility," Amanda said. "But there's another one that might fit."

"What?"

"Maybe another woman wanted Raymond and decided to get Kelly out of the way so she could move in on him."

Justin frowned. "We'll talk to Kelly's girlfriends and Fisher's male friends. Hopefully one of them can give us some insight there." He gestured toward the car. "We might luck out and find a print or hair that the kidnapper left behind."

The sound of an engine rumbling echoed from the road, and they all climbed the hill together. The crime van rolled up, techs spilling out with their kits. Amanda thanked the deputy and asked him to go back to the office to man the phones and follow up with the bank. By now, Kelly's photograph should have gone into the system. They could only hope someone would call in with a lead.

Another officer brought a police dog and began to search the area.

The head of the unit introduced himself as Lieutenant Gibbons, then pointed out the other workers by name. A redheaded woman named Petunia, a chubby guy named Larry, a rail-thin guy with funky glasses named Jerry, and the guy with the dog was named Herbert.

Amanda explained what they'd discovered so far and

handed over the shoe to be bagged and sent to the lab. The next hour they scoured the area in case Kelly had somehow escaped, but finally even the dog team gave up.

"We'll take a cast of the tire print," Lieutenant Gibbons said. "And we're going over the car with a magnifying glass."

"Run the paint sample through the lab, too," Justin said. "Maybe the paint was custom designed for a particular vehicle."

Amanda checked her watch. "It's getting late, but I want to talk to the bridal party tonight." She removed her phone and called Fisher. "Call everyone in the bridal party and tell them to meet me at the sheriff's office in half an hour."

"Did you find something?" The young man's voice warbled as if he'd been crying.

"We'll talk when Sergeant Thorpe and I get there."

She disconnected, dread balling in her stomach. Telling Kelly's fiancé and father about finding the car would be difficult. If they'd harbored any shred of hope that Kelly had simply gone away for a couple of days without telling anyone, the fact that they'd found blood would kill that hope.

JUSTIN STUDIED THE group of young men and women who'd gathered in the sheriff's office.

Kelly's bridesmaids and best friends—Betty Jacobs, Anise Linton, Mona Pratt and Eleanor Goggins—were all attractive women in their twenties, although they were a mixture of brunettes, blondes and redheads.

Any one of them could have fit the profile of the victims who'd disappeared over the past few years. So far, the kidnapper didn't have a clear MO, which had slowed down the police in connecting the cases in the beginning. Normally a kidnapper/killer chose a certain type—all blondes or brunettes or redheads. This unsub seemed to have no preference for hair color or body type or career choice.

Except they were all in their twenties and lived in Texas.

The groomsmen looked nervous as they settled into wooden chairs. Glenn Cates, Danny Latt and Lance Stephens. Fisher's father, Ernie, was his best man. He stood beside his son with a hand on his shoulder.

Raymond looked even worse tonight, the strain of the day wearing on him.

Amanda had taken Kelly's father to her back office to explain to him about the car and their findings.

"I want to thank you all for coming," Justin said.

"Did you find Kelly?" Mr. Fisher asked.

Justin shook his head. "I'm afraid not, but we did find her car."

Raymond jerked his head up, while the others exchanged worried looks.

"Where?" Ernie Fisher asked.

"Out on Old River Mill Road."

"What was she doing there?" Raymond asked.

Justin crossed his arms, studying the group for their reactions—any sign that one of them might have already known about the car. But he caught no signs of deceit on their faces, only fear and worry.

"Our tech department studied the text that you received, Mr. Fisher, the one supposedly sent from Kelly telling you she was spending the night with Betty."

"What do you mean, 'supposedly sent'?"

"That text was sent from a burner phone, not from Kelly's. That same phone sent a message to Kelly asking her to meet the person out on Old River Mill Road."

Fisher's eyes widened in horror. "Someone tricked her into going out there."

"That's correct," Justin said. "Whoever it was sent you that text so you wouldn't realize she was missing until the next day."

Gasps and whispers rumbled through the group.

Raymond paced over to Justin, his breath wheezing out. "Someone kidnapped her, didn't they?"

Justin swallowed hard. "It appears that way, Mr. Fisher. Her car had been run off the road and crashed into a ditch. We also found a small amount of blood on the seat."

Fisher's face crumpled with emotions. "Oh, my god. She might be…hurt or gone like those other women."

"Why her?" Betty sniffled. "Everyone loved Kelly."

"She was so excited about her wedding," the girl named Anise said.

"And the shower," Eleanor added. "She couldn't wait to open the gifts and move into her new house."

Mona wiped tears from her eyes and hugged Eleanor.

Justin made a low sound in his throat. "Can any of you think of anyone who'd want to hurt her?"

Heads shook, mumbled nos resounding through the room.

Amanda stepped from the back with Lambert who looked ashen-faced and distraught. "Please call us if you receive a ransom call," Amanda told him.

He nodded, then looked over at Fisher, pain radiating from him. "Have you heard anything, Ray?"

Raymond shook his head no, rubbing his bleary eyes.

Amanda rapped her fingers on the desk. "Ladies, I'd like to talk to you individually."

"And I need to interview each of the groomsmen," Justin added.

Mumbled questions and protests sounded.

One of the groomsmen, Lance, scowled, his arms crossed. "You think one of us had something to do with her disappearance?"

"That's not what we're implying," Amanda cut in. "But you might be able to help in some way. You *do* want to find Kelly, don't you?"

Heads nodded, everyone piping up with yeses.

Amanda gestured toward Betty. "Why don't you come

with me first? It'll only take a few minutes." She glanced at Justin. "You can use my deputy's office to interview the men."

Justin pointed to Raymond. "Come on, Fisher. There are a couple of things I need to ask you."

He looked sullen and nervous, but he followed Justin without a word. The moment Justin shut the door, the man turned on him.

"What else can I tell you? I don't know who would send me and Kelly that text. And I sure as hell don't know anyone who'd want to hurt her."

"Mr. Fisher," Justin said calmly. "You mentioned that Kelly's ex wanted to get back with her. I'm going to question him as soon as I leave here. But Sheriff Blair pointed out another possibility."

He hesitated, giving the man a moment to gather himself. "Do you have any ex-girlfriends that were unhappy about your upcoming wedding? Maybe a woman who wanted to get back with you? Or…one who wanted to get revenge against you for some reason?"

Fisher lapsed into a stunned silence for a moment, then dropped into a chair. "I don't think so…I mean…"

"What? There's something you remember?"

Fisher wiped his forehead with the back of his hand. "I did break up with my old high school girlfriend to date Kelly our senior year," he said. "But that was ages ago. Renee wouldn't do anything to hurt Kelly because of it. She's probably already moved on."

Justin gritted his teeth. "Where does she live?"

"Some small town north of here." He drummed his fingers on his knee, thinking.

"What else?"

A muscle twitched in his jaw. "She chaired the committee to set up the high school reunion."

"So she knew you were coming back for the reunion and

to get married. Perhaps facing old friends as a single woman while you two were together pushed her buttons?"

"I suppose it's possible," Raymond said, but he didn't sound convinced. "Although I just can't imagine it."

Justin shoved a pad toward him. "Write down her contact information. You do have it, don't you?"

A sliver of guilt streaked the man's face. "Yes, but only because of the reunion."

"Right." Justin watched him scribble the woman's name and number, wondering if she could have kidnapped Kelly out of jealousy.

Now they had two feasible suspects, Kelly's ex-boyfriend and Raymond's ex-girlfriend.

His cell phone buzzed, and he checked the number. The ME.

"Excuse me," he told Fisher. "I have to take this. You can go now."

Fisher looked wary as he rose. "You want one of the other guys sent in?"

Justin nodded. "Send Lance Stephens in." He'd start with the guy who'd protested. Maybe he had a reason to avoid questions.

His phone buzzed again, and he hit Connect. "Sergeant Thorpe."

"It's Dr. Sagebrush. We have an ID on the body from the creek."

Justin held his breath. "Her name?"

"Tina Grimes."

"Cause of death?"

"As we first thought—strangulation," Dr. Sagebrush said.

"Any sign of sexual assault?"

"No, she wasn't raped," Dr. Sagebrush said. "But there's something else that I noticed, too. I don't know if it's important, but her high school class ring was clenched in her hand."

Justin frowned. What did that mean? That she'd hung on to it as the perpetrator killed her?

Or had the perp put it in her hand as part of his signature?

THE YEARBOOK ANNUALS were all laid out in a row on the top of the dresser. All the high school students from Sunset Mesa, four years' worth of girls who'd finished their high school degrees and gone on to plan their futures.

They were successful, married, had babies of their own. One had even become a reporter who covered human-interest stories.

Ironic since the little witch had no sense of humanity.

Flipping the pages brought a sea of females who had to be punished.

Amanda Blair's photograph stood out. She wore her soft-ball uniform and was grinning from ear to ear after Canyon High won a game. Amanda had been a star player.

She'd also abandoned one of her friends, someone who'd needed her.

And she would have to be punished for that.

But there were others that had to be dealt with first. So many others...

Who would receive their penance next?

Chapter Six

Amanda had interviewed two of the bridesmaids and had two more to go. According to Betty and Anise, Kelly adored Raymond, couldn't wait until the wedding and had intentionally planned the ceremony the week after the reunion so more of her former classmates could attend.

Amanda studied Mona, aware the blonde was only a year younger than her. Man, she felt old. More worried about dead bodies and missing young women rather than a date for a mani-pedi and highlights.

"Did you sense any trouble between Raymond and Kelly?" she asked.

Mona twisted a strand of hair around one finger, reminding Amanda of the way the girl had behaved in high school. She had been a huge flirt. All the guys had eaten out of the palm of her hand.

"They were the perfect couple," Mona said, blinking back tears. "I just can't believe she's missing."

"Raymond said that her ex-boyfriend, Terry Sumter, wanted to get back with her. Did she mention that to you?"

Mona sighed. "She said she'd heard from him, but she blew it off. Every couple of years, Terry would contact her and want to get together, usually after he'd broken up with his latest conquest."

Amanda zeroed in on her word choice. "Conquest?"

She laughed softly. "Yes, he could be charming, and

whenever he met someone new, he poured it on. But eventually the girls wised up to his slick moves. When he was drinking, he had a bad temper. That's why Kelly broke up with him years ago."

"Did he ever get physical with her?"

Mona chewed her lip as if debating on her response.

"Mona, just tell me the truth. If you think he might have hurt Kelly, I need to know."

"Well, I can't imagine him actually kidnapping her. But Eleanor and I saw him at the pub one night and he was pretty trashed, mouthing off. He blamed Kelly for his life falling apart."

"Falling apart?"

"Yeah, he said she abandoned him, and after that his life spiraled downhill. Said he'd always wanted her. When she left, he didn't trust women anymore."

"That was her fault?"

"According to him, yeah. I think he just lost his job, too."

"What did he do?"

"He worked in construction. I think he was about to get his own crew," Mona said. "But it wasn't Kelly's fault he lost his job. He probably got caught drinking at work."

Maybe. Still, if he blamed Kelly for his problems, maybe he had come after her to get revenge.

JUSTIN FINISHED INTERVIEWING the three groomsmen, not surprised that the men all vouched for Raymond. After the phone call identifying Tina Grimes, he was looking for a connection between the two cases. But Raymond had no reason to hurt Tina.

Of course the killer, Raymond or otherwise, could have murdered Kelly, hoping the police would assume she'd been taken by the same perp who'd kidnapped the other girls.

Glen Cates and Danny Latt had attended high school with Kelly and Raymond as well as Amanda, and, as teens, had formed a bond that, according to them, could not be broken.

Lance Stephens had met Raymond in college and they were frat brothers, making their bond just as tight.

They also adamantly refuted the suggestion that Kelly might have cheated on Raymond, saying she was as devoted to him as he was to her.

Justin had never experienced that kind of devotion and wondered what it would be like.

Dammit, don't let the case get to you. You like being alone.

Sure, occasionally he wanted a hot body to warm him at night. Amanda's sexy face flashed in his mind, and for a brief second, he allowed himself to indulge in the idea of taking her to bed. Stripping her naked and tasting every inch of her. He'd bet his next dollar that she'd be as fiery and passionate in the sack as she was about police work.

But reality interceded. Facing the same woman day after day wasn't on the agenda.

His job was his wife.

And the last thing he needed was to get his butt fired for making advances toward a female sheriff. These days a man had to be careful.

Had to protect his reputation.

He'd learned a long time ago that the only person he could count on was himself.

Turning his thoughts back to the case, he left the men in the front office, strode to the back and knocked on Amanda's door. A second later, she opened it, ushering the young woman named Eleanor out.

"I've finished with the men," he said.

"Let's send them all home and interview Kelly's ex-boyfriend, Terry Sumter."

He agreed, but as his gaze met hers, his earlier thoughts taunted him. He'd tried to ignore those enormous eyes before, but now they intrigued him. Made him wonder what had made her so tough…and sexy at the same time.

An incredibly lethal combination.

She grabbed her jacket, and he dragged his mind away from sex and to the case.

"Thanks for coming in, everyone," Amanda said. "Go home and get some rest."

"Just let us know if you hear from Kelly," Justin said.

Bleak faces stared back, the young women's expressions full of fear as if they realized that they could become a victim just as easily as Kelly had. Especially if this criminal was choosing random women.

But he'd intentionally avoided linking Kelly's disappearance to the others to avoid panic.

Raymond stood on shaky legs. "Please find her, Sergeant Thorpe and Sheriff Blair."

Justin nodded and Amanda murmured she'd be in touch.

Raymond's father guided his son out, talking in a hushed voice, trying to offer words of comfort that Justin was certain fell on deaf ears.

"God," Amanda said as the door closed and they were left alone. "I'm afraid we may not be able to give him what he wants."

Justin gritted his teeth. He knew exactly what she meant. Because Fisher wanted his fiancé back alive, saying her vows at their wedding. He and Amanda both knew that might not happen.

He might be burying her instead.

That is, if they found her body. So many victims had never been found or their bodies recovered.

Amanda rubbed the back of her neck, and he realized she looked tired. Hell, she was probably exhausted. It had been a long day.

And it wasn't over.

Justin propped one hip against the desk. "We need to talk before we go."

A streak of panic darkened Amanda's face, and she poured another cup of coffee. She handed him a cup, then took hers and sank into her desk chair with a resigned sigh as if she knew he had bad news.

"The medical examiner called. They identified the body from the creek. Her name was Tina Grimes."

The color faded from Amanda's face, emotions clouding her eyes for a minute. "Jesus."

"You knew her?" he asked softly.

She nodded, then shoved a strand of hair away from her cheek. She was such a tough woman, but that one gesture seemed utterly feminine and made her look vulnerable.

Made him want to pull her into his arms and console her.

"We went to grade school together, then high school," she said. "Tina was a year ahead of me. The last time I saw her was at her mother's funeral."

And now she would have to attend Tina's.

"Were you good friends?" Justin asked.

"Not really. Tina was popular, more of a girly girl. Me...I was a tomboy."

"You played sports," he said, not surprised.

"Softball and I ran track and was on the swim team." She rolled her shoulders. "My father once asked me if I wanted to try out for cheerleading and I said, 'Why would I cheer for a bunch of boys when I could play my own sport and people could cheer for me?'"

In spite of the somber mood, Justin chuckled. He liked Amanda more and more every second.

Dangerous.

"Her father will be devastated," she said lost in her thoughts.

He simply nodded, giving her a moment to assimilate her feelings.

Finally she gave him a determined look. "Cause of death?"

He tapped his foot. "Strangulation. Killer used a belt. No sexual assault."

She sipped her coffee, mulling over that information. "So the killer is not driven by sex."

"Or he's impotent," Justin offered. "Although it could also suggest that the killer is a female. Strangulation is a common choice for murder with females. It also usually implies that the kill was personal."

Amanda jerked her head up. "Then again, we don't know if Kelly's disappearance is related to Tina's yet. They attended the same school but the first girls who disappeared did so as teens. Kelly is in her twenties."

Justin nodded. But there were too many disappearances for them not to be connected.

They just hadn't found the connection yet.

"We need more information," Justin said. "Who investigated Tina's disappearance?"

"The former sheriff, Lager. But I inherited the files." She rose, reached for a whiteboard on a swivel stand and turned it to face him. His eyebrows shot up. She had methodically listed each disappearance over the past nine years in chronological order along with details of the individual cases.

A map also showed highlighted markings. "The green indicates where the girls lived, the red is where they disappeared from or were last seen."

He studied the map, searching for a commonality. "The first two victims were Melanie Hoit and Avery Portland. Both grew up in Sunset Mesa although Melanie moved to Amarillo after graduation and was last seen at a shopping mall. Tina lived in Sunset Mesa at one time, as well."

He checked the map for Carly Edgewater and Denise Newman. "What about Carly and Denise? They went missing from neighboring counties. Did they ever live in Sunset Mesa?"

Amanda flipped through the file on her desk. "Hmm, Carly did when she was younger. She and her parents moved to Austin when she was fourteen."

"And Denise?"

She skimmed another file, her mouth thinning into a frown when she looked up. "Actually she lived here for a couple of years when she was fifteen. When her parents split, her father took her to a small town east of here."

She tapped the folders. "If all the girls lived here at one time, then Sunset Mesa is the connection."

"It looks that way."

"But why? What about this town triggered the unsub to kill?"

Justin remembered the rest of his conversation with the ME. "Dr. Sagebrush found a high school class ring in Tina's hand."

"So you think—"

"That whoever is taking or hurting these young women targeted your residents, specifically ones who attended Canyon High."

Except that Carly and Denise hadn't.

What the hell was going on?

JUSTIN'S WORDS REVERBERATED over and over in Amanda's head. "You're right, but at least two of the victims didn't go to the high school."

"They must have crossed paths with the perpetrator when they lived in the town though, enough for the killer to track them down."

She'd looked at each victims' past boyfriends, girlfriends and family problems, even issues at a job where the women could have made enemies, but found nothing to link them.

Still, she couldn't deny the truth—they had a serial kidnapper/killer in Sunset Mesa.

Were all the victims dead?

Whoever it was could be holding some of them hostage. But why? If he didn't want sex, what was his motive?

It could be a woman.

Although the percentage of women serial killers was so small that that scenario wasn't likely. But it was possible.

So far, they hadn't had a single person come forward claiming to have seen one of the abductions.

The person who'd taken Kelly had been smart and used texts to lure her to an isolated area. Maybe he'd done that with the others, as well. But he would have had to send the text as someone the girls trusted.

"The high school ring in her hand," Amanda said, thinking out loud. "That must be significant. Most of us stopped wearing them once we went to college."

"Right. That's normal."

"Kelly and Raymond planned the wedding shortly after the reunion so old friends could attend." Amanda's stomach roiled. "And with everyone coming back into town, that means the killer might be looking for another victim now."

SUZY TURNER HAD to die next.

She had been nothing but a two-faced, lying slut. Had stolen other girls' boyfriends and lied to her friends' faces. She'd worn short skirts to show off her long legs and tops that were three sizes too small and dipped down to her navel so all the guys would be drawn to her chest.

Yes, she had wanted attention, had craved having a trail of guys lusting after her and she'd teased them unmercifully, then made fools out of them so everyone in school would know.

The teenagers these days, the bullies, often showed up at school with guns and wiped innocents out while they exacted their revenge on the guilty and the ones who stood by and let it all come to pass.

But that wasn't the plan here. The plan was to eliminate the ones who'd been cruel. The ones who'd humiliated the geeks and nerds, the guys who hadn't been born with muscles and impeccable looks.

Yes, Suzy had been a bad, bad girl.

The door to her house stood open. She had a pool in back. She was out there now, skinny-dipping as if she didn't have a care in the world.

Little did she know that it would be her last swim.

Tonight she would say goodbye to her pitiful life. And all the world would be better that she was gone.

Chapter Seven

Justin didn't like the direction of his thoughts.

He jumped into his vehicle, antsy with the latest revelations. If someone was targeting young women from Sunset Mesa, especially ones around Amanda's age, then she might be in danger.

They needed to figure out the suspect's motive. Were there specific women being targeted or were all of the women who'd attended the local school in jeopardy?

For God's sake, with the reunion in less than a week, the kidnapper/killer could be stalking his next victim. And if that was the case, they would be hearing about another missing woman—or finding another body—soon.

He couldn't let Amanda out of his sight.

But if the unsub was targeting specific females from Canyon High, they needed to figure out the reason he was choosing those particular victims.

"We need to look at all the victims again, detail everything we know about them and see if there's a pattern. If they fit a type."

"They were all popular, well-liked cheerleaders, on the dance team, or color guard." Amanda frowned as she buckled her seat belt.

"So our killer doesn't like cheerleaders or dancers? That seems thin." Justin tapped his foot. "Was there any one male or female who hated all of them for some reason?"

"Not that I can think of. Of course there were typical girl rivalries but nothing that stands out."

"Like the bus accident in Camden Crossing?"

"Exactly. That incident changed the town. There were a lot of angry parents and friends. No one suspected that the soccer coach had been sexually harassing and assaulting the girls on his team."

Justin contemplated her statement as he veered onto the road leading to the apartment complex where Sumter lived. "How about any parties where things went wrong? Drugs? Kids getting arrested? A boy accused of rape by one of the girls?"

Amanda rubbed her temple. "I don't remember anything like that."

She fell silent for a moment, her brow furrowed.

"What?" he asked.

"Now that I think about it, there were two things that happened. Donald Reisling had a bad car accident his junior year and has been in a wheelchair ever since."

"What happened?"

"He was supposedly driving drunk, but there were rumors that his girlfriend at the time was behind the wheel, and that he covered for her."

"What happened to the girl?"

"She moved away after college, but I saw that she'd RSVP'd that she planned to attend the reunion."

"What about Donald?"

"He was pretty broken up. His family was irate. They tried to prove the girl was behind the wheel, but her father hired a fancy lawyer and the case was dismissed." Amanda pointed to a sign indicating the turnoff for the complex. The area was rundown, the concrete building outdated.

Odd for a man who was supposedly a builder himself.

"Donald's in a wheelchair, paralyzed from the waist down. There's no way he's strong enough or physically able to kidnap and kill anyone, then dispose of their bodies without someone noticing."

Justin turned into the parking lot, spotting a few battered cars, a black dusty Jeep, a Land Rover and a few pickup trucks holding supplies, obviously used for work.

"Unless he has a partner."

Amanda's eyes widened. "I suppose that's possible."

"What about his family? They have to harbor ill feelings about the court decision."

Amanda seemed to stew over that suggestion. "I don't know. I haven't seen him in years. But I know Donald's father still lives outside Sunset Mesa."

"And you said the old girlfriend is coming back for the reunion?"

Amanda sighed, sounding distressed. "Yes, her name is Lynn Faust. She's on the committee that organized the dinner dance."

Justin made a clicking sound with his teeth. "Maybe this reunion stirred up resentments. The father could be bitter that his son has spent the last few years in a wheelchair while this girl went on with her life. And now she's throwing it in his face that she's returned to dance at their reunion when he can't even walk."

"My God, you could be right. That might explain why Tina was left holding the class ring. But why kidnap or kill the others? Why not just go after the woman who ruined Donald's life?"

"Perhaps Donald or his father's resentment has grown, so he views all the victims as hurting Donald. After he was in the wheelchair, he probably didn't get many dates." Justin scraped a hand over his chin. "Lynn could be his endgame."

Fear streaked Amanda's face. "We need to warn her."

Justin shook his head. "Let's talk to the father first and test our theory. We don't want to cause unfounded panic."

She nodded although she fidgeted, obviously still worried.

He veered into the parking space, rolled to a stop, then cut the engine. "You said there were two incidents."

She shrugged. "The other was a suicide, a guy named Carlton Butts."

"What happened?"

Guilt flashed in her eyes. "He was a friend of mine," she admitted softly.

"You dated?"

"No. Nothing like that." Amanda bit her bottom lip. "He was a smart kid, but a nerd," she said. "I don't mean that in an ugly way, but he was one of those kids who was teased a lot. I... We grew up together and hung out some because I wasn't popular either."

Justin's gaze met hers. "I find that hard to believe, Amanda."

The vulnerable look on her face moved something inside him. Could she not see how beautiful she was? That he was turned on by her tough, stubborn drive and intelligence?

"It's true," she said, hands clenched. "But the difference between me and Carlton was that he cared and I didn't." Her voice dropped to a pained whisper. "I should have realized how deeply his depression ran. But it was spring and I was caught up in softball and swim meets."

A well of sadness and grief once again assaulted Amanda as she thought about Carlton. He was a classic case of a quiet kid with brains whose gangly body and glasses had caused him to be the butt of jokes from the testosterone-laden guys and silly teenage girls who'd treated him as if he was nothing.

Not that he was the only kid who'd been picked on. Which had made her wonder why he'd chosen suicide when he'd had a bright future and probably would have garnered college scholarships from more than one university.

"Amanda, his death wasn't your fault."

Justin's gruff voice made her glance across the parking lot. She couldn't look at him when she felt so raw. Exposed.

Guilty.

"Maybe not," she said. "But I should have been a better friend."

"I'm sure you *were* a good friend," he said. "But none of us can really know what's going on in another person's head unless they tell us."

She absorbed his words, knowing that on a rational level, they were true. But they still didn't alleviate the regret that filled her soul.

"Is Carlton's family still in town?"

She swallowed the lump in her throat. "His mother is. But she's not doing well. I think she has some kind of degenerative disease, bad rheumatoid arthritis. She has to use a walker to get around."

"Any other family?"

"A brother. Actually, he and Carlton were fraternal twins, as different as night and day."

"The brother was popular?"

"Yes. He was a wrestler so girls liked his body. He lives in a neighboring town."

"Were he and his brother close?"

Amanda wrinkled her nose. "Not really. I always got the impression they didn't get along, that Carlton's brother was impatient with him. He wanted Carlton to stand up for himself."

Justin narrowed his eyes. "Did the sheriff investigate the kid's death to make sure it was a suicide?"

"Not really," Amanda said. "Carlton's brother was away at the time at a wrestling tournament. And Carlton left a suicide note so no one really questioned it."

"Hmm. I'm still surprised there wasn't an investigation."

"I guess they had records from the shrink Carlton saw confirming his depression."

Justin reached for the door. "All right. Let's take it one step at a time. First Kelly Lambert's ex. Then Fisher's. Then we'll question Donald Reisling and his father."

Amanda climbed out, her nerves on edge. This case was even bigger than she'd first believed.

She just hoped they figured it out before anyone else died.

JUSTIN CHECKED HIS weapon to make sure it was secure and hidden beneath his jacket as he and Amanda walked up the sidewalk to Sumter's apartment. All this time they'd wondered if the missing girls were connected and looked for a psychopath who simply liked to kidnap young women.

But now they might have a lead. If the kidnappings/kills were personally motivated, finding the original trigger was the key to stopping the crimes. With the upcoming reunion, the killer had a whole pool of victims at his fingertips.

Whoever it was obviously had a bone to pick with the women in Sunset Mesa and was making a point.

He glanced at Amanda as she knocked on the door to Sumter's apartment. "Mr. Sumter, it's Sheriff Blair and Sergeant Thorpe," she yelled through the door. "We need to talk to you."

Justin kept his eyes peeled around the outside of the string of units, searching for trouble. If Sumter knew they were asking questions and he was the perp, he might ambush them.

Or he might have gone into hiding.

There were dozens of places in the deserted area surrounding Sunset Mesa to lie low and stay off the grid.

They waited for several seconds; then Justin raised his fist and knocked louder. "Mr. Sumter, if you're in there, answer the door."

"Were you friends with this guy?" Justin asked.

Amanda shook her head no. "Terry and Kelly were tight their freshmen and sophomore years. He was a big jock, but he had a cocky attitude." She gave a self-deprecating laugh. "Besides, by then I was more interested in the cases my father was working. I used to quiz him all the time."

"What about your mother?"

Sadness flickered in her expressive eyes. "She left when

I was fourteen. Said she couldn't take wondering if he was coming home at night any longer."

Justin understood that kind of worry, that marriage for lawmen was near impossible. The reason he'd avoided it altogether. No reason to put a woman or himself through the pain when things fell apart.

And things always fell apart.

"But what about you?" he asked. "Why didn't she take you with her?"

A self-deprecating laugh rumbled from her throat. "She said she knew I'd choose Dad, and she wasn't going to make me choose." She shrugged. "Maybe she was right. I don't know."

"But you wanted them both," he said, understanding. "Do you keep in touch with her?"

Her jaw tightened. "She remarried, has another family now."

A wealth of hurt underscored her words, but he didn't reply because shuffling sounded inside the condo. Feet pounded. Something slammed, like a window or a door.

Justin's senses jumped to full alert.

"He's trying to run," he muttered.

He slammed his shoulder against the door, knocking the thin wooden frame askew. Then he pulled his gun and rushed in, Amanda behind him.

A noise from a back room made him jerk his head to the right, and he ran toward the bedroom. The window was opening, wind swirling through the room. He rushed to it and saw Sumter climbing into the bushes. "Stay here and look around. I'm going after him!"

Not bothering to wait for her response, he ran back through the den and outside. He veered around the side of the building, then saw a figure dive from the bushes below the window and take off toward the woods in back.

"This is Sergeant Thorpe, Sumter. Stop. I'm armed." He sprang into motion and chased the man as he jumped a pile of trash in his backyard. "You're not going to get away!" Justin shouted.

The man tripped over something and nearly fell, but caught himself, glanced back and continued to run. Justin picked up his pace and caught up with him within seconds. He jumped him from behind and threw the man to the ground.

"Get off of me, I haven't done anything wrong," Sumter growled.

"You ran," Justin snapped. "That makes you look guilty."

Sumter spit on the ground as Justin dragged him to a standing position and shoved him back toward the building. Sumter smelled like booze and cigarette smoke and cursed as Justin forced him back into the apartment.

Amanda stood in the den, her expression angry. At him or Sumter?

He didn't have time to analyze it.

Justin shoved Sumter toward the couch, which was piled high with dirty laundry. The scruffy man collapsed on it with another round of expletives.

"You have no right to barge in here and harass me," Sumter muttered.

"We have every right," Justin said coldly.

Amanda crossed her arms and stepped in front of Sumter, staring down at him.

It made her look sexy as hell, but Justin refrained from commenting out loud.

"Why did you run, Terry?" Amanda asked.

"I thought you were a burglar," Terry said sarcastically.

Justin shook his head. "We identified ourselves."

"You know why we're here," Amanda said.

For a brief second, pain flashed in the man's eyes, before a smirk replaced it. "Yeah, I know, *Amanda*. You think that you're better than the rest of us now because you have that badge."

Justin squared his shoulders, irritated at the sarcasm in Sumter's tone.

He'd wondered if some of the younger people in town resented having one of their classmates assume the sheriff's position.

"I am better than you, Terry, because I'm not a drunk," Amanda countered.

He shot to his feet, rage seething from his every pore. "You bitch."

Justin shoved him back down. "You make another move toward her and your butt will be in jail."

Sumter made a low sound in his throat, then snapped his mouth shut.

"We have to ask you some questions about Kelly's disappearance," Amanda said calmly, showing no trace that his attitude affected her.

Sumter scowled at them, then scraped a hand through his already tousled dirty-blond hair. "I don't know anything."

Justin took a quick inventory of the inside of the apartment. It was just as rundown as the outside. Faded paint on the walls, worn furniture and stained carpet. The place reeked of cigarette smoke, stale beer and fast food.

A coffee cup filled with muddy sludge sat on the chipped coffee table and unwashed dishes filled the sink.

The man was not only a drunk but a slob.

"We heard that you wanted to get back with Kelly," Justin cut in sharply.

"I had a thing for her a while back," Sumter said, tugging at his ratty T-shirt. "But I've had other women since."

"Still, you wanted her back," Justin said. "Her fiancé told us that."

Sumter's eyes narrowed to slits. "She was too good for that jerk."

"He seems nice to me," Amanda said. "Like he really loves her."

"*I* loved her," Sumter said. "And she promised to love me forever. Then Fisher stole her from me."

"We were just kids back then, Terry," Amanda pointed out. "Everyone moves on from that first love."

Terry glared at her through glazed eyes. The man must have been sleeping off a hangover when they'd knocked. And the place reeked of pot.

Perhaps the reason he'd run?

"But you didn't move on, did you?" Justin asked.

"Yes, I did. I told you I've had other women." He smiled, a cunning evil in his eyes. "In fact, I don't have trouble in that department."

"Having other women doesn't mean you forgot Kelly or that you stopped wanting her." Justin took a menacing step toward him. "The reunion was coming up and so was Kelly's wedding. You figured you'd make one last attempt to win her back, so you called her and asked her to meet you."

Terry dropped his head slightly. "I did ask her, but she had other plans."

"Plans that didn't involve you. Plans to marry Raymond Fisher," Amanda said.

Justin poked Sumter with his finger. "That made you even angrier, didn't it?"

Amanda's voice hardened. "So you sent her a text pretending it was from someone else and lured her out to the Old River Mill Road."

"I did no such thing," Sumter snapped.

"You ran her off the road, then dragged her from the car," Amanda continued.

Terry shook his head no, his expression adamant. "No…"

"What kind of car do you drive?" Justin asked.

Terry glanced back and forth between them as if he suspected they were trying to trap him. "A pickup truck," he said. "I use it for work."

"What color is it?" Justin asked.

"Black," Terry said. Realizing he might be in serious

trouble, he gave Amanda a pitiful, lost-boy look. "Amanda, you really can't think I'd hurt Kelly. You've known me for years. You know I'm not capable."

"I know you have a temper when you're drinking," Amanda said. "And judging from your breath and the empty bottles in your kitchen, I'd say you've been doing a lot of that."

"Did you know Tina Grimes?" Justin asked.

Sweat beaded on Terry's forehead. "Tina? What the hell are you asking about Tina for?"

Amanda folded her arms across her chest. "She also went missing months ago—"

"Jesus, you think I took her and killed Kelly?" Sumter's panicked gaze darted toward the door. "Hell, you're crazy, Amanda. I'm not some serial nutcase."

"Just answer the question," Justin said firmly.

Terry clamped his mouth shut. "I'm done talking. I want a lawyer."

SUZY TURNER WAS such a stupid bimbo. She had fallen for the plan with no questions asked. Had even been friendly.

Friendly after what she'd done.

The sick bitch.

Her body now lay limp, her ivory flesh red and bruised where the belt had tightened around her throat.

Now, what to do with the body?

For so long the others had lain hidden inside the town. No one knew where they were, that they had never really left Sunset Mesa.

But now everyone had returned to town to celebrate, to relive their old high school glory days.

They had to see what had come from those days. That they hadn't been so glorious at all.

That not everyone felt like celebrating.

And it was time for them to pay for their sins.

Chapter Eight

"What do you think about Terry?" Amanda asked as they drove back to the sheriff's office.

Justin worked his mouth from side to side. "He looks good for Kelly's murder, but I'm not sure he fits the profile of a serial criminal. He's too out of control with the drinking."

"I agree. As volatile as he is, he would get sloppy and would have made mistakes by now."

"Maybe leaving Tina's body so it could be found was a mistake."

"True. But still, our killer has to be more organized, methodical."

"You're right." Justin glanced at the clock on the dash. "It's nearly midnight, Amanda. Let's call it a night. It's too late to visit Fisher's ex-girlfriend."

Amanda twisted her hands together. "I hate to go to bed knowing we haven't found Kelly."

Justin recognized a faint hint of despair in her voice and wanted to assure her they'd find the woman. But there were too many others missing that they hadn't yet located, so he couldn't make false promises.

"I understand," he said instead. "But we've done all we can today. Her picture is being run nationwide. Police everywhere are searching for her. You need to get some rest and we'll go at it again tomorrow."

Amanda nodded. He was right. But she wasn't sure she

could sleep when images of Tina Grimes's dead body floated in her head.

Was Kelly going to end up like that?

Was she still alive?

Justin parked, and the two of them climbed out and went inside. Darkness bathed the streets, most of the residents in the sleepy little town tucked in bed for the night.

But were they safe?

It was her job to make sure the residents were protected. What if she failed?

JUSTIN HAD WORKED in law enforcement long enough to know that Amanda was taking this case personally. As they entered the police station, she poured herself another cup of coffee.

And why wouldn't she take the case personally? She'd known some of the victims. She knew Kelly Lambert.

And now it seemed that members of her high school were being targeted by a serial criminal. She was probably racking her brain to figure out the reason.

Meaning she probably wouldn't sleep tonight.

"Have you eaten anything today?" he asked.

She looked at him as if he'd grown a second head. "I can't even think about food."

"Amanda," he said, his voice softening at the tortured look in her eyes. "You can't do your job if you don't rest and eat something. Is there anything open this time of night?"

"No."

"Do you have food at your place?"

She shrugged. "Eggs, I guess."

"Okay. Everything in the inn and hotel was booked, so I'm probably going to sack out in your jail. Let me follow you home and I'll make us an omelet while you grab a shower. With something in your stomach, maybe you can sleep and think more clearly tomorrow."

"You don't believe I'm thinking clearly?" she asked, her tone defensive.

"That's not what I meant." He released an exasperated sigh. "But once you relax, once we both do, maybe you'll remember something, or I'll come up with a more concrete theory than we already have."

In fact, he planned to spend the night studying the background and files on each of the cases. They had to be missing something.

She glanced at the files on her desk, then stuffed them in a worn shoulder bag. "All right, let's go. But you're not staying in the jail. You can sleep on my couch."

He started to argue, but she threw up a warning hand. "Trust me, it's not that comfortable, but it's better than one of the cots in the cell."

He conceded with a nod. "All right. I want to talk to Renee Daly in the morning. Then question Donald Reisling and his father."

He gestured for her to lead the way, and he followed her outside. She locked the office, then climbed in the sheriff's car while he followed her in his SUV.

She lived about a mile away in a small neighborhood with a mixture of older brick, stucco and adobe homes. Most looked well kept, the yards manicured, flowerbeds blooming. Judging from the kids' toys in the yards, it was a neighborhood of young families.

"Why did you choose this neighborhood?" he asked as he followed her up the cacti-lined walkway. Was she planning a family?

"It was close to town and affordable." She unlocked the door. "You'll have to excuse the mess. I don't have company very often."

Was that her way of telling him she didn't have a boyfriend?

"Hey, I'm not complaining. Like you said, anything's better than the prison cots."

In fact, he liked her place immediately. It was rustic inside, homey, with soft leather couches, throw pillows and folk art on the walls. The kind of place a man felt comfortable in, not one of those frou-frou women's showcase homes where the furniture was meant to be looked at but not touched.

He'd once dated a woman with white couches. Who the hell had white couches?

She flipped on a lamp, bathing the walls in a golden glow, then dropped her bag on a desk in the corner. His gaze was drawn to the sultry sway of her hips as she walked to the adjoining kitchen. Even though she was in uniform, he could tell she had enticing curves beneath the plain fabric.

Obviously exhausted, she released the ponytail holder keeping her hair from her face, and shook the wavy strands free.

Unexpected desire instantly bolted through him. The gesture seemed somehow intimate. Although she didn't seem aware of what she was doing to him. The scent of some kind of feminine spray, maybe a body wash, blended with vanilla.

"Want a beer?" she asked, one hand on her hip as she stopped by the fridge.

"Sure." She grabbed two from the refrigerator, popped the top on both of them and handed him one while she took a long pull of the other.

His gut tightened as he watched her tip the bottle back. Her slender throat worked to swallow the cold liquid. Then she flicked out her tongue to lick her lips and raw need seized him.

Damn. He wasn't supposed to be attracted to her. She was a sheriff, for God's sake.

But she was still a woman. A very sensual one.

"Go shower," he said, desperate for her to leave the room so he could regain his composure. "I'll whip up an omelet."

She studied him for a long moment, an odd look in her eyes. Friendly? Wary? "I've never brought a man here," she admitted softly.

So she didn't have a boyfriend?

Ridiculous, but relief made him smile.

"Of course this is just work," she said. "Maybe we can review the files while we eat."

Disappointment tapped at his desire.

Hell, though, not enough to destroy it. He still wanted her. Sex was the best stress reliever.

But how would she feel if he suggested a one-night stand? No complications, just hot, raw sex.

She'd probably slug you, sue you for sexual harassment and laugh in your face.

"Sure, just go shower," he said a little more sharply than he intended.

Her eyes flickered in confusion, but she shrugged it off a second later and made her way down the hall.

Traitorous thoughts of her naked in the shower with rivulets of water streaming down her bare back pummeled him. The sound of the shower kicking on taunted him with what-ifs.

What if they weren't working a case and they'd just met in a bar and shared a night of passion?

Dammit to hell and back. It did no good to torture himself with the idea of holding her and tasting her. He needed a distraction.

Food. He needed to concentrate on the food he could eat and the investigation.

Sweat beading on his forehead, he scrounged through her refrigerator, hoping an omelet would satisfy this sudden unsettled feeling clawing at him.

Because bedding Amanda was not an option.

IN SPITE OF the hot water, Amanda shivered. Had she misread that hungry look in Justin's eyes a few minutes ago? Her body tingled as the soapy bubbles coated her skin and the water sluiced over her bare breasts.

Heat speared her as she imagined Justin stripping and stepping into the shower with her. His fingers would trail over her naked skin, making her body come alive with desire.

Desire that would bring them both pleasure as they slid their naked bodies against each other, then melded their mouths and tasted the heat simmering between them.

His hands would skate over her back, then lower, over her hips and she'd open wide for him. He'd lift her and she'd impale herself on his rigid length. He would feel so good inside her....

Struggling for control, she ducked her face beneath the water.

Good heavens alive. The tension of the day had definitely gotten to her. She was not the kind of girl to fantasize about sex.

Especially with another law officer.

She would ruin her career forever if she let him know how she felt.

Furious with herself, she scrubbed her body and hair, then rinsed, climbed out and dried off. Whistling a tune her father used to hum beneath his breath, she towel dried her hair and slid on a pair of shapeless sweatpants and a long sleeved T-shirt. Nothing that looked remotely sexy or inviting.

Not that Justin was interested. Was he?

He's a man. Men are always interested in sex.

But there would be nothing more than that, and she couldn't indulge in a one-night stand with a coworker.

Heck, she'd tried to be a modern woman and pretend sex wasn't personal, but she couldn't do it. Her emotions always got in the way. Besides, she couldn't give her heart away and chance having it broken.

She tousled her damp hair with her fingers, then headed back into the kitchen. The scent of bacon and eggs filled the space, and her stomach growled. When she entered, Justin had set the table with two of her mismatched plates and poured them both orange juice.

She set the rest of her beer on the table and noticed that he'd opened a second one. Hot buttered toast sat in a stack on another plate in the center of the table. He scooped the bacon on a paper-toweled plate, then flipped one omelet, then another, onto their plates. He'd obviously raided her refrigerator and found the green peppers and mushrooms in the crisper.

"You were pretty stocked," he said.

She sank into the chair, suddenly ravenous. "I enjoy cooking when I have time. I have a bad habit of making up my own recipes though."

"Sounds creative. This is about my limit," he said. "Although I can grill a mean steak."

Her mouth watered, but just as much for him as the steak.

Their gazes locked for a heartbeat, a moment of charged heat rippling between them. Her nipples hardened as if he'd touched them, and arousal speared her.

"Amanda?" he said in a gruff tone.

"It looks great," she said, pasting on a cheery smile to diffuse the tension. "Let's eat."

She dug in with gusto, and he did the same, both obviously deciding to ignore the moment.

Amanda spotted her series of yearbooks on the bookshelf by the fireplace in the den, retrieved the last two years', then started flipping through them while she ate. Justin finished off his meal and took another swig of his beer.

She pointed out some random shots of the football games, cheerleaders and pep rallies.

"Here are Avery and Melanie," Amanda said. "They were the first two girls to disappear." She flipped the page to a shot of Kelly, Anise, Mona and Julie Kane, the prom queen. "All these girls were friends."

"What about Renee Daly, Fisher's ex?"

Amanda searched the photos and frowned as she found a candid of Raymond and Kelly beneath the big tree where the students used to gather to talk. "Here she is." In the background, Renee Daly stood by the breezeway shooting daggers at the couple.

Was she jealous enough to carry a grudge all these years?

And if so, why not just go after Kelly to begin with? Why carry out a ten-year-old vendetta?

Serial killers often came from abused families. None of these girls fit that description and neither did Terry Sumter or Donald Reisling.

She flipped to another page, her pulse hammering at the sight of Donald Reisling in his wheelchair at a basketball game. He was sitting all alone beside the bleachers, his expression angry as if he had no friends.

Because they'd abandoned him. "Now that I think about it, some of the girls said their parents didn't want them hanging out with Donald, not after they knew he'd been driving drunk."

"Did he go to college?"

Sympathy for Donald mingled with suspicion. "He lost his basketball scholarship. I heard he went to some kind of technical school, maybe on the internet."

She pointed to the front row of the bleachers. "That's Lynn Faust beside Jimmy Acres. He took over the lead spot on the basketball team after Donald was paralyzed."

Could Donald or his father have hated Lynn and the other girls for turning their backs on him after the accident?

Hated them enough to kill them?

Chapter Nine

Justin wrestled with images of Amanda all night while he tossed and turned on her couch. Maybe it would have been better if he'd stayed at the jail.

No woman had ever made him lose his focus before. He couldn't afford it this time either. Innocent women's lives depended on him.

His phone buzzed, and he reached for it, the nerves along his neck prickling. It could be news of another body or another missing woman.

But it was his superior, Chief Stone Stabler.

"Morning, Chief." He rose and went to look out the kitchen window. Last night it had been dark when they'd arrived and he hadn't noticed the view out back. The sun rising over the canyon took his breath away.

This must be the reason Amanda had bought the house. The canyon loomed behind her, vast, rugged and beautiful.

"Where does the case stand?" Chief Stabler asked.

"We think that the disappearances are all related to Sunset Mesa. So far, most of the girls attended the same high school. The ones who didn't lived here at one time. The body discovered in the creek belonged to a woman named Tina Grimes. Her class ring was found in her hand."

"Any suspects?"

Justin spread the pictures of the missing women across

the desk in the corner. His gut told him yes. "I think so, but I'll know more after I finish questioning some of the locals."

"All right. How is it working with that sheriff? Is she co-operating?"

Justin swallowed back an image of her in the shower, the one that had kept him awake half the night. "She's fine. Competent." And sexy as all get out.

They agreed to talk later and disconnected; then he scribbled a note to Amanda saying he'd meet her at the station. He was going to notify Tina Grimes's father that her body had been found.

He quickly dressed, then went through the drive-in doughnut shop for a doughnut and coffee. Thirty minutes later, he knocked on the door of Mr. Grimes's house.

It was a nice Georgian home on an estate lot in the next town. Colorful flowerbeds adorned the front lawn, twin lion statues flanking a water fountain in the center of the circular drive.

He rang the doorbell, his mouth tasting gritty. This was the worst part of his job.

A maid answered the door, so he flashed his badge and identified himself. "I need to see Mr. Grimes please."

She mumbled, *"Si,"* then escorted him to a study to the right and disappeared. Justin scanned the library, noting that Grimes had a collection of antique books as well as travel and finance magazines.

Footsteps clattered, and an astute man with graying hair entered through the arched doorway. Age lines fanned his tanned face, and his clothing indicated he was dressed for a golf game.

Justin hated to ruin his day, but the man probably hadn't had a good day since Tina disappeared.

Grimes took one look at his Silver Star and paled. The man instinctively knew the reason he'd come.

"You found Tina?" he asked, his voice thick with desperation.

Justin nodded. "I'm afraid so. I'm sorry, Mr. Grimes."

Grimes stumbled toward his desk chair, then sat down and dropped his face into his hands. Silent sobs wracked his body, and Justin simply waited, giving him time to absorb the shock.

Finally Grimes heaved a breath, wiped his eyes with a handkerchief and looked up at him. "Where?"

"In Camden Creek."

"Did she…suffer?"

He grimaced. The man didn't need to know details. "She was strangled."

"God…" Another sob erupted, making Justin's heart squeeze with compassion.

Grimes looked up at him with tear-filled eyes. "Do you have any idea who did it?"

"We're working on a couple of leads." He hesitated, leaned forward and steepled his hands. "I understand you're grieving, sir, but I need to ask you a few questions."

A weary sigh reverberated from the man. "I already told the sheriff everything I knew months ago."

"I understand. But we found a high school class ring from Sunset Mesa in Tina's hand. Was the ring special to her?"

Grimes pulled at his chin. "We moved here from Sunset Mesa her senior year. She didn't graduate from Canyon High."

"Did she keep in touch with her old friends there?"

He hesitated, thinking. "Some of them. Kelly Lambert and Suzy Turner. She and Suzy went to college together."

Justin's mind raced. "How about old boyfriends from Canyon High?"

Grimes rose, went to the bar and poured himself a scotch even though it was barely breakfast time. Under the circumstances, Justin cut him some slack.

After Grimes downed the scotch, he turned back to Justin. "Before we moved, she dated a guy named Donald. But he broke up with her to date some other girl. I think he ended up in a wheelchair, some drunk-driving accident."

"Did she keep in touch with Donald?"

"He called her a couple of times after the accident, but he was a wreck. And since he dumped her, she didn't take him back."

Motive for Donald.

"Thank you, Mr. Grimes. And again, I'm sorry for your loss. The ME will contact you about retrieving Tina's body for burial."

At his words, the man broke down again.

He laid his card on the desk. "Call me if you think of anything else that might help."

"Please, Sergeant Thorpe," the man said, his voice filled with anguish. "Find out who did this to my little girl."

Justin met his gaze. "Don't worry, sir. I intend to."

Justin let himself out, climbed into his SUV and phoned the ME. "Dr. Sagebrush, did you find any DNA on that class ring in Tina's hand?"

"I was just about to call you," Dr. Sagebrush said. "As a matter of fact, I did."

Justin's pulse jumped. This could be the lead they needed. "Whose was it?" The man who abducted and strangled her?

"That's the interesting part," Dr. Sagebrush said. "I thought it might be the killer's, but it's not a male's DNA. It's a female's."

Justin sucked in a breath. "Do you have a name?"

"Melanie Hoit," Dr. Sagebrush said. "The DNA belonged to one of the first women to disappear. Also, I found her initials inside the ring."

The ring didn't belong to Tina as he'd originally thought.

Justin's fingers tightened around the phone. That DNA meant that the cases were connected. The killer had taken Melanie's ring and placed it in Tina's hand as his signature.

To taunt them with the fact that he'd been abducting and killing young women and getting away with it for years.

And he obviously wasn't finished.

BY THE TIME Amanda met Justin at the sheriff's office, she'd reviewed the missing-persons files again and combed through her yearbook.

She hated the fact that every face she saw now looked like a suspect. The mayor had also called for an update on the Lambert case, pushing her to make an arrest, and two reporters had called, requesting an interview.

She passed Julie Kane driving toward the school on her way to the office and was tempted to pull her over and warn her that a madman might be after her and their classmates.

But that would cause panic. She needed more information first.

She was on her third cup of coffee when Justin strode in. Wow. The man looked as if he'd grown another inch. He'd shaved, too, although she had to admit she'd liked his five o'clock shadow. Still, she wanted to run her hands across his jaw and feel those big arms of his flex beneath her touch.

Lack of sleep. That was the only explanation for her racy thoughts.

"Morning," he said in a deep, throaty voice. A voice laced with fatigue that told her he hadn't slept any better than she had. Of course, he'd probably been focused on the investigation, not fantasizing about her.

That thought burst her bubble, and she handed him some coffee. "Are you ready to question Fisher's ex?"

He gave a clipped nod. "Yes, but I have some information for you first."

A shiver rippled up her spine at his tone. "What?" Please not another dead body.

"I talked to the ME. He found some DNA on the class ring Tina Grimes had clenched in her hand."

That was good news. "Who did it belong to?"

"Melanie Hoit."

Questions pummeled Amanda. "I don't understand. Melanie disappeared years ago. How could Tina have her ring?" The truth dawned, ugly and disturbing. "The same person abducted both of them."

He nodded.

Amanda rubbed her arms with her hands. "Do you think Melanie is still alive?"

"I doubt it," Justin said, his expression grave. "The killer probably took Melanie's ring as some kind of trophy. He may have kept all his victims' class rings as souvenirs."

His theory made sense. She'd heard of serial killers personalizing their MOs. "But we haven't found any other bodies. And Tina didn't graduate from Canyon High."

"Her father said she dated Donald before Lynn did, and that he contacted Tina after the accident, but she wouldn't take him back."

So all roads were leading back to Donald.

"The unsub has been lying low, picking off these young women one at a time. For some reason, they all spark his hatred or anger, probably of a specific woman who hurt him."

"And the reunion triggered him to escalate," Amanda said, following his logic. "The perp has stayed off the grid all these years, but this ten-year reunion means something to him. It's an anniversary of sorts."

"Exactly. He can't stand the thought of everyone gathering to party and celebrate their accomplishments when he feels hurt, betrayed by them."

"When his life didn't work out the way he wanted," Amanda said, thinking of Donald. She hated to suspect him after all he'd suffered.

But she had to do her job.

Justin gestured toward the door. "Let's go talk to Renee Daly. Then we'll confront Donald Reisling and his father."

He was right. Donald had good reason to hate Lynn Faust.

He could be taking all his rage out on the other girls who had shunned him and still be planning to kill Lynn.

Probably on the night of the reunion.

They walked to his SUV in silence, but as soon as they settled inside and she gave him directions, she voiced her concerns. "Justin, maybe we should plan a press conference for the town. Warn the women that they're in danger."

"They probably already realize that," Justin said. "Besides, all we have is a working theory now. No proof."

"No, but if the reunion is his trigger, he may strike at one of the events. I should tell Julie Kane and the other organizers to call off the events until we catch the killer."

"Continuing with the events might be the best way to trap this guy," Justin said as he made the turn. "We can assign extra law officers to watch for trouble."

Amanda's stomach somersaulted. That was a good, solid plan. Except that it meant endangering more women.

Women she knew personally, had known most of her life.

Not that they were best friends, but she'd sworn an oath to protect them and Justin's idea would do the opposite.

"Think about it," Justin said. "We have a couple of days to figure it out. Maybe we'll get lucky and catch the suspect and the reunion plans can go on without a hitch or panicking the town."

AMANDA WAS WORRIED about the residents in town.

But he was worried about her.

Until he knew the unsub's specific motive, and whether or not Amanda was on the hit list, she wasn't leaving his side.

"There, Renee works at the dress shop on the corner," Amanda said. "She has a boutique that supposedly sells the latest designer wear."

He shot her a wry look. "In Sunset Mesa?"

Amanda chuckled. "I know. This little town is old-school Western all the way. She wants to class it up."

Amanda was probably the classiest thing they had.

She indicated the corner down the street on the left, and he drove past the bank and diner. Kelly Lambert's father was exiting his Mercedes and entering the bank, but his shoulders were hunched, and he looked tired as hell.

Another night where his daughter hadn't come home.

And they had no good news to tell him.

Justin parked in front of the boutique, noting the short skirts and five-inch heels in the window. For a brief second, he wondered what Amanda would look like in nothing but those heels.

Oblivious to his wandering thoughts, Amanda shoved her door open and slid from the seat. The sign on the shop door indicated it didn't open until ten, but he could see movement in the back through the front window.

Amanda rapped on the door. "Renee, it's Sheriff Blair. We need to talk to you."

A heartbeat passed; then footsteps tapped on the floor inside. A woman's voice answered, "Hang on," and the door opened. A bell tinkled above them and Renee, a tall, leggy blonde wearing a miniskirt and tube top that looked absurdly out of place in the small town, appeared.

Justin had to admit she was attractive, but she did nothing for him. Didn't stir his hunger like Amanda did in her dull uniform.

"What's going on, Amanda?" Renee's eyes darted from Amanda to him, obviously curious.

"Renee, this is Sergeant Thorpe of the Texas Rangers. We need to talk to you about Kelly Lambert's disappearance."

A frown pulled at Renee's eyes, barely registering on her Botoxed forehead. "I heard about that. It's awful," Renee said. "Do you have any idea who abducted her?"

Amanda gave her a deadpan look. "Not yet. We're talking to everyone who knew her and trying to piece together what happened."

"You used to date her fiancé, Raymond Fisher?" Justin cut in.

Renee rolled her eyes. "Yes, but that was ages ago. We're just friends now."

"So friendship is all you wanted from him?" Amanda asked.

Renee looked shocked at the implication that she might want more. "Of course. I have boyfriends in three different cities. I don't need an old high school tagalong."

"Are you seeing anyone specific now?" Justin asked.

She lifted a blood-red fingernail and raked it along the buttons of his shirt. "Not anyone serious. How about we get together later for a drink?"

Amanda stiffened beside him.

Justin clenched his jaw. Most men would have been pleased at her advance. But Justin was simply annoyed. He wrapped his fingers around her hand and stopped her playful tease.

"No, thanks. We're working a case," he said. "Do you know anyone who would have wanted to hurt Kelly?"

Renee shook her head. "No. But poor Raymond. I bet he's distraught."

"Yes, he appears to be," Amanda said.

Renee's eyes twitched with a devilish gleam. "I guess I'll have to console him at the reunion."

Justin's stomach twisted. He really didn't like women like Renee. Teases. She probably flirted with anything in pants.

"What about that dead girl they found at the creek?" Renee asked. "I heard she used to live around here, too."

"She did," Amanda said. "Other women in Sunset Mesa have disappeared over the past decade, too, and we suspect it might have something to do with our class. That our reunion might be triggering someone's anger toward the females."

Renee paled, and she stepped backward, her hand gripping the door. "Are you saying this maniac might come after me?"

THE TEENAGERS OF Sunset Mesa would wake up today, wolf
down breakfast, go to school and find one of their alumni
lying on the bleachers waiting for them.

Kelly Lambert didn't look so pretty right now.

Getting her onto the football field had been an ordeal.
But it was worth it.

Maybe the bullies and mean girls would think twice about
how they hurt others the next time.

Yes, all the members of that class were counting down
the days till they partied together again.

But their party might be moved to the cemetery when they
realized how many of them would end up dead.

Chapter Ten

"What did you think of Renee?" Amanda asked, hoping the sliver of jealousy she'd felt when the wicked woman had flirted with Justin hadn't shown through.

She had no reason to be jealous. Justin was his own man. He could flirt or sleep with anyone he wanted.

They weren't even remotely involved and never would be.

"I think she's a big flirt and probably a liar. But that also tells me she probably wasn't serious enough or obsessed enough with Fisher to carry a ten-year-old torch for him."

"True, she has always been superficial," Amanda said, surprised but relieved that Justin hadn't fallen for the woman's charm. Most men did.

"I also think she's too concerned with fashion, her looks and appearances to dirty herself enough to commit a murder." Justin folded his hands, flicking his fingernails. "Did you see those fake claws? Girls like that are too worried about breaking a nail to strangle someone."

Amanda laughed. "You're right. Let's go talk to Donald."

"His home or work?" Justin asked.

"I looked him up this morning. He has a home office, works in computer graphics."

She gave him the address and pointed out directions as he drove. But her nerves remained on edge as they passed the high school, and she saw teachers arriving for work, buses beginning to pull up. The marquis out front announced that prom was fewer than two weeks away. The same night Kelly's wedding had been scheduled. Amanda wondered if she'd planned it that way.

The reunion date was also posted.

A bad feeling crept over her, and she clenched the seat edge. Had something else happened?

"Is this the right road?" he asked.

"Yes." Amanda pointed to the subdivision. "Go to the end of the road and turn left."

He pulled down the row of houses, all older with a spattering of well-kept single-family homes mingling with rentals that had seen better days. He turned left and they wound down a mile-long private drive to the Reisling estate.

Justin parked and Amanda caught his arm before they got out. "If you don't mind, let me take the lead. Donald might be...defensive."

"He also might be guilty," Justin said. "I don't intend to cut him any slack just because he's in a chair."

"Fair enough," Amanda said, although her heart squeezed. She felt like Donald had been dealt a shoddy deal in life.

Yet he'd chosen to say he was driving instead of turn Lynn in.

He'd probably regretted that a thousand times over. If so though, why hadn't he changed his testimony later?

The enormous estate house sat on several acres, grandiose and stately.

"What the hell does this man do to own this place?" Justin asked.

"Family money," Amanda said. "Donald's father is an entrepreneur, works in investments and has done well. But Donald's grandfather invented some kind of farm equipment that he patented and it earned them a fortune."

Justin followed her up to the door, where she rang the bell. A few minutes later, a voice sounded and the door opened to reveal Donald in his wheelchair.

But instead of looking scruffy and angry, as if he was

living in the past, he was well dressed in dress slacks and a blue shirt and his hair was groomed.

"Amanda?"

"I'm the sheriff now," she said.

"That's right, I heard that," he said, his mouth quirking to the side.

"This is Sergeant Thorpe with the Texas Rangers," she said. "Can we come in?"

"Sure. What's this about?"

"Kelly Lambert's disappearance."

"That was shocking. I don't know how I can help, but come on in." He turned and wheeled his way through the two-story foyer to an office equipped with a state-of-the-art computer system.

Reisling parked his chair behind his desk and indicated a coffee decanter on the sideboard. "Help yourself."

Amanda and Justin both declined. Her gaze was drawn to the high school trophies on a bookcase behind him. If his basketball career hadn't been cut short, he would have most likely added college ones to that collection.

"Donald, when was the last time you saw Kelly?" Amanda asked.

Donald rubbed his temple as if he had to think about the question. Because he was fabricating a lie?

"Honestly, it's probably been months. She dropped by one day to ask me if I wanted to help with the committee organizing the class reunion." He grunted. "Imagine that."

Justin cleared his throat. "Sheriff Blair told me what happened years ago. Her visit must have angered you."

Donald chuckled. "Actually I thought it was funny. I asked her why she thought I'd even want to attend, much less help organize the thing. It's not like I've stayed friends with anyone from back then."

Anger hardened his tone. She couldn't blame him. Hadn't she thought the same thing when she'd opened her own invitatlon? And she didn't have the reason to dislike their class-mates that he did.

"So why didn't you move away?" Justin asked.

Donald shrugged. "Takes money to have a place set up for handicap access," he said matter-of-factly. "I'm not proud that I live at home—then again, my father is rarely here. He has his own office and travels. And I stay in the guesthouse. He also fronted me startup money for my own business. Now, I'm doing pretty well," he said. "I've been looking at buying a condo in the city."

Amanda offered him a smile. "It sounds like you've made a success of yourself." Not as if he was stuck in the past.

He gave a sarcastic laugh. "Business is good. But not a lot of women can handle the chair."

Sympathy for him stole through Amanda.

"Where were you day before yesterday?" Justin interjected.

Donald's expression turned to steel. "What? Why? You don't think I had something to do with Kelly's disappearance, do you?"

The strained second that followed answered his question.

He cut his eyes toward Amanda. "Amanda, why would you think that?"

"You suffered a terrible tragedy and got the raw end of the deal. Everyone said Lynn was driving the night of your accident."

"That must have eaten at you all these years," Justin said in a dark voice. "Watching her go on with her life, date other guys, have everything you missed out on with no consequences."

Any semblance of friendliness faded from Donald's face. "Even if I did harbor resentment toward Lynn, why the hell would I hurt Kelly?" His voice rose an octave. "Besides, I thought some sicko stalker was kidnapping those women."

Justin crossed his arms. "It's possible that the kidnapper hates all women who remind him of the one who first hurt him."

Tension stretched between the two men as Donald realized the implications of Justin's statement.

Donald pressed a hand over his chest. "Look, that person is not me. I decided a long time ago that anger was only holding me back."

"That's very mature of you," Justin said.

Amanda pursed her lips. "So you forgave Lynn?"

"Yes." A mixture of emotions seethed in Donald's eyes. "You may not believe me, but look at me." He gestured at his chair. "Even if I wanted revenge or was this sick person you're talking about, how the hell would I kidnap anyone and get away with it?"

"Donald, we're just trying to get to the truth," Amanda said calmly. "One of the missing women was found in Camden Creek. She'd been strangled and was holding one of our class rings."

"So you think someone in our class murdered her?"

Justin spoke up. "Someone who had a beef with the females. After your accident, we heard that the girls turned you down for dates."

Pain wrenched Donald's eyes. "I admit it was a rough time, but that doesn't make me a killer."

"We're talking to everyone still in town and everyone coming in for the reunion," Amanda said.

"What about your father?" Justin asked.

A muscle ticked in Justin's jaw. "What about him?"

"You may have forgiven Lynn and accepted your situation, but did he?" Justin asked. "He probably enjoyed watching you play basketball. He had big dreams for you. Then those dreams were crushed because some teenager caused your paralysis. That would be enough to set off any parent."

Donald gripped the wheels of his chair and flew around his desk. "I think you need to leave now."

"Please, Donald," Amanda said. "If you know anything

about Tina's death or Kelly's disappearance, tell me. I don't want to see anyone else hurt."

Donald gestured toward the door. "I told you what I know. Now, if you want to talk to me again, go through my attorney."

"I WANT TO talk to Reisling's father," Justin said as they left the estate.

Amanda fastened her seat belt. "He has an office in town."

"You feel sorry for the guy, don't you?" Justin asked.

Amanda twisted sideways to look at him. "I don't know what to think. If he's truly forgiven Lynn, then maybe he's found some peace and happiness and he's not our perp."

"But his father might be," Justin pointed out. "A parent's love is the strongest bond there is. I've seen fathers, especially fathers of athletes, do outrageous things to help their kids succeed."

"I know there are stories of fistfights at little league games, and dopers at the Olympics—"

"And parents who sought revenge against another person for hurting their child."

Amanda bit her lip as they lapsed into silence.

Ten minutes later, they arrived at Reisling's office on the corner of town. Justin faintly wondered why the man hadn't kept his office at home as his son had, but figured Reisling had other employees working for him and needed a professional space.

He was worried about Amanda, too. Knowing the people in town made it more difficult for her to treat them as suspects.

She obviously hadn't seen the harsh realities he had on the job. Teenagers killing their parents. Husbands and wives taking out hits on one another.

Babies abused and children mistreated in heinous ways.

"Were you and Donald friends growing up?"

Amanda shook her head. "I told you before, I wasn't in the popular crowd. He was."

"Until the accident," Justin clarified. "Coupled with the loss of his scholarship, losing his social status and the extra burden of helping him start his business, his father could have broken."

Amanda sighed wearily. "I know logically you're right. But it's hard for me to believe that a serial killer has been living in Sunset Mesa all this time and no one caught on."

Justin wanted to cut her some slack. "Sometimes people are blinded because they're too close to the situation."

"To see the forests for the trees," Amanda finished. "But surely a friend or family member would have noticed something suspicious."

Justin parked, noting as they walked up the sidewalk that the office space was the nicest building on the street. Reisling must have spent some major bucks on renovations. "It's possible that the killer lives alone. Or that if a family member noticed something suspicious, he or she is in denial."

Amanda sighed. "Or they feel indebted enough to the unsub not to turn him in."

He reached for the door to the office. "That would fit Donald. He has to feel indebted to his father."

"I don't like this," Amanda said. "But I like even less the fact that a killer might have been hiding in town right under my nose."

Justin squeezed her arm. A dangerous move because heat blazed through him instantly. Amanda glanced down at his arm, then licked her lips, drawing his gaze to her mouth.

Damn. She had luscious full lips. Lips he wanted to taste.

"Don't beat yourself up, Amanda," he said softly. "This string of disappearances started long before you took office. You were only a teenager back then."

"Yes, but when I think about my classmates, I can't imagine any one of them committing these crimes."

He dropped his hand and opened the door. "Let's talk to Reisling."

The inside of the office was plush and modern, nothing like the Western feel of the town. Steel gray and chrome furniture, a high-tech computer where a receptionist sat and expensive artwork.

He didn't feel as if he was in Texas anymore.

Amanda led the way to the receptionist's desk. "We need to talk to Mr. Reisling."

The middle-aged woman with platinum hair frowned up at Amanda, giving her a jolt of surprise.

"Mrs. Kane, I didn't realized you worked here." Or that she worked at all. She had been the country-club type.

"Yes," the woman said with a sheepish look. "I've been here a couple of years now. Mr. Reisling's good to me."

Amanda glanced sideways at Justin. "Is he in, ma'am? It's important we talk to him."

Confusion marred the woman's face, which obviously had had some touch-up work. "Can I tell him what this is about?"

Justin flashed his badge. "Tell him it's urgent police business."

She rose, diamonds and jewels glittering, then disappeared through a doorway that probably led to more offices in the back.

"You seemed surprised to see her here," Justin said.

Amanda jammed her hands in the pockets of her jacket. "I am. She was one of those tennis moms who had maids and martini lunches."

Justin started to say something more, but the door opened, and Mrs. Kane waved them through, then led them into a hallway and to an office space that was even plusher than the entry and waiting area. The computer system outdid the sheriff's office's ancient one by thousands of dollars.

Mr. Reisling greeted them with shakes of their hands and indicated for them to seat themselves in the area in the corner. A sparkling water decanter sat by crystal glasses, along with a fancy espresso machine, and a fully loaded bar ran along the back wall. Reisling offered them a drink, but Amanda shook her head and Justin cut straight to the chase.

"Mr. Reisling, we're investigating the disappearance of several young women from this area over the past ten years, the most recent being Kelly Lambert. We also recently recovered the body of Tina Grimes."

Mr. Reisling smoothed a hand over his red tie. "I don't understand what that has to do with me." He glanced pointedly at Amanda. "What's going on, Sheriff?"

"A class ring from Canyon High was found in Tina's hand, Mr. Reisling. Added to the fact that all the girls lived in the town at one time and that the majority of the victims attended the local high school, we believe the abductor/killer is from this area. That he has some personal beef with these young women."

Reisling shook his head, his right eye twitching. "I still don't get why you're here."

"Because we know what happened to your son," Justin said flatly. "How unfair it was that he was permanently paralyzed and persecuted for driving under the influence when the girl that was with him escaped and then dropped him."

"Good God, that happened ages ago," Mr. Reisling said, his face reddening with anger. "And yes, I was bitter, sometimes still am bitter, because that little tramp lied and hurt my son. But—" he stepped closer to Amanda, eyes flaring "—my son forgave her and managed to make something of himself. So I'm incredibly proud of him."

"That doesn't mean you didn't harbor hatred for all the girls who turned him down for dates after the accident." Justin matched the man's intimidating stance.

If the guy laid a finger on Amanda, he'd deck him.

"Maybe I did hate them," Reisling said, his lips curled into a snarl. "But that doesn't mean I've been kidnapping or killing them! I'm a businessman and well respected in this town." He jerked his thumb toward the door. "Now, unless you're here to arrest me, get the hell out of here. And leave my son alone. He's suffered enough."

Amanda's phone buzzed, cutting into the tension, and she snatched it up and headed to the door.

Justin clenched his jaw. Reisling was the kind of man who used his power and money to get what he wanted. The man might not be guilty, but Justin didn't like him. Reisling was smart, calculating and, he suspected, vindictive.

If he was methodical in his business, he was probably also meticulous, organized and patient—patient enough to wait ten years to build toward his endgame.

AMANDA GLANCED AT the caller ID on the phone, surprised to see the number for Canyon High. Was this call about the reunion? Maybe the staff had heard about the discovery of Tina's body and decided they should postpone it.

"Who is it?" Justin asked.

"The school." She punched Connect. "Sheriff Blair."

"Sheriff, it's Principal Blakely at the high school. You need to get out here."

Amanda gripped the phone tighter. "What's wrong?" Not a school shooting. God, there were too many of those....

"This morning when our track team met at the track, they found a body on the bleachers in the stadium."

Amanda's legs threatened to buckle. "Who is it?"

"Kelly Lambert. She was murdered, Sheriff. Murdered and left here for the kids to find."

Chapter Eleven

Amanda staggered toward the car. "Lock the school down, Principal Blakely."

"It's on lockdown and we've confiscated cell phones, but I can't say for sure that one of the students hasn't already texted or sent this out. There may be photos already on the internet."

Oh, God…

"We have to contain the situation," Amanda said. "Keep everyone away from the field. I'm on my way."

Her vision blurred with the mind-boggling implications of the phone call. "We need a CSI team at the school along with extra officers," she told Justin as he met her at the car.

"What's wrong?"

"Kelly Lambert's body was found on the high school bleachers in the football stadium."

Which meant everyone in the entire school needed to be questioned. And that whoever had killed her was ready to make a bolder statement… and to make that statement in a public way.

AMANDA'S FACE PALED as she disconnected, and Justin couldn't help himself. He reached out and steadied her with his hands.

"Amanda?"

"I have to see her family before word gets out about this. If it hasn't already."

"With teens and their cell phones, it probably is out," Justin said in disgust. "People have no respect for privacy anymore. The more morbid or shocking the better."

Amanda visibly shook herself as if to pull herself together. "We need to go."

"I'll call for backup and for a crime scene team," Justin said. "Hell, we'll need a whole crew to question all the students."

Her phone was beeping again and she checked it. "Dammit, it's Mr. Lambert."

"He knows." They jumped into the car, and Justin started the engine and headed toward the school.

"Sheriff Blair, Mr. Lambert—" A pause and Amanda massaged her temple with her fingertips. "I just heard, Mr. Lambert. I'm so sorry that you found out through a text."

Justin punched in his chief and explained the situation, and he agreed to send teams to help canvass the students. Phones would have to be kept, photographs of the victim and crime scene analyzed.

Had someone touched the body? Changed anything?

All details that would affect the investigation.

They could only hope a witness had seen the killer leaving the body…

No, the drop-off had probably been done during the night when the place was empty.

But…if the perp was getting daring enough to leave a dead victim at a public place, maybe he'd gotten sloppy and they'd find some evidence this time.

He glanced back at Reisling's business and wondered if the rich cocky jerk had been at the high school last night dumping Kelly's body.

Was Reisling cool enough to fake his calm when they'd arrived at his office?

"No, sir, you cannot come to the school," Amanda said. "The school is being locked down, Mr. Lambert. Police and

Texas Rangers will be all over the place. I promise you I'll let you know as soon as we move her body so you can see her."

Justin heard the man's sobs as he ended the call. Traffic was picking up with morning commuters, but Justin flipped on his siren and careened around cars and trucks, knowing every minute counted.

This case was about to blow up in their faces. The crime scene was probably already contaminated six ways till Sunday. And now the suspect pool would only mount.

Not to mention the press...

He saw the first media van roll up just as he and Amanda did. He wished he'd had that coffee Donald Reisling had offered.

It was going to be a helluva long day.

Worse, the unsub would probably be watching the circus and gloating, adding up his body count and choosing his next victim.

AMANDA AND JUSTIN met the school's security guard for the school at the front door and were immediately escorted out to the football stadium where the principal and football coach were keeping watch. The students who'd found the body had been sequestered in the gym with the track coach while all other students had been retained in their homerooms.

Principal Blakely looked haggard as he greeted them at the entrance to the stadium and led them over to Kelly's body where it had been staged on the bleachers at the fifty-yard line.

Emotions caught in Amanda's throat when she saw the young woman's matted hair, ashen skin and eyes glazed with the shock of death. Amanda snapped on latex gloves and handed Justin a pair, and he did the same.

"Who found her?" Justin asked.

"Coach Turner came out here with the track team. The team captain, Naomi Carter, spotted her first. She screamed and everyone else came running."

Amanda winced. "Did the students touch anything?"

"I don't think so," the principal said. "Coach said he shouted at them to stay back. Some of the kids are pretty shaken up."

"Get the counselors with them right away."

"Already done." Blakely shook his head sadly. "I don't understand why a killer would leave her at school."

"To send a message," Justin said.

"There's a string of young women who've gone missing the past ten years from this area," Amanda filled in. "We think their disappearances are related to a former student from Canyon High."

Amanda stooped down to examine Kelly's neck and saw the telltale markings indicating strangulation. Wide marks reddened her throat, marks that looked as if they'd been made by a belt.

"Do these look like the marks on Tina's throat?" she asked.

Justin stooped down to examine them. "Yes. Looks like the same belt was used."

She snapped several photographs with her camera phone while Justin focused on the surrounding area, the bleachers beside the body and the ground beneath her.

Kelly's skirt and blouse were wrinkled, one sleeve torn, but at least her clothing was intact, and she saw no evidence of sexual assault. The ME would have to confirm that though.

"Did you check her hand?" Justin asked.

A bevy of voices sounded behind them, and Amanda realized the ME and backup officers had arrived.

"Get the officers set up to interview the students," Justin told the principal. "We'll need all their phones to look at pictures and contacts they've had since then."

"You think one of them killed her?" Blakely asked.

"No," Amanda answered. "But they may have caught some important detail on their cameras that could help us."

The principal headed over to meet the county police and ME and to do as they asked.

Amanda glanced at Kelly's hands. Her left hand was splayed open, her nails jagged as if she'd fought for her life. Hope budded. If she'd fought with her attacker, maybe they'd find the suspect's DNA beneath her fingernails.

Gently, she stroked Kelly's right hand, the one folded up. It was stiff, rigor having set in. "I'm so sorry, Kelly. I wish I'd found you before this happened. But I promise you, I'll catch whoever did this and make them pay."

She uncurled Kelly's fingers, her suspicions confirmed. A class ring was clutched in her palm.

"Same MO," Justin said.

Amanda snapped a picture of it, then lifted the ring, knowing immediately it wasn't Kelly's but had belonged to a boy.

She turned it over and peered at the inside of the band for the engraving. TS. This was Terry's ring.

How had the killer gotten it? And why put it in Kelly's hand?

Had Terry done so as a message that Kelly had always been his?

She bagged it for evidence, hoping they would get something useful from it.

The crime scene team approached, Lieutenant Gibbons in charge. "What did you find?"

Amanda showed him the ring. "A class ring was found in Tina Grimes's hand that had DNA from a previous missing victim. This ring belonged to Terry Sumter, Kelly Lambert's former boyfriend."

"Did she keep it all these years, or did someone plant it in her hand to turn suspicion toward Terry?" Justin said, speculating aloud.

A ruckus sounded near the fence to the stadium, and Amanda saw a media frenzy pushing at the gate, cameras flashing as reporters volleyed for footage.

The sound of more cars roaring up rumbled from the parking lot, then more shouts and voices.

Principal Blakely strode toward them, visibly upset. "Good grief. The word spread and parents are starting to storm the school."

"Get officers out there to control the crowd," Amanda said. The crime scene techs went to work examining the bleachers and football field while Dr. Sagebrush approached the body.

The ME looked reverent as he knelt beside Kelly. "So sad to see someone in their prime taken this way."

And so needless, Amanda thought. But she bit back the words. Her emotions were teetering close to the surface.

So she stepped aside to let him do his work while she phoned her deputy. She quickly explained what had happened and asked him to bring Sumter to the sheriff's office for questioning.

Suddenly, shouts erupted and she looked up to see Mr. Lambert scaling the fence and running toward them.

"Oh, my God," Amanda whispered.

A deputy was trying to catch him, but Amanda threw up a hand to warn him that it was okay. Not that it really was okay, but the last thing she wanted was the officer pulling a gun on the victim's father and the situation spiraling out of control.

"I've got it," she told the officer.

She rushed toward Mr. Lambert, blocking his view. "Mr. Lambert, I told you to wait and I'd call you."

"I have to see her," he cried. "It's my little girl...."

"I know, and I'm so sorry," Amanda said softly.

She pulled him into a hug and let him sob on her shoulder, her own chest aching with grief and guilt.

JUSTIN DIDN'T DO emotional scenes and had to admit that Amanda was handling it well. Although he noticed the slight shiver in her body. The man's outburst was definitely weighing on her.

Sympathy for her registered. She knew the victim personally and felt responsible because she was the local sheriff. Everyone was looking up to her, counting on her.

She probably viewed today as a failure.

But she'd inherited this mess and he'd make sure she knew it wasn't her fault.

She coaxed Lambert back near the gate, and Justin watched as the ME examined the body.

"The MO consistent with Tina?" Justin asked.

"Belt marks look the same width." The doctor peered at him over the rim of his glasses. "But your killer didn't keep Kelly long."

"He's escalating, wants to show off, taunt us with the fact that he hasn't gotten caught and that he'll keep killing until we stop him."

Shouts near the gate made him jerk his head up, and he saw Lambert still arguing with Amanda, so he strode toward them. Someone had to defuse the situation. The media were taking pictures left and right.

"Mr. Lambert, I'm really sorry for your loss," Justin said as he coaxed him beneath the awning of the snack stand. "But right now you need to go home. Call a friend or family member to stay with you. Someone who can offer you comfort while we investigate."

Lambert's anguished look turned to anger that he directed toward Amanda. "You said you'd find her. I came to you for help and look what happened."

Amanda's hurt look tore at Justin. He understood about grief and anger, but Amanda didn't deserve this.

"Mr. Lambert," he said, his voice turning to steel. "Sheriff Blair did everything in her power to find your daughter, but Kelly's disappearance is related to a string of missing-persons cases that has spanned a decade. She has already made more strides in this investigation than your former sheriff."

Amanda gently took Mr. Lambert's arm. "Please go home, Mr. Lambert. I swear that I'll find the person who did this and lock him up."

She gestured toward the officer who'd been chasing Lambert earlier, and he escorted Lambert toward the exit. Justin saw the feeding frenzy of reporters and parents converging and silently cursed.

But another deputy stepped up to intervene and push them back so he headed over to the principal, who was talking with one of the crime techs.

"Excuse me, Mr. Blakely," Justin said. "Are there security cameras outside the school?"

The principal nodded, although his mouth thinned into a grim line. "We have a few, but not as many as we should, and I think a couple are broken."

Unbelievable with all the school shootings these days. "I want to look at all the feed of the parking lot and area by the stadium for the last twenty-four hours."

Justin gestured toward the crowd in the parking lot. "It's possible that our killer is in that crowd right now watching the commotion. He'll get off on our reactions and the drama."

Because he enjoyed inflicting pain and suffering on the town.

THE VIDEO FEED was all set up so Suzy Turner could watch the commotion. The reporters running to the school for the story. The students in upheaval.

The parents worried and racing to protect their spoiled offspring from the ugliness of the world.

Except they were hypocrites.

Those same parents allowed their teenagers to bully others. To taunt the weaker and berate the less intelligent and to shun the less attractive as if they were lepers.

Suzy Turner was one of them.

When the cameras finally showed Kelly Lambert's dead body sprawled on the bleachers, Suzy would know what her future held.

Not parties and bragging about her looks and money to her classmates.

Oh, she thought she was popular and that everyone loved her.

But they were a fickle lot. They'd quickly forget her just like they'd forgotten the others.

Chapter Twelve

Amanda and Justin approached the local news reporter, deciding they needed to gain control before the press made things worse. Parents and families were becoming increasingly agitated.

Amanda stepped up on one of the platforms on the outer edge of the stadium. "Folks, I need everyone to listen."

Angry voices shouted at her.

"Was there a teenager killed here this morning?"

"Who was murdered?"

"Why won't you tell us anything?"

"Are there shooters in the school?"

Amanda waved her hand. "Please listen. There was no school shooting, and no students at the school have been injured. Nor do we believe they're in danger."

"Then why is the school on lockdown?"

"A body was found!"

Amanda's hand shot up again. "This morning when the staff and students arrived, they did find the body of a young woman. She has been identified as twenty-seven-year-old Kelly Lambert, who was reported missing two days ago. Miss Lambert was not killed on the school grounds, but rather whoever murdered her left her body on the bleachers."

"Why leave it at the school?"

"Do you think one of the students is responsible?"

"Is the killer in there with our kids?"

Amanda shook her head. "We do not believe any current student at Canyon High is responsible or that the killer is inside the school. However, some students did see the body and we're keeping everyone contained until we can investigate. Your children are only being questioned in case they saw something pertinent to the case, and only with adult counselor supervision." She forced a calm firmness to her voice. "Now, I urge you to go home and go about your day. I promise you the students are safe and sound."

"What if you're wrong and the killer is in the school?" someone shouted.

Amanda tensed. What if she was wrong? No…the killer/kidnapper was now targeting women in their twenties, not teenagers. "Again, we do not think that is the case. Kelly Lambert was left here sometime during the night. The killer was long gone before the students and staff arrived."

But even as she tried to reassure the crowd of restless concerned parents, she wondered if that was true. She didn't think the killer was inside, but what if he'd waited around to see them find Kelly's body?

JUSTIN'S GAZE SCANNED the group as Amanda addressed them. Some asinine reporter had been talking to parents and onlookers, stirring up suspicion and panic by asking questions that were off base.

Everyone was restless and imagining the worst, but hopefully Amanda's reassurances would calm them. He saw doubt on many faces though, as if they weren't convinced she was telling the truth.

Principal Blakely took the microphone next, also urging parents to go home. "Folks, we have policies in place for situations like this, and we need your help. As Sheriff Blair stated, your kids are not in danger. If, however, any one of them suffers emotional duress as a result of today's events, we will be offering counseling services.

"Classes are resuming as normal, although sports activities and practices will be cancelled for the day. Buses will run on schedule, as well. Rest assured that if anything changes we will contact you."

He stepped down and began to move through the crowd, personally shaking hands and chatting with individuals until some of the panic settled and individuals began to disperse.

Justin studied the group, his senses honed for anyone who looked overtly nervous, someone filming the pandemonium, someone on the run.

"You did a good job," he told Amanda as they wove past a set of older folks, probably grandparents of some students. The small cluster looked worriedly at Amanda, then bowed their heads in whispers and finally clung to each other as they walked toward the exit.

Justin took Amanda's elbow. "Let's study the footage from the security cameras. Maybe something will stick out."

They walked together to the school guard, who escorted them to the security station inside and showed them the surveillance cameras. One camera was situated on each of the corners of the building with two more covering the gym and football stadium. The emergency exits also had cameras, but the angles were poor.

Unfortunately two of the cameras overlooking the entry points to the stadium had been broken.

Probably by teen pranks, the security guard said. They had been out for six weeks. The principal was waiting on budget approval to have them repaired.

But after surveying the films of the night, they found nothing. No one dragging a body into the stadium. Meaning the killer knew where the broken cameras were.

They moved on to look at the feed of the media and crowd gathered outside.

"What do you see?" Justin asked.

Amanda rubbed her temple. "A town full of concerned parents. I can't blame them. If my child was inside the school and I didn't know what was going on, I'd be anxious, too."

Justin covered her hand with his. An innocent gesture of camaraderie but one that made him want more. "We will find out who did this."

"I still think we should warn the classmates returning for the reunion."

"Then we'd tip our hand," Justin reasoned. "Right now the perp has no idea we're on to him."

"But that's just it. We're not," Amanda said, her voice riddled with frustration.

Justin squeezed her hand. "Yes, we are. We know he has a reason for targeting your female classmates. Reisling's father looks good for the crimes. And he has enough money to pay someone to alibi him if needed." He drummed his knuckles on the table as he searched the feed. "Do you see Reisling or his father in the crowd?"

Amanda leaned closer, searching. "No."

"Anyone else look out of place?"

"I know a few of the folks but not all of them," she said. "Wait, there's Suzy Turner's mother."

"Who's Suzy Turner?"

"Another classmate," Amanda said. "She looks upset. And she's talking to the principal."

Amanda's phone buzzed, and she snatched it up. "Sheriff Blair."

"It's Principal Blakely. Mrs. Turner is here and says she has to talk to you."

"I'll be right out," Amanda said. She disconnected, then turned to Justin. "Keep looking at the feed. Let me go talk to Mrs. Turner."

He nodded, but a bad premonition hit him. Kelly Lambert had been taken two days ago. And now she was dead.

And Mrs. Turner looked panicked.

Had the unsub taken another victim?

AMANDA RUSHED THROUGH the hallway and outside to the roped-off area around the bleachers, her heart hammering as Suzy Turner's mother rushed toward her. "Amanda," the woman cried. "I'm scared. I can't find Suzy anywhere. I think she's missing." She glanced at the crime scene tape. "When I heard a body was found here, I was terrified it was her."

Amanda's chest constricted. "No, now tell me what happened, Mrs. Turner. Why do you think Suzy is missing?"

"Because she was supposed to come to our house for dinner last night," Mrs. Turner said. "She always comes on Thursday nights. Ever since her father got sick, she never misses a week."

"I'm sorry, I didn't know your husband was ill," Amanda said.

Tears glittered in the woman's eyes. "He has Alzheimer's. Early onset. Suzy didn't like to talk about it, but she knew her time with him was limited, so she wanted to see him while he still remembered her." Her voice broke on the last few words. "You have to find her. I can't lose her, too...."

Amanda squeezed Mrs. Turner's hands. "When was the last time you saw or spoke to her?"

"Yesterday morning. She called and said she'd pick up dessert for that evening. Then she...didn't show."

"Did she tell you what her plans were for the day?"

"Just that she had errands to run. She was in charge of decorations for the reunion." Mrs. Turner rubbed her hands as if to ward off a chill. "I called and called her all night, but there was no answer. So I went to her condo this morning to check on her, but nobody was there."

"What about her car?"

"It was gone."

"Doesn't she travel for her job?" Amanda asked. She faintly remembered that Suzy was in pharmaceutical sales.

"She does travel, but she cancelled work trips until after the reunion."

Everything pointed back to the reunion.

If Amanda didn't call it off soon, there wouldn't be any

females left to attend. The unsub had killed Kelly in two days, meaning Suzy's life was in terrible danger.

"I'll need to search her condo, her phones, computer. Maybe something in there can tell us where she went. Hopefully she just had an emergency business meeting."

"I hope so, but it's not like her not to call." Mrs. Turner wiped tears from her eyes. "Do you think the person who killed Kelly has my Suzy?"

Unfortunately she did, but she refused to panic the woman. "We can't jump to that conclusion. Was Suzy upset with anyone, or was she having problems at work or home?"

"No," Mrs. Turner said. "Her job was going great. She just got a promotion."

"How about problems with coworkers?"

"Not that she mentioned."

"Did she have a boyfriend?"

"No one serious. She said there was someone at work, but she wouldn't tell me who he was."

Which made Amanda wonder if he was married. "I'll get over to Suzy's and look around as soon as possible. Do you happen to have a key to her place?"

The woman fidgeted, then pulled one from her purse and gave her the address. "Here, I water her plants when she's out of town." She pushed the key into Amanda's hand. "I can't lose her, Amanda. You have to find her before she ends up like Kelly."

"I promise I'll do everything I can." Of course she'd made the same promise to Kelly Lambert's father and fiancé and she'd failed.

Amanda had to ask one more question. "Did Suzy have trouble with anyone from our class?"

"No," Mrs. Turner said. "Why would you ask that?"

"Just routine questions, ma'am."

"You remember Suzy. She was popular in school, head cheerleader, class vice president and all. Everyone loved her."

Except for the not-so-popular girls who'd been jealous of

her. But were any of them jealous enough to hurt her? And after ten years?

That seemed extreme.

"Mrs. Turner, do you remember Donald Reisling and his accident?"

"Of course, that was awful. I felt so sorry for his father, the way Donald shamed him and all."

Hadn't she heard that Lynn had really been driving? Of course, no one had ever proved that….

"Did Suzy date Donald?"

"No…I mean she was nice to him after the accident, tried to be a friend. But I think he wanted more and that would never have worked." Mrs. Turner's eye twitched. "Why? What does Donald have to do with Suzy?"

"I don't know, maybe nothing," Amanda asked.

Still, if she'd rejected Donald, either he or his father might have wanted revenge.

JUSTIN CONTINUED STUDYING the camera feed, his instincts kicking in as he noticed a young man, late twenties to early thirties, with sandy hair and a goatee.

He looked nervous, his gaze shifting back and forth between the spectators as if he was searching for someone. He pushed his way to the front until he reached the edge of the football field and peered over the fence.

One of the officers in charge of clearing the parking lot motioned for people to head back to their cars, and the guy pulled a ball cap lower on his head, jammed his hands in the pockets of his jeans and hurried away.

Justin searched the other cameras to see which vehicle the man went to, but lost him when he faded into an area where the cameras had been broken.

Who was the man and what had he been nervous about?

SUZY TURNER HAD struggled and fought for her life, but to no avail. Now she lay like a limp rag doll, her white blond hair tangled around her face, those sparkling green eyes blank of the normally coy smile that lit them up.

It had been fun to watch her die.

The pictures of the others lined the wall. Julie Kane. Lynn Faust.

Then the final one—Amanda Blair.

Killing her would make the revenge complete.

Chapter Thirteen

Amanda hurried back to the security station to talk to Justin. He waved her in, his brows furrowed. "I've narrowed the window of time when the body was dumped," Justin said. "Sometime after two a.m." He pointed to one of the cameras near the left entryway to the field. "One of the cameras had been out, but that one was working. Someone shot it out around two-fifteen."

"That could be helpful," Amanda said. "The crime scene team should search for the bullet casing."

"I'll let them know. There's something else I want you to look at."

Amanda eased up beside him. "Okay, but we've got another problem. Mrs. Turner is worried, Justin. She thinks her daughter, Suzy, has disappeared."

Justin cursed. "All right, look at this, then we'll talk about the Turner case." He rewound the camera and zeroed in on the young man with the hat. "Do you recognize him?"

Amanda narrowed her eyes. "Yes, that's Carlton Butts's brother, Ted."

"Did they have a younger sibling at Canyon High?"

She shook her head no.

"Then what's he doing here?"

"I don't know," Amanda admitted. "Maybe he heard about the body and was just curious like half the town."

"Could be. But he looks awfully nervous."

"He does, doesn't he?" Amanda tried to recall the last time she'd seen Ted, but couldn't.

"You said he and his brother weren't close?"

"No, they were too different," Amanda said. "At Carlton's funeral, he told me that he didn't understand Carlton. Ted knew his brother was depressed and had been picked on by the other kids, but he said Carlton brought some of the antagonism on himself."

"So he wouldn't want revenge against the girls who refused to date his brother?"

"I don't think so," Amanda said "But we can talk to him if you want."

Justin said, "We need to look at Suzy's life, her schedule, figure out her movements the day she went missing. Maybe we'll find something to link her disappearance to Kelly's."

She hoped so. The bodies were piling up way too quickly.

Together they walked outside, then drove back to the police station, the gray clouds adding to the gloom mounting inside her.

Terry Sumter sat by the front desk, looking belligerent as they entered the station.

In another chair Mr. Reisling sat beside another man she assumed was his attorney. Reisling looked confident, almost smug.

"Deputy, please escort Mr. Reisling and his lawyer to my office," Justin said. "I'll interview them while the sheriff talks to Mr. Sumter."

Amanda nodded, knowing the interrogations would go quicker if they split up. They'd spent most of the day at the school. Afternoon was fading into early evening and they needed answers.

Needed to find Suzy before it was too late.

Terry glared at her with hate-filled eyes. "You aren't really going to arrest me, are you?"

"Where were you two nights ago?" Amanda asked.

He crossed his feet at the ankles. "You mean the night Kelly disappeared?"

"Yes."

"On a work detail," Sumter said.

Amanda raised a brow. "I thought you lost your job."

"My company fell apart when the building business hit bottom," he said. "But I do some renovations with Harvey Mabry. Two nights ago I was laying floors in Cedartown. Call Harvey and ask him."

"I will." Amanda shoved a notepad in front of Terry. "Write down his contact information."

Terry's hand shook as he took the pen.

"Nervous, Terry? You hiding something?"

His eyes pierced her again. "I just need a drink, that's all."

So he was an alcoholic. "They have AA meetings at the Methodist church."

He dropped his head with a grunt that said he didn't appreciate her advice, scribbled the number, then handed it to her.

"Terry, have you seen Suzy Turner lately?"

"No, she left a message on my machine about the reunion, but I didn't call her back. No one there I want to see."

"Stay put while I call Harvey." She stepped aside and punched the man's number, then explained that she needed to know if Terry was working the night Kelly disappeared.

"Yeah, he was with my crew all day and half the night laying floors. Didn't get done till after four a.m. Terry's not a bad guy when he leaves the booze alone."

She wondered if that was why his business had failed instead of the economy.

She thanked him, then hung up. "Terry, do you still have your class ring?"

"No, I gave it to Lynn years ago. When we broke up, I didn't want it back." He flexed his hands, looked at his empty ring finger. "Why are you asking about my class ring?"

Amanda gritted her teeth. "I can't say at this point."

But if Terry had given Lynn his class ring, how had it ended up in Kelly Lambert's hand?

JUSTIN STUDIED REISLING. Interrogating him again would probably be a waste of time. The man had money and power and wielded it like a sword.

But he was the most viable suspect they had.

"First of all, let me introduce myself," the astute grayhaired man in the three-piece suit said. "I'm Mr. Reisling's attorney, Jay Edward Fuller."

Justin tapped his badge. "Sergeant Thorpe, Texas Ranger. And before you start throwing up a bunch of legal jargon, I want you to know why we asked Mr. Reisling to come in."

"He explained that you're investigating a missing woman named Kelly Lambert."

"Actually she's no longer missing, as I'm sure you're aware if you've seen the news today. Her body was found at the high school this morning. So now we're dealing with a homicide."

Mr. Reisling averted his eyes. "Such a shame. She was such a nice young woman."

Justin's brow shot up at Reisling's sarcastic tone. "I understand that you disliked her because she didn't want anything to do with your son after the accident that paralyzed him. At least that was my earlier impression."

"All those snotty kids did abandon him," Reisling shot back.

"Don't say anything else," Fuller warned in a low tone.

Justin's mouth twitched as he fought a smile. He enjoyed seeing the jerk put in his place. And if he was the killer, he wanted to see him rot in jail.

"Where were you two nights ago?" Justin asked.

Reisling smoothed down his tie. "In Austin on business."

"You have someone who can verify that?"

Reisling glanced at his attorney and his attorney gave a clipped nod. "I met with a client. And yes, she'll alibi me."

Justin propped himself on the edge of the desk, folded his arms and leaned forward, scrutinizing him. "What about last night?"

Reisling fidgeted and looked at his lawyer for guidance. Fuller's expression was a complete blank. The man had a great poker face.

"What time?" Fuller asked.

"Between two-fifteen and six-thirty," Justin said. "That's when the guard comes on duty at the school."

Reisling's lips compressed into a thin, straight line. "I was home in bed like everyone else in this godforsaken town."

"Not everyone," Justin said. "Someone was dropping off Kelly Lambert's body so the teenagers at school would find her this morning."

Reisling scowled and started to say something, but Fuller placed a hand on the other man's arm and shook his head. "We came in as a courtesy, Sergeant Thorpe, but I've heard enough. Unless you're going to arrest my client, we're done here." Fuller stood and Reisling followed.

Irritated, Justin worked his jaw from side to side. "Mr. Reisling, do you know Suzy Turner?"

Hatred flashed in the man's eyes for a millisecond before he disguised it with a phony smile. "Of course. She went to school with my son."

"What's going on?" Fuller asked.

"We believe Kelly Lambert's murder is related to a string of other disappearances from this area and counties across the state. The common link is the high school, more specifically the girls who attended school with Mr. Reisling's son."

Awareness dawned in the lawyer's eyes, and Justin realized that Reisling hadn't filled his attorney in on his son's background. Fuller must not be from Sunset Mesa or he'd already know.

"You're looking for a serial kidnapper/killer?" Fuller asked.

Justin nodded. "And your client had motive to hurt each of the missing girls."

"How DID IT go with Reisling?" Amanda asked as she drove to Carlton Butts's mother's house. She wasn't sure if his brother still lived there, but since Mrs. Butts relied on a walker and had trouble getting around, she took a chance that the woman didn't live alone.

The home was located in a low-rent section of town that kids used to call the poor houses, another reason Carlton had literally been the butt of other kids' taunts. Ten years had intensified the weathered paint and rotting boards, proving no one, real-estate developer or individual, had decided to keep up the properties. Dark clouds shrouded the sky, adding an eerie look to the area. Weeds and dead flowers choked the yards, trees that had blown down in a storm still hadn't been cut and hauled away and the vehicles parked in the drives confirmed that the owners were low-income families barely able to survive.

Too bad Terry Sumter hadn't taken it upon himself to upgrade this property. He could probably pick up the houses for a song and flip them, then turn his life around.

But he was not Amanda's problem. Unless he'd killed Kelly and Tina and kidnapped the other victims.

She parked and cut the engine. "I used to come out here to work on science projects with Carlton. I still can't believe he committed suicide."

"Did his mother see the signs?"

"I don't know," Amanda said as they walked up the cement driveway.

She rang the doorbell, but it wasn't working, so Justin knocked. He was studying the property and woods behind it as if he expected trouble.

Footsteps shuffled inside, and the sound of a key being

turned echoed through the door. Finally, Mrs. Butts cracked the door open and peered out, but she was leaning heavily on her walker.

"Mrs. Butts," Amanda said. "It's Amanda Blair, Sheriff Blair now." She gestured toward Justin. "This is Sergeant Thorpe with the Texas Rangers. We'd like to talk to you and your son."

"My son is dead," she said bitterly.

Amanda detected the strong scent of whiskey on her breath and realized Carlton's mother must, like Terry, have a problem with booze. Her once-brown hair had gray stripes and was uncombed, and she tugged a ratty bathrobe tighter around her neck as if they'd just woken her.

"I know Carlton died," she said, wondering if the woman simply wanted to make a point or if she was senile. "But we'd like to talk to your other son Ted."

Mrs. Butts put more weight on her walker. "What about?"

"Is Ted here, ma'am?" Justin asked.

"Why would he be? He don't live here anymore."

"Where does he live?" Amanda asked.

"Other side of town. Got one of those cabins near the creek."

Tina Grimes's body had been found in Camden Creek.

"Is that where he'd be now?" Amanda asked.

"Naw, he should be at work. What you want with Ted?"

"He was at the high school earlier when Kelly Lambert's body was found."

Mrs. Butts's eyes widened, tinged with fear. "I'm sure a lot of other folks were there, too."

"Most of them were parents of students in the school," Amanda pointed out.

Justin gripped the edge of the door. "Where does your son work?"

"He owns a cabinet shop. Does custom work for those big fancy developments going up in the neighboring counties."

"Has he kept up with any of his former classmates from school?" Amanda asked.

Mrs. Butts shook her head. "No, why would he? After the way they treated Carlton, he decided they weren't worth his time."

"So he was still mad at people over Carlton's death?" Justin asked.

The woman's eyes darted back and forth between them as if she suddenly realized she'd said too much. "Ted's a good boy," she said defensively. "He went to college and got a degree in business. Manages his own shop." She wagged her finger at Amanda. "Don't you dare turn on him like you did Carlton."

Guilt suffused Amanda. She hadn't turned on Carlton. But she also hadn't remained close friends. She'd been caught up in her own life. "Is Ted going to the reunion?" Amanda asked.

"You'll have to ask him," Mrs. Butts said. "Although he may want to show those little twits that he made something of himself."

Amanda thanked the woman; then she and Justin walked back to the car.

Mrs. Butts's comment about her turning on Carlton gnawed at her. If she'd stayed closer to Carlton, could she have saved him from committing suicide?

Ten minutes later, they stood inside Ted's cabinet shop. Amanda was impressed with the details of his carpentry work and understood why he'd landed projects with the developers building high-end estate homes.

She spoke to the receptionist, a redhead with streaks of black in her hair and red cowboy boots. "Howdy. What can we do for you?"

Amanda and Justin both identified themselves. "Can we talk to Ted?"

"Let me check and see if he's busy with a customer." She rose, teetering on her high-heeled boots, and disappeared through a doorway. The sound of voices echoed from the back; then she reappeared and led them through a set of double doors to an office that surprised Amanda with its modern design.

"Hello, Amanda," Ted said.

Gone was the ball cap from the camera feed. His hair was close cropped, his button-down shirt and jeans giving him a professional but casual look. He'd aged some since she'd seen him, but there was such a stark difference between him and Carlton that she understood how Carlton had felt like the underdog in comparison.

"It looks like your business is doing well," Amanda said.

He shrugged, but his eyes glittered with pride. "Yeah, I like my business." He glanced at Justin. "But you two didn't come to talk to me about my cabinets, did you?"

Amanda shifted. "Why were you outside the school today?"

Unease flickered in his eyes. "I heard the news and was curious like everyone else, I guess."

"Did you keep up with Kelly?" Justin asked.

He shook his head. "She called about the reunion and left a message. I never called her back."

"Are you going to attend?" Amanda asked.

He smoothed a hand over a wood sample. "Not sure yet. It's not like I kept close friends with anyone there. After Carlton died, it was…hard."

"What about Suzy Turner?" Justin asked. "Have you seen her lately?"

"Suzy?" His voice cracked. "Don't tell me she's missing, too."

"Her mother thinks so," Amanda said.

"Answer the question," Justin asked. "Have you seen her lately?"

"No. But she left a message about the reunion, too. Said she was bringing a new boyfriend. You know she always liked to brag about herself."

"Did you have a thing for her?" Justin asked.

"You've got to be kidding. Snotty girls aren't my type." His eyes flashed with annoyance; then a mask slid over his face. "Listen, Amanda, I didn't hang out with those girls in school, and it's been ten years since Carlton died. If you think I've held some grudge against them, you're wrong." He rubbed a finger along one of the ridges of a cabinet. "I loved my brother, but I told him he needed to grow thicker skin. Then he killed himself and I had to pick up the pieces of my mom." Anger hardened his voice. "I don't blame the kids at school. I blame Carlton. He took the coward's way out and destroyed our family in the process."

"WELL, THAT WAS a surprise," Justin said as they left the cabinet shop. "Ted had good reason to harbor a grudge against the girls who ridiculed his brother, but he doesn't seem to."

"I told you I didn't think they got along," Amanda said. "He's obviously still angry with Carlton for killing himself."

"He's right, that is the coward's way out," Justin said. "But since he doesn't seem to hold a grudge, he doesn't seem like a likely suspect."

Amanda punched in Mrs. Turner's number, hoping for a miracle—that Suzy had shown up by now. The woman answered on the second ring, her voice raspy as if she'd been crying. "Hello, Amanda."

"Have you heard from Suzy?"

"No, did you find her?"

Amanda winced at the desperate hope in the woman's voice. "Not yet. I'm on my way to her place right now to look around."

"Do you need me to come over?"

"No, just let me know if you hear from her." Amanda hung up and swung the vehicle onto the main road leading to the condos. Night had fallen, the land bathed in darkness as she left town and sped down the road.

Suddenly a dark car shot out of a side street, raced up

behind her and started around her. Irritated, she flipped on the siren, but the car simply sped up instead of falling back or pulling over.

The windows were tinted so dark she couldn't see inside, but the window slid down a fraction of an inch and suddenly a gunshot blasted the air.

Amanda ducked, swerving right as the bullet shattered the driver's window. Glass sprayed her and a burning sensation shot through her left arm.

Justin cursed and grabbed the steering wheel as the squad car spun out of control and slid toward the ravine.

Chapter Fourteen

Justin jerked his gun from his holster, hoping to get off a round at the shooter, but Amanda had been hit, and the car was out of control.

"I've got the wheel," Amanda said, struggling to right the car and keep it from crashing.

He swung his gun up behind her head and fired, but the dark sedan surged forward, its taillights disappearing into the night. His breath rasped out as he squinted to read the license plate, but the car had no tag.

The squad car slammed into the bank to the right, then spun sideways and screeched to a stop. He jerked forward, but the seat belt caught him, and Amanda gripped the steering wheel. He expected the air bags to pelt them, but the impact must not have been strong enough to trigger them.

"Dammit, he got away!" Amanda shouted.

Justin's heart hammered. "Where are you hit?"

"My arm, but it's just a flesh wound." Amanda shoved hair from her face. "Did you see the shooter?"

"No, did you?"

She shook her head. "The windows were too dark."

"There was no license plate either," Justin said.

"It was a planned attack." Amanda closed her eyes and leaned back against the seat, and Justin wondered if she'd lied about the seriousness of her injury. Flesh wounds still stung like the devil and now her adrenaline was wearing off, she might be feeling the pain.

"Let me see your arm," he said, forcing his voice to be gentle when he wanted to tear after that car and beat the hell out of the SOB who'd shot her.

Amanda sighed, twisting around to look at him. "I'm fine. But obviously the killer wants to stop us from asking questions."

He pulled her hand toward him. "Let me see, Amanda."

Emotions swirled in the depths of her eyes. It had been a hell of a day and she looked exhausted.

"I should have stopped this guy before now," she murmured.

Guilt deepened her voice, making his heart tug. Kelly Lambert's father had blamed her for not finding his daughter in time. Mrs. Butts blamed her for abandoning her son.

Amanda blamed herself for another classmate's disappearance.

It wasn't right.

Unable to stop himself, he pulled her into his arms. "None of this is your fault, Amanda. You're doing a great job."

She shook her head, her hair brushing his chin, but she didn't pull away. "But I promised Mr. Lambert I'd find Kelly, and now Suzy is missing."

Justin stroked her back, soothing her. "I've worked cases like this before. The killer seems like he's one step ahead, but eventually he screws up. We will find him, Amanda."

He felt Amanda's soft breath on his neck as she lifted her head to look up at him. "But it's not enough. If I don't make an arrest soon, Suzy might end up like Kelly."

Justin bit his tongue to keep from telling her that if the unsub had Suzy, she was probably already dead. Since there was no sign of sexual assault, it was clear the motive was murder.

Only the suspect had disposed of the bodies where they

couldn't be found with the first few cases, but had recently decided to claim the kills.

Because he was ready to send a message and receive the glory for the crimes.

He cradled Amanda's face between his hands. "Listen to me, Amanda. We're law officers. We hunt down the bad guys, but we're still human. We can't save everyone."

"But we have to try," she whispered.

He nodded, his heart hammering. "Yes, and we will get him."

She looked so vulnerable that his eyes were drawn to her mouth. He wanted to kiss her. Hold her.

Promise her everything would be all right.

His lips touched hers. Soft. Gentle. Hungry.

She parted her lips in invitation, and he deepened the kiss, tracing her mouth with his tongue. She moaned softly and clung to him, her fingers stroking his back.

A heartbeat later, her phone rang and she eased away from him. For a brief second, he felt bereft, as if he'd lost something important.

Only how could he lose something he'd never had?

AMANDA SHIVERED AT the intensity in Justin's expression. Lord help her, she could drown in those sultry bedroom eyes.

He was so strong and in control, so masculine and confident, so protective—exactly like her father had been.

She'd been devastated when she'd lost him.

How would she survive if she allowed herself to fall for Justin and something happened to him?

He could have been killed a minute ago.

So could you, and you would never have known what it was like to be in his arms. To feel his kiss.

Her phone buzzed like a siren again, and she jolted back to reality. Good grief, she was supposed to be working.

She snatched up the phone. "Sheriff Blair."

"It's Deputy Morgan. I wanted to let you know I looked

at the list of people Lambert turned down for loans. Two of them have moved on. The other is old man Gentry. He's almost ninety so I don't see him kidnapping or killing anyone."

"Thanks for checking it out, Deputy."

She disconnected and reached for the keys, but Justin caught her hands.

"Let me look at that arm first."

Her arm was stinging, and he would persist unless she proved that she was okay. The bullet had grazed the upper part of her shoulder so she had to undo the top few buttons of her uniform shirt to show him.

Heat blazed in his eyes as he watched her unfasten the buttons. She knew the plain khaki shirt wasn't sexy, but she was still a woman and had donned a lacy black bra beneath it.

His smile of appreciation made her belly flutter with awareness and desire. Her nipples budded, practically begging for him to touch them.

But she leaned sideways so he could examine her arm, ignoring the pull of attraction. The bullet had skimmed the skin, tearing her shirt, and her flesh was red like a burn. But the bullet hadn't lodged inside her arm.

"We need to find that bullet," Justin said.

Amanda nodded, her heart squeezing when he bent his head and placed a kiss on her flesh wound. "We'll treat that with some cream later."

"It's fine," Amanda said, swallowing back the emotions his tenderness stirred. Since when had a man been tender with her?

Most guys thought she was such a tomboy they didn't bother. Of course that was when she had a rare date. She was more the "friend" type. They treated her as if she was one of the guys.

Unable to stand being so close to him and not touching him or kissing him again, she hurriedly fastened her blouse while he searched the floor for the bullet casing. Several seconds later, he plucked it from the door on his side.

He used a penlight to examine it. "Looks like a .38. I'll send it to the lab for analysis."

Amanda focused back on the case, then pulled onto the highway before she did something insane like throw herself at him.

JUSTIN SILENTLY CURSED himself as Amanda drove toward the Turner place. What the hell was wrong with him?

He never allowed himself to become involved with a suspect or a law enforcement officer. He normally liked sexy women who wanted a romp in the sack with no baggage, no ties, no commitments.

No expectations.

Amanda fit none of those requirements.

Well, maybe she fit one. She didn't seem as if she was looking to settle down. She was just as career focused as him. Growing up under the thumb of a Ranger, she obviously wanted to follow in his footsteps.

But her job could get her killed.

Protective instincts that had reared their ugly head at him when that bullet zinged through the window fought their way to the surface again.

Dammit, he shouldn't care. She was just another coworker.

Except she might be a target of this nutcase.

"Did Donald Reisling ever ask you out?" Justin asked.

Amanda slanted him an odd look. "Why would you ask that?"

"Just curious. Did he?"

Amanda's pretty lips formed a pout. Or maybe they simply were plump from his kisses.

Damn, he wanted to plump them up some more.

"No, he was a star athlete," she said, self-deprecation in her voice. "I told you I wasn't in the popular crowd."

"But you're attractive and you were athletic and smart. The guys had to see that."

"We're talking about *teenagers*," Amanda said, emphasizing the last word. "The only thing on their brains was sex. And I wasn't that kind of girl either."

He hadn't expected that she was. Which also made him like her more.

And want her more.

He balled his hands into fists. He had to get a grip.

"So after the accident when the popular girls rejected Reisling, did he seek friendships with you or anyone that he hadn't befriended before?"

Amanda chewed her bottom lip. "No, not that I remember. I heard he fell into a deep depression for a while. And of course, he underwent physical therapy."

"That's understandable."

"Why the questions about Donald?"

"Because someone just shot at us. Rather you," he said. "And Donald Reisling's father is one of our primary suspects."

A frisson of alarm splintered her face. "You think that he might target me?"

Justin hated to voice the thought aloud. But he had to follow the clues and evidence. And if that didn't work, he'd rely on his gut instincts.

Someone had just tried to kill Amanda.

He wanted to find the SOB and lock him up before he finished her off like he had Kelly, Tina and the other victims whose bodies hadn't yet been found.

AMANDA STIFLED THOUGHTS of that heated kiss as she and Justin entered the high-rise condo development. They stopped at the security desk, identified themselves and explained the situation.

One look at Justin's credentials and her badge, and the beefy guy escorted them to the elevator.

"You have surveillance cameras?" Justin asked.

"Yes, sir. If Suzy was abducted, it wasn't from here."

Amanda frowned. Nothing was impossible. But the fact that this building had built-in security points at the front and cameras stationed throughout the hall and elevators would definitely make a kidnapping more difficult.

With Kelly, fake texts had been sent to lure her into a trap. Had the same thing happened to Suzy?

The guard pointed out the camera near the elevator, only three feet from Suzy's door, making Amanda even more sure that the perp hadn't abducted Suzy from her condo.

She inserted the key into the lock, and opened the door. Justin reached out a hand and urged her to stay back.

"Let me check out the interior first."

Even though she doubted the killer was there, Amanda pulled her own gun.

Suzy might be inside the condo.

But she might not be alive.

Suzy Turner could still wear her cheerleading uniform after ten years. All those exercise classes and body-toning treatments and personal trainers had paid off.

Too bad she wouldn't need them anymore now she was dead.

But wouldn't her mother be proud she'd kept her figure?

Her darling, pretty daughter had danced and cheered and teased all the boys ten years ago.

She'd broken dozens of hearts. Trampled on them as if they were ants that needed stomping out at a picnic.

No more.

Now Suzy would lie dead instead of partying with her friends.

The circus at the school had been fun to watch today.

Tomorrow would be even better. Even if they didn't find Suzy tonight, they would find her.

Then another one would die.

Chapter Fifteen

Justin hesitated at the doorway of the condo, studying the scene. Amanda gasped beside him.

The cushions on the white sofa had been slashed, the stuffing pouring out, something black that looked like ashes smearing the fabric.

Was it symbolic? Was the unsub trying to send a message, or had Suzy's place simply been an opportunity for the perp to vent his rage?

Amanda eased inside, her gun poised to fire, and they swept the living room and kitchen. He gestured that he would search the room off the right side of the hall and she took the left.

One look into the master bedroom, and he realized Suzy was compulsive with organization and design. The condo was a showcase, not a place he'd want to live in. Expensive furniture, artwork, vases, white carpet.

Nothing that felt like home.

No personal photographs or worn tennis shoes or holey jeans. Did the woman really live here, or was it just a stop between travels?

Her closet had been opened, several evening gowns slashed and strewn across the floor. Others had been left hanging, neat and at equal intervals, designer shoes still encased in their original fabric dust bags or boxes.

But no one was inside.

He inched to the master bath, half expecting Suzy's dead body to be lying on the floor or in the bathtub, although he didn't know why. So far, only two of the missing women had been found, both strangled.

Neither in their own homes.

He scanned the bathroom, again noting plush white towels and a glass shelf filled with cosmetics.

Although some bottles had been broken, thrown against the wall, the contents spilled out.

Then he noticed there was water in the garden tub. He stepped closer, leaned over and spotted a corsage floating in it.

Questions ticked in his head.

A class ring had been found in Tina's and Kelly's hand. Rings that signified the class preparing to gather for Canyon High's reunion.

Was this corsage significant? Violets. Were they the same type of flowers she'd worn to homecoming or prom?

AMANDA'S LUNGS STRAINED for a breath as she eased her way through the hall and into Suzy's home office. She'd already noted the destruction of the entertainment system in the living room, but a laptop sat on another desk in the office.

This one hadn't been smashed. Instead it was open, and a screen saver displayed a ten-year-old photograph of Suzy and the cheerleading squad. Suzy's blond hair gleamed beneath the camera lights, her smile boasting no telling how many dollars' worth of dental work.

Amanda's heart began to pound.

Was there a specific reason the intruder had left this computer unharmed? Did the photo of Suzy and the other cheerleaders mean something?

She quickly checked the closet, but it was empty. Relief spilled through her that she hadn't found Suzy's body. Not that it meant Suzy was still alive.

But until they had her body, there was hope.

Amanda noted dozens of fliers and stacks of mail on the chrome desk, one file box designated for work. But most of the other mail pertained to the reunion and the upcoming plans for the celebration.

"The bedroom's clear," Justin said, startling her.

She glanced over her shoulder. "Did you find anything?"

"Her bedroom was trashed like the living room. The bathtub was full of water, and a corsage was floating inside."

Amanda's pulse jumped. "A corsage?"

"A wristband of violets a teenage girl would wear to homecoming or prom."

"Good grief," Amanda said. "Class rings. Corsages. It all keeps coming back to the school."

"And whatever happened ten years ago to tick off the perp."

Perspiration trickled down the back of Amanda's neck. "Look at this." She gestured toward the screen saver. "I doubt even Suzy was still stuck in time enough to keep this on her computer. Especially one she uses for work."

Justin leaned toward the screen, studying the photos. "Who are the girls?"

Amanda swallowed hard and pointed them out from left to right. "Melanie Hoit, Julie Kane, Lynn Faust, Kelly Lambert and Suzy in the front row. Anise Linton, Mona Pratt and Eleanor Goggins in the back row."

"Two of the girls in the front row are dead and now another is missing," Justin surmised.

Worry kicked in Amanda's gut. "I wonder if that means Julie and Lynn are next."

"There's the back row, too," Justin said.

Amanda contemplated what they knew so far. "But Avery Portland, one of the original victims, wasn't a cheerleader. And neither was Tina Grimes, Carly Edgewater, or Denise Newnan. At least not at Canyon High."

"True. But somehow they fit the victimology or knew the unsub."

Amanda glanced up at Justin. "We have to warn the rest of the cheerleaders that they're in danger."

Justin hesitated.

They had already questioned Anise, Mona and Eleanor about Kelly's disappearance. "Let's think about that. We don't want to panic anyone. And with Kelly's death, they're probably already on edge."

Unease prickled Amanda's spine. "What if we're looking at this all wrong? We know Donald Reisling had a reason to hate the women. But what if our killer is a female? A woman from our class who feels like these girls cheated her out of something."

"Like making the cheerleading squad?" Justin asked.

"That does seem thin for a motive, doesn't it?" Amanda said.

Justin shrugged. "Not if the girl has mental problems. Sometimes unstable people zero in on a specific event as the pivotal moment in their life, the event that destroyed their future. The perp could have tried out, failed and been shunned by the ones who did make it. She thinks that if she'd only made the squad, she would have been popular, would have had more friends, success…a different life."

"Then we need to look at the roster and find out who was cut." Amanda felt a burst of adrenaline. "I'll talk to the cheerleading coach. She might have some insight."

"We should speak with the school counselor, too," Justin said. "The counselor would know if a specific student had emotional issues that fit the profile."

"Good idea."

"Have you seen a purse or cell phone?"

"No."

"I'll search for one while you scan her emails." Justin glanced around the condo. "If the unsub didn't take her from here, he might have sent her a text to lure her away like he did Kelly."

Amanda frowned. "But even if he didn't take her from

the condo, the suspect was here. We should look at the surveillance tapes and see who came in and out."

"I'll ask the guard to get tapes of the last twenty-four hours for us."

Amanda's pulse pounded. Hopefully they would finally catch a break.

JUSTIN QUICKLY PHONED the guard, filled him in and asked him to pull the tapes. Then he hurriedly searched the office bookcase, various shelves, the hall closet and the bedroom, but found no purse or phone. Another sweep of the den didn't turn up anything either.

Had Suzy left of her own accord to meet someone, then been ambushed?

"I didn't find the phone or purse," he told Amanda. "I'm going to look at those tapes while you finish with her computer."

"Call me if you find anything," Amanda said, her attention on the screen. "I'll see what her schedule looked like before she disappeared."

He rushed into the hallway, and rode the elevator to the main floor and met the guard.

The guard escorted him down the hall into a large room with several screens showing views of the building, hallways and elevator.

"This is from the last twenty-four hours."

Justin slid into one of the chairs and watched as the guard set the tapes for him to review. The guard identified each of the residents as they appeared outside and inside the building, seemed to know the make and model of cars they drove and other tidbits of personal information he'd picked up on the job.

One unit had had furniture delivered the previous day, but the resident had been home to sign for it and let the deliveryman in. UPS delivered several packages along with FedEx. A cleaning service that worked the building came and went, cleaning the common areas, while several of the units had obviously hired them, as well. The residents consisted of young singles or couples in their thirties who worked.

He sat up straighter as Suzy Turner exited her unit at eight a.m. the previous morning. She looked distracted, was checking her phone messages and juggling her briefcase as she rushed toward the elevator.

She'd been very much alive.

He wanted to know what was on her phone.

"What kind of car did Suzy drive?"

"A silver BMW," the guard said. He recited the license plate off the top of his head.

Justin punched his chief's number and requested the tech analyst get copies of Suzy's phone records, then asked him to put an APB on her car.

"I'll get back to you," his chief said.

Justin's mind churned as he scoured through the rest of the tapes. The same cleaning crew that had worked the building entered Suzy's apartment around 1:00 p.m.

Or was it the same crew?

There was only one woman. Her head was wrapped in a scarf like one of the workers from the company, but she was alone.

"Does the crew ever split up on jobs?" he asked.

The guard shrugged. "Sometimes they do for individual cleaning jobs."

He studied the woman again, frowning when he noticed she was wearing a pair of black boots. Hadn't she been wearing tennis shoes earlier?

He rewound the tape and studied the footage, his pulse spiking. Yes, the woman with the scarf had worn tennis shoes in the previous shot.

Why would she change her shoes?

Unless it wasn't the same woman…

Could Amanda be right? Was their unsub a female, maybe a former classmates who held a grudge?

AMANDA MET THE crime team at the door to Suzy's condo and explained the situation. "Any forensics you can find might help stop this guy."

They went straight to work while she finished combing Suzy's computer files. Suzy was active on social media, but most of her posts pertained to business and her active social life. Apparently she had hit the million-dollar sale mark at work, traveled to Europe constantly, and liked to shop on-line at expensive boutiques.

Amanda faintly remembered her once saying that she wouldn't be caught dead in a department-store find or in a dress that another girl might own.

Amanda searched for a boyfriend and found several flir-tatious notes between her and a man named Syd who lived in London, but nothing definitive. Another flurry of notes discussed the upcoming reunion with Kelly, Julie and Lynn.

She found a photo gallery of old high school candids in a file that had been organized into a slideshow accompa-nied by music. It seemed to be intended to be shown at the reunion dinner. One shot captured her attention—Suzy in her prom dress standing beside her date.

Amanda immediately zeroed in on the corsage.

Violets, just like the ones floating in Suzy's tub.

She scrolled through the photos again, searching for signs of a classmate who might be jealous of Suzy and the other cheerleaders, but no one stuck out. Most were shots of pep rallies, dances, ball games and couples at parties.

Another photo showed Suzy, Julie Kane and Lynn Faust working the kissing booth at the county fair. In the back-ground, Amanda spotted Donald in his wheelchair watch-ing from a distance, looking sullen.

A bad premonition tightened Amanda's throat. Julie and Lynn were the next victims. She knew it in her soul.

She checked the latest emails Suzy had received and found one from Julie telling Suzy to meet her at the malt shop where they used to hang out as teens.

Amanda punched Justin's number. "I might have something." She explained about the email.

"Meet me downstairs and we'll go together," Justin said. "If the email was a lure to get both Julie and Suzy at the same time, and they met, maybe we'll find a witness who saw one of them."

Amanda's pulse clamored as she told the head of the crime team where she was going. Justin met her in the lobby, and they rushed outside to the squad car. She started the engine, praying she was wrong, that Julie hadn't been abducted along with Suzy.

LURING SUZY AND Julie to the diner had been brilliant. Neither one had suspected a thing.

Suzy would be appalled to know that everyone would see her looking so pale in death. Normally her makeup was perfect. Now mascara streaked her cheeks and her skin was a pasty yellowish white.

And Julie…ahh, Julie, the prom queen. She had expected to return in full glory, showing off the fact that she'd married her high school lover and accumulated a fortune.

But money and looks hadn't saved them.

Now everyone in town would see them as they should have all along. Silly, ugly girls who gave nothing back to the world. Silly, ugly girls who'd hurt others.

Silly, ugly girls who'd had to die.

Chapter Sixteen

Images of Suzy and Julie haunted Amanda—images of them dead.

She had to hurry.

"Call information and get Julie's telephone number," she said. "If the unsub doesn't already have her, we need to warn her."

Justin snatched his phone from his pocket and stabbed the number for information while she sped from the condo development and veered onto the highway leading back toward town.

Darkness bathed the rugged landscape between the two towns, worry gnawing at her. Julie's phone rang over and over, but no one answered. Finally the message machine clicked on, and Justin left a voice mail asking Julie to call the sheriff as soon as she received the message.

"I have a bad feeling we're too late," Amanda said.

"No one has reported Julie missing," Justin pointed out, offering her a tiny thread of hope to cling to.

"That doesn't mean she's safe," Amanda said. "Did you find anything on the surveillance tapes?"

"Maybe. There's a cleaning service that works the building. I saw them go in and out of several units. There were three women and a man. Later, I saw a woman go in Suzy's condo who looked suspicious."

"How?"

"She was wearing a scarf like the woman in the cleaning group, but this time she wore black boots instead of tennis shoes."

Amanda jerked her gaze toward him. "You think it was a different woman?"

He nodded. "She might have been the one to trash the place."

"Could you tell who it was?"

"Didn't get a look at her face. She kept it hidden from the cameras," Justin said. "But I asked the guard to courier it to the lab for analysis. Hopefully they can do something to help us identify her."

It was a long shot, but with technology today, they could look at different angles, shadows, reflections, enhance the image...

Amanda took the turn on two wheels, then braked, reminding herself that an accident would only delay the search. But as she wove through town, the fear in the pit of her stomach intensified.

Memories of watching Suzy and Julie cheer flashed back. The class picnic before graduation. The floats for the homecoming parade.

The football win celebrations at the diner.

And the dances at the gym and local party event center. A center Lynn's mother owned and ran.

She squeezed the steering wheel tighter and made the turn into the square, noting that the diner was practically empty tonight, the dinner crowd having thinned out. With people starting to come into town for the reunion, she was surprised there weren't more cars.

If the suspect was following the time line—a countdown—he or she might be planning their endgame for Saturday night.

She had to put an end to this before anyone else in her class died.

JUSTIN'S GUT TOLD him that Suzy was already dead and Julie might be with her. But he refrained from commenting, not wanting to add more pressure on Amanda.

She looked strained and exhausted, and the case wasn't over yet.

She parked in front of the diner, gold and orange lights forming the name, a string of green ones in the shape of a cactus decorating the door. The place looked like a cross between a Mexican cantina and an old-fashioned soda shop, he noted as they entered and he saw the orange vinyl booths and stools at the bar.

"Why would they choose this place to meet?" Justin asked. It certainly didn't look like the martini bar he'd imagined the women frequenting.

"Because this was the old hangout spot in high school," Amanda said. "Teens used to come here after all the ball games. They still do." She pointed to the menu. "No alcohol, but they have the best burgers and milkshakes of any place I've ever been."

His stomach growled. "Maybe we should grab something while we're here." They hadn't bothered to break for lunch.

"You can order us some burgers while I talk to the owner, Max, and his wife."

Justin slid onto a bar stool and picked up a menu. He ordered three burgers and two fries, his gaze scanning the room. An elderly couple sat in a corner booth sharing a chocolate malt. Three middle-aged women had huddled in another one chatting and laughing as they shared coffee and pie.

Teenagers eating burgers and drinking sodas and shakes sat to the left, half of them glued to their cell phones while the others were griping about a school project that was due soon and that nobody had even started yet.

Deciding he'd let Amanda question the owner and waitress, he went to look around. A hall led to the restrooms so he headed that way, but he didn't see anything suspicious.

Not that he'd expected to find a body in the hall, but he had considered that the perp might dump Suzy outside.

He noted a back door and pushed at the knob. It swung open to an alley with a Dumpster.

His breath whooshed out in relief. Suzy's body hadn't been left here.

Maybe she was still alive.

AMANDA APPROACHED MARY LOU, Max's wife, where she sat refilling napkin holders at a table near the kitchen.

"Mary Lou, can I talk to you for a minute?"

"Sure, Amanda. I mean, Sheriff." The older woman clucked. "Lordy, I can't get used to seeing you in that uniform. Seems like yesterday you were in here drinking chocolate shakes and doing algebra."

Amanda forced a smile. It seemed like eons ago to her. "I still love those shakes."

Mary Lou smiled. "Your daddy did, too. God rest his soul."

A pang of longing seared Amanda. She still missed her father every day. "I'm sure you heard about Kelly Lambert's death."

Mary Lou closed the napkin holder. "So sad. I can't believe she was murdered and left at the school like that. What kind of person would do such a thing?"

"That's why I'm here, Mary Lou. We believe that Suzy Turner is missing now."

Mary Lou gasped, one hand flying to her chest. "Oh, no. Not Suzy."

Amanda wanted to soothe her, but she couldn't lie. Not now. Not when they needed everyone in the town's help to find this unsub.

"We searched Suzy's place, and discovered that someone trashed her condo. We also found an email indicating that she was supposed to meet Julie here to discuss the reunion plans. Were they here yesterday?"

Mary Lou filled another napkin dispenser. "I don't think so. At least not during the day. But let me ask Myra. She worked the night shift."

Mary Lou used her cell phone to punch the woman's number. "Myra, did you see Suzy Turner or Julie Kane in the diner yesterday?" A pause. "No? All right. Thanks."

She hung up and turned to Amanda. "She said they didn't come in last night."

Amanda frowned. If the emails had been a lure, the assailant could have caught them outside. But how would the unsub force two women to go with him? Or her...

And where had the perp taken the women?

As soon as Justin returned to the counter, the waitress sat the food he'd ordered on the counter. Amanda appeared next to him, grabbed the glass of water and sipped it.

"Suzy and Julie weren't here yesterday."

Justin gestured for her to sit down and eat. "I checked out back just in case but didn't see anything."

Her features softened in relief, and she sank onto the stool and picked up her burger. "I've been thinking about the possibility of a female suspect. We need to talk to the school counselor and the cheerleading coach."

"Eat and then we will." Justin dug into his food ravenously.

Amanda dipped a few fries in ketchup and inhaled them, then retrieved her phone and punched in a number. Seconds later, she spoke, "Lynn, this is Sheriff Blair. I need to talk to you ASAP. It's urgent. Please call me back."

"No answer at her place either?"

Amanda shook her head. He hoped that wasn't a bad sign.

They finished their food in silence; then he reached for the bill. Amanda reached for it at the same time, and their fingers touched. A current of awareness shot through him, and his gaze was drawn to her mouth. She flicked her tongue out to lick away a drop of ketchup, and hunger bolted through him.

The memory of that kiss teased at his senses.

Hell, he could become obsessed with her mouth.

If they weren't working together, looking for a murderer, he might give in and take her to bed. Get his fill so he could put her out of his mind.

Once would do it. No, twice. Maybe three times.

Dammit. She was getting to him bad.

"I've got it," he said, his voice harsher than he'd intended.

She jerked her hand away. "Fine. I'll meet you at the car." She headed toward the ladies' room, and he forced himself not to watch her hips sway as she walked.

He paid the bill and left a nice tip, then strode outside. Sunset had long come and gone, and the town was quiet.

As if nothing bad had ever happened in Sunset Mesa.

Not as if a murderer had been kidnapping and killing young women for a decade.

"I called and talked to Deidre Anderson, the cheerleading coach," Amanda said when she got in the car. "She's expecting us."

Amanda drove two streets over and turned into a small neighborhood with stucco houses. A bicycle and skateboard had been left in the drive, indicating the woman had teenagers herself.

They walked to the door in silence, feeling tension that had as much to do with the heat building between them as it did the case. Maybe it was more intense because of the case and the fact that Justin was afraid Amanda might be targeted next.

Justin knocked, and a slender woman who was wearing a warm-up suit and had ash-blond hair opened the door. "Hi, Amanda," she said. "You must be the Texas Ranger who was at the school today. I'm Deidre Anderson."

"Sergeant Justin Thorpe. Thanks for letting us stop by. Can we come in?"

"Please." She gestured for them to enter and five minutes later they were seated at a modest kitchen table with coffee.

"How can I help?" Deidre asked.

"It's about Kelly's death." Amanda filled Deidre in on the information they had on the missing-persons case so far and their speculations about Donald Reisling and his father.

"We've been operating under the assumption that the killer is male," Justin said. "But I saw an unidentified female disguised as a cleaning woman enter Suzy Turner's apartment last night, so we are considering the possibility that we might be looking for a female."

Deidre stirred sweetener into her coffee, then added a hefty amount of hazelnut creamer. "I don't understand how I can help."

"We found some evidence linking the girls' disappearances to the class reunion at the high school, so we've been looking at the students from that graduating class, their connections and any enemies who might want to target them. That's the reason we wanted to talk to you."

"A photo of the cheerleading squad was used as Suzy's screen saver," Amanda explained. "It started me thinking that perhaps a classmate at the time, a girl who tried out for cheerleading and didn't make it, might have harbored a grudge against the ones on the squad."

Justin sipped his coffee. "Can you think of anyone who fits that description?"

"Gosh." Deidre traced a finger along the rim of her mug. "There are girls who try out and don't make it every year. It's hard for me to remember ten years ago." She walked over to a bookcase, pulled a yearbook from the shelf and flipped through it. "I can't imagine anyone being so angry over not making the squad to kill because of it."

"It was most likely someone who already had emotional problems. Maybe someone from a bad home life," Amanda said. "She probably suffered from low self-esteem."

Deidre sank into a chair and continued thumbing through the yearbook. She paused at a photograph of the cheerleaders at a pep rally, then seemed to be scrutinizing the teens gathered on the stands.

Her finger paused on a brunette in the second row who wore thick glasses and had buck teeth.

"Hmm, I do remember this girl trying out. Her name was Bernadette Willis. I think I cut her the first day. Poor girl just wasn't coordinated."

Or pretty enough, Justin thought. "How did she handle the rejection?"

"She seemed upset, but so did the other girls who didn't make it."

"Why does she stick out to you?" Justin asked.

Deidre tapped the photo again. "It's just…I faintly remember something about her family, that her father had run out on her and her mother that year."

"What about the mother?"

"She was an alcoholic. Crashed her car into a tree a few weeks after the father left. Bernie had to live in a group home for teens after that."

Amanda heaved a breath. "Her whole life fell apart," Amanda said. "Then she was dumped into the system. No telling what happened to her there."

AMANDA STRUGGLED TO recall if she and Bernie had shared any classes together. Maybe chemistry or biology lab? She faintly remembered rumors about her having emotional problems, that she was angry all the time.

They needed to talk to the school counselor, then maybe the social worker, and find out all they could about her.

If she'd suffered some kind of breakdown, it might explain why she'd started exacting her revenge.

Amanda's phone buzzed, sending a wave of fear through

her. She checked the number, her chest clenching as she answered. "Sheriff Blair."

"Sheriff, it's Eileen Faust. You have to get over to the event center."

"What's wrong, Mrs. Faust?"

"Suzy Turner…I found her here and… Amanda, she's dead."

Chapter Seventeen

"We have to go, Justin," Amanda said. "That was Lynn Faust's mother. She found Suzy Turner's body at the event center."

Deidre gasped. Justin's jaw tightened as he stood.

"Let us know if you think of anything else, Deidre," Amanda called over her shoulder as she and Justin rushed to the door.

A gusty breeze hit her as she stepped outside, and a hint of rain scented the air. She couldn't believe that Suzy was dead, too.

How many more women had to die before she stopped this maniac?

Her hand trembled as she tossed Justin the keys. "You drive. I'm going to try and reach Julie and Lynn again on the way."

Justin jumped in, started the engine and called for a crime team and the ME as he backed out of the Anderson driveway.

For once Amanda was glad to have someone else to rely on. She felt frail and vulnerable and…as if she'd failed.

Emotions welled inside her, threatening to overflow.

But she had to maintain control. When she found this unsub and had him—or her—in custody, then she could fall apart.

Justin maneuvered through the subdivision and turned onto the road leading into town. She punched Julie's number again, but, just as she'd feared, no one answered, so she left another voice mail.

Next she tried Lynn, and got her voice mail, as well. "It's Sheriff Blair. It's important I talk to you, Lynn. You may be in danger. Call me immediately."

The event center slid into view, and she pointed it out to Justin. "Park in the lot on the left."

Justin veered into the space, turned to her and placed his hand on hers. "If you need me to handle this, I can, Amanda. I understand that you knew these women and their families and that this case is tearing you apart."

Tears burned the backs of Amanda's eyelids, but she blinked them back. The last time she'd cried had been at her father's funeral. She couldn't break down now.

"I did know them. That's why I have to stop this madness." The temptation to hang on to his hand fluttered through her, but she had to resist.

Suzy's mother was waiting for news. News that was not going to be what she wanted to hear because Amanda had failed to find this psycho.

If Julie and Lynn died, their blood would be on her hands, too.

JUSTIN CURSED AS he climbed from the squad car. Amanda was blaming herself, but Suzy's death was just as much his fault as hers.

He should have figured out who this perp was by now. Instead, he felt as if they were chasing leads all over town. First Terry Sumter, then Donald Reisling and his father, then Carlton Butts's brother and now this Bernadette Willis was a suspect.

The fact that Amanda hadn't been able to get hold of Julie or Lynn meant they might already be in trouble.

Dead on his watch.

Amanda straightened her spine as they approached the front door of the building, but a middle-aged woman wearing a white skirt and sweater rushed out, her face streaked with horror and tears.

"Sheriff, it's so awful," she cried. "Suzy…she's in there…. Why would someone do this?"

Amanda paused to calm her, her voice soft. "I'm so sorry, Mrs. Faust. When did you find her?"

"Right before I called you," she said, hysteria lacing her voice. "What's happening in this town? First Kelly Lambert and now Suzy! And that horrid mess at the school. Who's doing this?"

"We're doing everything we can to figure that out," Amanda said firmly.

Justin tried to telegraph to her that it would be all right.

But both of them knew that was a lie.

The town's residents, more specifically the young women of Sunset Mesa in Amanda's very own graduating class, were being targeted by a killer who was growing bolder by the minute.

"How did the killer get into your building?" he asked.

Mrs. Faust pressed two fingers to her forehead as if thinking about the question. "I don't know. I didn't have anything here today, so I stopped by tonight to drop off some flower arrangements for a luncheon we're having tomorrow."

"What type of luncheon?" Amanda asked.

"It was a mother-daughter event, one we set up every year to honor the mothers and daughters the day before the reunion begins. The country club mothers put it together."

"So not every female in the class is invited?" Amanda said. "Just the ones whose parents belong to the club?"

Mrs. Faust wiped at her eyes. "That's right. Why? Does that mean something?"

"It means whoever left Suzy's body here chose this spot to make a point just as they chose the school," Justin said.

"Because he or she felt left out of the group," Amanda pointed out.

"Stay here with her," Justin told Amanda. "I'll go in and

examine the scene. Send the crime scene team and ME in when they arrive."

Justin headed inside to check out the body. He heard Amanda asking about Lynn as he entered the building, then only the echo of his footsteps as he walked across the slick marble floor. The exterior of the building was nondescript, but the inside was upscale. White tablecloths were draped over several round tables and more rectangular serving tables jutted up against the wall. Silver and china plates had been set, rose-colored napkins tied with white lace atop the plates and bouquets of fresh roses filled a cart, obviously centerpieces waiting to be distributed.

The room looked formal and classic, just waiting for the socialites to adorn it.

Except for the dead body perched in a sitting position on a dark green velvet sofa on the stage.

Justin had never seen Suzy Turner in person, but in her photograph she was a pretty girl. Yet the green eyes that had been lit up in the photograph were now wide, glazed with shock and fear, and her normally olive skin was pale with death.

He yanked gloves from his pocket and inched toward her, a wave of anger and sadness hitting him. Suzy Turner might have made mistakes as a teenager; maybe she'd even been mean to some guy or girl. But she had been a kid ten years ago and didn't deserve to die and be left like this.

He knelt and brushed his hand across her cheek in a silent apology, giving her a moment of quiet reverence before he did anything else.

Swallowing back emotions, he examined her neck. The same type of bruise pattern indicated she'd been strangled with a man's belt. Her dress looked disheveled, probably from the killer moving her body, but again there was no visible evidence of sexual assault.

Heart hammering, he checked her hands. One lay across

her heart as if the killer had positioned it there, while the other dangled open by her side.

Using his cell phone, he snapped some photos of her exact body position and the area, then lifted her hand from her chest and slowly uncurled her fingers.

Just as he'd expected, inside lay a class ring.

He lifted it up and examined the inside and saw the initials JK.

Julie Kane.

Was the killer sending a message that Julie Kane was next?

AMANDA FELT MRS. FAUST'S horror deep in her bones. "Listen to me, Mrs. Faust. I promise Sergeant Thorpe and I will find out who did this. But right now, I need you to talk to me. Did you see anything out of the ordinary when you arrived? An open window? Broken lock? A car leaving the place?"

"No, no," Mrs. Faust murmured. "The parking lot was empty. I don't know how the killer got in. Maybe he broke the lock."

"Did you touch anything when you went inside?"

"The door," she said. "The kitchen counter in the back room." She looked frazzled. "Maybe the walls. I brought the flowers in the back door, then put them on the cart to move them to the ballroom. That's when...I found Suzy." She gripped Amanda's arms. "Does Suzy's mother know?"

Dread balled in her stomach. That would be the worst part. "Not yet. I'm going to send my deputy out to tell her while Sergeant Thorpe and I investigate."

"Do you know who did it?" she cried.

"We have a couple of suspects we're interviewing. I need to ask you something else."

Fear deepened the grooves around her mouth. "What?"

"Have you seen or talked to Lynn today?"

Mrs. Faust shook her head. "No, we spoke yesterday. She was shopping for a dress for the dance Saturday night, then she said she was going to meet Suzy..." Realization dawned, and the woman gasped. "My God, no..."

Her legs buckled, and Amanda caught her before she collapsed. She eased her down on the front steps to the building and urged her to take deep breaths.

But the woman's fingernails dug into Amanda's arms. "You think this maniac has my daughter?"

"I don't know, but I called and left her a message to phone me ASAP. Where does she live?"

"In Austin," Mrs. Faust said. "But she's been staying at the inn in town. A couple of her friends were supposed to be coming in tonight, and they wanted to be together. It was Julie Kane's idea." Her voice cracked. "Lynn said it would be like old times, a big slumber party."

Amanda's throat thickened. "Keep trying to call her and let me know if you hear back. Maybe she and her friends are out shopping and having dinner and took in a show or something."

She prayed that was true, but her gut instinct warned her it wasn't the case. She remembered her conversation with Deidre Anderson. "Mrs. Faust, do you remember a classmate of ours named Bernadette Willis?"

The woman's eyebrows bunched together. "Just that the mother was a drunk. Someone in town said the daughter was crazy, too. That she had to go to some kind of juvenile delinquent home before she came here because she tried to kill her mother."

Amanda's heart stuttered. If that was true, it meant Bernadette had a history of violence.

She might be the unsub they were looking for.

JUSTIN GREETED THE crime scene team and ME, the sight of Suzy's body giving the team pause as it had him.

"How did the killer get her in here without anyone seeing or hearing something? This building is right on the edge of town," Lieutenant Gibbons said.

Justin had already checked out the exits and entry points. "I took a look around. There's a back exit that connects to the parking lot. He probably waited until it was dark. There are no surveillance cameras, and apparently no security system."

Unbelievable for a place that catered nice events, but it was a small town and everyone knew everyone else, so Mrs. Faust had probably thought they were safe.

"Look carefully—even a hair might be able to help us nail this perp," Justin said. "And keep in mind that we may be looking for a female."

"What makes you suggest that?" Dr. Sagebrush asked.

Justin explained about Bernadette Willis and the cleaning woman at Suzy's condo complex.

The crime scene team went to work snapping pictures and searching the room. Another tech went outside to rope off the area as a crime scene. They wouldn't be having the luncheon here tomorrow.

Amanda entered, her mouth in a grim line.

Emotions darkened her face at the sight of Suzy, a battle raging for control in her eyes.

"She was strangled?" Amanda asked.

"MO is the same as Kelly and Tina," Justin said. "The ring in her hand belonged to Julie Kane."

Amanda muttered something beneath her breath. "Lynn and Julie were staying at the Sunset Mesa Inn. Mrs. Faust hasn't heard from Lynn since yesterday. She was supposed to be shopping for a dress for Saturday night."

"Did you talk to the inn's manager?"

Amanda clenched her phone. "Next on my list. Then I want to talk to the school counselor."

One of the crime techs motioned that he'd found something, and Justin walked over to him and saw him holding up a long brown hair with a pair of tweezers. "The victim is blond. You may be right. This may belong to the unsub, a female."

Or hell, this was an event center; there was no telling how

many people had been in and out. They probably needed the names of all the employees, vendors, cleaning staff. Another list to sort through.

"Bag it and anything else you find. And don't forget to search the door and floor for prints. If our suspect is female, she probably had to drag the body inside. At some point, she might have touched the wall or floor for support."

Amanda returned, her phone in hand. "Neither Lynn nor Julie showed up at the inn last night. I told the owner to call me if they did. And I asked my deputy to check out the rooms where Lynn and Julie were staying to see if there was any indication where they might be."

"I'll call and put a trace on Julie's and Lynn's phones." He punched in the number for his chief and made the request as he and Amanda rushed to her car. This time she took the wheel and, ten minutes later, they were seated in the living room of Faye Romily, the school counselor.

"I don't understand how I can help you," Ms. Romily said.

Amanda explained the connections they'd made between the missing girls and the recent murder victims.

"You really think one of your classmates is behind this because of some deep-seated jealousy?" Faye asked.

"The unsub has to be mentally unstable," Justin explained. "The class reunion was a trigger for the rage that has been eating at him or her for years, so the perp escalated."

"Deidre Anderson said that Bernadette Willis was cut from the cheerleading squad that year, and that she suffered emotional issues."

A stricken look crossed Faye's face, and she stood and wrapped her arms around her waist. "Amanda, you know I can't discuss the sessions I had with any of the students. That's confidential."

Amanda sighed wearily, but Justin squared his shoulders. "Ms. Romily, we believe there are two other young women missing now. If the suspect follows the pattern, those girls may be dead before morning. We don't have time for a court order—"

"Please, Faye," Amanda said. "You don't have to divulge details—just tell us about Bernadette. Did she suffer emotional problems?"

Faye inhaled sharply and gave a quick nod.

"Did you think she was dangerous?"

"I don't want to say—"

Justin cut in, "Did she ever talk about hurting anyone in her class?"

Faye winced and cut her eyes sideways. "She was a troubled young girl. I…tried to follow up and see what happened to her after graduation and was told she was institutionalized at one point."

"Do you remember the name of the hospital or mental-health center?"

Faye hesitated a moment, then scribbled it down on a piece of paper.

Amanda flashed Justin a look of concern. They both were watching the clock.

"I'll call them," Justin said. "See what they'll tell me or if they have an address where she lives now."

Amanda's phone was buzzing. "That's the mayor calling. I'm going to tell him to set up a press conference for the morning. I think it's time we inform everyone what's going on and warn them there's a serial murderer in town."

Justin punched the number for the mental hospital. How many more women did the unsub plan to kill?

Chapter Eighteen

Justin punched Disconnect on the phone with a curse. "The receptionist at the hospital wouldn't tell me anything about Bernadette. Patient confidentiality."

"Let's go there in person," Amanda said. "Maybe if we talk to one of the doctors they'll help us. I'll start working on a warrant."

Justin gritted his teeth as she put in the request and drove toward the mental hospital.

"Yes, Judge, we think two more women may be missing and possibly dead. Every second counts." A pause, then Amanda thanked him and hung up.

"He's going to do it. I set the press conference up for ten in the morning."

"Hopefully we'll have the killer in custody by then and you can deliver some good news."

She rolled her shoulders as if to relieve tension. "From your lips to God's ears."

She accelerated, and ten minutes later they parked at a concrete building set off from the road surrounded by barbed wire fencing.

"This place looks like a prison," Justin muttered.

"It's the only mental health facility within a hundred miles," she said. "I guess they have some dangerous cases."

"Like Bernadette?"

She shrugged, and they identified themselves at the security gate, then parked in the visitor lot. Other than the few cars in the employee lot, the place looked virtually empty.

Justin glanced at the clock. Of course, it was late for visitors. But he had the uneasy sense that this was a place where unwanted people were discarded by loved ones and forgotten.

His impression of the place continued to go downhill as they entered. The building smelled old, like sick people, medicine and despair. Amanda squared her shoulders as she spoke to the receptionist, who eyed Justin over the rims of her bifocals.

"Judge Stone is working on a warrant for your records on Bernadette Willis. I need to speak to the director of the hospital and the doctor who treated Bernadette."

The nurse fiddled with a pencil stuck in her bird's-nest hair, then punched a button and paged the director along with a Dr. Herbert.

The director arrived first, a portly man with a white beard, and led them to his office. Seconds later, Dr. Herbert, a rail-thin fiftyish bald man appeared, reading glasses perched on his head.

Justin explained the reason for their visit.

"We need to know everything you can tell us about Bernadette," Amanda said. "What was her diagnosis?"

"You know I'm not comfortable discussing my patients," Dr. Herbert said staunchly.

"We are investigating the disappearance of a string of girls, at least three of whom are dead," Justin said in a dark voice. "If Bernadette exhibited signs of violence or verbally threatened any of them and you don't tell us, then you'll be responsible for their murders."

Dr. Herbert and the director exchanged concerned looks; then the director gestured for Herbert to speak up.

Dr. Herbert fiddled with the pocket of his lab coat. "Bernadette was suffering from bipolar disorder when I treated her. Our sessions were private and yes, she did express hatred for several of her teenage classmates, girls she felt shunned her and made fun of her, but as far as I know, she didn't act upon that aggression." He paused, and Justin and Amanda both remained silent, waiting for more.

"What aren't you telling us?" Justin finally asked.

Dr. Herbert released a wary sigh. "She did attack another girl who was here at the time."

"What do you mean, she attacked her?" Amanda asked. "What exactly happened?"

Dr. Herbert tensed. "She tried to strangle her."

AMANDA'S ADRENALINE KICKED in, charging her with hope. "What happened after that?"

"We reevaluated her and changed her medications," Dr. Herbert answered. "She received intensive therapy and was released a year later."

"Where did she go from here?" Justin asked.

Herbert slanted the director a questioning look. "I referred her to a home for troubled young women so she could continue her recovery with group therapy."

"What was the name of the place?" Amanda asked.

"Hopewell House."

Justin cleared his throat. "Did you follow up with her?"

Dr. Herbert shrugged. "I did. But I was told she left after a couple of weeks. I have no idea where she went from there."

Amanda ground her teeth. Bernadette could have moved anywhere.

"You should try her aunt," the director said. "She visited her once in the hospital, but said she was too old and that Bernadette had too many problems for her to take her in permanently."

Amanda's heart constricted. So Bernie had felt abandoned and alone. Even her only living family member hadn't wanted her.

"Do you have her contact information?" Amanda asked.

The director drummed his fingers on the desk. "I'm not supposed to give it out."

"Do you want more women to die?" Justin asked bluntly.

The man scraped a hand over his beard, then jotted down the address.

Amanda shook their hands. "Thank you for your help. If you think of anything else that might be of use, please call me."

She jangled the keys in her hands as they rushed to the car. Seconds later, she peeled from the parking lot and headed out of town toward the aunt's house.

"What do you remember about Bernadette?" Justin asked.

"Not much. She was quiet, withdrawn. Obsessed with science fiction characters and movies. Rumors circulated that she was really a guy."

"Was she gay?"

"I don't know. Her clothing and mannerisms and hair seemed masculine."

"Gender confused," Justin suggested. "Maybe she was struggling with her sexual identity and the popular girls accentuated the fact that she didn't fit in."

Amanda swerved onto a side road that seemed to lead nowhere. Raw land and rugged countryside sprawled ahead of them, an eerie feeling encompassing her.

Bernie's aunt lived out here—alone?

The car bounced over ruts in the road, a sliver of moon offering little light against the shadows. Her headlights blazed a trail on the dirt road that finally led her to a small trailer. No other houses or trailers were around, making her wonder why the woman lived in such an isolated area.

"What's the aunt's name?" Justin asked as she parked and they walked up to the door. The trailer was rundown. A clothesline out back held a string of ratty jeans and housedresses, and a mangy-looking dog lay slumped on the ground near the stoop.

"Oda Mae Willis. She is Bernie's father's sister. I heard she is eccentric, that she never married."

Three cats also roamed the yard, and when Amanda knocked, a screeching sound like cats fighting echoed from the inside. Shuffling followed. Then the door squeaked open, and a stoop-shouldered gray-haired woman wearing an orange flowered housedress stood on the other side. The scent of cigarette smoke surrounded Amanda, and the acrid smell of cat urine wafted through the door.

Amanda fought back a gag. "Ms. Willis, it's Sheriff Blair and this is Texas Ranger Sergeant Thorpe."

The woman glared up at her with rheumy eyes. "What you want?"

"We need to ask you about your niece. Is she here?"

"Hell, no," the woman muttered. "I told those folks at the hospital I couldn't take her in. That girl's too much trouble."

Amanda's heart squeezed for Bernadette. First to lose her parents, then to be a misfit in school, and to have her aunt refuse to give her a home. "Have you seen or talked to Bernadette lately?"

The woman clacked her false teeth. "Hadn't seen her in years and she just showed up here a couple of days ago. Said she was back for that reunion. Wanted to show all those kids that was mean to her what she'd made of herself."

"What was it she wanted to show off?" Justin asked.

"Hell if I know," Oda Mae muttered. "But she had that mean look in her eyes like she did the night I sent her to that hospital."

"You sent her there?" Amanda asked.

Oda Mae's head bobbed up and down. "Didn't have no choice. She killed one of my cats. Strangled the poor baby to death. Then she started on another and I got my shotgun and made her stop."

Amanda's pulse clamored. Killing animals was a sign of sociopathic behavior.

An indication that Bernie might have been practicing for killing a human.

And becoming a serial killer.

"IF BERNADETTE ISN'T staying with her aunt, where would she stay?" Justin asked as they settled back in the car.

Amanda rubbed her finger along her temple and started the engine. "The inn is the most popular place." She punched the number for the inn, then asked if Bernadette was registered there. "Okay, thanks. If she shows up, please call me." When she hung up, she shook her head.

"There are a couple of motels on the outskirts of town. Try those."

She gave Justin the names and he made the calls. The first one was a bust, but the clerk who answered at the Canyon Resort Motel confirmed that Bernadette was registered in room twelve.

Amanda steered the car back onto the dirt road, then hung a left when she reached the main highway. Five miles down the road, they reached an adobe building painted a burnt orange that boasted a view of the canyon. Amanda parked, and they rushed to the lobby.

They both flashed their credentials. "We're looking for Bernadette Willis," Justin said.

The tiny lady behind the counter looked as if she were ninety. "What's going on, Sheriff?"

"We just need to talk to her. Do you know if she's here?"

"Saw her leave this morning."

"Can you give us a key to her room?" Amanda asked.

"I don't think I'm supposed to do that," the little woman said.

"Look, we need to get in there. We have reason to believe she might be in danger," Justin said, hedging.

Fear splintered the lady's face, and she reached behind her and retrieved a key. Her hand trembled as she handed it to Amanda.

Justin led the way outside and down the row of rooms until they reached room twelve. He knocked and identified them as police officers, but no one answered so he used the key and let them inside.

The room was dark, and he flipped on a light by the door.

"Bernie?" Amanda called as she brushed past him to check the bathroom. But there was no answer. The bed was unmade, a duffel bag tossed on the floor, a wet towel thrown across the bed.

Justin scanned the rest of the room and saw a yearbook on the bed. He picked it up, his pulse clamoring as he flipped the pages. He found the photo of the cheerleading squad on Suzy's screen saver.

Bernadette had drawn big black x's across the girls' faces.

Amanda's phone buzzed, and she snatched it from her belt. "Sheriff Blair." She hesitated. "Okay, we'll be right there."

"What?" Justin asked.

"That was Delores at the inn. Bernadette is there now."

Justin flipped the yearbook around. "Look at this."

Amanda took one look and motioned to the door. "Let's go. If we hurry, maybe we can arrest her tonight and this ordeal will be over."

AMANDA SWUNG THE squad car toward town, hit the gas and wove around a tractor trailer pulling out from a side street.

Her thoughts strayed to Lynn and Julie. Were they all right?

She hoped they'd snuck away to the city for a while.

The other option was too disturbing because it meant they might be dead.

But if she had them, why go to the inn tonight?

The temptation to turn on the siren hit her, but she didn't want to warn Bernadette she was coming.

Justin pointed to an SUV across the street from the inn. "Look, there's a black SUV with a brunette in it."

Amanda slowed and parked several cars back on the side of the road. "Come on, let's move in quietly."

Justin slid from the car, his gun drawn, and they crept along the sidewalk toward the SUV. They inched past a sedan and a minivan. Then Justin gestured that he'd take the right side of the SUV and she'd move in on the left.

A car whizzed by, forcing her to duck between cars, and Bernie glanced up in the mirror. Panic flashed in her eyes when her gaze met Amanda's in the rearview mirror.

She reached for the keys, and the car engine rumbled to life. Amanda didn't intend to let her get away. Keeping low, she ran toward the SUV. Justin reached it before she did and tapped on the passenger side of the vehicle.

His knock distracted Bernie long enough for Amanda to reach the driver's side. She rapped on the driver's door, but Bernie saw her and gunned the engine.

Amanda had to jump back to keep from getting run over. "Stop, Bernie!"

Justin gestured toward the squad car, and they jogged back to it. Amanda jumped in and floored the engine. Tires squealed as she chased the SUV through town and onto the country road leading toward the motel.

Another car darted onto the highway in front of Bernie, and she swerved to miss it. She lost control, and the car wove back and forth, brakes squealing.

Amanda slowed to avoid hitting her as the SUV careened into a ditch.

Amanda's breath caught. If Bernie died, they might never find the other missing women.

Chapter Nineteen

Amanda steered the car to the side of the road and cut the engine, and she and Justin ran toward the SUV.

By the time she reached it, smoke was billowing from the hood. Justin beat her to the driver's side, yanked open the door and dragged Bernie from the vehicle.

Blood dotted her forehead and lip, and her eyes looked glazed. From drugs or shock?

Amanda gripped her phone. "I'll call an ambulance."

Justin eased Bernadette down onto the ground a few feet away from the SUV and checked her pulse.

Amanda punched 911 and gave the dispatch officer an address, then knelt beside Justin and Bernie. "How is she?"

"Her pulse is low and thready, and she's banged up, but the air bag worked, so she might be all right."

Amanda noted a few differences in the girl she'd once known. Gone was her pointed nose; instead she had a petite rosebud of a nose. Her teeth had been straightened, her coke-bottle glasses were gone and…she had implants.

Was this what her aunt had meant about Bernie wanting to come back and show off what she'd made of herself? That she was a beauty now, not the geeky masculine awkward teen they'd made fun of.

"Bernie." Amanda caught Bernie's hand in hers. "Can you hear me?"

Bernie gave a low groan; then her eyelids fluttered. Wild panic darted through her eyes.

"You've had an accident," Amanda said. "The ambulance is on its way."

Bernie reached her hand up to touch her face as if to make sure her remodeling hadn't been affected.

"You're fine," Justin said. "Just some bruises from the air bag. But the medics need to check you out."

"Why did you run?" Amanda asked.

Bernie's lips quivered, making Amanda's stomach knot.

"You were outside the inn," she continued. "Were you looking for Julie and Lynn?"

Bernie coughed, wincing as she gripped her chest in pain. "They wouldn't let me stay there," she growled. "Stupid jerks haven't changed at all."

"Is that why you made all those girls disappear over the years?" Justin asked. "Why you killed Kelly Lambert and Suzy Turner?"

Bernie hissed through clenched teeth. "They deserved to die. All of them…they deserved exactly what they got."

THE AMBULANCE ROARED to a stop and two medics jumped out. Amanda directed them to Bernadette.

"This woman is a suspect in a homicide so I need to ride with her," Justin said.

The blond medic checked Justin's badge while the dark-haired one hurried to Bernie and took her vitals. He instructed Amanda not to let her move; then he and the second medic retrieved the stretcher, secured Bernie's neck with a brace and boarded her.

"I'll ride along if you want to meet us at the hospital," Justin said.

Amanda agreed, her expression torn. "I'll search her car and find her phone and meet you there."

Justin climbed in beside Bernie, hoping to solicit a confession on the way to the hospital.

But the minute the doors slammed shut, she closed her eyes and clammed up.

"Bernadette," he said in a gentle voice. "If you abducted Julie Kane or Lynn Faust and they're still alive, you need to tell me now. Things will go a lot easier on you if we find them alive."

She opened her eyes and gave him a cold stare.

"The D.A. can cut you a deal for their safe return. And we can arrange psychiatric care instead of putting you in a maximum-security prison."

A blink of her eyes was her only response.

"Think about it," Justin said as the ambulance careened around a curve and into the hospital emergency room entrance. "A psychiatric hospital versus a prison with murderers, rapists and gangs."

A sinister smile curved her lips. "They deserved to die," she said again. "Every single one of them."

Justin urged her to say more as the ambulance screeched to a stop, and the medics pulled the stretcher from the ambulance. But she maintained her silence.

Was she the sociopath who'd committed all these crimes?

By the time Amanda arrived, they'd carried Bernadette off for X-rays and a CAT scan. The two of them went to get coffee and Amanda paced the waiting room while they waited on Bernadette to be moved to a room.

"Did you find a gun in her car?" Justin asked.

"No." Amanda lifted her cell phone. "I've been checking her calls but so far, nothing we can use against her. And no calls to any of our victims."

The doctor entered and cleared his throat. "She's going to be all right. She sustained a blow from the air bag, but no broken ribs. We'll watch her overnight for a concussion." His brows arched in question. "We did a tox screen, and it showed that she is taking medication that's used to treat bipolar disorder."

"She was a mental patient at one time," Justin filled in.

"That explains it," the doctor said. "Do you know who her doctor is?"

Amanda relayed their conversation at the mental hospital. "We're putting her under arrest," Amanda said. "I'm sure the court will order a psych evaluation. I'm assigning my deputy to stay at her door all night. But I want to talk to her again before I leave."

Justin followed her inside, and they found Bernadette sleeping.

"Damn, Bernie," Amanda said, her tone laced with irritation. "Have you been kidnapping and murdering our classmates all these years?"

But Bernadette had lapsed into a deep sleep and didn't respond.

"I offered her a deal," Justin said. "But she just reiterated that the girls deserved to die."

"No, they didn't," Amanda said fiercely. "There are a lot of jerks in high school, but people grow up and some of them change."

Justin rubbed his hands down her arms in a soothing gesture. "You have to remember that she's mentally ill, Amanda. Her thought processes don't work like a normal person's."

Amanda knotted her hands into fists. "She has to wake up and tell us where Julie and Lynn are."

A knock sounded at the door, and the deputy poked his head in. "Reporting for duty, Sheriff."

Amanda updated him on the situation. "Make sure she stays handcuffed to the bed. I want to question her if she wakes up."

He claimed a seat in the vinyl chair in the corner. "I'll call you the minute she stirs."

"Thanks."

Justin checked his watch as they left the hospital. It was midnight already. They'd been working nonstop since he'd arrived in town. Something nagged at the back of his head as she drove from the hospital though.

Julie and Lynn were still missing. And he'd wondered if Amanda was a target.

Was she safe now that Bernadette was in custody?

AMANDA PARKED AT the station, her adrenaline waning, and Justin retrieved his SUV.

Clouds rolled above, obliterating the moon as he followed her to her place. Amanda kept reliving the past few days, seeing the dead girls' bodies in her head.

Bernadette had been cunning enough to remain under the radar for years. But now that she was in custody, they could hope the town would be safe again.

But they still needed to find Julie and Lynn and the bodies of the other missing victims.

Weary, she parked and walked up her porch steps, aware Justin was close behind her. She could feel his big body, his strong presence, his intensity...

She halted on the porch, her heart stuttering. A picture had been tacked on her door.

One of her cut out from her class yearbook. A big X had been drawn across her face.

A deep shudder coursed through her body.

"What the hell?" Justin snarled.

"It's a message to me, that I was going be next," Amanda whispered hoarsely.

Justin yanked gloves from his pocket, tugged them on and removed the photo from the door. "If she left her prints on it, this will help us build the case."

"Bag it and we'll send it to the lab tomorrow," Amanda said. "We need to check in with them and see what they found at the event center, too."

Even though they had Bernadette in custody, she removed her weapon before unlocking the door. Behind her, Justin did the same and she slowly crept inside.

Everything looked just as she'd left it, yet she had the uneasy sense that someone had been inside. She visually swept the attached kitchen while Justin eased his way to the hall and her bedroom.

"Clear," he called.

She walked to the bedroom and looked inside, then checked her bathroom. "It doesn't look like anything's been touched."

"She's taunting you, wants you to know she's watching."

"She wanted to kill me, too," Amanda said, the truth harsh. "For some reason, she lumped me with that group even though I wasn't a cheerleader or dancer or part of their crowd."

"Maybe she thought you were protecting them."

"That could be," Amanda admitted.

Justin pulled her near him, his dark gaze raking over her. "Bernadette is a sick woman. No one could have predicted what she would do." He tucked a strand of hair behind her ear, and her heart fluttered with a feminine awareness that she rarely felt.

It was probably just the situation, she told herself. She was upset. Women her age had died all around her and she'd been helpless to save them.

"Amanda," Justin said in a husky whisper. "You're nothing like the students who were mean to Bernadette. You know that, don't you?"

Her chest ached with suppressed emotions. "But I should have seen how disturbed she was." Her voice cracked. "The people in town depended on me to solve this case instead of letting it go on so long."

Justin stroked her arms with his hands, making her want to lean into him.

"You did solve it. Bernadette is handcuffed, and we'll get her confession in the morning and find out where Lynn and Julie are." He lifted her chin with his thumb. "Not only did you do a good job, but you showed compassion to the victims and their families. That's a lot more than some law enforcement officers do."

Her breath caught as she looked into his eyes. For a brief second she felt totally vulnerable, feminine, wanted.

Desire heated the air between them, desire charged by emotion, danger and adrenaline from the case and horrors they'd seen.

Desire that made her forget all her reservations.

Pulse throbbing, she laid her hand against his cheek. Coarse beard stubble grazed his jaw and his lips were thick, parted as if hovering, waiting for a kiss.

She answered him by rising on her tiptoes and pressing her lips to his.

RAW HUNGER BLAZED through Justin as Amanda fused her lips with his. She was tough but tender, smart but vulnerable, shy yet aggressive. A mixture of sensuality that fueled his desire with an intensity he'd never felt before.

Some part of his brain shouted at him to stop this madness, but the week had been filled with another kind of madness that made him crave this kind. A physical connection charged with want, need and passion.

He deepened the kiss, teasing her lips apart with his tongue. She moaned and captured his face between her hands, moving against him in a seductive torture.

Wind whistled behind them, and he realized they'd left the door open. He kicked it closed with his foot, then trailed his hand down Amanda's side. When his hand hit her holster, he paused.

"Amanda?"

She murmured a soft whisper of need against his lips, then dropped her hands and unstrapped her holster. He quickly did the same, and they set their weapons on the end table.

The plush rug in front of her fireplace beckoned, and he threaded his hands into her hair and kissed her again, leading her to the rug, where they knelt, slowly undressing each other in a seductive tease.

Even in a uniform, she was beautiful, but in red satin

panties and a sheer lace bra, she was exquisite. Her hair fell around her bare shoulders, inviting him to play in the tangled strands, and the rise of her chest as she exhaled with desire drew his eyes to the soft flesh above the lacy cups of her bra.

He dipped his mouth and tasted her skin. Succulent. Sweet. Heady.

She moaned and stripped his shirt, buttons popping in the breathy silence, the heat between them igniting as he lowered his mouth to tease her nipples through the lace. Her breasts were larger than he'd expected, her nipples dark, achingly enticing. He cupped them in his hands, molding them and lifting them so he could tease the turgid peaks before he stripped the bra and held her bare in his hands.

"You're so beautiful, Amanda," he rasped.

"You feel so good," she whispered as she unsnapped his jeans and pushed them down his hips.

His length surged and hardened, aching to be free, inside her.

Desperate for her touch, he helped her shuck his jeans and then she was climbing on top of him, pushing him back against the rug, straddling him and stroking him.

His sex throbbed, begging for release, but he moved her hand and shifted her hips so he could strip her panties. Her hair fell around her face like a curtain as she bent over him and kissed his neck.

Erotic sensations flooded him, but a moment of rationality returned, and he reached for his jeans, grabbed a condom from his pocket and ripped it open. Amanda helped him roll it on, her eyes darkening as she straddled him again and lowered herself onto him.

He gripped her hips, barely hanging on to control as his length filled her. With a whispered sigh of pleasure, she rotated her body, moving up and down on top of him in a frantic rhythm. The friction was erotic, her body a haven for him as he thrust deeper and deeper.

She braced her hands on his chest, her breath gushing

out with a moan as her body quivered. Euphoria carried her away, and she moved faster and faster, circling her hips and riding him until his own orgasm teetered on the surface.

He tugged one nipple into his mouth, suckling her until she cried out his name, and they rode the wave of pleasure together.

AMANDA GROANED, HER body convulsing, every nerve cell in her alive with erotic sensations. Justin gripped her hips, pumping deeper inside her until colors exploded behind her eyes and she soared over the edge.

Her breath rasped out, and she clutched his shoulders, savoring the feel of his thickness inside her.

She had never felt more complete. More…of everything. Pleasure blended with emotions, making her throat close as feelings for Justin overpowered her.

Fear immediately seized her.

She could not have feelings for him. He was a Texas Ranger married to his job just as she was. He could die on the job just like her father had.

And then she'd be left behind again, alone and…broken.

Instincts warned her to stop this foolishness now. To forget that she'd needed him and that he'd seemed to want her just as much as she wanted him.

That it was the best sex she'd ever experienced.

But that was it—just sex. Yes, just sex.

Sex was normal. A tension release. They were two consenting adults simply working off the strain of the past few days.

As long as she kept their lovemaking in perspective.

She should pull away.

But when she looked down into his passion-glazed eyes, and hunger heated his expression, she couldn't make herself leave the rug.

Justin must have felt the same way and wanted her to

know the sex meant nothing because he rolled her sideways, then stood up and strode into the bathroom.

She closed her eyes, reminding herself that they were on the same page, but disappointment made unwanted tears swell in her eyes.

She wanted him again.

The door creaked open, and she took a deep breath, expecting him to leave. Instead, he crawled back onto the rug with her, slid his arms around her and spooned her.

Amanda wanted to turn around and kiss him again, but forced herself to lie still.

Just for tonight, she'd let him hold her.

IT WAS ALREADY Friday. One more day until the reunion.

One more day until the town would see that they couldn't stand by and let innocent teenagers be bullied and brutalized and tormented.

They thought words couldn't hurt a child. But words could be cruel and cut a frail person to the bone just like a knife could.

Anticipation rose, exhilarating and sweet. Ten years of watching those who'd sinned climb their way to the top in spite of their shortcomings.

This week they'd returned to brag and gloat as if the ones they'd trampled on didn't matter.

But they did matter.

Tomorrow when they gathered to celebrate, they would be talking about funerals and goodbyes and the end of their glory days.

And justice would finally be served.

Julie and Lynn would attend that party, but they wouldn't be dancing.

No…dead girls didn't dance.

Chapter Twenty

Justin started to leave Amanda's bed a half dozen times during the night. But each time he'd felt her lush, warm body against his and hadn't been able to bring himself to go.

Because he wanted her again.

They had made love over and over during the night. Finally they'd slept.

Both of them had been exhausted from the investigation and the tension had triggered their need for raw sex.

Nothing more.

Then why don't you want to walk away?

He climbed from bed, unable to answer that question because the answer terrified him. Because he was starting to care for Amanda.

She turned over and murmured his name, and he lowered his head and kissed her. "Time for reality. That press conference is this morning. And I need to question Bernadette again."

Her so-called confession had haunted him during the night. She'd said the girls deserved to die. But she'd never actually admitted that she'd killed them.

He needed to grill her for details. Make sure they had the right unsub.

Amanda's life depended on it.

THE MENTION OF the press conference drove thoughts of another lovemaking session with Justin to the back of Amanda's mind. She heard her shower kick on, and she was tempted to join Justin, but with daylight streaming through the window, she had to face reality and the truth.

She and Justin were coworkers who'd relieved their stress in bed together. It happened.

She'd get over it.

Hoping to end the nightmare today, she dragged on a T-shirt, then went to the kitchen to make coffee. Her stomach growled, and she checked the fridge, then pulled out eggs and bread and whipped up some French toast.

Finally the shower turned off, a relief as it was much too tempting to think of Justin naked in there alone. When he entered the kitchen, his hair was damp, and he looked sexy as hell.

God help her. She was seriously falling for him.

His dark gaze met hers, stirring erotic memories of the night before. His jaw tightened as he glanced at the table, and she suddenly wanted to forget breakfast and make love on the table.

He cleared his throat, hunger flaring in his eyes as if he'd read her thoughts. But the look faded and his professional mask fell back over his chiseled face.

"Thanks," he said. "I'm starving."

So was she. But not for food.

Still, she kept that comment to herself. Couldn't invite more personal interaction today. They had to finish this case.

So she handed him a mug of coffee and set their plates on the table. Still, the ordinary routine felt intimate, his masculine body taking up all the air in the room.

He wolfed his food down, then studied her while he sipped his coffee. "I'm going to question Bernadette, make sure we tie up details while you hold the press conference."

His statement made her refocus. "I've been thinking about

that," she said. "Maybe I should postpone and go with you. We need to find out what she did with Lynn and Julie."

He shook his head. "No, go ahead with the meeting. The town has to be up in arms now and panicking. Talking to them is the right move. But I wouldn't reveal Bernadette's name."

"I don't plan to," she said. "But I do want to urge people to come forward if they have any information." She stood, carried her dishes to the sink and rinsed them.

"I'll clean up while you shower," Justin offered.

Unaccustomed to having a man in her kitchen, she rushed to the bedroom to get ready for the day. After the conference, a family picnic was scheduled to jumpstart the reunion.

She wanted to be there and study the group just in case they were wrong about Bernadette.

Hopefully Lynn and Julie would show up safe and sound.

As soon as she finished showering and dressing, she phoned her deputy to check on Bernadette.

"She slept like the dead all night."

"Sergeant Thorpe will be there soon to talk to her. When he arrives, go home and get some rest. I'm heading to the office to hold a press conference with the mayor."

An hour later, she stood with the mayor in front of the county courthouse and greeted the media. Reporters immediately hurled questions at her.

"What's happening in Sunset Mesa?"

"Did you find the missing girls?"

"Is this a serial killer?"

Amanda held up her hand in the universal signal for them to hold the questions. "At this point, we do believe that the disappearance of several women from this town and neighboring counties is related. The bodies of three victims have recently been found—Tina Grimes, Kelly Lambert and Suzy Turner. Police believe that they were kidnapped and murdered by the same perpetrator and that the upcoming ten-year class reunion at Canyon High triggered the perpetrator to escalate."

Hands shot up, but she waved them off and continued. "We do have a suspect in custody although I'm not at liberty to disclose the name yet as we're still investigating. That said, there are still other women missing at this time. If you have any information regarding the whereabouts of Lynn Faust and Julie Kane, please call my office immediately."

"How were the women murdered?" someone shouted.

"Do you think Lynn Faust and Julie Kane are dead?"

Amanda gritted her teeth. "As I said, if anyone has any information, please call my office immediately."

She glanced at the mayor and turned to duck inside so he could smooth ruffled feathers, but another shout echoed behind her.

"What if you have the wrong person? What if the women in town are still in danger?"

Amanda slowly turned around to see who'd voiced the question and frowned at the sight of Kelly Lambert's maid of honor, Betty Jacobs. "Are we still in danger, Sheriff?"

Amanda wanted to tell the young woman no, that she was sure they had the right perpetrator. But she couldn't lie. And if she assured the residents and her former classmates they were safe and another woman was abducted, it would be her fault.

"All I can say is that we have a suspect in custody. Until we confirm that this person is the one we've been looking for, I would urge all the women in town to be on guard. Travel in pairs and don't trust anyone."

JUSTIN BROUGHT A mini recorder in with him to see Bernadette. The deputy sheriff met him at the hospital room door.

"I talked to Sheriff Blair and told her the suspect has been asleep all night."

"She didn't wake and say anything? Talk in her sleep?"

The deputy shook his head. "They must have given her some heavy-duty drugs. Not a peep all night."

"Thanks. I'll handle it now."

The deputy left, and Justin stepped inside and closed the door. He walked over to the bed and studied Bernadette. Granted, she had suffered emotional problems and had killed her aunt's cat, but was she a serial murderer?

Considering her emotional issues, did she have the organizational skills and patience to wait months before abductions and to commit this many crimes without being caught?

He touched her hand. "Bernadette, it's time to wake up and talk."

Her eyes suddenly popped open as if she'd been faking sleep. They looked cloudy, hazed with drugs, but the same sinister smile he'd seen the night before stretched across her face.

"Talk to me," he said in a low voice. "You came back to town for the reunion to show off your new face, didn't you?"

"Yes," she murmured. "But do you think those bitches cared?"

"But *you* cared, didn't you? You've been angry since high school. You decided to start taking your revenge out on them ten years ago."

Bernadette reached for the water on the steel table beside the bed, and he handed it to her. She took a long sip, then laid her head back down.

"They should have noticed," she said. "Should have let me stay at that inn. But they thought they owned the school, and now they think they own the town."

"That's wrong," he said. "I understand why you're upset. They hurt you ten years ago and now they're still doing it."

"I wasn't the only one," Bernadette said. "There were others. The geeks like me. Like Carlton Butts. You know he killed himself because of them."

"Yes, I heard that. But you decided to fix yourself and to make them pay instead of committing suicide."

"They're not worth dying for."

"But they deserved to die. You said that."

"Yes, they deserved to die."

"So you practiced killing with your aunt's cats?"

Bernadette's eyes widened. "You talked to that mean old hag?"

"You hated your aunt, didn't you? Like everyone else, she abandoned you."

"She loved those damn cats more than she did me. She threw me out, but she kept taking in those mangy strays. They pissed all over the place. Her trailer smelled like garbage and cat urine, but she chose that over me."

"She hurt you so badly that you killed one of her cats. Then the teens at school wronged you, so you retaliated by abducting and killing them one at a time."

Bernadette twisted sideways, clutching the sheet to her neck.

"You can talk to me here or down at the station," Justin said. "Either way, Bernadette, you have to tell me what happened. I'm on your side."

She pierced him with a look of rage. "You're not on my side. No one is."

"I can stand up for you if you tell me what happened. Who was the first girl you abducted?"

She looked down at her fingers where they were wrapped around the sheet. "I took them all, made them suffer for what they did."

Suffer? She'd strangled them, but there was no evidence of torture or sexual assault. Or that the victims had been beaten.

"How did you make them suffer?" he asked.

She chuckled. "You know how. You found Kelly and Suzy."

"You humiliated them by leaving them in public places. But Tina's body was found in a creek. What about Melanie and Avery and Carly and Denise? Why didn't you leave their bodies for us to find?"

"Because I had more on my list who had to pay." A bitter laugh sounded. "And it was fun watching the police run in circles."

He narrowed his eyes. "Who was the first one you took?"

She shifted restlessly, then rubbed her temple as if she had to strain to think. "I don't know, I get them all confused. It's been a long time."

"Avery Portland, wasn't it? Or was it Melanie Hoit?"

A heartbeat passed and Bernadette breathed deeply. "Avery was supposed to be at the school dance."

"But she disappeared and no one heard from her again," Justin said. "And Melanie?"

"From the mall. She was a shopaholic. A rich daddy's girl." Her eyes hardened. "Everyone wanted to be like Melanie."

"What did you do with their bodies?"

Bernadette looked him straight in the face then gave a small shrug. "I don't remember."

"How did you kill them?"

Her eyes darted sideways. "I told you I made them suffer."

"How? Did you beat them? Stab them? Torture them before you ended it?"

"I choked them," she said. "I watched them beg for another breath, but I took it away." She snapped her fingers. "And just like that, they were gone. The world's a better place without them."

"What about Gina Mazer? Where did you abduct her?"

Bernadette pinched the bridge of her nose. "I told you I can't remember them all. They were all alike, one blending into another." Her eye began to twitch. "The stupid meds the doctor gave me…they make me forget."

Or maybe she wasn't the killer. Because there was no one named Gina Mazer in the case files.

"So now you're ready to finish it," he said quietly. "You're ready to go public. You did all this for the glory, to prove something. You can't do that, Bernadette, if you don't let everyone know you're responsible."

"Then tell them to take my picture and put it all over the news. Bernadette Willis finally gets payback for the abuse she suffered."

Justin hesitated. "Okay, but for the record, you have to tell me how you carried out the crimes."

"I told you I choked them."

"How?" Justin pressed. "With your hands? A scarf? A rope?"

Bernadette began picking at her fingernails. "With a scarf. One I took from my aunt's house. It smelled like cat urine. I wrapped it around their throats and squeezed it so hard they choked on the odor."

A hysterical laugh echoed from her, and Justin silently cursed.

Either Bernadette was just plain crazy and wanted to taunt him with her sadistic games.

Or…she hadn't killed the women.

Because the killer had used a man's belt to strangle the victims. That was one detail they'd held back from the press.

The one detail that only the police and the real killer knew.

THE POLICE HAD a suspect in custody. Some classmate of all the dead girls named Bernadette.

Another one of the odd ducks in school. One those mean girls had picked on.

Bernadette understood the reason they'd had to die.

Maybe when this was over they could be friends.

Chapter Twenty-One

Justin met Amanda at the reunion picnic, surprised she'd shown up wearing her uniform.

"You trying to make a statement to your former classmates?"

She shrugged. "Yes, that they're safe. And that I'm on the job."

"Not here to mingle."

"Not here to mingle," she said in a wry tone. They walked across the field by the lake. Dusk was setting, the ducks nibbling for food at the edge of the water, a breeze stirring the trees and whipping Amanda's hair around her face.

He wanted to reach up and tuck it behind her ear, but they were in public and he couldn't touch her. Although he imagined making love to her again tonight and need speared him.

Not a good idea, man. One night was just sex. Two could lead to something more, could mean she is getting in your head.

And your heart.

No one got into his heart.

"What happened with Bernie?"

Justin chewed the inside of his cheek. "I don't know, Amanda. She wants credit for the crimes, but when I asked her about the details, there were discrepancies in her story."

Amanda paused by a tree and looked up at him, her eyebrows furrowed. "What do you mean?"

"She claimed the drugs made her memory foggy. I threw in the name of a fake victim to test her. And she said she couldn't remember all the names."

Amanda shaded her eyes with her hand as she scanned the picnic area and pavilion where her former classmates and their spouses and kids had gathered. Grills were heating up for burgers and hot dogs, and one of those bouncy houses had been set up for the kids, along with face painting, music and games.

"It is possible that the medication messed with her memory," Amanda said. "Of course that will make it harder to get a conviction unless we find other evidence to support her story."

And so far, they hadn't. "When I asked her how she killed the girls, she said she choked them to death with a scarf."

Alarm flared in her eyes. "Not a belt?"

"No."

She pursed her lips. "Maybe she's trying to throw us off with the details because she still has plans for Saturday night."

"That's possible. Either way, we have enough to hold her for twenty-four hours."

"She wouldn't tell you where Julie and Lynn are?"

He shook his head. "They haven't turned up at the picnic?"

"No. But I'll keep watch." She headed down the hill. "I guess I should canvass the crowd in case anyone's heard from them."

Justin had a bad feeling that the women were dead.

The question was—where were their bodies? And if Bernadette hadn't murdered them, who had?

AMANDA THREADED HER way through the throng of classmates, listening to the normal chitchat about how much everyone had changed, or hadn't, the questions about marriage and kids and jobs. She remained on the periphery, avoiding ongaging in conversation, listening and hoping for information that might help with the case.

Because if Bernadette wasn't the murderer, one of her other classmates might be.

Or was Bernadette just toying with them now? Dragging out the inevitable to make them wonder and throw suspicion off of herself?

Two of Kelly Lambert's bridesmaids cornered her by the sodas. "We saw the press conference," Anise said. "You found the person who killed Kelly?"

"Who was it?" Mona Pratt asked.

"I'm sorry, but I can't divulge that information yet," Amanda said.

Anise touched her arm, her voice pleading. "But you're sure you have him in jail?"

"We think so," Amanda said, then because these women might be in danger, added, "but until we have the evidence we need to confirm that we have the right person in custody, please be careful. This killer targeted our classmates. Watch your backs."

Worry darkened both women's faces. "Is that why Julie and Lynn aren't here?" Mona asked. "You think they're dead, too?" Panic strained her high-pitched voice and several other people turned to her with questioning eyes.

Amanda lowered her voice. "I don't know, but if you hear from them, please call me."

She moved to the edge of the crowd, feeling as out of place as she had ten years ago.

But that feeling reminded her that the killer felt the same way. So she sipped her soda and watched the picnic—old friends reconnecting and rehashing memories, the couples introducing spouses and children, and the occasional whisper and somber expressions of sorrow and regret that several of the students at Canyon High had died or disappeared and were presumed dead.

But as she studied the faces, she didn't see anyone who

looked suspicious. Carlton's brother was there, laughing with a couple of guys he used to run track with. Donald Reisling sat in his wheelchair, although he wasn't alone. Three of the former basketball players were crowded around him asking for financial advice, listening raptly to what Donald had to say.

Raymond Fisher, the man who had been Kelly's fiancé, had even shown up although he and Terry Sumter passed each other with mutinous glares.

Then Renee cornered Raymond, hovering close, obviously consoling him for his loss.

WHEN JUSTIN AND Amanda left the picnic, they wanted to move Bernadette to the jail. But the doctor who'd treated her had called for a psych evaluation, and instead they transferred her to the psychiatric ward to stabilize her medication.

While Justin called the crime lab to check on forensics and to ask if the tech team had found any leads on Julie's and Lynn's phones, Amanda called her deputy to ask him to stand guard by Bernie's room again that night.

Amanda didn't know whether it was the meds or if Bernie had realized that she wasn't going free and that, if she'd planned another murder for the big reunion Saturday night, that she wouldn't get to follow through, but apparently she'd shut down again.

When she and Justin arrived back at the sheriff's office, Lynn Faust's mother was waiting along with Julie Kane's parents.

"Where are our daughters?" Lynn's mother cried.

"You said you arrested someone. Where is he?" Mr. Kane demanded.

Mrs. Kane swiped at tears. "Let us talk to him. Maybe he'll tell us where our daughters are."

Lynn's mother clutched her arm. "Please, Amanda, please find them. Lynn's all I've got."

Emotions thickened Amanda's throat. "We're doing everything we can."

"Damn you, Sheriff, it's not enough." Mr. Kane raised a fist and shook it in the air. "Tell us who kidnapped our daughters, and I'll get him to talk."

Justin rapped his knuckles on the desk. "Listen here, everyone. We understand you're upset, but the sheriff is doing her job. We do have a suspect and are continuing to question her—"

"It's a woman?" Mrs. Faust shrieked.

"Let us see her!" Mr. Kane shouted.

"I can't do that," Justin said, kicking himself for mentioning the suspect's gender. "But I promise you as soon as we know anything, we'll inform you."

"But our babies are still out there..." Mrs. Faust sobbed.

Mrs. Kane leaned into her husband. "We have to know what happened to them. Julie, she was so bright and smart... She can't be gone."

Their grief ripped at Amanda's heart, and she silently vowed that somehow she would find the answers the families sought.

Even if it meant finding Julie's and Lynn's bodies so they could bury them and put them to rest.

BY THE TIME Justin managed to coax the families to leave, he knew Amanda was wrung out. He saw the guilt and pain in her eyes, and felt helpless to do anything about it.

Because he wasn't sure they had the right unsub.

Meaning Amanda might be in danger and wouldn't be safe until the perp was caught.

He suspected tomorrow as the big day, the reveal—if the killer had one. That Julie's and Lynn's bodies would turn up in some way connected to the reunion so all their classmates could bear witness.

And so Amanda would feel even worse.

The CSI team had found little. Nothing to connect Bernie to the crimes. Her cell phone showed calls to the inn and motel, but not to Julie, Lynn, Kelly or Suzy. If she'd used a burner phone, it hadn't been in her purse or car.

Together he and Amanda made rounds in the town, checked the inn again to see if there had been any word from the women, then picked up some dinner from the diner and drove back to Amanda's.

Tension vibrated between them, the uncertainty hovering around Bernie and the case needling both of them. Once they ate, Amanda poured herself a drink and offered him one.

He liked a woman who drank brown whiskey.

He liked Amanda period. She was strong and gutsy and fought for her town.

Worn and worried though, she looked vulnerable again. He sipped his whiskey with her on the porch, the night sounds echoing around them.

The memories of the night before taunted him.

He wanted her again.

Amanda sighed and leaned against the rail, looking out over the woods and canyon, and he couldn't help himself. He stepped up behind her, needing to hold her, aching to pull her into his arms and touch her everywhere.

To make her sigh and moan with pleasure and erase the dark shadows in her eyes.

He gently stroked the hair from her cheek and pressed a kiss behind her ear. Amanda leaned back into him and whispered his name softly, a protest to stop. A plea for more.

He took her hand and led her inside, then swept her in his arms and carried her to the bedroom, where they stripped and made love all through the night.

FOR A FEW blissful short hours, Amanda felt at peace. Safe. Cared for. As if everything might be all right.

But daylight brought reality and uncertainty. When the case ended, Justin would leave Sunset Mesa. His job carried him all over Texas. She understood that from her father.

She also understood that he might not come back.

Daylight also reminded her that Julie and Lynn were still missing. And that Bernadette might not be the killer.

Justin joined her in the kitchen for coffee and breakfast again, the two of them silently agreeing not to discuss the frantic sex they'd had during the night.

"Let's question Bernie again," she said as they cleaned up the kitchen.

Justin nodded, and they drove to the hospital, the tension between them vibrating with dread. The reunion dance was tonight.

The tick tock of the clock was like a time bomb echoing in her ears.

If Bernadette wasn't the suspect, then they could expect trouble tonight. The killer probably had something big planned for today. Plans that didn't involve celebrating the good times from years past, but adding to the death count and celebrating her revenge.

Amanda led the way to the psych floor and they identified themselves to the head nurse, who escorted them to Bernie's room. Bernie was sleeping, her face pale beneath the hospital lights.

Amanda shook her gently. "Bernie, I need you to wake up and talk to us."

Bernie made a low sound in her throat, then slowly opened her eyes. Gone was the wild, panicked, angry look. Her eyes looked flat, empty, as if she was far away.

"Bernie, it's Sheriff Blair. Amanda," she said, hoping to connect with her on a more informal basis. "We need to talk."

Bernie pushed hair from her face and looked around, disoriented. "Where am I?"

"The hospital in Sunset Mesa," Amanda said. "Yesterday you told us that you killed Suzy Turner and Kelly Lambert. That you've been punishing classmates who were mean to you."

Her eyes darted back and forth. "I didn't say that. You're lying."

"You told me they all deserved to die," Justin said. "That you choked them."

"No," Bernie bellowed. "I didn't. You're making up stuff to have me locked up again."

"That's not true," Amanda said. "You were at the inn. You—"

"I didn't do anything wrong!" Bernadette yelled. "I didn't kill anyone."

The hospital door suddenly opened, and a barrel-chested doctor rushed in. "What's going on?"

"They're saying I killed someone!" Bernie shouted. "They want to lock me up. It's just like before, everyone turned against me."

The doctor gestured for Amanda and Justin to step outside, and a nurse rushed in and gave Bernadette a sedative to calm her.

"I'm afraid she needs intensive therapy," the doctor said.

"But yesterday she ranted about killing several women," Justin said.

"Bernadette has taken heavy medication for years. She suffers from delusions. When she's off her meds as she was yesterday and probably has been for days, she doesn't know what she's saying."

"She was in a delusional state when we brought her in?" Amanda asked.

He nodded grimly. "Off her meds, she's susceptible to suggestions from others. If you'd told her she was a green alien, she probably would have agreed."

Amanda knotted her hands into fists. "So we can't believe anything she said yesterday? And even if we did, it would never hold up in court."

A sliver of unease rippled through her. She and Justin had both doubted whether or not Bernie's confession had been real.

Now she had even more doubts.

Which meant that the killer might still be out there planning to snatch another victim.

SHE WATCHED THE group decorating the float, laughing and talking and reminiscing about the fun times they'd had.

High school was supposed to be the time of your life.

But for some it had been torture.

They added strings of crepe paper and made a papier-mâché school mascot, even fashioned the canyon for which the school had been named out of clay and paper.

One of the women laughed as she placed two dolls in cheerleading uniforms on the float while a young man planted a football in the middle of the football field onstage.

Tonight that float would sit outside the dance for everyone from Canyon High to see. It was tempting to leave Julie and Lynn in place of those stupid dolls.

But she had another plan. The big finale.

Then Amanda Blair had to die.

Chapter Twenty-Two

Tension knotted Justin's muscles as he waited on Amanda to dress for the dance. He had changed into clean jeans and a blue Western shirt, but he strapped on his gun and covered it with his jacket.

When Amanda stepped from the bedroom, she looked so stunning she robbed his breath. In deference to the occasion, she wore a short black dress that hugged her curves and made her look more like a sex siren than the sheriff.

She rubbed her hands down her hips in a self-conscious gesture. "Too much? I'll go change." She turned to go back into the bedroom.

He caught her arm. "No, you look beautiful."

"I don't care about that," she said. "I have a job to do."

He chuckled. "Perhaps you'll look less intimidating dressed up for the reunion. Your uniform might spook the killer if she's there."

"The killer will be there," Amanda said with conviction.

He silently agreed and walked her out to his SUV. "I'll drive tonight."

"Maybe my car should be there. It might make the other guests feel more secure."

"You'll be there," Justin said. "And so will I. We'll stay on our toes."

Except at the moment, all he wanted to do was strip that slip of a dress and make love to her again.

God, he was like a sinking ship. He not only liked and admired Amanda—and she was the best sex he'd ever had—but he wanted to protect her tonight. Lock her here where she'd be safe, off the killer's radar.

But he couldn't even suggest that. Amanda wouldn't go for it, and it would be unprofessional of him.

He squeezed her hand as they settled in the SUV. "Amanda, you know the killer left that photo of you on your door as a warning."

She lifted her chin. "I know. The unsub wants to punish me, too."

"That means you're in danger," he said in a hoarse voice. "I don't want you to get hurt."

She lifted the hem of her dress and he saw the gun strapped to her thigh. It was the sexiest thing he'd ever seen.

"I'm a pro," she said. "Don't worry about me."

But he did worry about her, and that scared him. Caring might make him sloppy and distracted.

He couldn't afford that. Not tonight.

THE CRIME SCENE techs had released the event center in time for the dance, but the committee had decided to move the party to another venue, a hotel ten miles north with a ballroom. Lynn's mother had recommended the place, saying she couldn't have a party at the center where Suzy's body had been found, especially not when her own daughter was missing.

Volunteers from the school committee had scurried to decorate the place and make the arrangements. The float classmates had created was parked in front, a testament to the class that they were honoring the past and refused to allow the recent traumatic events to stop them from celebrating their friendships.

When she and Justin entered, a band was playing, the lights were low and couples filled the dance floor.

She had opted not to attend the dinner before the party,

although she and Justin had staked out the outside, watching to see if anything went wrong.

She scanned the room, looking for anything suspicious.

"You look different out of uniform."

Amanda turned to see Donald looking up at her from his chair.

"I'm still on the job though." She sipped her club soda. "What about you, Donald? Are you enjoying seeing the old crowd?"

He shrugged. "I'll never forget how some of them treated me after the accident. But it's nice to be vindicated in that I made a success out of myself in spite of them."

"Good for you," Amanda said, wondering if she'd been wrong about Donald.

Across the room, she noticed Carlton's brother dancing with Eleanor Goggins, one of Kelly's bridesmaids.

Near him, Raymond Fisher stood talking to Renee Daly, his former girlfriend and one of their original suspects. The couple looked chummy, raising Amanda's doubts again. Was Renee simply consoling him, or did she have another agenda?

Suddenly a commotion broke out near the door, and a small crowd gathered. Justin squeezed her arm. "Stay here and keep an eye on everyone. I'll check it out."

Amanda's nerves prickled, and she wove through the room, studying the faces of the people she'd known as teenagers, hating that she was now viewing them as possible murderers.

Her phone dinged that she had a text and she slid it from her purse and checked it, expecting to see a message from Justin.

But the text was from an unknown.

She squinted in the dim lighting, her heart hammering as she read the text.

I have information on the killer you're looking for. If you want to know who it is, meet me in the stairwell.

Amanda jammed the phone back in her purse, then scoured the room for Justin to tell him about the message, but she didn't see him anywhere. He must still be outside.

Determined to follow up, she wove through the dancers and people hovered around the bar and ducked through the back exit to the hallway. She veered down the hallway toward the dark stairwell.

When she reached it, she heard a muffled footstep, then the brush of clothing, as a shadow appeared from the corner. Something shiny glinted in the darkness. A gun.

Shock immobilized her when she recognized the person aiming the weapon at her.

JUSTIN SHOULDERED HIS way through the shouting and voices outside the ballroom exit, then jogged over to where a small crowd had gathered.

"What's going on?" he asked one of the young men.

The guy pointed to the right. "Someone trashed the float."

Justin inched his way closer and saw two women about to climb on the float. "Who would do such a horrible thing?" someone cried.

"We have to get those dolls off the float," the other one shouted.

"Wait." Justin caught up with them and gently grabbed the first woman's arm. Then he saw what had upset them. Two dolls in cheerleading clothes were set up on a football field on the float. But their clothes looked as if they were covered in blood and the dolls had been hung by their necks from the goalposts.

"This may be related to the crimes in town. We'll need to examine it." He addressed the group. "I don't want anyone to touch this float." He gestured toward one of the men. "Get one of the security guards. I need him to watch this until the crime team arrives."

The gentleman jogged toward the door to the ballroom while Justin tried to quiet the crowd. He circled the float searching for anything else out of place. A knife. Forensic clues. A note or photo of some kind.

But he saw nothing else out of the ordinary. The hair on the back of his neck prickled, and he scanned the group outside in search of someone on the periphery watching.

The killer was here. She wanted to enjoy her classmates' reactions.

But the group had thinned, milling back into the dance. The guard approached, and he explained that he needed him to cover the float while he phoned for a crime team. Of course dozens of hands, maybe a hundred, had touched that float so it would be hard to weed out the killer's prints. But maybe she'd messed up and they could find some forensic clues on the dolls.

He punched in Lieutenant Gibbons's number while he hurried inside to tell Amanda and monitor the group. But he didn't see Amanda anywhere. He explained to the lieutenant that he needed a crime scene unit, then tried Amanda's number, but she didn't answer.

Anxiety mounted.

The only reason she wouldn't answer was if there was trouble.

He spotted Betty Jacobs, one of Kelly's friends, and approached her. "Have you seen Amanda?"

She shook her head no, and he moved along the bar asking others.

"She was heading toward the stairwell a few minutes ago," Donald said. "She received a text and rushed out of the room."

Justin thanked Donald, then rushed into the hallway toward the stairwell. The area was dark, but he noticed something shiny on the floor below the stairs. He bent down, a seed of panic sprouting.

Amanda's gun lay on the floor by the wall. Scuff marks marred the floor leading toward the back door.

The killer had been here. And he or she had Amanda.

AMANDA SILENTLY CURSED herself for letting the woman get the jump on her with the gun. Of all the people she'd suspected, it had never occurred to her that Carlton Butts's mother had been vindictive or strong enough to carry out a series of crimes for ten years.

But the woman had coldly shoved a pistol to Amanda's head, then tied her hands behind her back and was shoving her into an old van. "I thought you had trouble walking."

"And I thought you were Carlton's friend, but you were just like the others. You deserted him when he needed you."

"I didn't mean to do that," Amanda said. "I cared about him."

"Then why have you been running all over town trying to stop me." The woman's eyes blazed with rage as she slammed the door shut, jumped in the front of the van and sped from the parking lot.

"Because killing those women isn't right," Amanda said, hurling herself to a sitting position in the backseat as she struggled with the ropes behind her back.

"You know how they treated my son," she snarled as she took the curve on two wheels. "They killed him."

"I understand how you feel and that you're angry," Amanda said. "But Mrs. Butts, a lot of teens and kids get picked on. Not all of them commit suicide."

"No, some of them go in and shoot the bitches," she said. "But my Carlton was too sweet for that. But they drove him crazy, drove him to such despair that he never thought anyone would like him, much less love him."

She sped down the highway, mumbling incoherently about each one of the women she'd hurt and what they'd said and done to her son. "He was a bright boy, so smart," she continued on a rant. "He could have been something one day. You know he loved science. He might have worked on one of those space stations or discovered a cure for some rare disease."

Amanda worked at the knot behind her back, slowly

threading the end through the loop. "I think he could have done that, too," she said. "But he gave up, Mrs. Butts. He made the choice not to fight back and—"

"Don't you dare badmouth my son," Mrs. Butts cried. "See, you're just like the others. All you care about is your life, like he never existed at all."

"That's not true," Amanda said. "I mourned for Carlton and still do. I've never forgotten what happened to him. That's one reason I chose law enforcement. So I could help others."

"But you took up for those mean girls who hurt Carlton. I saw you on the news. You made out like they were innocent, like they never did anything wrong."

"We found Tina, Kelly and Suzy," Amanda said, knowing her time might be running out to find the information she needed. "What did you do with the other bodies? With Melanie, Denise, Avery, Carly...how many have you killed?"

"Just the ones who deserved it," Mrs. Butts said, her voice brittle. "And don't you worry. All of the early ones are together. All in one big grave."

A shudder of horror ripped through Amanda. Mrs. Butts sounded demented. "Except for Tina. I thought someone saw me with her so I left her in that river. That was a mistake. But I had to get rid of her fast." Mrs. Butts cackled. "I thought she'd just float away. Bye-bye, bye-bye."

"But she didn't and the fish ate at her body," Amanda said. "That was cruel."

A nasty laugh escaped the woman. "Cruel? Do you know what she did to poor Carlton? She sent him a note that she wanted to meet him behind the bleachers in middle school. He thought she wanted to kiss him, but she pulled his pants down, then tied him to the bleachers and left him for the whole class to see."

Amanda's heart hurt at the story, her hand aching from tearing at the rope. So far, it hadn't budged. "What about Julie and Lynn?"

Mrs. Butts threw the van to the right and raced down the drive to the canyon behind the high school.

A cold chill enveloped Amanda. She knew exactly where the woman was going and why.

She was going to kill her at Carlton's Canyon, where her son had taken his life.

Chapter Twenty-Three

Justin retrieved Amanda's weapon and stuffed it in the back of his jeans as he ran to the back door and glanced outside. Except for a couple of vendor vans, the back lot was empty.

He scanned the hallway and stairs but didn't hear or see anything. Frantic, he raced back into the ballroom. The first person he saw was Donald Reisling. Could Reisling's father have come after Amanda?

Shoulders tense, he grabbed the microphone from the DJ and tapped it to get everyone's attention. "Listen up, folks. The prank outside with the decimated cheerleader dolls was a diversion. Someone abducted Amanda—I mean Sheriff Blair. She supposedly received a text and went into the hall. Her gun was left on the floor so someone either overpowered her or had a gun. Did anyone see her?"

"The last I saw she was going into the hallway," Donald said.

"I saw her near the stairs," a young woman spoke up.

"Was she with anyone?" Justin asked.

He glimpsed Carlton's brother sneaking out the side door and yelled at him to stop. "Where do you think you're going?" Justin vaulted off the steps and lunged at him. "Did you do something to Amanda?"

Ted shook his head, pain lining his face. "I've been in here with Debby all night."

"He has been with me," a buxom redhead said. "I swear."

Anise ran over, her breath rasping. "I didn't see Amanda, but I saw Carlton's mother near the stairs."

Justin narrowed his eyes at Ted. "Your mother is here?"

"I...didn't know she was," Ted said in a choked voice.

Justin grabbed the young man by the collar. "But you know something. Now spill it."

Ted shook his head in denial, but emotions shrouded his features. "It can't be. My mother...she's messed up, but she wouldn't hurt anyone..."

"She wasn't using her walker either," Anise said. "She was actually standing upright."

A muscle jumped in Justin's jaw. "Your mother faked her handicap?"

Ted scraped his hand over his goatee. "I...don't know, I'm sorry. I didn't think...didn't want to believe that she'd hurt anyone."

"She never recovered from Carlton's suicide," Debby said in a whisper.

"Where would she take her?" Justin asked.

Ted rubbed his goatee again. "I...have no idea."

"Let's try your house. You can call her on the way."

He shoved the young man outside to his SUV and roared from the parking lot.

He hoped he'd find something at Wynona Butts's house to tell them where the woman had taken Amanda.

He had to hurry before Mrs. Butts killed her.

He couldn't lose her now.

AMANDA'S LUNGS CLENCHED for air as she spotted Julie and Lynn beside the drop-off for the canyon.

They were alive.

"Mrs. Butts—Wynona—you can stop this now," Amanda said as the crazed woman yanked her from the car and shoved her toward the other women.

"You're going to watch them die," she hissed, "then you'll join them."

Amanda fought with the rope. She had one end through the loop. Now if she could just loosen it and slip her hands free.

Wynona nudged her forward with the gun at her back.

"Is this where you dumped the other bodies?" Amanda asked.

A cynical laugh echoed behind her. "It was fitting, don't you think? They've been lying at the bottom, looking up at the school where they tormented my son."

Nausea rose in Amanda's throat. All this time, all these years, the missing women had been dead, their bodies lying in the elements.

So close to home yet no one had known. And the families had no answers.

Julie and Lynn both looked up at her with terrified eyes. Their hands and feet were bound, their mouths gagged and Carlton's mother had secured them to a tree with thick ropes.

Amanda tried to communicate to the women that she'd save them. She didn't know how, but she'd die trying.

Surely Justin had realized she was missing. Somehow he'd find her. She had to stall.

Wynona pushed her to her knees beside Lynn and Julie. Tears streamed down Julie's cheeks. Lynn made muffled sounds of fear and protests behind her gag.

"Tell me how you did it," Amanda said to Wynona. "How you managed to trap your victims over the years."

Wynona cackled again. "It was easy. I met them in different places, mentioned Carlton." She gestured at herself. "With that walker, none of them suspected a thing. Stupid twits."

"They thought you were an innocent grieving woman," Amanda said, disgusted at the depth of the woman's depravity.

"And you...Carlton looked up to you, Amanda. He thought you'd be his friend forever." She placed the barrel of the gun at Amanda's temple. "But you let him down worse than everyone else. I think that's what sent him over the edge. Now you have to die."

JUSTIN DROVE LIKE a madman to Wynona Butts's house while Ted frantically phoned his mother. But she didn't answer, and when they arrived at the house, there was no car in the drive.

He hit the ground running.

"Why didn't you tell someone what your mother was doing?" Justin snapped as Ted let him in the house.

"I told you I didn't know," Ted said, panicked. "You aren't going to hurt her, are you?"

Justin glared at him. "I'm going to do whatever necessary to stop her from killing Amanda."

Justin shouted to identify himself as he and Ted entered the house.

"Look around, see if your mother left any indication where she might take Amanda."

Justin jogged into the woman's bedroom, searched the desk in the corner, then the dressers, but found nothing but old bills and clothes.

Desperate, he swung open the closet door, his chest heaving at the sight inside. Mrs. Butts had cut out pictures of all the victims from the yearbook and taped them on the back of the door with big black X's marked across the faces just like the one she'd left on Amanda's door.

Then he noticed a photograph of Carlton when he was a teen. Beside it was another picture, this one of the canyon behind the school, more specifically a grassy area by a tree where she'd obviously planted flowers in a tribute to her dead son.

That was it. The canyon behind the school where Carlton had ended his life—that was where she'd taken Amanda.

He rushed back to the den and saw the brother slumped on the couch staring at the yearbook with all the pages that had been cut apart. A shoebox sat beside him on the couch, open. Justin gritted his teeth at the sight of the class rings inside the box.

"She did it," Ted mumbled in shock. "She kidnapped our classmates all these years...."

He looked lost as he stared up at Justin.

"Stay here and call me if she returns. I'm sending a crime scene team out here to pick up this stuff," Justin said.

Ted nodded, sagging on the couch with emotions. Justin felt sorry for him, but he had to save Amanda.

"I'm going to the canyon where Carlton jumped. I think your mother took Amanda there."

Pulse hammering, he ran to his SUV and raced from the drive, calling Lieutenant Gibbons on his way. He prayed he was right about the canyon as he sped down the road to the high school.

Seconds crawled, but it felt like an eternity until he reached the sign for Canyon High. He flipped off the lights and siren and parked in front of the school to avoid alerting Mrs. Butts of his arrival.

He eased the car door open and slid out, checking his weapon as he scanned the area. He wondered if the security cameras had been fixed.

He crept around the side of the school to the back, searching for signs of Amanda and Mrs. Butts. Then he spotted it.

The door to the gate that separated the school property from the deepest part of the canyon. It stood open, making a grating sound as it swung back and forth in the wind.

His heart pounding, he moved along the bank of trees to the left, his weapon at the ready. Voices sounded to the right, and he inched closer.

Fear seized him when he saw Amanda on her knees with a gun to her forehead.

Breath tight in his chest, he took another step. Suddenly Mrs. Butts jerked Amanda up and dragged her closer to the edge of the canyon.

He couldn't wait. He had to make a move.

Vaulting into action, he crossed the next few feet, aiming for a clean shot at the woman. But suddenly Amanda lunged at Mrs. Butts, knocking her to the ground.

The gun fired, a grunt of pain echoing in the silence, and he ran forward, fear choking him. Was Amanda hit?

To the left, he spotted two other women he recognized from the yearbook as Julie and Lynn. They were struggling to free themselves.

The Butts woman had collapsed on top of Amanda. Was she hurt?

Amanda shoved the woman off of her with a grunt. Mrs. Butts lunged for her gun, but Justin raised his.

"It's over, Mrs. Butts," he said in a menacing tone. "Give it up or I'll shoot."

The woman stilled at the sound of his voice, then swung a sadistic look his way. "She has to die. It's not over till they're all punished."

"It is over," Amanda said calmly. "You've punished enough people. Carlton wouldn't want you to hurt Lynn or Julie or me."

"But you let him down!" she cried.

Justin inched closer. Julie and Lynn were sobbing and struggling with their bindings. Mrs. Butts slid her hands around Amanda's throat and tried to strangle her.

Justin was tempted to shoot. But Amanda was fighting the woman, and he was afraid he'd hit her. So he ran to them, grabbed the woman and dragged her off of Amanda.

She kicked and fought, but he was stronger, and he wrapped his arms around her waist, hauling her away. Amanda gasped for a breath, then pushed herself to her feet and ran to free the other women.

Justin threw Mrs. Butts down on the ground, rolled her to her stomach, jerked her arms behind her and slapped hand-cuffs around her wrists.

"Now it's over. And this time you're the one who's going to be punished."

WHEN AMANDA THOUGHT she might die, her life flashed in front of her. A life filled with police work, cases, murders and…living alone.

She suddenly yearned for more. A life with someone who loved her. With someone she loved.

Like Justin.

But that was crazy… He wasn't in love with her.

Sirens wailed as an ambulance arrived to examine Lynn and Julie. Except for shock, they appeared to be okay, but she had to play it by the book.

Her deputy arrived, along with Justin's supervisor, a crime team and another team that brought equipment to locate the bodies at the bottom of the canyon.

The next few hours were an ordeal as they began work to excavate the bodies. She left Justin to oversee the process while she drove Wynona Butts to the jail and locked her up.

"You can't do this," Wynona yelled. "They deserved to die."

"But not all the victims even attended our high school," Amanda said, mentally reviewing the list.

"No, but they knew Carlton, met him at different times. Middle school, church. They were all mean to him."

"You need help," Amanda said, her chest aching for all the lost lives. "I'll see that you get it for Carlton's sake."

The woman continued to rant and scream as Amanda shut the door behind her. But Amanda tuned her out. At one time she'd felt sorry for her. But not after all the lives she'd taken and the pain she'd caused the victims' families.

Finally exhausted, Amanda slept on a cot in her office, determined to make sure Wynona didn't attempt suicide, and worried that when the victims' parents heard the news they'd bombard the jail and try to exact their own revenge.

By dawn, fatigue knotted her muscles, but she called a team to move Wynona to a more secure facility. By ten, she and Justin met for another press conference.

"We can now safely say that the missing women from our

state have been found. Their families have been notified and will finally be able to put their loved ones to rest." A lump lodged in her throat, but she swallowed it back as she explained about Wynona Butts's arrest. "I suppose if there is a lesson in this it's that we, as parents and members of the town, should watch our teenagers more closely and teach them to be tolerant of others."

Hands flew up with questions, but she shook her head. "We're done here, folks. Justice will be served in a court of law."

And now maybe everyone in town could sleep soundly again.

THE REST OF the day Amanda and Justin spent meeting with family members of the missing women whose bodies had been recovered. Emotions ran high, relief to finally have answers mixing with anguish, shock and the sad realization that the missing women had been so close yet no one had guessed where they were.

Arrangements for autopsies were made, along with funerals, and a memorial service was held that evening at the church in town. A sunset vigil to mourn for the lives of the dead and the tragedies of the families who needed the town's support also was organized.

As Justin and Amanda left the service, a quiet descended between them.

The case was solved. It would take time for the residents to heal, but now that they knew the truth, they could begin the process.

He glanced at Amanda as they walked back to the jail. Maybe they could have one more night together, an evening to celebrate before he left Sunset Mesa.

His cell phone buzzed, and he checked the number. His chief. He punched Connect. "Sergeant Thorpe."

"Thorpe, listen, I know you just finished this case, and you did a fine job—"

"A lot of the credit goes to Sheriff Blair," he said, wanting to give Amanda her fair due.

"Sure, all right. I know you just finished, but we just caught another case. If you want it, it's yours, but you'll need to go to Laredo right away."

Adrenaline surged through Justin. Another case on the heels of this one. He'd never turned down an opportunity to solve a crime.

Chasing bad guys was his life.

"I'll leave right away."

Amanda left the podium and walked toward him, and his heart did an odd flutter. A few minutes ago, all he could think about was getting her in bed again. Touching her. Loving her. Holding her another night. And maybe another…

Shaken by the thought, he squared his shoulders. "Good job, Amanda."

"You saved my life," she said. "Thank you for that."

He shrugged. "Just doing my job. Speaking of which," he said, his chest twitching with an odd pang, "I have to leave right now. Another case."

Something akin to disappointment flared in Amanda's eyes. Then again, maybe he'd imagined it, because a second later, she smiled, the professional, distant look she'd given him when they'd first met.

Before he'd seen her naked and touched and tasted every inch of her.

He wanted to do it again.

But she extended her hand for a handshake. "Thanks, Sergeant Thorpe. It's been a pleasure working with you. Good luck."

His gaze met hers, and a moment of tension rippled between them. His chest squeezed, the urge to say something more nagging at him.

He felt as if he was leaving something important behind.

But she shook his hand, then turned and walked toward

her car, and he felt like a fool. She obviously didn't have feelings for him.

She was independent, smart…and beautiful. And married to her job just as he was.

The perfect woman for you.

And if he didn't snap her up, someone else would.

That would be for the best, he reminded himself as he climbed in his SUV and headed out of town.

He didn't do emotions. And he didn't have room or time for anything else in his life.

Chapter Twenty-Four

Amanda bit her lip to keep her emotions at bay as she watched Justin drive away. She was a big girl. A strong, independent woman.

She did not need a man.

She'd always known that her time with Justin was limited. Work related. Nothing more.

So why was she crying?

Because Justin was the first man she'd met who understood her drive to do her job, understood her need to solve crimes.

And respected her for her work.

He'd also made her body sing with erotic sensations that she'd never experienced before.

But that wasn't all. She had fallen in love with him.

Stupid, stupid, stupid.

Falling for any man was crazy in her line of work, much less for a Texas Ranger who might leave one morning to go to work and end up in a body bag that night.

So could she.

She swiped at her tears as she parked at her house, let herself in and jumped in the shower. The memory of looking down at that canyon and imagining herself at the bottom taunted her.

Yes, she could have died last night. And if she had, would anyone have cared?

Would she spend the rest of her life alone because she was too afraid of losing someone to actually allow love in her life?

JUSTIN STOPPED AT the crossroads leading out of town, the moonlight dappling a golden glow across the horizon. If he drove all night he could make it to Laredo by morning. Find a hotel, grab a shower and hot breakfast and be working the case before noon.

The canyon to the left caught his eye, its vastness stretching far and wide, from behind the high school to the edge of town. A hollow emptiness resounded from the canyon tonight as if the ghosts had finally been raised and the dead could rest.

Amanda had almost died there. If he'd been a few minutes later, they might be dragging her broken body from the bottom.

His stomach seized into a knot.

He'd never been so afraid in his life.

Because he loved her.

He punched the steering wheel with his fist and spun the SUV around. He didn't want to drive all night to a new crime scene. The chief had other agents who could do the job.

He wanted the night off. Wanted to hold Amanda in his arms and make love to her again and whisper sweet nothings to her while he could.

His heart throbbed as he raced to her place, and when he arrived and saw a dim light glowing in the bedroom, adrenaline surged through him. He jumped from the SUV and hurried up to the door. He had no idea what he'd say, but he couldn't leave Sunset Mesa tonight.

He couldn't leave Amanda.

He pounded on the door, perspiration trickling down the back of his neck. A second later, she opened the door. Her eyes looked red rimmed as if she might have been crying, and he wondered if something else bad had happened.

He inhaled a breath, but the scent of some feminine body wash wafted from her, and he realized she'd just come from the shower. Her gorgeous hair lay in damp tendrils around her shoulders, a bead of water lingering at the top of her breasts where her satin robe had parted.

"What's wrong?" she asked. "I thought you had to leave."

"You've been crying," he said in a hoarse whisper. "Why?"

Her eyes misted over, and she squeezed them shut as if to stem more tears. Fear clogged his throat and he gripped her arms. "What happened?"

Her gaze met his, other emotions filling the depths. Hunger, passion, need.

"I missed you," she said, her cheeks stained with a blush. "Why did you come back?"

"For you," he said, emboldened by the fact that she'd actually cried over him. It was foolish, but it gave him hope. "I…don't want to go to Laredo tonight."

"I don't want you to go either," she said softly.

"I want you." He lowered his head and kissed her. "Tonight. Tomorrow. Always."

She slid her arms around him and kissed him back. "What are you saying, Justin?"

"That I love you," he murmured against her ear. "I almost lost you last night and that scared me."

"We could both die on the job."

"We could." He teased her neck with his lips. "So we might as well enjoy what we have together."

"I love you, too," she said, a seductive smile lighting her eyes. "Come on in, cowboy."

He chuckled and let her lead him to the bedroom. Seconds later, they lay naked in each other's arms, words of love spilling out as they joined their bodies again and again through the night.

* * * * *

"Thank you," she said. "For every-thing."

Her face was close. Close enough that he could see the tears that still clung to her long lashes. Her skin was a lovely mocha and her lips were pink and inviting. He leaned forward. She stilled.

He bent his head and kissed her. She tasted like spaghetti sauce and red wine, sweet with just a hint of sharpness. And when she pulled back quickly, he had to force himself to let her go, to not demand more.

Her dark eyes were big.

"I hadn't planned on that," he said, proving that adult men lied, too. Maybe he hadn't exactly planned it, but for months, he'd been thinking about kissing Carmen.

She didn't answer. She just looked as shaken as he felt. A few more strands of her silky hair had fallen down, and her lips were trembling.

DEAD BY
WEDNESDAY

BY
BEVERLY LONG

Published in Great Britain 2014
by Mills & Boon, an imprint of Harlequin (UK) Limited,
Eton House, 18-24 Paradise Road, Richmond, Surrey, TW9 1SR

© 2014 Beverly R. Long

ISBN: 978 0 263 91345 3

46-0114

Harlequin (UK) Limited's policy is to use papers that are natural, renewable and recyclable products and made from wood grown in sustainable forests. The logging and manufacturing processes conform to the legal environmental regulations of the country of origin.

Printed and bound in Spain
by Blackprint CPI, Barcelona

As a child, **Beverly Long** used to take a flashlight to bed so that she could hide under the covers and read. Once a teenager, more often than not, the books she chose were romance novels. Now she gets to keep the light on as long as she wants, and there's always a romance novel on her nightstand. With both a bachelor's and a master's degree in business and more than twenty years of experience as a human resources director, she now enjoys the opportunity to write her own stories. She considers her books to be a great success if they compel the reader to stay up way past their bedtime.

Beverly loves to hear from readers. Visit www.beverlylong.com, or like her at www.facebook.com/BeverlyLong.Romance.

To my good friends, who have always believed it was possible. Your support made the difference.
Now, please pass the wine.

Chapter One

Wednesday

Robert Hanson looked up from his computer screen when Lieutenant Fischer approached his desk. He wasn't surprised or worried about the anger that flashed in his boss's eyes. He knew what had put it there. Had heard the news before he'd gotten off the elevator. Even though it wasn't his case, it had been enough to make him shove his half-eaten bagel back into the bag and toss his untouched orange juice into the nearest waste can.

"Got another dead kid," his boss said.

Robert had really, really hoped that the pattern would break. For the past three weeks, there had been a new dead kid every Wednesday morning. This was week four. "I heard," Robert said.

"Did you hear he was Alderman Franconi's nephew? His sister's kid."

Robert shook his head. Franconi was tight with the mayor. The heat was going to be turned up high. Not that every detective on the force wasn't already aware of the case and keeping his or her eyes open 24/7 looking for some kind of clue.

"Where's Sawyer?" his boss asked.

"On his way. He's dropping Liz and the baby off at Options for Caring Mothers."

"Okay." His boss started to walk away. Then stopped, turned and edged close to the metal desk. "Carmen Jimenez still work there?" he asked, his inquiry casual.

"I guess so," Robert said, working hard to keep his tone neutral. He hadn't seen Carmen since the wedding three months ago, where his best friend, Sawyer Montgomery, had married her best friend, Liz Mayfield. Robert had been the best man. Carmen had been the maid of honor. Her dress had been an emerald-green and it had wrapped around her body in a way that had made him break out in an instant sweat.

The groom had been calmer than he'd been.

Which was ridiculous because everybody knew that Robert Hanson never got rattled by a woman. He *managed* relationships. Not the other way around.

"Pretty woman," Lieutenant Fischer said.

Robert raised an eyebrow. The lieutenant had been married for twenty years and had kids in high school.

"Just making conversation, Hanson. If it's any consolation, probably nobody but Sawyer and me realized that it was taking everything you had to keep your tongue from hanging out. We just know you better than most."

Robert shrugged and tried his best to look innocent. "I don't know what you're talking about, sir."

Lieutenant Fischer let out a huff of air. "Of course you don't. When Sawyer arrives, get your butts out to the scene. Blaze and Wasimole are still there. They could use some help talking to neighbors. Details are online in the case file."

Robert shifted in his chair and reached for his computer keyboard. But he let his hands rest on the keys.

Visions of Carmen Jimenez weren't that easy to push aside.

They'd danced, just once. It was expected, after all. And she'd felt perfect in his arms. And her scent had danced around him, making his head spin. He'd made small talk. *Nice wedding, wasn't it? Is your brother starting high school soon? Are you busy at work?*

She responded, her voice soft and sexy, with just a bare hint of a Spanish accent. *Very pretty. Yes, he is looking forward to playing in the band. Always lots to do.*

And when the music had ended, he hadn't wanted to let go. But she'd stepped away, murmured a quick thank-you and left him standing in the middle of the dance floor.

And later, when he'd tried to catch her eye, she'd looked away, and he wondered if it was deliberate. Toward the end of the evening, he hadn't had to wonder anymore. He'd finally worked up the courage to ask her to dance again and when she'd seen him approaching, had practically run into the ladies' restroom to avoid him.

He didn't need it written on the damn marquee. She wasn't interested. So he'd forgotten about her.

Right.

Well, he was working on it.

He tapped on his keyboard and brought up the case file. In their system, every entry was date- and time-stamped. Detectives Blaze and Wasimole, two veterans, had been on the scene within fifteen minutes of the call coming in at four o'clock this morning. Shortly after that, they'd entered a brief narrative into the electronic case file and updated it twice after that.

Victim had been discovered by a couple of sanitation workers. They hadn't touched the body. That was good. More than fifteen residents of nearby apartment buildings had already been interviewed and nobody had seen anything. That was bad.

There were multiple stab wounds, and fingers on his right hand had been severed and removed from the scene.

That wasn't a surprise.

The first victim had lost two fingers on his left hand. The second, two on the right. The third, two on his left hand.

Left, right. Left, right. There was a crazy symmetry about the handiwork but the end result was always the same. The kids were dead. Although it hadn't come easy. Coroner had determined in the first three deaths that the mutilation had occurred prior to death, which meant that they'd suffered the pain, then the blood loss; and finally the bastard had killed them by suffocating them by covering their noses with duct tape and stuffing a red bandanna in their mouths.

The killer hadn't bothered to remove the bandanna once the kids were dead.

Robert checked the notes. Yep. Victim had been found with his nostrils taped shut and a red bandanna stuffed in his mouth. He clicked on the pictures that had already been uploaded and started scanning them. They were gruesome and made his empty stomach twist.

When he heard Sawyer's footsteps, he was grateful for the interruption. His partner shrugged off his heavy coat, pulled out his desk chair and sank into it.

"You look like hell," Robert said.

"It's amazing the trouble one little tooth can cause," Sawyer said, his lazy drawl more pronounced than usual. "Catherine was up several times during the night. That doesn't happen very often."

"How's Liz?" Robert asked.

"Fabulous," Sawyer answered, sounding like a very

happy man. "Although she wasn't too crazy about me giving Catherine my leather belt to chew on. That is, until she saw how well it worked."

"Southern tradition?" Robert asked.

Sawyer shook his head. "Midwest desperation."

Robert stood up. "Well, we got another kind of tradition going on here and quite frankly, it sucks." He pointed at his computer. Sawyer got up, rounded the desk, stood behind Robert, and quickly read through the information.

"Henry Wright," Sawyer said, resting his eyes on the text that had been added just an hour or so ago once the body had been identified.

"Alderman Franconi's nephew," Robert added. That wasn't in the notes.

"This is going to get interesting fast," Sawyer said.

"I know the area," Robert said. "Residential, mostly multiunit apartments. Some commercial."

Sawyer picked up the gloves that he'd tossed on his desk. He pulled them on. "Let's go knock on some doors. But take pity on me, for God's sake, and stop and get some coffee on the way. It's freezing out there."

"It's January in Chicago. What do you expect?"

"It would be nice if it got cold enough that all the killing stopped."

"It's cold," Robert said, "but I don't think hell has frozen over yet."

The two men piled into their unmarked car, with Robert driving. He pulled out of the police lot and five minutes later, found street parking in front of their favorite coffee shop. Once inside, he waited patiently while Sawyer had to flash a picture of six-month-old Catherine after the woman behind the counter asked for an update on the little girl.

Robert was damn happy for his friend. Liz was a great woman, and given how much she and Sawyer were enjoying their adopted daughter, Robert figured they'd be adding to their family in no time.

He wasn't jealous.

Hell, no. He had the kind of freedom that married men dreamed about.

Back in the car, he sipped his coffee, grateful for the warmth. It hadn't been above twenty degrees for two weeks, which meant that the four inches of snow that had fallen three weeks ago lingered on. Most of the roads were clear, but the sidewalks that hadn't been shoveled right away now had a thick layer of hard-packed snow, making walking dangerous.

It was dirty and grimy and very non-postcard-worthy. Even in the high-rent area known as the Magnificent Mile, things were looking a little shabby.

Ten minutes later, Robert left the car in a no-parking zone. Five feet away, the alley entrance was still blocked off with police tape. He looked around. When he'd been a kid, he'd lived just a few blocks from here. For a couple years, he and his mom and husband number three had shared an apartment in one of the low-income high-rise buildings. His mom still lived less than ten blocks away.

He'd spent a fair amount of time on these streets. The area still looked much the same. There were a couple small restaurants, a dry cleaner, a tanning salon and one of those paycheck advance places where the interest started doubling the minute your loan payment was late. There was a church a block down, and the neighborhood school was just around the corner.

Buses ran up and down these streets in the daytime, leaving the snow-packed sidewalks tinged with black exhaust.

Sawyer crushed his empty coffee cup. "Ready?" he asked, pulling the collar of his heavy coat tighter.

"Sure," Robert said. He tossed his empty cup over his shoulder into the backseat.

It wasn't hard to see where the body had been found. The hard-packed snow was an ugly combination of black soot and fresh blood. Detective Charlene Blaze was talking to one of the evidence techs, who was still scraping the snow for something. He didn't see her partner, Milo Wasimole.

"Hey, Charlene," Robert said. "How's it going?"

She was a small woman, maybe mid-fifties. Her first grandchild had been born the previous week. Her face was red from the cold. "Okay, I guess. I lost feeling in my toes about a half hour ago."

"Lieutenant Fischer asked us to swing by."

She nodded. "Yeah, all hands on deck when an alderman's nephew gets it," she said, her tone sarcastic.

Robert understood. Hell, there were teenagers killed almost every night in Chicago. Most of the killings were gang-related. And nobody seemed to get all that excited about it.

But after week two, when it had become apparent that they might have a serial killer on their hands, the cases had started to get attention.

Week three, local newspapers had gotten hold of the story, noting the similarities in the killings. Two days later, they got television exposure, when the twenty-four-hour news channels picked it up. Then the dancing had started. Because nobody in the police department wanted it widely known that three kids were dead and they didn't have a clue who was responsible.

"Press been here yet?" Robert asked.

Charlene nodded. "Oh, yeah. Can't wait to see tomorrow's headline." She nodded goodbye to the evidence tech, who was putting away his things. "I know you guys already have your own caseload but I have to admit, I'm appreciative of every set of eyes I can get. This is getting really creepy. Based on what we know at this point, this was a good kid. Fourteen. Just made the eighth-grade honor roll. Played the trumpet in the middle-school band."

Robert had read the files of the other three dead kids and knew they had similar stories. First victim had been thirteen. Second, fifteen. Third, fourteen. All male. All good students. All without known gang ties. "Any connection to the previous three victims?"

"No. All four lived in different parts of the city and went to different schools. We don't have any reason to believe they knew each other or had common friends."

Robert shook his head. "Nobody ever said it was going to be easy." He pulled his gloves out of his pocket. "Sawyer and I'll start knocking on some neighbors' doors. Maybe we'll get lucky and somebody saw something."

CARMEN JIMENEZ SWAYED back and forth with six-month-old Catherine on her hip. "I can't believe how big she's getting," she said to Liz, who was busy making coffee. "I saw her just a few weeks ago and she already looks different."

"I know. I'm almost grateful that her regular babysitter got sick. It's nice to bring her to work with me." Liz pushed the button on the coffee machine.

"Did Sawyer get her room finished?" Carmen asked.

Liz smiled. "It's gorgeous. I can't believe he had the patience to stencil all those teddy bears. You should come see it. We're getting pizza tonight. You and Raoul could join us."

"Raoul has band practice tonight. Even so…" She stopped.

Liz frowned at her. "What's wrong? You look really troubled."

"Nothing," Carmen denied automatically. Then remembered this was Liz, her best friend. "I was going to say that even so, he probably wouldn't want to come with me. I haven't said much, but I'm worried about Raoul."

"What's wrong with your brother?" Liz reached for Catherine and settled the little girl on her own hip.

"He's not talking to me. By the time I get home from work, he's already in his room. He comes out for dinner, shovels some food in, and retreats back to his cave. I'm lucky if I get a few one-word answers."

"He's an adolescent boy. That's pretty normal behavior. Aren't you almost thirty? That automatically makes you too old to understand anything."

"I know. It's just hard for me. It seems as if it was just weeks ago that he and his best friend Jacob were setting up a tent in our living room, laughing like a bunch of hyenas until the middle of the night."

"I can see why you'd miss that," Liz said with a smirk.

Carmen rolled her eyes. "I know, I know. But in the old days he couldn't wait to tell me what had happened at school." She swallowed. "He used to confide in me."

Liz wrapped her free arm around her friend's delicate shoulder. "That, my friend, is the difference between ten and fifteen. Give him a couple more years and he'll start talking again. In the meantime, you need something else to focus on."

"Maybe I'll take up knitting," Carmen said. "I couldn't find my scarf this morning."

Liz shook her head. "That's not what I was thinking."

Carmen sighed loudly. She and Liz had had this conversation. "I know what you were thinking."

"I never thought I'd play matchmaker. Really, I didn't. It's just that I'm so happy. I want that for you."

"I know. That's the only thing that's keeping me from

tripping you on these stairs." She leaned forward and kissed Catherine's soft cheek. "Take care of your mother, darling. Her head is in the clouds."

Liz shook her head. "Just think about it, please. Maybe try the online thing?"

"Sure. I'll think about it. But right now, I have more pressing issues. I'm meeting my new client in fifteen minutes. Alexa Sage is sixteen, seven months along and lives at home with her parents, who have no idea that she's pregnant."

Liz nodded. "Winter clothes make it easier to hide a pregnancy, that's for sure." She took another step. "Will you come for pizza tonight? Please?"

"No need to beg. My middle name is carbohydrate. I'll be there." Carmen stopped at her office door, unlocked it, opened the door and immediately walked across the small space to pull open the heavy curtain on the lone window. Most days the sun offered some warmth but today, everything outside was gray. Wednesday. Hump day. By five o'clock tonight, the workweek would be more than half over. Although for the counselors who worked at Options for Caring Mothers, their workweeks didn't tend to be so carefully defined. Babies came at all times of the day or night, and none of the staff wanted their teenage clients to be alone at that time.

Alexa Sage arrived five minutes later. She wore a big black coat and jeans tucked into black boots. Her short hair was a white-blond and her pale skin was clear and pretty, with nicely applied makeup. Her eyes were green and wary.

"It's nice to meet you, Alexa," Carmen said, motioning for the girl to take a chair. "I hope you didn't get too cold getting here."

"I took the bus," she said. She sat but didn't take off her coat.

"Better than walking," Carmen said, keeping up the small talk. "I have a younger brother, and when I don't have early-morning meetings, I drop him and his best friend off at school."

"My mother doesn't work. She takes my sister and me to school every day. Picks us up, too. That's what Frank Sage wants."

"Stepdad?" Carmen asked, noting the use of the first name.

"Nope. His blood is my blood. Let me tell you, that has kept me up a few nights. He doesn't like it when I call him Frank. My mom thinks it's disrespectful, too."

"Do you say it to be disrespectful?"

"I say it because I can."

Maybe that's why she'd had sex. Because she could. And now she was in a heap of trouble. "How did you find out about Options for Caring Mothers?" Carmen asked.

"My counselor at school. She gave me an OCM brochure."

That was how many of their referrals came. "I'm glad that happened," Carmen said. "Did you tell her that you were pregnant?"

"I think the school nurse told her. I got sick a couple times at school. The nurse thought I had the flu and wanted to send me home. I had to tell her the truth."

"But you haven't told your parents?"

"No."

"Why not?"

Alexa chewed her lip. "My dad works in some little factory and he hates his job. He gets mad when my sister or I get a B. Says that if we're not careful, we're going to be trapped in some dead-end job. When he finds out that I'm going to quit school to take care of the baby, he's not going to be happy."

"So, you're planning on keeping your baby?"

The girl nodded.

"What about the father of the baby?"

This got a shrug. "He's a junior, too, so we're not, you know, getting married or anything, but he's cool with it."

"He hasn't told his parents?"

"There's only his mom. And no, we both agreed that we wouldn't say anything to anybody."

Alexa was mature, but was she mature enough to handle a child? "Have you considered adoption?" Carmen asked.

Alexa shook her head. "So that she can be raised by somebody like my parents? No, thanks."

Carmen nodded. Not much to say to that, was there? "Have you had any prenatal care?"

Alexa nodded. "At the health department. Everything is fine. I'm twenty-eight weeks. The baby is due April 15."

"How much longer do you think you can hide your pregnancy from your family?" Carmen asked.

"Probably not much longer. In a week, I have a family wedding. I'm not going to be able to wear a sweatshirt and baggy pants or my coat. I think the cat is going to be pretty much out of the bag."

"You should tell your parents before then," Carmen said.

"I know. That's why I'm here. Frank doesn't do so good with surprises. Goes a little crazy sometimes."

"What kind of crazy?" Carmen asked. "Crazy yelling or crazy something else?"

"When my mother hit a post with the fender of our car, he slapped her so hard that he split her lip."

Carmen felt sick.

"You were the counselor who helped my neighbor, Angelina. She said you were wonderful. I was hoping you could be there when I tell him."

Chapter Two

Raoul almost dropped his trombone when a skinny man stepped out of the dry cleaner's doorway, right into his path. His dark hair was slicked down on his head and pulled back into a short ponytail. His skin was really pale and he had gray eyes.

"Hi, there," the man said.

He was about six inches taller than Raoul, which basically wasn't all that tall. His shoulders were wide and he had on a really ugly plaid coat.

Raoul tried to step around him.

The man stepped with him, blocking his path.

"Hey, man," Raoul said. He'd already had a really bad day and all he wanted was to go home.

"Is that how you treat your friends, Raoul?"

Friends? "Who are you? How do you know my name?" Raoul asked, feeling uncomfortable. He looked around. There were other people on the sidewalk, but nobody seemed to be paying any attention to him.

"I know a lot about you. Your brother Hector and I were friends. Real tight."

Hector had been dead for eleven years. Whenever anybody said Hector's name, his sister, Carmen, got a real funny look on her face and she got sad. Once, when he asked her about it, she said that she was just so sorry that Hector had died.

That made him feel even worse that he couldn't remember Hector. He'd only been four when he'd died. He couldn't tell Carmen the truth. That would probably make her even sadder.

"You really knew Hector?"

"Oh, yeah. One time, before he died, he told me that if anything ever happened to him, that I should watch out for you."

Raoul didn't know what to say to that and anyway, his throat felt tight.

"Your brother used to talk about you all the time. Said that having a kid brother was cool."

Hector would have understood how hard it was to be the smallest kid in the class. He'd have known how humiliating it was to have someone jam your head into a toilet. He'd have known how ridiculous it felt to be tripped going down the hall and have your books fly everywhere.

He'd have known how much it hurt when everyone laughed.

"What's your favorite song?" the man asked, giving Raoul's shoulder a light punch.

Raoul didn't want to talk music. Even though this guy had been a friend of Hector's, he sort of gave him the creeps. "What's your name?" he asked again.

The man shook his head. "We'll talk soon, Raoul. I know what your brother wanted for you. I'm here to make sure you get it. Now, go home. Practice your music like a good boy."

BY THE END of the day, the police knew just a little more than they had that morning. The boy had not been killed on site. No, somewhere else, and then brought into the alley.

One of the neighbors said that he'd left the neighborhood bar and walked home, cutting through the alley shortly before two in the morning. He swore that the body hadn't been there. If he was right, then the drop-off had occurred sometime between two and four, which was earlier than the other three killings. Those bodies had been found late in the day, and the coroner had estimated time of death to be late afternoon, early evening.

Was the killer getting more anxious?

That thought kept Robert and Sawyer and a half dozen other detectives knocking on doors, for six blocks in every direction, in the hopes that somebody had seen something. Maybe they'd also walked through the alley, maybe they'd seen a car idling nearby, maybe they'd heard something unusual.

It was the proverbial looking for a needle in a haystack, but dead kids got feet on the street.

Early evening, Robert and Sawyer returned to the parking lot behind their police station. They parked the department-issued cruiser and walked toward their own cars. "I'm starting to really hate Wednesdays," Robert said.

Sawyer nodded. "Yeah, me, too. At least I have dinner to look forward to. I'm picking up pizza at Toni's. Liz invited Carmen over to look at Catherine's room. I painted it this weekend."

All damn day Carmen Jimenez had been on his mind. "I've been thinking of doing some painting," Robert said.

Sawyer smiled. "Yeah. But for some reason, I doubt you're thinking pink."

Robert shrugged. "What did you use? A gloss, semi-gloss or a flat?"

Sawyer waved a hand. "I have no idea. I used the paint in the can that Liz brought home from the paint store."

"Oh, good grief. Now I've got to see this paint job. If

you get the pizza, I'll get a couple bottles of wine on my way. As long as you think it will be okay with Liz."

"Liz adores you. Why, I'm not a hundred percent sure."

Robert shoved his friend, then had to grab him to keep him from slipping on the snow, which was gathering a top layer of ice as the temperature continued to drop.

"Be careful," Robert said.

"Be on time," Sawyer said, getting into his car. "I'm hungry."

Less than forty-five minutes later, Robert knocked on his partner's door. He'd had time to run home, take a five-minute shower and grab a couple of bottles of wine off the rack in his kitchen.

While he was perfectly happy in his ultramodern high-rise, he had to admit that he loved Sawyer's house. A month before Liz and Sawyer had gotten married, Liz and Catherine had moved into the eighty-year-old brownstone. Now the family occupied the first two floors and rented out the top floor to a single woman who spent most of the week traveling.

The house had good bones. Before meeting Liz, Sawyer had already refinished the oak floors, replaced all the lighting and hung artwork that reminded him of the Deep South. Liz had added feminine touches that had turned the wonderful structure into a home.

"Hi, Robert," Liz said as she opened the door. She leaned forward for a kiss on the cheek. "Come in quickly. It's freezing."

He stepped inside, closing the door behind him. He could hear the soft murmur of voices from the living room. He heard Carmen laugh, and there wasn't a cold bone in his body.

Liz peered at the wine. "Very nice," she said. "The pizza is good but this may put it to shame."

Robert set the wine on the entryway table, shrugged off his coat, stuffed his gloves in one pocket and handed it to Liz. She hung the coat in the hall closet. There was a royal-blue cape hanging there and he suspected it belonged to Carmen.

It was crazy but he liked seeing his coat next to hers.

He picked up the wine and followed Liz into the family room. Like any good cop, he took in the details quickly. Fireplace was lit. Soft jazz played in the background. Catherine lay on her back, on the very nice rug that had been one of Liz's contributions to the house. Both plump little legs were moving, as if she were pedaling an invisible bicycle. Sawyer was stretched out next to her.

Carmen was sitting in the chair, leaning forward, looking at the baby. The light from the fireplace cast a soft glow around her. She wore a red sweater and black slacks. Her long dark hair flowed over her shoulders.

She was beautiful.

And when she turned, he saw that she wasn't surprised to see him. Her face was composed, polite. And he should have felt much the same. After all, he'd known that she was going to be here. That was why he'd wheedled an invitation with some crazy excuse that he was interested in paint. Paint, for God's sake. It was ridiculous.

And it was pretty damn ridiculous, too, that just looking at Carmen made him feel short of breath and a little unsteady on his feet.

"Hi," she said.

"Hi," he managed.

Sawyer sat up. "Cold beer in the fridge."

Robert nodded. "I'll stick with this," he said, holding up the wine. He looked at Carmen. "Can I get you a glass?"

She nodded. "Yes, thank you."

Liz reached for the wine. "I'll get some for both of you.

I need to check the pizza anyway. We put it in the oven to keep it hot." She took a step. "Have a seat, Robert," she said gently.

He sat. And felt like an awkward sixteen-year-old at his first prom. His shirt felt too tight and his heart was racing in his chest.

The only noise in the room was Catherine's happy squeals. Carmen stared at the fire. He stared at the antique umbrella stand in the corner of the room.

Sawyer looked from Carmen to him and back again. Finally, his friend sprang to his feet. He reached for Catherine and cupped her in the crook of his elbow. "Liz probably needs my help in the kitchen," he said as he left the room.

Now there was just silence.

Sawyer had probably been gone for less than a minute when Carmen turned her head. "I don't think Liz really needs his help."

He relaxed. "Maybe if we were having grits and chicken-fried steak."

"Ugh," she said with a smile that made her even prettier. "I'd suddenly have to run an errand."

"I'd drive you," he said. "Although to be fair, the man makes a great gumbo. He brought some into work one day, and it made me nostalgic for my last trip to the French Quarter."

"I think I'd love New Orleans," she said. "Maybe someday."

The kitchen door swung open, and Liz emerged holding two wineglasses. "Follow me," she said, leading them to the dining room. There was a huge pizza in the middle of the table with a big bowl of salad next to it. Sawyer was clipping Catherine's high-chair tray on.

They sat, and Catherine immediately started squealing

and pounding her plump fists on the high-chair tray. Liz smiled apologetically. "Sorry. This is the kind of ambience we have now."

Robert dished out a slice of pizza and handed it to Carmen. "No problem. Table manners like her father."

They were done with their pizza and cutting into the cheesecake that Carmen had picked up at the bakery after work when Robert's phone buzzed with an incoming text message. He glanced at it, shook his head and turned his phone upside down on the table. "Sorry about that," he said.

"Bad news?" Liz asked.

"A reporter from the newspaper," he explained. "She's evidently not getting enough of a story from Blaze and Wasimole, so she tracked me down. I imagine she got the number from one of the people we talked to today. We generally leave a card in case they think of something that might be helpful."

"These killings are the only thing the local talk show hosts were discussing today," Liz said. "It's getting very scary."

It was horrible, thought Carmen. With Raoul being about the same age as the other victims, it made her sick to hear people talking about the stories. Her heart ached for the terrible loss that the families had suffered, for the pain the boys had endured. "I didn't know if I should say anything to Raoul," she admitted. "I didn't want to scare him unnecessarily but I also didn't want him to be naive."

"Where did you land on it?" Robert asked.

"I left the newspaper on the table one morning, folded so that he could easily see the headline. He read the story and that gave me the opportunity I was waiting for. I tried to gently suggest that it was important to be careful, to always be watching."

"What did he say?" Liz asked.

Carmen rolled her eyes. "He said, and I quote, 'Sis. There are three million people in the city of Chicago. Eight million if you count the suburbs. I don't think anybody is looking for me.' I didn't push it. I'm crazy enough about other things, like brushed teeth and pants that stay up around his waist."

"Raoul's such a smart kid. You didn't need to say anything else," Liz said. "He gets it."

"Yeah, and we're going to *get* this guy," Sawyer said, his tone confident. "He's going to make a mistake. In fact, he already has."

"What's that?" Liz asked.

"He mutilates and suffocates his victims. That's been reported in the press. What hasn't been reported is that the victims have all been found with red handkerchiefs in their mouths. We've been successful in keeping that out of the press. But that shows an arrogance on his part—that he's so confident that he won't be caught that he can afford to leave clues at the scene. Arrogance makes criminals sloppy."

"Can you trace the handkerchiefs?" Carmen asked.

"We've tried. No luck so far," Robert said. "They're sold in a bunch of stores. But something will break, soon. It has to." He leaned across the table and tickled Catherine's belly. "Right, darling?"

She giggled, breaking the tension at the table.

Carmen felt more relaxed than she had in months. That wasn't how she'd expected the evening to go. She'd gotten to Liz's house and her friend had quickly pulled her aside. *Sawyer just told me he invited Robert, too. Are you okay with that?*

Heck no, she wasn't okay with that. She'd met Robert Hanson just weeks before Catherine was born, when

Catherine's mother was kidnapped by a gang leader who wanted to steal the baby. Robert had been a little brash, maybe even a little cocky, but he'd been helpful to both Liz and Sawyer.

And she had tried to ignore that whenever he was close, it seemed a little harder to focus. She'd done pretty well with that until the wedding and then the dance.

Robert Hanson knew how to hold a woman. For a big man, his touch had been light and his steps graceful.

But she'd known that he was a man who knew what to do. And her skills were rusty. Real rusty. She was twenty-nine years old and hadn't been on a date in thirteen years.

No worries, she'd assured her friend. After all, they'd had one little dance. She remembered it but he'd probably forgotten it the next day. She told herself it was silly to think for even one minute that the evening would be the least bit awkward.

But when the door opened and she heard his voice in the foyer, her senses had become more acute. She felt her skin get warm and knew it had nothing to do with Sawyer's nice fireplace.

And she'd tried to remember that it was just a DWF night. Dinner With Friends. They'd have a little pizza, some wine, a few laughs.

And she'd prayed that the butterflies in her stomach would get the message.

She'd worried for nothing. Robert Hanson, in his usual charming way, had made the night perfect.

Now that they'd finished with their cheesecake, Robert pushed back his chair and began to gather up the dirty plates. Liz started to get up. "I've got this," he said. "I'm anxious to see the paint job that your husband did. I must admit, he's never impressed me as being all that artistic."

Sawyer wadded up his cloth napkin and threw it at Robert. "If I get tired of wrestling with the bad guys, maybe I'll start my own painting business."

"Not a chance, Michelangelo," Robert said. "You're not leaving me on my own."

Liz shook her head. "Like either of you would ever stop being cops. Come with me."

They followed Liz back to Catherine's room. It had been painted a pale mint-green. Waist-high was a border of dancing teddy bears in yellows and pinks.

"It's adorable," Carmen said. "Very impressive. Can I hire you? My kitchen desperately needs paint."

Sawyer smiled and shook his head. "I don't want to see another stir stick for quite some time. Robert, you seemed to know a lot about painting earlier."

"I work cheap," Robert said, his tone casual.

"I'll keep that in mind," Carmen said, grateful to get out of the conversation so easily. The idea of sexy Robert Hanson in her kitchen, face smeared with paint, looking all adorable, had the butterflies double-timing it. Her stomach lining was getting scratched. "I should probably get going," she added.

Sawyer and Robert grabbed coats out of the closet and Carmen hugged her friend. "Thank you so much. Everything was delicious. Remember, I'm going to be late tomorrow."

"Be careful, okay?" Liz replied, her tone serious.

Both Sawyer and Robert immediately stopped their conversation. "What's going on, honey?" Sawyer asked, moving close to his wife.

"Carmen has a new client. Unfortunately, the girl hasn't told her parents that she's pregnant. She's afraid to. Dad evidently has a history of a violent temper. Anyway, she asked Carmen to be there when she breaks the news."

Robert took a step forward. "He's coming to OCM?"

"No," Carmen said. "That won't work. The minute she tells him that she wants to meet him at a pregnancy counseling center, he's going to have a pretty good idea of what's going on."

"You're not going to this guy's house?" Robert asked, his tone challenging.

Carmen shook her head. "No. I'm not that crazy," she said, trying to make light of it. She saw that it wasn't working. "Frank Sage evidently stops for coffee every morning at a little place on the corner of Taylor and Minx. His daughter and I are going to meet there and uh, break the news. It's a public place where he'll probably feel inclined to behave. It was the best plan I could come up with."

Robert was frowning at her. "You do this kind of thing often?"

"Not often, but I've had cases where we've had to quickly remove a young girl from a situation when her parents or her boyfriend or somebody else couldn't handle the news of the pregnancy. We need to protect our clients and their babies."

"You think that's what's going to happen here?" Robert asked.

"I don't know. I should be able to tell. If I have any reason to believe that he's going to harm my client physically, I'll take the necessary steps."

Liz stepped in and wrapped an arm around Carmen's shoulder. "She's little but she's tough. I'll see you tomorrow," she said. "Be careful driving home."

She and Robert left. She saw a red SUV parked behind her car. She assumed it was Robert's. "Well, good night," she said when they got to her car.

"It's pretty late," he said. "How about I follow you?"

Was Robert Hanson asking to be invited in? The idea

was absurd. And terribly exciting. She felt sixteen again. "I drive all the time at night," she said.

"That doesn't make it a good thing. Please let me do this."

Liz had always said that both Sawyer and Robert were real gentlemen. "Okay. Do you need my address?" she asked. "In case you lose me at a light?"

He shook his head and smiled. "I won't lose you."

And he didn't. She drove a sedate thirty-eight miles an hour and he stayed a couple car lengths behind her. The whole time she worried about what she should say if he asked to come in. When she parked at her apartment building, she still didn't have an answer.

He pulled up next to her.

"What floor?" he asked.

"Second. That window is my kitchen," she said, pointing at the end of the building closest to them.

"Okay. Flip the light twice and I'll know you're in safe. Have a good night, Carmen."

"Uh…sure. Thanks." She practically ran into the building. She got inside her apartment and pressed herself up against the hard wall. Her heart was pounding in her chest, and she didn't think it was from the physical exertion.

Then she remembered to flip the light twice.

Robert Hanson wasn't interested in coming inside, and she was a fool to think so.

Chapter Three

Thursday

Carmen was just slipping on her shoes the next morning when she heard Raoul's door slam. "You're up early," she said, ruffling his hair as he walked past her.

He didn't answer. Just went to the cupboard and pulled out a box of cereal. He poured a big bowl, added milk, grabbed a spoon from the drawer and stood at the counter. "I have band practice this morning," he said with his mouth full.

She ignored the poor manners. Lately, Raoul hadn't offered much conversation; she wasn't inclined to shut him down. "Practice before and after school?"

"Winter concert is next Thursday," Raoul said. "Mr. Raker said we better improve fast or we're going to be an embarrassment to ourselves and our families."

Carmen smiled. Mr. Raker could get a little over-the-top sometimes. "You'll pull it off. I know you will."

"I guess." He chewed. "Hey, Carmen. Did Hector have a lot of friends in high school?"

Hector. He'd been two years older and in every way possible, her hero. And then he'd made a few bad decisions that changed the course of his life. All their lives, really.

And then he'd died.

"I guess," she said. Raoul never talked about Hector. "Why do you ask?"

He stared at her and put his half-eaten cereal down. "He was my brother. Can't I ask about my brother?"

"Of course," she said. "It's just…you surprised me, that's all. What would you like to know?"

He grabbed his coat. "Never mind," he said. "I have to go. It's Mrs. Minelli's turn to drive. She's probably already here."

"Raoul," she said.

A slamming door was her answer.

"Say hi to Jacob," she said, her voice trailing off at the end. She sank down on one of her kitchen chairs. Over the years, she'd had a few clients who were as young as fourteen or fifteen, but girls were different. They communicated. Boys just shut down.

It was driving her crazy.

She turned the lights off, grabbed her coat and patted her pockets to make sure she had gloves. She normally drove to work, but she knew that parking near the coffee shop would be hard to find. It was easier to take a cab.

When she was just a few blocks away, she texted Alexa's cell phone. *Are you there?*

The response came almost immediately. *No. Five minutes.*

Carmen checked her watch. Alexa's father stopped in on his way to work. Same time, every day. He was due in ten minutes.

The cab stopped, and she handed over a ten and got out. She considered waiting outside for Alexa but across the street, the flashing sign on the bank indicated it was ten degrees.

And in Chicago, the wind never stopped blowing. Which made the windchill about twenty below.

She opened the coffee shop door, took her place in line and studied her choices. When it was her turn, she ordered a large hot chocolate and a glass of water. Then she turned to find a table.

And saw him.

Robert Hanson.

He smiled at her and held up his own cup. "Morning, Carmen. They make a great cup of coffee here, don't they?"

He looked fresh and handsome and as delicious as one of the scones in the front display case. "This is not your coffee shop," she hissed.

"I drink coffee all day long, all over the city. Why not here?"

She rolled her eyes. "Look, there's no need for you to be here. Everything is going to be fine."

"Good. Then you can just ignore that I'm here."

Robert Hanson was six-two and two hundred pounds of muscle. His eyes were a brilliant blue, his bone structure was strong and his thick light brown hair looked as if a woman had just run her fingers through it.

He was hard to ignore.

"Do not interfere," she said.

"As long as Dad behaves, that shouldn't be a problem."

Carmen shook her head and took the table in the corner. She turned her chair so that she could see the door but not Robert. She concentrated on taking deep breaths. When she felt she had it under control, she took small sips of her hot chocolate.

Alexa came in, wearing the same big, dark coat. The young girl got a cup of coffee and headed for Carmen. "I'm sorry I'm late. He should be here really soon."

"No problem." Carmen decided that now wasn't the time to lecture on the evils of pregnancy and caffeine.

"When he arrives, make eye contact and motion him over to the table. Then I'll introduce myself and let him know that you have something that you'd like to tell him. Just be calm. It's going to be okay."

"You don't know my dad," Alexa said. She looked tired, as if she hadn't had much sleep.

Carmen reached over to pat the girl's hand but stopped when the teen stiffened in her chair. Carmen turned and immediately saw the resemblance between daughter and father. Their coloring was the same; the nose, too. Frank Sage was a big man, probably at least six feet. He wore gray work pants and a big black coat that hinted at a well-fed stomach. His blond hair was thinning on top.

He was frowning at his daughter.

Alexa motioned and the man hesitated. Then he walked across the room, bumping into a chair on the way.

"Alexa, what are you doing here?" he asked. He had a deep voice, somewhat raspy, likely from years of ciga-rettes. Carmen could smell smoke on his jacket.

"Hi, Dad," Alexa said.

Carmen stood up. She did not like him towering over her. She extended her hand. He stared at it. "Mr. Sage, I'm Carmen Jimenez. I am a counselor and I've been working with your daughter."

When it didn't appear that he was going to return the shake, Carmen dropped her arm. "Will you please have a seat?" she asked.

The man hesitated, then sat on the edge of his chair. "A counselor? Working with my daughter," he repeated. "What the hell is this about, Alexa?"

Carmen sat down. "Alexa has something that she wants to tell you, Mr. Sage. And this is difficult for her. It may also be difficult for you to hear. All I'm asking is that you hear her out, give her a chance."

The man nodded. His eyes were narrowed.

"Dad." Alexa stopped and licked her lips. "I'm pregnant."

The man's face turned red. He shook his head. "No," he said, staring at his daughter.

Alexa nodded. "I'm going to have a baby around April 15."

"No," he repeated, his voice louder, as if by proclaiming it so, he could simply get the problem to disappear.

Alexa's face turned pink and she looked quickly around the coffee shop. A few people in line were staring in their direction. "Please, Dad. Carmen is a counselor at Options for Caring Mothers, a pregnancy counseling center. She's helping me."

The man swiveled in his chair, looked at Carmen, then stood up fast, catching the edge of the table. Cups and water glasses flew. Carmen felt the hot splash of liquid on her face and heard Alexa yelp. She looked up to see Frank Sage's big red face coming toward her.

ROBERT WRENCHED THE man's arm behind his back, put pressure on the back of his knees with a well-placed foot, and in seconds, had him facedown on the tile floor.

He looked around the room. "My name is Detective Robert Hanson. I'm a police officer with the Chicago Police Department. I need all of you to remain calm and to stay in your seats. I repeat, remain calm and stay in your seats."

He turned to look at Carmen. She was standing up. Her mouth was open and she looked shell-shocked. There was hot chocolate on her blouse, and some had splashed on her face and hair. He tightened his grip on Sage's arm, pulling it just a little higher. "Are you okay?" he asked her.

She nodded and turned to look at the girl who had also

stood up. "Alexa?" She wrapped an arm around the girl's shoulder.

"I told you," the young girl said, her tone soft. She was looking at her dad.

There was a disgusting combination of hot chocolate, coffee and water pooling on the table. The uneven slate floor was causing a small trickle to drip off the side.

A helpful server walked by and offered Carmen a towel. Robert shook his head. "Leave it," he said. He wanted pictures.

Robert leaned close to the man's ear. He spoke quietly. "If you didn't hear it the first time, my name is Detective Robert Hanson, with the Chicago Police Department. I'm going to let you get up, Mr. Sage. But if you make one wrong move toward your daughter, Ms. Jimenez, me or anybody else in this room, you're going to be in even bigger trouble than you are now. Do you understand?"

He waited until the big man nodded. Then he loosened his grip and let the man get to his knees. He kicked a chair toward him. "Sit there," he ordered.

The man did as he was instructed. His face was red and his eyes were wild, but he didn't try anything. He did not look at Alexa or Carmen.

Robert moved behind him. Quietly but distinctly, he read him his Miranda rights.

The man let him finish and then immediately said, "I didn't do anything wrong."

He'd had his arms up, coming toward Carmen, and if Robert hadn't been there to stop him, Carmen's injuries would have been far worse than some splashes with a hot drink. It was taking everything he had not to punch the son of a bitch.

"You caused hot liquid to land on Ms. Jimenez. That's battery, Mr. Sage. And by virtue of your size, your proximity and your aggressive posture, I'm adding criminal threatening to the list of charges."

Frank Sage said nothing. Then he looked at his daughter. "I didn't mean to upset the table. I caught it with my legs. And I wouldn't have hurt her. I was…surprised. You surprised me. This wasn't the way it should have happened. Not with some stranger here."

Alexa stared at her hands.

Carmen stepped forward. "No closer," Robert said.

She nodded and sat down. "I believe Mr. Sage when he says that he didn't purposefully lift the table. And I'm sure we did catch him by surprise this morning with some very difficult news. If Mr. Sage feels that he can now have a reasonable conversation, I think we should forget the last five minutes and move forward. Alexa has a lot of decisions she needs to make and she needs her father's help." She motioned for Alexa to take her seat again.

No, Robert wanted to yell. In his head, he could still see Sage lunging over the table, his big hands ready to wring Carmen's neck.

"Please," Carmen said, looking at him. "Robert?"

Damn. Like he was going to be able to deny her anything. He squatted next to Frank Sage. "You're lucky. She's a nice person. I'm not that nice, in case you were wondering." He pulled a business card out of his pocket and handed it to Sage. "Take this, as a little reminder that I'm going to be watching you."

He stepped back and watched while Carmen used the towel to sop up enough of the liquid to keep more from hitting the floor. Then, the three of them conversed for a few minutes. She talked and Alexa and Sage listened. Then it was Alexa's turn. Sage said very little. After a few minutes, Carmen stood up. She extended a hand to Sage. He hesitated, then extended his own arm, giving her hand a quick shake. Then he left without a backward glance at the two women.

Alexa stood up next, hugged Carmen, said something that made Carmen smile and then left. Carmen finally looked at him.

She was sitting at a dirty table, a large splotch of brown liquid on her pink shirt, with more on her face and in her hair, and he'd never seen anyone more beautiful.

He moved over to the table. "You're sure you're okay?" he asked.

She looked down at her shirt. "Oh, yeah. This is the look I was going for." With two fingers, she rubbed at the sticky substance on her face. "By the way," she said, "thank you. I mean it. I know I wasn't very gracious about you being here but you were a big help."

He nodded. "What's next for Alexa and her parents?"

"They're going to tell her mom tonight. Alexa didn't want to tell her first because she was afraid that her father would be mad at her mom, thinking that she'd been hiding information from him. This way, he'll see how surprised his wife is by the news. Then they'll have to start talking about next steps. Alexa is determined to have this baby and take care of it. She probably could do it by herself, but it would be a whole lot easier if she had her parents' help."

"And where do you come in?"

"I'll continue to work with her throughout the remainder of the pregnancy and then after delivery, too. There are resources available to both her and her baby that I can help her with."

"Sage didn't look happy."

"He's not. Hopefully he'll work himself into the stage of acceptance. If he can't, then I'll help Alexa with finding a new place to live. I'm not going to let her live with somebody who can't get over his anger."

"I don't want you to ever go to their house," he said.

She narrowed her dark brown eyes. "Detective, I'm must have heard that wrong because it sounded as if you were telling me how to do my job."

He shook his head and rolled his eyes. "Come on, I'll walk you to your car. I assume you're going to want to go home and change."

She nodded. "Yes, but no car. I took a cab."

He frowned at her. "I'm not going to let you stand around in a wet shirt when it's freezing, waiting for a cab. I'll drive you home."

He could tell she wanted to argue, but her shirt was probably uncomfortable enough that it changed her mind. "If it's no trouble."

Carmen Jimenez had been causing him trouble since the first day that he'd seen her. She'd been standing outside OCM, waiting while bomb specialists removed an explosive device that had been left on her boss's desk. He'd taken one look and his world had changed. His sleep was disturbed, he rarely got through a day without thinking of her and his sex life had taken a turn down a dead-end road. He still dated, made himself pretend that he was having fun, but he hadn't slept with anybody since that morning.

And she had barely given him the time of day.

If Sawyer or their boss knew that he was such a fool, Robert would never hear the end of it.

"No trouble," he said.

ROBERT DROVE WITH an ease and competence that impressed Carmen. She'd grown up in the city and had been driving in it for years, but all the traffic still made her nervous. Raoul had been hinting that he was going to get to take driver's education soon and that he'd need lots of practice hours. The thought of it made her ill. But she would do it. She would do anything for Raoul.

She pulled her cell phone from her purse, intending to check in with Liz. There was a missed call and a voice mail. She didn't recognize the number.

She listened to the voice mail and felt sick. She played it again. Then let her phone drop back into her purse.

"What's wrong?" Robert asked, checking his rearview mirror.

There was no reason to tell him. She'd been handling things on her own for a long time. She'd handle this, too.

"Carmen?" he said, his voice soft. "Was that Sage?"

She was so tired of being strong and so damn worried about Raoul. "That was Raoul's homeroom teacher. She wanted me to know that Raoul is failing two of his classes. He rarely turns in homework and on the last essay test, over half of his answers were wrong."

Robert nodded. "Is he a pretty good student, usually?"

"He's always made the honor roll. Oh, my gosh, I've never gotten a call like this. Never dreamed I'd get one."

"So talk to him. You're good at that," Robert said with an encouraging smile.

Carmen chewed on the corner of her lip. "It's not just the grades. There's something else going on but I have no idea what it is. He's changing. Right in front of my eyes. He won't talk to me. It's as if he doesn't even like me."

Robert slipped the car into a parking place in front of her apartment, shut it off and turned toward her. "Look, take it from somebody who used to be a boy," he said with a smile. "It's tough being a freshman in high school. He likes you. He just doesn't know how to show it."

"That's what Liz says."

"She's right."

Carmen shook her head. "I know Raoul better than I

know anybody. It's been just the two of us for a long time. Our older brother, Hector, died when I was eighteen and Raoul was barely four. About a year later, our parents were killed in a car accident. I raised Raoul from that point."

"You were really just a kid yourself. That was a big responsibility you took on."

"I guess. It never entered my mind to do anything different. I was in college by then. We both did our homework at the kitchen table," she said, smiling at the memory.

"Good bonding time," Robert said.

She nodded. "I know him as well as I know myself. That's how I know that there's something else going on here. I just have to figure it out before it's too late." She swallowed hard. "Hector was shot by a rival gang member. He had just turned twenty." She closed her eyes for just a second, then opened them and looked at him. "I can't lose another brother. I just can't."

"You lost a great deal in a short period of time. Yet you went on, made a good life for yourself and your brother. It could not have been easy."

He seemed so sincere in his praise. She hadn't told him to impress him. She'd just wanted him to understand.

"I'll figure something out," she said, trying to change the subject.

"I could talk to him," Robert said.

It was a nice offer but it wouldn't work. "He doesn't know you. He's not going to trust you."

Robert shrugged. "Okay. So I get to know him. Invite me over for dinner tonight. I'll pick something up on my way—maybe Chinese?"

"That's impossible," she blurted out.

"Okay. No Chinese. Italian? Although we just had pizza," Robert said.

He was deliberately misunderstanding her. "I'm sure

you have better things to do than have dinner with a paranoid twenty-nine-year-old and a snarling teenage boy." When Liz had first started dating Sawyer, she'd confided that Robert was a bit of playboy.

"You're not paranoid, and unless he's rabid, I can take a little snarling from a fifteen-year-old."

"I don't know why you'd want to do this," Carmen said, shaking her head.

"Come on. It's my version of community service," he said easily. "You're not going to deny me the opportunity for that, are you?"

Chapter Four

From Carmen's apartment, Robert drove directly back to the police station. When he got there, he saw that Alderman Franconi was in Lieutenant Fischer's office. The door was closed, but the blinds were open just enough that Robert and every other person in the squad room understood that Alderman Franconi wasn't happy.

He made eye contact with Sawyer, who was sipping on a cup of coffee and eating some kind of pastry. He had a newspaper spread out on his desk. The headline said it all. Police Frustrated with Lack of Progress.

Frustrated? Oh, yeah.

As was the alderman, who spent another three minutes in the lieutenant's face before turning and leaving. When he walked through the squad room, he didn't look at or talk to anyone. Once he was out of the room, all heads turned toward the lieutenant's office. The man was standing in the door, not looking any worse for wear. It would take more than a frustrated alderman to rattle him.

"Well," Lieutenant Fischer said, his tone dry. "As you may have gathered, Alderman Franconi wants us to find the killer and string him up at Daley Plaza. Or we'll all be looking for new work."

Nobody reacted to the last line. It was this particular alderman's style to threaten jobs. He did it when the crowd control at the summer festivals didn't go well. He was certainly going to do it now. The alderman was a jerk about most things. He did have a dead nephew, however, so everybody was more inclined to cut him some slack.

Robert didn't have to have family to understand family. It had just been his mom and him, with a progression of husbands and live-ins over the years. His mom had been married five times, no, make that six. He sometimes forgot number four. That one had lasted less than six months. One had continued on for five years but Robert was convinced that was because the man was an over-the-road trucker and gone most of the time. That was actually the one guy he'd liked.

The weird thing was, his mother wasn't a bad person. People generally liked her. She was the life of the party. Had a good sense of humor, knew how to tell a joke. She drank too much, perhaps. But she was a pleasant drunk, not a mean one. She mostly made bad choices. Because she couldn't stand being without a man, couldn't stand being alone. And so whatever loser came along got credit for having testosterone, and was immediately a viable prospect.

Robert had been three when his biological dad had been killed in a car accident. His mother, who had been a beautiful woman with her blond hair and green eyes, had remarried within the year, although Robert didn't even remember that guy.

Now, if he felt inclined to ever look back, which he did not, the only way he could keep the parade straight in his head was to go to the pictures that his mother had stuffed in a shoe box. Every year, on his birthday, she'd taken a picture. And the man of the hour had always been in one of the shots.

None of them had been inclined to adopt him, or maybe his mother had never wanted that. He wasn't sure. From a very early age, before he even knew what the word meant, he'd considered them boarders in his home. There but not important. Certainly not family.

Her latest husband was retired military. He wore black shoes that always had a nice shine and he grew orchids in the small garden behind their house. His name was Norman. She called him Normie.

The man didn't say much when Robert visited. But then again, getting a word in edgewise was a feat when his mother was revved up. As Sawyer would say, she could talk the ears off a chicken.

Robert sat down at his desk and was surprised to see two pink message slips in Tasha's scrawling handwriting. Hardly anybody left messages anymore. They either knew him well enough to call his cell phone or they left a voice mail on his office line.

These were both personal. One from Mandy, the other from Janine. They both had his cell number.

But then again, he hadn't been answering any of their calls for the past couple of weeks. He looked up when a shadow crossed in front of his desk. Tasha, an unlit cigarette hanging from her mouth, was buttoning her coat. Every morning at exactly ten o'clock, their department clerk went outside to smoke. It didn't matter how hot or how cold. "Who's the lucky one tonight?" she asked.

He shrugged.

"When in doubt," Tasha said, "use FIFO. First in, first out. Janine gets the nod. Your phone was ringing when I got here this morning. If you ask me, she's a bit needy."

He folded the slips and put them under his stapler. "I'll give them both a call later."

Tasha frowned at him. She leaned over and laid the back of her hand against his forehead. "Are you sick?"

"I'm fine. Busy." Robert yanked open a file drawer so hard that it jarred the pencil holder on his desk.

Sawyer folded his paper and frowned at him. "Everything okay?" he asked. Then his expression changed. "Damn. Something happened at the coffee shop, didn't it?" He pushed his chair back and started to stand up.

"I handled it," Robert said, motioning for Sawyer to sit back down. "Everybody is okay, but I don't like the dad. Frank Sage is a big guy and I think he's used to intimidating people with his size."

"I've known you for a long time, Robert, and I've never seen you intimidated by anything."

Good thing Sawyer had no idea how nervous he'd been last night, when suddenly it was just him and Carmen sitting in Sawyer's living room. He'd felt as if his tongue had grown until it was too big for his mouth. Then she'd broken the tension and everything had been fine.

Better than fine. It had been one of the nicest nights that he'd spent in a long time. And he hadn't wanted it to end. When it had and he'd offered to follow her back to her apartment, he'd been afraid that she might have been offended.

She'd been on her own for a long time, successfully supporting her brother and herself. He understood feminism. Other than Sawyer, his two best other partners had been women. Both highly skilled and competent as hell.

And Carmen Jimenez was likely every bit as smart as they had been. But she didn't have the same training and she sure as heck wasn't packing a gun. A lone female, traveling at night, was a target.

It had just made sense for him to offer to follow her home. What hadn't made sense was that for the entire drive he'd debated whether he should ask to come in. In the end, he'd decided against it. Maybe it had been the memory of her running into the bathroom to avoid dancing with him. Maybe it had been that the night had been so nice that he didn't want to take the chance of spoiling it with a refusal.

Maybe it was because he hadn't figured out what to do about Carmen. He'd spent months trying to forget how she'd felt in his arms but he hadn't been able to. What the hell did that mean?

So, he'd made sure she got inside safely and he'd gone home. He'd gone to bed thinking about her, had dreamed about her, and when he'd gotten out of bed at the crack of dawn, he'd known that he was going to be waiting in that coffee shop.

Good instincts. That's what his boss had written on his last performance appraisal. Robert liked to think that he listened to his gut. And his gut had been telling him to be there.

Those instincts had been front and center when he'd pushed for the invitation to have dinner tonight with Carmen and Raoul. And he'd been happy when she'd finally said yes, insisting that she would cook.

But for some reason, he didn't feel inclined to share that information with Sawyer. "What's the plan today?" Robert asked.

"More knocking on doors. Somebody saw something."

"Maybe not. The body was found early Wednesday morning. It was below zero on Tuesday night. There probably weren't that many people out and about after midnight, not like they would have been on a summer evening."

"Well, we have to hope somebody was taking their dog out, or maybe they made an emergency run for cigarettes. We need a witness," Sawyer said.

They needed something. Right now, Robert would settle for some old-fashioned luck.

WHEN RAOUL UNLOCKED the apartment door, he could smell the sauce. Something else, too. Something chocolate.

"Raoul," his sister greeted him. She pinched his cheek as he walked past. "How was band practice?"

"Okay," Raoul said, leaning his trombone case up against the counter. "Some girl who plays the flute had a meltdown. We had to stay late to make up the time."

"No problem. I'm running behind, too."

"Something smells good," he said. He started to reach for the brownie pan.

She stuck out her wooden spoon and tapped his hand. "You have to wait. It's for dessert."

"You never make dessert."

She shrugged. "We're having company."

They never had company. Well, almost never. Sometimes Old Lady Curtiss from down the hall ate with them. She smelled like lilacs and cough medicine.

"An acquaintance I met through work," Carmen said.

"Who?"

She turned her back to him and stirred the sauce. "His name is Robert Hanson."

A man? The only man at OCM was Jamison, his sister's boss. "What does he do there?"

"He's a police officer. A detective. You might remember him from Liz and Sawyer's wedding. He was the best man."

"Oh, yeah. He gave a funny speech at the reception."

"Yes, that's him."

"Why is a cop coming for dinner?" He walked around to the other side of the stove so that he could see her face.

"Because I asked him to. He's been helpful with a situation at work and I thought it would be nice if I fixed him dinner." She looked at her watch, then at the clock on the wall. "Shoot. I've got to get dressed. He'll be here any minute." She thrust the spoon in his hand. "Keep stirring."

She left the room as Raoul dropped the spoon in the sauce and watched it sink to the bottom.

ROBERT JUGGLED WINE, bread and a bouquet of fresh flowers as he walked up the apartment stairs. He stood outside the door and tried to remember that he'd probably gone to dinner at some woman's house at least a hundred times before.

But Carmen wasn't just some woman. She was Liz Montgomery's best friend, for one thing. She was totally hot for another. And when she smiled, it seemed as if the world suddenly became a better place.

Damn. He should take up writing greeting cards.

He'd worried that he might be late. His mother had called just as he'd walked into the florist. He'd stepped outside the small shop and stood in the cold so that he could have some privacy. It had been a short conversation. She'd apologized for bothering him, he assured her it was no bother, and then she'd dropped what might have been a zinger if he hadn't been waiting for the call for some time. *Normie is leaving.*

He'd promised to stop over the following night. That had seemed to make her happy. It was a pattern of behavior they'd perfected over the years.

He'd hung up, bought his flowers and here he was. He glanced at his watch. One minute early.

He kicked the bottom of the door with the toe of his shoe, then stepped back so that he could be seen through the peephole. He smiled and held up the loot. The door opened. A young Hispanic boy, dark and fine-boned like his sister, stood there. He was holding a fat orange cat.

"I'm Robert," he said. "You must be Raoul."

The boy didn't say yes or no. He simply stepped aside and motioned him in. "Carmen's changing her clothes."

"No problem. Where should I put this?"

Raoul pointed to the counter. The cat squirmed in his arms and he immediately bent down and placed her gently on the floor.

Robert bent down to scratch her head but she skirted away. Okay. The cat and the kid had the same sort of attitude.

Robert watched the boy walk over to the stove, immediately noting the limp, as though his right leg might be just a bit shorter than his left.

"I hear you play the trombone." Robert leaned against the counter.

"That's right," Raoul said. The kid took tongs and dug a spoon out of the sauce.

"Where do you go to school?"

"Mahoney High."

"Really? That's pretty far from here. How come you don't go to a neighborhood school?"

"Because I won't let him."

Robert whirled around. Carmen stood in the doorway. She wore a white sweater and a black skirt. It wasn't short, but tight enough to be very interesting. Her hair was piled up on top of her head in a haphazard sort of fashion.

He was struck again by how small she was. She couldn't have been more than five-three and a hundred and ten pounds soaking wet. Not his type at all.

Why was his heart pounding as if he was at the end of a 5K?

"Mahoney High School," she said, as she walked over to the stove and sniffed the sauce, "graduates more than eighty percent of the students who start there as freshman. That's almost twice as good as some of the neighborhood schools."

"Did you go there?" Robert asked, handing her the wine.

She shook her head. "No. I did the neighborhood thing."

"Looks like you turned out okay."

She shrugged. "Looks can be deceiving."

He started to make some quip about liking bad girls, but in deference to Raoul, he kept it to himself. "Should I slice the bread?" he asked.

She nodded, handed him a knife and pointed toward a wooden cutting board on the counter. "The flowers are beautiful," she said. "Thank you."

Her tone was almost wary, and he wondered if he'd gone too far. "It's January," he said. "We should grasp on to every sign of spring we can."

She smiled. "You're right. At lunch today, Liz and I sneaked out and bought spring soap. We put some in every bathroom at OCM."

"Spring soap?" he repeated. He put the bread that he'd sliced into the basket that she passed to him.

"Yeah, you know. There are winter soaps, like cranberry-apple or peppermint-spice. Spring soaps are totally different. When you wash your hands, you can almost image that you're somewhere tropical."

"I never gave that much thought before," he said.

She laughed. "Perhaps you could buy some for the police station?"

He shook his head. "I don't think I want to be known as the spring soap guy."

"Perhaps not," she admitted. She drained the pasta and motioned for Raoul to set the table.

"I didn't know you had a cat," he said.

"Lucy is low-energy but high-strung," Carmen explained. "We got her from a shelter. She spends a lot of time hiding under the bed." She set a big bowl of spaghetti on the table. "Let's eat."

"Food's great," he said ten minutes later, meaning every word of it.

"Spaghetti is easy," Carmen said, pulling at the neckline of her sweater.

She was cute when she blushed. Robert smiled at her and then shifted his attention to Raoul. "So band keeps you pretty busy?"

"I guess."

"Your friends play instruments, too?"

"My best friend, Jacob, plays the drums."

Robert took another bite and took his time chewing. "Mahoney's got a good football team. They went to state tournaments last year."

"Yeah," Raoul said. For the first time, Robert heard the bitterness. "If you're an athlete, you've got it made."

"No special treatment for the band?"

That just got him a look. Didn't mean anything, but Robert filed the information away. "What's the gang situation like there?"

Raoul shrugged. "I'm sort of busy with my classes. I wouldn't know."

"I was just curious. I know they mix it up every once in a while in that neighborhood. I suppose drugs are a problem?"

"Not for me."

"Have you ever had anyone try to sell you something?" Carmen asked.

Raoul shook his head. "Trombone players don't get a lot of attention from the drug dealers." He stood up. "I've got a lot of homework." He carried his plate over to the sink and rinsed it.

"How are your classes going?" Carmen said.

"Fine." Raoul grabbed his backpack off the kitchen counter and walked out of the kitchen. Seconds later, a door at the back of the apartment slammed.

Carmen sat at the table and put her head in her hands. Robert scooted his chair closer. He reached a hand out and with one finger, gently stroked the back of her hand.

Carmen lifted her face. "He's lying to me. He's never done that before. Something is wrong. Very wrong." There were tears in her eyes.

"Kids lie," he said. "It doesn't mean he's in trouble. Maybe he's embarrassed about his grades and intends to bring them up."

She shook her head.

"I'll tell you what," he said. "We have cops in all the high schools. I'll talk to the ones who are at Mahoney High School. I'll see if they recognize his name. Okay?"

"Thank you," she said. "For everything."

Her face was close. Close enough that he could see the tears that still clung to her long lashes. Her skin was a lovely mocha and her lips were pink and inviting. He leaned forward. She stilled.

He bent his head and kissed her. She tasted like spaghetti sauce and red wine, sweet with just a hint of sharpness. And when she pulled back quickly, he had to force himself to let her go, to not demand more.

Her dark eyes were big.

"I hadn't planned on that," he said, proving that adult men lied, too. Maybe he hadn't exactly planned it, but for months he'd been thinking about kissing Carmen.

She didn't answer. She just looked as shaken as he felt. A few more strands of her silky hair had fallen down and her lips were trembling.

"Look," he said, "I—"

"I know you were just comforting me," she said.

He started to protest but realized that she was rational-izing the action. In her own way, she was as skittish as her cat. If she thought that he was romantically interested in her, her first instinct might be to run and hide, too. Car-men Jimenez might be twenty-nine, but he suspected she hadn't had the experiences of other twenty-nine-year-old women. She'd been too busy raising her brother.

For the first time, he felt better about what had hap-pened at Liz and Sawyer's wedding. Maybe it hadn't been *him* that Carmen had objected to? Maybe it had just been her lack of experience and her generally shy demeanor that had sent her scurrying into the ladies' room.

This was going to require very careful handling.

If it made her happy to think the kiss had been about comfort, so be it. "Did it work?" he asked.

"I'm fine," she said. "Really, I just needed a minute."

"No problem. I'll call you tomorrow once I've talked to the cops at Raoul's school." He got up, gave her a little wave and opened the door. "Thanks again for dinner. It was great."

When he got to his car, he didn't even turn on the heat. He was plenty hot enough. One kiss and he'd been about to implode.

Very careful handling indeed.

Chapter Five

Friday

As Robert walked past Tasha's desk, she extended a long arm. Her fingernails were bright purple. "I found the name of the cop who is pulling regular duty at Mahoney High School. Horton Davis."

He took the pink message slip from her. "Thanks," Robert said. After leaving Carmen's last night, he'd left a message for Tasha, hoping that she'd work on it first thing in the morning. He pulled his cell phone off his belt.

He got the man's voice mail and he left a brief message, asking for a return call. He hoped that Raoul wasn't involved in something bad at school. He sure as hell didn't want to break that kind of news to Carmen.

Hot, hot Carmen Jimenez. Some women worked hard at being sexy. They wore the right clothes, the right makeup, had the look. He'd dated women like that and had appreciated their efforts and the end result.

But Carmen didn't seem to work at it at all. She just was.

Didn't matter if she was wearing a turtleneck and a skirt that almost reached her knees. It was the way she moved. Her natural grace. The effortless way she tossed her long, dark hair when it got in her way.

She smelled sexy.

She laughed sexy.

Damn. He was in trouble. Had known it last night when he'd gotten to his car and had sat in the cold for five minutes, letting his body temperature return to normal. After one kiss.

He fingered the pink message slips on his desk, the ones Tasha had handed him the day before. Mandy and Janine. Hell, maybe he should give one of them a call. Get things back into perspective.

He didn't pick up his phone.

Instead, he nodded at Sawyer, who was standing across the room, in conversation with Charlene Blaze.

In the morning report, there'd been the usual litany. Two gang shootings. A couple home invasions, one with injuries to the invader. Jewelry store robbery. A bank located in a grocery store had been held up. The feds were taking that one.

Just another day. More files for the desk. Especially now because, like most every detective in the city, he and Sawyer had been told to put their own cases on the back burner if possible and help Wasimole and Blaze on the serial killer case.

Their neighborhood search had turned up nothing yesterday. Nobody had seen anything. It had been cold, frustrating work, all the more so because everybody knew the clock was ticking. Another Wednesday was just around the corner. And with that came the good probability of another dead kid.

It had kept them moving even when they could no longer feel their toes and their faces were chapped from the brisk wind. They'd covered a six-block radius and had talked to countless people.

He saw that Sawyer had finished his conversation with

Blaze. "What's the plan?" Robert asked when his partner approached.

"Friends and family detail," Sawyer said.

Robert had figured as much. As each of the dead boys had been discovered, Blaze and Wasimole had interviewed family and friends at great length, trying to find some thread that might tie the deceased together. But they hadn't come up with anything. Lieutenant Fischer had suggested that another team of detectives do the same, thinking that now that a few weeks had gone by for some of the distressed families, their heads might be a little clearer and they would remember something that would be helpful.

It was possible that there was nothing that connected the boys. That the serial killer was picking random victims. That certainly had been the case before. But given that the age range was so tight, the cops weren't discounting the fact that they'd missed the thread that tied all the victims together and maybe even to the killer.

"I guess we drew the short straw," Robert said.

"It's indoor work. At least mostly," Sawyer said.

Yeah, but it would be brutal, nevertheless. It was never fun talking to people who were torn up about losing their child, their nephew, their best friend. The list went on. They'd answer a few questions and then start down a tangent, recalling a special time or place that had meant something to the young victim.

He and Sawyer would listen and try to sort through the memories to try to find something that made some sense out of what seemed to be a senseless crime.

"Okay, let's get going," Robert said. "Where do you want to start?"

"Victim one. Johnnie Whitmore."

BEFORE ARRIVING AT the Whitmores' home, Robert and Sawyer reviewed the notes they had on Johnnie Whitmore. At age thirteen, he was the youngest of all the victims. Eighth-grader at Thornton Middle School. B student. Had been in Boy Scouts up until last year. Lutheran, but the family weren't regular churchgoers. On the basketball team but mostly warmed the bench. Played the clarinet. Lactose intolerant. One sister, age seven. Two-parent family. Biological mom, Michelle. Stepfather, Tom.

Their lives had been going pretty well until their son had been found by a night security guard near the entrance of a factory on Boughten Avenue.

The Whitmore family lived in a white house with green shutters. Their sidewalks were clear with snow piled two feet high on each side.

Some of that snow had fallen before Johnnie Whitmore had died. Robert wondered if the young man had shoveled the walk; maybe he'd even had a snowball fight with his younger sister.

On the porch, they could hear piano music. Sawyer cocked his head. "We had that song in our wedding," he said. "I don't know the name of it," he added. "Liz would."

Yeah, that kind of stuff was important to women. He'd dated a tax attorney the previous year and she'd spent valuable time over several years planning her wedding and documenting it on some online social networking site. Music. Dress. Everything down to the bacon-wrapped asparagus she was having for appetizers. When she'd started looking at him, sizing him up for a tux, he'd run like hell.

That was one family tradition that didn't need to be carried on.

They knocked. Michelle and Tom were expecting them. Blaze had set up the appointment the night before. Both he and Sawyer showed their badges and settled down on the leather couch in the small living room. The Whitmores sat on the love seat. There was one empty chair, a flat screen on the wall and a big, shiny piano that took up most of the far wall.

"Thank you for seeing us," Robert said. "I know that you've spoken at length to Detectives Blaze and Wasimole but given the circumstances, we wanted to have one more conversation. I know this is difficult for you."

"We want to do everything we can to catch this animal," Michelle said. She held her husband's hand.

For the next three hours, they labored over Johnnie's life, their lives. Minute details. Where was he born? Who was his doctor? Where did he go to preschool? Do you remember any of his teachers? Have you ever lived anywhere else? Did Johnnie spend time with aunts, uncles or grandparents who lived somewhere else? Where did he get his hair cut? What grocery store do you shop in? Where do you get your car fixed?

"I hope this has been helpful," Tom Whitmore said when it appeared they were finally finished.

"Yes. Thank you," Robert said. He stood up and discreetly stretched his back. "Nice piano," he said. "I saw in one of the reports that you teach lessons out of your home, Michelle."

She nodded. "I started doing that shortly after Johnnie was born. I wanted a way to be able to be at home with my kids more. Our daughter is very good for her age. Johnnie never took to it as well but at least when he started playing the clarinet, he already knew how to read music. He said that helped."

"What's that song you were playing when we arrived?" Sawyer asked.

"Beethoven's 'Ode to Joy.' I hire out for weddings. That's how I met Tom. I played at his brother's wedding.

It was great extra money after I was divorced, and there's something about a wedding that just makes me happy." She licked her lips. "I need a little happiness right now," she said.

Of course she did. She'd lost her son to a maniac.

Robert and Sawyer pulled on their coats and left. Once they were back in the car, they sat there for a minute, letting the engine warm up.

"What are you thinking, Robert?" Sawyer asked.

He shrugged. "I'm thinking that I'm going to rip this guy apart when we find him."

Sawyer nodded.

"On a more practical level," Robert continued, "based on what I've seen in the other files, I didn't hear anything that rang a bell. But maybe once we talk to a few more people."

Sawyer pulled away from the curb. "First we get coffee."

TINA JOHANSON, the mother of Ben Johanson, the second boy killed, was too thin, and she chain-smoked. They met with her at her apartment right after lunch and she still had on the waitressing uniform from the overnight shift she pulled at Dill's Diner. There was no husband. Had never been a husband, according to the notes Blaze had taken. Ben was an only child. Fifteen. Freshman in high school. He qualified for free lunches.

Halfway through their questions, she pulled out her scrapbooks, slowly flipping pages, walking them through her son's short life. Robert was surprised to see the album. Most people kept their pictures on their computers and rarely printed them. But she had dutifully printed and labeled each one.

First day of kindergarten. Broken leg in second grade.

Science project in fourth grade. Youth camp when he was ten. Playing the tuba in the eighth-grade band concert.

The instrument had been almost as big as the kid.

It made Robert think about the trombone case that had been propped up against Carmen's counter.

Tina had already flipped the page before Robert held up a finger. "How long had your son played the tuba?" he asked.

"Started in sixth grade," she said, wiping away a tear. "I wanted him to play the violin but no, he insisted upon the tuba." She gave them a shaky smile. "And he was really good at it. I picked up a couple extra shifts every week so that he could take lessons from the Gottart Studio."

Robert added a line to the pages of notes he and Sawyer had already collected. *Band. Tuba. Gottart Studio.*

"I'm not familiar with the Gottart Studio," Robert said.

"On Peach Street. It's one of the best," she said proudly, as if that still brought her some satisfaction that she'd been able to provide that small luxury for her son.

They talked for another hour before finishing up. Then it was back to the cold car. Sawyer rubbed his hands together. "Her son was her life," he said.

Robert had been thinking the same thing. Now Tina Johanson was truly alone. "It's Friday," he said, stating the obvious. "If something didn't break soon, they'd have another mother grieving over her son.

Robert's cell phone rang. He looked at the number and realized it was one he'd called earlier. "I need to get this," he said.

"No problem. There's a deli on the corner calling my name," Sawyer said. He got out fast, but still cold air came in and Robert turned the heater dial to the max.

"This is Robert Hanson."

"It's Horton Davis. I had a message from you, Detective."

"Yeah. Thanks for calling back. I'm working with a family who has a teenage son at Mahoney High School," Robert explained. "I wanted to see if you recognized his name. Raoul Jimenez. Dark hair, slight build. He's a freshman. No sports. Plays in the school band."

"Not ringing a bell," the man said. "But then again, there are fifteen hundred kids at this school. I can do some checking."

"Thanks. I don't want the kid to know that I'm asking about him," Robert said.

"No problem. I'll call you in a couple days," Horton Davis said.

Robert thanked the man and hung up. Then he took a deep breath and dialed Carmen.

She answered on the third ring. "This is Carmen."

"Hi. It's Robert. Robert Hanson. Are you busy?"

She seemed to hesitate. "I have a few minutes," she said finally.

"I…uh…wanted to thank you for dinner last night," he said. "It was really good."

"You're welcome," she said. She paused. "Was there something else, Detective?"

Yeah. I'd like to kiss you again. "Uh…I talked to the officer who has primary duty at Mahoney High School. He didn't recognize Raoul's name."

"Oh."

"That's a good thing," Robert said. "They know the kids who are in trouble or who *are* trouble."

"Thanks for checking," she said. She sounded disappointed, and Robert knew it wasn't because she wanted Raoul to be a known troublemaker. She just wanted some explanation for why he was pulling away.

"I wanted a chance to pay back your hospitality. How about I treat for dinner tonight?"

"Dinner?" she repeated.

Her tone suggested that she was figuring out a way to say no.

"Now, I know you're familiar with the concept. I can't promise, however, that the food will be as good as last night." He kept his tone light, which was a damn miracle of the human body, because he was literally holding his breath. "We did talk about the need to spend time together. Of course, I'd want Raoul to come, too."

There was absolute silence on the other end. He covered his phone and gulped in some air.

It was his nature to push, to force the solution he wanted, but he backed off to give her some space. He counted to ten.

"I guess dinner would be okay," she said finally.

Robert smiled. If he always needed an enthusiastic welcome, he wouldn't have become a cop. "Good. I'll see you about seven." That would give him time to swing by his mom's house first. He hung up before Carmen could think of a reason to change her mind.

He was still staring at his phone when Sawyer opened the door. He reached out and accepted the large coffee and the plastic container. Blueberry pie. And it felt warm.

"Thanks," he said.

"News?" Sawyer said, looking at Robert's phone.

"No. It was...personal."

"I should have figured a woman. It's so cold that there are parts on my body that I'm not even sure Liz can heat and yet, you're sitting here, grinning like a fool. Mandy or Janine?" he asked, proving that Tasha didn't keep secrets well.

"Neither," Robert said, brushing off the question. "The pie looks good." He opened his container and dug in.

Sawyer stared at him, then very deliberately reached over and flipped the lid shut on the plastic container. "Damn. Please, please, tell me that you are not smiling over Carmen Jimenez. I know we all had some good pizza together and that you were helpful at the coffee shop and that she made you dinner as a thank-you. But Robert, it does not have to go beyond that. Really, it doesn't."

It was the longest spiel that he'd heard come out of Sawyer Montgomery's mouth.

And he would not lie to his friend. Was not above evading the truth, but would not lie.

"I'm taking Carmen and Raoul out to dinner tonight."

Sawyer pointed a finger in his face. "I swear to God, Robert Hanson. If you screw up and hurt Carmen and that makes Liz even just a little bit sad, you and I are taking it outside."

Robert smiled. "It's too cold outside for a Southern boy like you to want to fight. You'll get snow down your pants."

"I mean it, Robert." Sawyer leaned close. "Carmen is a very nice person."

And while his own smile didn't fade, it hurt just a little. "And I'm Jack the Ripper?"

"Of course not," Sawyer said. "Don't be ridiculous. You're my daughter's godfather. I'd trust you with her life. But I don't know if you and Carmen want the same thing."

"I think we both want to have dinner," Robert said. "It's no big deal. She's worried about Raoul."

Sawyer nodded. "Liz told me something about that. I've met him. Quiet but polite. He likes video games and one time I saw him eat about half a chocolate cake. That was after he'd wolfed down four tacos. I think he's just a normal adolescent boy."

"I agree. But Carmen is concerned. I said I'd make a few inquiries with the cop at Mahoney High. And I said that I'd try to get to know Raoul a little better. You're worrying about nothing, Sawyer. Now get your ugly hands off my pie."

Chapter Six

Raoul walked down the empty hallway, his trombone case bumping his leg with each step. Man, he'd be glad when the winter concert was over. His band teacher might just blow a gasket before that happened. Tonight, he'd actually taken a set of drums away from the kid who stood next to Jacob.

He was starving. Lunch had been seven hours earlier. Most of the time, he got some food out of the vending machines before practice started. Today, he'd been pulling his money out of his pocket when trouble had stepped around the corner.

He'd looked around but it was only him and JJ and Beau. He wasn't sure what JJ's real name was because everybody just called him JJ. He and Beau were both juniors and Raoul hated them. They'd been pretty much making his life difficult since football had ended in November and they'd suddenly had too much free time.

Beau had held out his hand and Raoul had dropped the dollar bills into it. It wasn't the first time they'd ripped him off. He'd thought about telling somebody but they'd already told him that they'd beat the crap out of him if he did that.

He believed them. They could probably bench-press his weight without breaking a sweat. He hadn't even told Jacob and he usually told Jacob everything.

It was just too embarrassing.

He'd gone to band practice hungry and been so angry that he hadn't even been able to stay with the music. He was looking forward to the brownies left from dinner the night before.

Raoul turned the corner and almost bumped into JJ and Beau. He veered to the left, hoping to get around them. Twice in one day was too much.

Beau stepped directly in front of him. "Where you going, band boy?"

Raoul didn't answer. He took a side step. "I don't have any more money," he said, hoping he sounded more confident than he felt.

"That's not band boy, that's Limpy." JJ lounged against the locker and laughed at his own joke. "That's your name, right?"

Raoul wanted to pound their stupid faces into the wall. But he knew if he tried, they'd kill him first. So he didn't say a word. He just stood there and took it.

"I saw you get dropped off for school this morning," Beau said. "Somebody told me that's your sister. She is hot, sizzling hot." He touched the gray lockers with his index finger and made a sizzling noise. "I'd like to do her."

"Shut up," Raoul said.

"Maybe we could both do her," JJ said, "at the same time."

The two of them laughed like they were the funniest things on earth. "Stay away from my sister," Raoul said.

"Oooh," Beau said, pretending to be frightened. "Like we care what you tell us to do." He grabbed Raoul's trombone case and threw it, sending it end-over-end down the hallway. It banged against the metal lockers. "Go get it."

He took a step, trying to walk around Beau. JJ stepped away from the lockers, reached out, put his hand on Raoul's shoulder and pushed down.

"Crawl."

Beau laughed. "Yeah, on your hands and knees. Like a dog. A scrawny pup from the pound."

Raoul thought about running in the other direction. But what would he tell Carmen about his trombone? She wasn't going to believe that he'd forgotten it somewhere. And if she knew these kids were hassling him, she'd be in the office, demanding that something be done.

Then it would get worse.

Raoul dropped to his knees. Then like a stupid baby, he started crawling. His backpack felt heavy and awkward and the floor hurt his knees. He could hear Beau and JJ laughing. He didn't look back until he reached his case. When he did, they were gone.

He couldn't breathe. He freakin' couldn't breathe.

He tried to stand up but he couldn't. With his back against the lockers, he slid down to the floor.

And then he started to cry.

And he hated more than he'd ever hated before.

He finally picked himself up off the floor and left the school. He got on his regular bus, rode for thirty minutes, and got off at his stop, which was three blocks from his house. He hadn't walked more than fifteen feet when the man claiming to be Hector's friend approached from behind and started walking next to him. "You're late today," the man said. It was so cold that his words came out in a puff of steam.

Raoul didn't answer. He didn't feel like talking to anybody. He walked faster.

The man kept pace. "I've got something of Hector's that he wanted you to have," he said.

That got Raoul's attention. There was nothing of Hector's at their apartment, except for a couple of pictures that had Hector in them. "What?"

"I don't want to ruin the surprise," the man said. "Give me your number and I'll text you later and let you know where you can meet me."

Raoul considered the suggestion. It wouldn't hurt to give the man his number. If he decided he didn't want to go, he'd just ignore it. He rattled it off and the man entered it into his own cell phone.

"I still don't know your name," Raoul said.

"Apollo," he said. "Just call me Apollo. I'll be in touch."

AT TEN MINUTES after six, Robert pulled up in front of his mom's pale yellow house. It was a nice two-bedroom, two-bath Cape Cod in a neighborhood that had been predominantly Polish at one time.

She wasn't Polish. But she'd fallen in love with the house four years ago after her fifth marriage ended and she'd needed a place to live. Robert had bought it for her.

At least this time she wouldn't have to move. Norman had moved in with her.

His mom greeted him with a kiss on his cheek and pulled him into the house. It smelled like vanilla and he could see candles burning on the mantel of the fake fireplace.

"How's it going?" he asked.

"Normie has a girlfriend, someone he met at last year's Flower and Garden Show. They're moving to Florida. I'm being dumped for a longer growing season," she added.

He smiled, knowing that's what she expected. Wanted. Humor, even at her own expense, had always been his mother's fallback position.

"You going to be okay?" he asked.

"Oh, sure," she said, wiping a tear from her cheek. At sixty-seven, her face was showing the signs of age.

"What are your plans for tonight?" he asked. He hated

the idea of canceling on Carmen, but he couldn't leave his mom crying at her kitchen table.

"Bingo at the church," she said. "I'm going with my friend Margie."

"You don't play bingo," he said.

She sucked in a big breath. "I do now. Margie says there's a group of retired gentlemen there, most of them widowers."

"Good Lord, Mom. Has Norman even moved his things out?"

"This afternoon. I helped him pack his truck." With the palm of her hands, she smoothed down her shirt. "At my age, you can't wait around forever. And they only play bingo twice a month."

Rebound bingo. At least he didn't have to give her the lecture about practicing safe bingo.

He stood up, pushed his chair in and kissed his mother's cheek. Ten years ago, he'd have tried to convince her that it wasn't wise to jump from the frying pan into the fire. That was two husbands ago. "Call me if you need anything," he said.

It only took him fifteen minutes to get to Carmen's apartment. At twenty minutes before seven, he parked down the block. He left his car running, knowing that the temperature inside would drop in minutes if he killed the engine.

He closed his eyes and tried to block out the last half hour. It didn't work.

He had a bad gene pool. Maybe Sawyer was right to be worried about Carmen. What was it that he'd said? *Not sure Carmen and you want the same thing.*

What did he want from Carmen?

He wanted to kiss her again. That was a given. He'd managed to keep from blurting that out, thankfully.

He wanted more, though. To hear her laugh. And watch her move around her kitchen in a tight black skirt with a towel tossed over one shoulder. To see her eyes, content with pride, when she watched her brother shovel in his spaghetti.

None of that spelled danger for Ms. Jimenez. Sawyer was worried about nothing.

Robert checked his watch and decided to wait another five minutes. He didn't want to appear overanxious, yet he wanted to be prompt.

That was respectful.

Sawyer would be proud.

At seven minutes before seven, Robert pulled into a parking space in front of Carmen's building. He opened the main door of the three-story building and walked up the stairs to the second floor. Then, as he had the night before, he knocked on the door.

Carmen opened it. She wore a high-necked, long-sleeved cream-colored sweater and matching slacks. She'd left her dark hair down and it fell over her shoulders to midback.

She looked fabulous.

And she smelled even better. Something spicy that hinted that there was more to Carmen than met the eye.

Or was that wishful thinking on his part?

"Hi," he said. "You look nice."

She blushed. "I wasn't sure where we'd be going."

"Maxine's."

She frowned. "That's expensive, isn't it?"

He waved a hand. "They're running a winter special," he said. "Where's Raoul?"

"In his room. I'll get him. Excuse me," she said.

Robert stood near the door. He could see the cat. She was scrunched under the couch, watching him. "I'm not here to steal the silverware, Lucy," he said, trying to sound friendly.

No response from the cat.

He could hear the murmur of voices from the back room. They went on. And on. And he was just about to barge down the hall and fix whatever needed to be fixed when Carmen appeared.

"Raoul is sick," she said. "He thinks it's something he ate for lunch."

Okay. Plan B. "No problem. We can order in," Robert said.

The words were no more out of his mouth when Raoul appeared behind his sister. He was dressed in jeans and a sweatshirt and his hair was sticking straight up on his head.

"I told you, sis. I want you to go. I'm not three. I can take care of myself. You deserve to have a nice dinner."

Robert could see the indecision in Carmen's eyes. He kept his mouth shut. He didn't want to take the chance of reminding her that the dinner invitation had been about the three of them bonding.

"You're sure?" Carmen asked.

Raoul rolled his eyes.

"I'll bring you back some chicken noodle soup," she said.

"Fine." He turned and went back into his room.

Robert worked hard to keep the smile off his face. "He probably just wants to get some sleep."

Carmen grabbed her bright blue cape from the closet. She stuffed her hands into dark gloves. "I know that I need to treat him more like an adult. It makes him crazy when I baby him. It's just that I've been taking care of him forever," she said, her voice quiet.

"You have been. And you've done a great job. If you

don't mind me asking, what's the story behind Raoul's leg?"

"He's had it from birth. It's actually a problem with his hip but it looks as if his legs are not the same."

"Doesn't look as if it slows him down much." Robert wrapped an arm loosely around her shoulder. "Give him some space. It'll be fine."

They had barely pulled away from Carmen's apartment building when she dug her feet in. "If we go to Maxine's, I want to pay my half."

Robert counted to ten. "That's not necessary."

"Yes, I insist. I wouldn't be comfortable any other way."

Well, hell. She'd been right earlier. Maxine's could get a little pricey. There was no way that he was imposing that kind of expense on her budget. He had some idea of what social-worker types made and he doubted there was much left at the end of the month.

"Maybe we could go somewhere else?" he suggested.

"Gordon's is close. I love their soup."

He made a quick right. Gordon's had been a neighborhood favorite for years. It had a tile floor, worn booths, surly waitresses and great comfort food. Sometimes he and Sawyer had lunch there.

It wouldn't break anybody's budget. "Whatever floats your boat," Robert said easily. He found a seat as far away from the door as possible, knowing that every time the door opened, cold air would blow in. They read the plastic-covered menu, and then he ordered the meat loaf special, and Carmen got a turkey club with broccoli soup.

There was a young couple in the corner with a squealing baby. An old couple was in the next booth, both reading sections of the newspaper. A young black man, wearing a white apron that came to his knees, was unloading clean glasses and cups onto the shelves.

He'd never brought a woman to Gordon's before. Never even considered it. The women he dated were generally successful in their own careers, had discretionary spending and expected him to have the same.

Both Mandy and Janine would have been severely disappointed in Gordon's.

"What's so funny?" she asked.

He hadn't realized that he was smiling. "Nothing," he said. "Just thinking that Sawyer will be jealous. He loves the hot beef sandwiches here."

She glanced around. "I imagine it's not your usual place for dinner."

There was an underlying message in her simple words. It went sort of like this. *I realize you had something different in mind, but this place is really more me, which is just one more sign of how different we are.*

She wasn't the only one who had studied human behavior in college.

"I think I'm ready for the unusual," he said.

Her dark eyes widened. But at that moment, the waitress returned, slapped their food down and refilled their water glasses. Carmen picked up her turkey sandwich and chewed. She looked very thoughtful.

Robert dug into his meat loaf. It was delicious. And the potatoes were equally good. Neither of them spoke for several minutes. Finally, she pushed her plate away. She'd eaten her soup and most of her sandwich.

"I should be getting back," she said.

He nodded and motioned for the waitress. He ordered a large chicken noodle soup to go. Carmen unzipped her purse and started pulling out money.

"Please," he said. "It's on me. Consider it payback for the spaghetti, although I certainly got the better end of the deal."

She hesitated and then nodded. She leaned back against the booth and yawned.

"Tough day?" he asked.

"Sort of. Uncooperative pregnant teens can be a bit trying on the nerves."

"How are things with Alexa Sage?"

"Okay. I got a message from her today. In the presence of her father, she told her mom the news. I guess there were lots of tears but it sounds as if everybody held it together."

He felt a chill run down the back of his neck. Which was crazy because the air from outside was blowing in his face. "Don't let your guard down around that man. There's something about him that I really didn't like."

"I won't. But I'm hopeful that he'll get past his disappointment in his daughter and give her the support she needs."

"I don't think his daughter was too confident of that and she knows him best, right?"

"Yes, but teenagers don't have the reasoning skills to understand that adults, once they've had time to assimilate new information, have the capability to deal with all kinds of things. When a kid messes up, she can't imagine that her parent will ever be able to understand why she did it or how she could have made such a mistake."

Her eyes were serious and her voice soft. There was pain in both and he wasn't sure what had put it there. "But I bet you're good at painting the picture that things can get better," he said, wanting to make her smile again.

It must have worked. She lifted her water glass. "Here's to sharp crayons," she said. And she took a big drink. "How was your day?"

"Cold," he said. "Irritating because we're not making more progress on the case. Plus," he added, "I had to go see my mother. Her husband is leaving her." He wasn't sure why he told her. He never talked about his mother.

"Oh, no," Carmen said.

He waved a hand. "It's okay. I mean, she's sad and all. But she's been through this before. Sometimes she's even the leaver, not the leavee."

She was looking at him as if he had two heads.

"I know that sounds bad. But she's been married six times and she's had a couple live-ins, as well."

"I see," said Carmen.

There was no way. Nobody could understand it.

"She likes being with someone, being part of a pair," Carmen said.

That was a nice way to put it. "Yeah, well, she's the left shoe and she enjoys the search for the right shoe very much, but then she quickly tires of wearing the same pair so she has to go shoe shopping again."

She smiled. "I bet she's fun."

He nodded. "She is and she's my mom so I can't stay irritated with her for very long."

"Of course not," Carmen said.

Five minutes later, they got in the cold car and he drove to her apartment. "It will probably be hard to find parking," she said. "You can just drop me off."

He smiled and kept driving. She wasn't getting rid of him that easily.

As they neared the building, she put her hand on the door handle. It looked as if she was ready to make a break for it.

"I'll walk you in," he said. "I want to make sure Raoul's doing okay," he added.

He found a parking spot, pulled in and was around the car before she could get her seat belt undone. They walked up the stairs to her apartment and she unlocked her door.

When she opened the door to the apartment, he saw that almost every light in the apartment was on. They hadn't been when they'd left. That was a good sign that Raoul had been up and about, so maybe the kid was feeling better.

"I'm going to check him," she said.

He watched her walk down the short hallway, appreciating the view. Her slacks weren't tight but just snug enough to hint at a nicely rounded bottom.

He heard the door open and then slam shut. When Carmen returned to the living room, her face was pale and her eyes were big. Robert's protective instincts shot up a notch.

"What's wrong?" he asked, already moving closer.

Chapter Seven

"He's gone," she said. "He's not in his bedroom."

"Check the other rooms," Robert instructed.

It didn't take her long. There was only her room and the bathroom. She came back into the hallway and shook her head.

"Does he have a cell phone?" Robert asked.

Carmen nodded.

"Okay, check your cell phone for messages and then try his phone," he said. "I'm going to take a look at his room."

He supposed it was a typical teenage boy's room. It looked a little bit like he remembered his own room. Posters on the walls. Dirty clothes in the corner. A single bed with covers in disarray.

There were no signs of a struggle.

No hastily prepared note propped up against the pencil container. No clue as to why a sick fifteen-year-old boy would suddenly be gone.

He looked up. Carmen stood in the bedroom doorway, cell phone in hand. "Nothing. And he's not answering. It went straight to voice mail."

"Does he ever do this? Go out without letting you know?"

Carmen shook her head. "No. I mean, he goes out on his own, of course. But not usually at night. Not without telling me. And he was sick. Oh, my God, maybe he had to call an ambulance." She stopped. "No, that's ridiculous. He would call me before he'd call an ambulance."

Robert could see when the full realization of the situation hit Carmen. Raoul hadn't called her. So either something had prevented that or he simply hadn't tried.

There was no sign of struggle, and the door had been locked.

"It's possible he was lying," she said. "Maybe he wanted to get me out of the apartment and figured he'd have a couple hours of free time. He thought we were going to Maxine's."

He appreciated that she wasn't going to refuse to consider alternate realities. Her work with teenagers had taught her that teenagers lied.

"He had on jeans and a gray sweatshirt earlier. Do you see them anywhere?" Robert asked, sweeping his hand around the room.

Carmen shook her head. "His coat is a red jacket with a hood. I don't see it, either."

"Okay. We'll assume that's what he has on. I'll call it in. Get our guys watching for him."

She reached out a hand, stopping him. "Robert," she said, her voice subdued. "I don't know what he's up to. I want to hope it's not something bad. And I know that I don't have any right to ask you to look the other way. But—" her voice cracked "—I don't want him to be arrested. When that happened to Hector, things got so much worse. It was the beginning of the end."

He hoped like hell Raoul hadn't done something stupid that was going to make this woman sad. He was going to really have to kick his butt. He put two fingers under her chin and tilted her head up. "Here's what I think," he said. "Raoul is a good kid. I don't think he's involved in anything that's going to get him arrested. Stop worrying. We're going to find him. Now, why don't you start with his friends?"

He watched while she scrolled through the numbers in her phone. He believed everything he had said to Carmen. The kid was probably fine. But just in case, he called in Raoul's description to dispatch. He felt immediately better after doing that. It wouldn't hurt for a whole lot of eyes to be looking. He sent a text to Sawyer, letting him know. Within seconds, Carmen's phone rang.

She grabbed for it. "Liz," she said, looking at him.

Robert nodded. "I figured it wouldn't take long."

Carmen answered and the women talked for a few minutes. While he couldn't hear Liz's side of the conversation, she evidently was volunteering to come over because Carmen repeatedly assured her it wasn't necessary, that she should stay home with her baby. Carmen ended the conversation by assuring her friend that she'd call her if anything changed.

A half hour later, nothing had changed and they didn't know anything more. Robert and Carmen had both tried his cell phone multiple times.

Carmen had talked to some kid named Jacob twice. She'd explained that he was Raoul's best friend and that they often carpooled in the morning. After school, they each took different buses because Jacob's house was a couple miles from their apartment. After the first call to Jacob and learning that the boy hadn't talked to or seen Raoul since band practice had ended, she'd waited while he also tried to reach Raoul. She'd called a second time only to learn that Raoul wasn't answering any of Jacob's texts or calls, either.

Carmen sat at the table, her shoulders bowed, her head in her hands. Robert pulled his chair close and put an arm loosely around her shoulders. She seemed even smaller than usual, as if she were deflated.

He was so going to kick the kid's butt if he was out fooling around and making his sister worry needlessly. If it was something more serious, he hoped he had the wherewithal to help Carmen deal with it.

He wanted to be out on the street, looking for Raoul. But he knew that he couldn't leave Carmen.

So he simply sat with his arm around her. Maybe they'd sat for ten minutes when they heard footsteps on the stairs. Carmen's head sprang up.

"Relax," Robert whispered.

They heard the key in the lock and the door opened. Raoul, wearing his red jacket, his gray sweatshirt and his blue jeans, walked in. He was carrying a bag from Walgreens.

"Hi," he said. He looked surprised to see them.

Carmen ran to him and hugged him tight. He tried to duck her embrace. "What's going on?" he asked.

"Where have you been?" she asked. She held his face in her hands. "I've been worried sick. You didn't answer your phone. I called you at least ten times."

Raoul pulled his cell phone out of his pocket. "It's dead," he said. "I was going to charge it when I got home."

"You said you were sick. Too sick to go to dinner with us."

"I started to feel better. I remembered I needed some things for school. I'm sorry, Carmen. I didn't mean to worry you."

"Don't ever do that again," she said, her tone gentle. "I mean it. For goodness' sake, we had the police looking for you."

That got Robert a swift and unfriendly look. Which Robert might have been inclined to ignore if his gut wasn't telling him that something was very wrong. The kid had looked like death warmed over an hour ago. Yet minutes ago, his steps on the stairs had been quick and light. His color was good.

Maybe it was possible that within minutes of their departure, he'd suddenly felt much better and had remembered the school supplies. But it was Friday night. There was no school tomorrow. He'd have had the whole weekend to buy school supplies.

Maybe he needed them for a project he had to complete this weekend?

Or, maybe, as Carmen suggested, he'd heard Maxine's, figured that his sister would be out of his hair for at least two hours and took off, fully expecting to be back before she was any the wiser.

He'd pulled similar stunts when he was Raoul's age.

And rarely gotten caught. His mom had been busy wooing the next potential husband, and that had left little time to watch over a busy and sometimes rebellious teen.

"You need to get some sleep," Carmen said. "I'll see you in the morning."

Raoul mumbled good-night as he walked past Robert. Very quietly, Robert took a deep breath. He waited until he heard Raoul's bedroom door shut. "He smells like grilled onions," he said.

Carmen frowned. "I guess."

Robert shrugged. "I don't want to make too big a deal out of it but the kid didn't want anything besides chicken noodle soup to eat an hour ago. Now he smells like he swam in a vat of cooked onions, like maybe he got one of those steak sandwiches from the guy on the corner two blocks down."

Carmen chewed on her pretty lip. "I'm just grateful that he's okay," she said finally. "Thank you," she added. "For being here. For being a voice of reason. For knowing what to do. I swear my brain just stopped working."

"I still want to do dinner with the two of you. Maybe tomorrow."

She shook her head sharply. "Tomorrow. No. That's impossible."

Robert had learned years ago that sometimes retreat was an essential component of an effective offense. "No problem. I'll give you a call," he said. He gathered up his coat and gloves. "Take care," he said.

And he left without touching her.

RAOUL HEARD THE apartment door shut and pulled his sack out from underneath his bed. His hands were still shaking. He'd seen Carmen and that cop sitting at the table and thought for sure that they would want to see what was in the bag.

He opened the thin plastic and pulled out the heavy black gun. He pointed it at the Spider-Man poster on the wall. *Bang. Bang. Take that, superhero.*

Apollo had sent him a text about ten minutes before his sister knocked on the door to tell him that Robert was there. He'd already agreed to go to dinner and he had to do some fast talking to get out of it so that he could meet Apollo. But he'd been really anxious to see what Apollo had of Hector's.

He'd sure as heck never expected that it would be a gun. Raoul ran his hand across the barrel and could almost feel his brother in the room with him.

Carmen didn't like guns. Didn't even like it when Raoul played video games where there were guns.

She never had to know.

But just having it made him feel better. Made him feel

closer to Hector. Made him feel like he wouldn't always be the kid who got pushed around.

He put the gun and the box of bullets that Apollo had given him in his backpack, underneath his history book.

Chapter Eight

Saturday

At ten the next morning, Robert was impatiently standing in line at a coffee shop. Sawycr usually took coffee duty, but they'd split up this morning. Sawyer was running down the Gottart Studio and Robert was following up on red handkerchiefs. They had identified three more retailers that carried the product. That was in addition to the four large retailers that they'd already spoken to.

Unfortunately, these three stores were small shops and they didn't have information systems that tracked all their sales data and could spit out reports at the push of a button. The big stores had been able to tell them the day and time the product had been sold. Had even been able to tell them if the merchandise had been purchased with a credit card or cash. Unfortunately, all the red handkerchiefs purchased in the last six months had been bought with cash.

The three places this morning hadn't even been able to tell him that. And they had no recall of any specific customer who had purchased one or more of the handkerchiefs, which generally came in packages of three.

It made Robert sick to think of how many packages their guy might have bought.

He shuffled forward and gave his coffee order to the

sixteen-year-old girl at the counter. She'd just given him his
change when his cell phone rang. "Hanson," he answered.

"Horton Davis here," the caller said. "I had a chance to
check out Raoul Jimenez late yesterday afternoon and figured you might be anxious to hear. He's a freshman. Plays
in the band, just like you said. Quiet kid. Small for his age.
No known gang affiliations. That's about all I can tell you."

"That's enough," Robert said. "I appreciate it."

"No problem. Wish this school had fifteen hundred just
like him." The man hung up.

Robert waited about fifteen seconds before dialing Carmen's cell phone. There was no answer. He scanned the
numbers in his phone until he found Options for Caring
Mothers. He remembered adding it last summer when
Sawyer had been fixated on Mary Thorton and her pretty
counselor, Liz Mayfield.

He figured it was a good idea to call the office. Carmen seemed the conscientious type who might work a few
hours on a Saturday morning even if she didn't have to.

The phone was answered on the third ring.

"Carmen Jimenez, please," he said.

"I'm sorry, but Carmen isn't in today. Can I take a message?"

Not in. Holy hell. She wasn't doing something stupid
like meeting Frank Sage and his daughter again, was she?
"Is she out of the office on business?" he asked.

The receptionist didn't answer. "May I take a message,
sir?" she asked again.

"Can I talk to Liz Montgomery?" he said.

"Just a moment, please," she said.

Liz picked up within seconds. "This is Liz Montgomery."

"Hey, Liz, it's Robert." He heard the quick inhale of
breath and knew that she'd immediately jumped to the

worst possible conclusion. "Sawyer is fine. This call is not about him," he said quickly.

There was a shaky laugh. "Sorry," she said. "What can I do for you, Robert?"

"I tried Carmen and she's not in. Do you know where she is?"

Liz sighed. "Robert, you are my husband's best friend and I think the world of you. I know you were at Carmen's last night and I'm really grateful that she wasn't alone, waiting for Raoul to come home. But Carmen is like a sister to me. I just have to ask. What's going on here?"

He adored Liz but he'd been a cop way too long to put all his cards on the table. "Carmen asked me to check with the officer at Mahoney High School to see if he knew anything about Raoul. I heard from him this morning and wanted to pass on the message. She didn't answer her cell phone."

"You just want to pass on a message? That's it?"

"Yes, ma'am."

Liz sighed, loudly. "I swear, what is it about cops? Haven't you heard that transparency is the new thing? And don't you 'Yes, ma'am' me. That's what Sawyer does just before he convinces me to get up, put my feet on the cold floor and fetch him coffee in the mornings. But if you must know, I did expect Carmen for a couple hours this morning but she called in sick. I'm sure she's at home sleeping and didn't hear her phone."

"Thanks, Liz. Appreciate it."

He tried Carmen's cell one more time, and again there was no answer. He grabbed his coffee from the counter where it had been sitting for a couple minutes and was out of the building in less than thirty seconds.

Ten minutes later, Robert knocked on Carmen's door and stepped back so that he could be seen through the peephole. He heard a noise on the other side. He waited but no one opened the door.

He knocked again. "Hey, Carmen, it's Robert. I called your work and they said you were at home."

No answer, but he heard a quiet sniff and he got nervous. "Carmen. Either open the door or I'm going to break it down. Your choice."

No answer.

"Okay. Stand back because I'm going to shoot your door lock off."

Because he was watching the peephole, he saw the quick flash of dark, proof that she'd looked out. She must believe him. Robert rubbed the bridge of his nose, where a full-blown, knock-you-on-your-butt headache was started to brew.

She opened the door a crack. "I'm busy," she said.

He could see the middle six inches of her face and body. "What's wrong?" he asked.

"Nothing's wrong."

"I don't think that's true," he said in a very conversational tone. "I can only see a little bit of you but your nose is red and your voice sounds like you've either been on an all-night smoking binge or you've been crying. I'm guessing crying. Did something else happen with Raoul?"

He heard her sigh. "I don't want to talk about it."

"I talked to the cop at Mahoney High School," he said.

There was no response. "What did he say?" she asked finally.

"Open the door and I'll tell you." He'd learned to play dirty in preschool.

Slowly, the door opened. She had on old jeans, a sweatshirt and absolutely no makeup. Her eyes and nose were both red and she had a box of tissues in one hand.

"What did he say?" she asked again.

"Just tell me one thing," he said. "Are either you or Raoul hurt, sick or in danger?"

She shook her head. He smiled at her and wrapped an arm around her shoulder. He pulled her toward the couch. "Good. Then whatever else is wrong, we'll fix it."

She tried to pull out of his embrace. He let her go but when he sat down, he grabbed her hand and pulled her down next to him. When she immediately scooted several inches farther away, he smiled at her again. Smart woman. Having their thighs touch was probably not a good idea. Especially if they intended to have any conversation.

"Want to tell me about it?" he asked.

She shook her head.

Okay. That stung. He had this overwhelming urge to comfort her, to make it all better. "I'm a really good listener," he said. "They teach you how in cop school."

That got him his first smile. As absurd as it sounded, he thought the room lit up a bit. That even the plants in the window glowed a little greener.

"I can't," she said. "My issue. My problem. What did your contact say? Did he find out anything about Raoul?"

Robert looked down the hallway. "Is he sleeping still?"

Carmen shook her head. "Music lessons and then his friend Jacob is having a birthday party. He won't be home until late afternoon."

"Okay. Well, the cop at the school figured out who he was and basically doesn't think you've got anything to worry about. He's not a troublemaker and he's not running with any gang. I'm guessing his problem is that he's fifteen. Nothing worse than that."

"I hope you're right," she said, not sounding convinced. "But thank you for checking. I really do appreciate it."

"Okay. Show me," he said.

Her eyes widened.

He stood up. "I need somebody to share my popcorn with at the movies. You've got your choice between a Gerard Butler action movie, a Keanu Reeves action movie, or a Matt Damon—"

"Let me guess," she interrupted. "Action movie."

"How did you know?"

She laughed. "Just lucky."

He felt the first easing of the pressure on his heart. He didn't want this woman to cry. Ever again.

"But I'm sorry," she said. "I just can't."

"Philosophically opposed to cinematic entertainment?"

She shook her head. "No. That's a ridiculous question. But my reasons don't really matter. You can't go anyway. I've read the paper. Every cop is working overtime on this case."

"True. I'm working all day tomorrow. But I do get a couple hours of R & R today. You like ice cream, right?"

She frowned at him, not following his abrupt change of topic. "Of course, but what does that have to do with it?"

"Near the movie theater is the best ice cream shop in all of Chicago."

"It's freezing outside."

Robert smiled. "The lines will be shorter."

Carmen took a deep breath and looked around her apartment. Finally, her gaze settled on him. "I need some time to shower."

"No problem. I'll just sit here and wait. I've got my phone, which means I've got my emails, and I'll work on those while you're getting ready."

"You've got an answer for everything, don't you?"

She was giving him way too much credit. He felt as if he were on a train and it had run off the tracks. He was hurtling through time and space. All he knew was that he wanted an afternoon with Carmen, with no worries about work or Raoul or anything else to cloud the horizon. He held up his phone. "If I don't have the answer, I'll just search for one on Google."

She shook her head. "I'll be ready in forty-five minutes. And I need to be home by six."

CARMEN COULDN'T REMEMBER ever having more fun at the movies. Of course, she hadn't been to the movies with a man in a very long time. The last time someone had paid for her ticket, it had been four dollars. She'd been almost embarrassed when Robert plunked down a twenty for the two of them and hadn't gotten any change back.

They walked up to the snack counter. She pulled money out of her pocket and after a quick glare, he let her pay for the treats. They each got a soda and a large popcorn to share. Robert picked out a bag of M&M'S candy. He raised one eyebrow at her and when she nodded, he dumped the whole package into the popcorn.

"Now we have to get married," he said.

She shook her head at him. "I never marry on the first date."

"Okay. We can probably go out a couple more times before we tie the knot."

He looked so serious. She could feel her heart rate accelerate. She thought she might pass out until he winked at her.

She started to feel a little dizzy again, however, halfway through the movie, when Robert reached over and gently held her hand, his thumb caressing the soft inner flesh of her palm. She knew it meant nothing to him. But when she closed her eyes, she could shut away the world, shut away her memories, shut away the knowledge that thirteen years ago to the day, something had happened that had changed her whole life. His warm hand, his soft touch, it all gave her a little bit of peace.

They left the theater shortly after four, her hand still in his, and walked along the frozen lakefront. The weather was the warmest it had been in days, maybe weeks, and the wind was almost nonexistent. The sun wasn't as warm as it had been at noon but still it had to be at least thirty degrees.

"It feels almost tropical," she said. "That is, if one wears a hat, scarf and mittens in the tropics."

He looked around. "Seems like a spring soap kind of day."

She nodded. "Yes. Very mangoish."

"Mangoish?" he repeated. "Is that a word?"

"It is in the spring soap world." But he was right. It was as if someone had opened the cage and let all the mice out to play. Old people in pairs, young women in knee-high boots and moms pushing baby strollers that probably had a baby in them but all you could see was blankets.

She turned away from the strollers, not willing to let them intrude on her happiness.

"Ready for the ice cream?" Robert asked.

"I guess. I'm going to need to get home soon. I like to be there when Raoul comes home."

"He's having cake. That's means you've got time for a double chocolate chip in a waffle cone."

"Okay. But one scoop."

He took her to an old-fashioned ice cream shop with white tables and red chairs. It was at least half-full, proving that it was never too cold for ice cream. Of course, the owners had the place toasty warm, making it easy to forget that winter raged outside.

She ordered a single scoop of butter pecan in a cup, and he got the waffle cone with two scoops of chocolate chip. He found them a booth in the corner, and they took their coats off. A young girl wearing a short red skirt, a white ruffled blouse and a red hat brought the ice cream to the table.

Halfway through her ice cream, Carmen sighed. "This is so good. Raoul is going to be mad when I tell him that I had homemade ice cream. He loves desserts."

"Based on the meal I had at your place, I think the kid is eating pretty good most nights. I dreamed about those brownies and I woke up craving caramel and chocolate."

She waved a hand. "They're easy," she said, dismissing the compliment. But it left her feeling warm inside.

"Where did you learn to cook?"

"From my grandmother. She lived with my family. There was always a pot simmering on the stove and something baking in the oven. I'm sure she'd think I was a terribly lazy cook." Carmen mockingly glanced over both shoulders. "Don't tell anyone," she said, her voice soft, "but I buy my refried beans in a can. No soaking and boiling for me."

He smiled. "No problem. I buy mine already spread on a burrito shell and topped with melted cheese. And they get passed through the drive-through window."

She shook her head in mock disgust. "They should not call that Mexican food."

"Maybe not, but the city has some great Mexican places. I'll take you to my favorite spot for enchiladas."

She swallowed hard, feeling as if she had a pecan stuck in her throat. He'd said it so casually, as if it was a foregone conclusion that they'd be seeing more of each other.

As if they were going to start dating.

Which was preposterous. Yeah, maybe she had told Liz that she'd consider the online thing. Raoul was getting older. Maybe she could start dating. But she needed to start with someone who was equally green at the game—

maybe some nerdy guy who lived at home with his mother and collected comic books.

Like one of the guys from *The Big Bang Theory*.

She certainly wasn't going to start with Robert Hanson.

She quickly finished her ice cream and pushed the empty dish aside. "I should be getting back," she said.

Robert nodded and helped her with her coat. Once outside, she saw that the streetlights were on and darkness was fast approaching. "Do you want to catch a cab?" Robert asked.

She shook her head. This was her favorite time of day to be out. It still felt safe and the city was always prettier when the lights were on. "It's only seven blocks," she said. "Let's walk."

Two blocks down on the corner, a travel agency had big posters of tropical locales in their front window. She stopped to take a better look. "Speaking of tropical," she said, "doesn't that look wonderful? This time of year I'm envious when anyone talks about their warm-weather vacations."

"Aruba, Bermuda or the Cayman Islands?" he asked, letting his eyes run down the alphabetized list of destinations. "What's your pleasure?"

She smiled. "All of them. One right after another."

He reached for the door handle. "Let's see what they've got."

He was serious. Oh, good Lord. "I was only kidding," she said, pulling his hand off the door handle.

He looked her in the eye. "Too late. I can see the way to your heart is hot sand and an icy rum drink."

The way to her heart? He was teasing, but it made her feel warm all over to think that he was looking for a path. Robert Hanson was a very nice guy, and she really couldn't remember ever having a better day.

"I really have to be getting home," she said.

"Okay. We'll put this conversation on hold for now."

When they got to the front steps of her building, it suddenly seemed awkward. She still didn't know why Robert Hanson had knocked on her door or why he'd spent the afternoon with her.

"Thanks for the movie," she said.

"My pleasure."

"And the ice cream, too."

He nodded. "Likewise. The popcorn and M&M'S were great."

Too bad they hadn't had time for more food. Their conversation could have lasted through the night. She climbed up two of the steps. "I guess I better go."

"Can I ask you something?" Robert asked. He looked serious.

No. "Sure."

"Can I call you?" he asked.

So he hadn't missed that she'd been evasive back at the ice cream store. He'd evidently decided on a more direct approach. Well, maybe she should follow suit. "Why? Something tells me that you're not the type to spend your time going to movies and eating ice cream."

He considered. "I think you're wrong. I had a great time this afternoon."

He sounded as if he meant it. "Maybe," she said, letting him know she wasn't convinced. "I guess you could call me."

He nodded. "Good. You know we're going to talk about why you were crying," he said, so casually that she almost missed it.

"Not today," she said.

He nodded. "Okay, not today. Maybe not even tomorrow or the next day. But soon. I don't want you to be upset. When you are, I want to know why."

"You can't fix everything, you know?"

He shrugged. "Who says?"

She rolled her eyes. "I have to go." She took a step and her cell phone rang. She pulled it out of her purse and looked at the number. *Alexa Sage*.

"Hi, Alexa, this is Carmen." She listened, interrupting just once. "Slow down, Alexa. You're hard to understand."

After a minute, she nodded. "Okay. I'll meet you at the coffee shop in twenty minutes. Pack an extra outfit in your backpack and we'll worry about the rest later. It's going to be okay, honey."

She put her phone back in her purse and met Robert's eyes. "Alexa and her dad had a big fight. She's leaving home. I'm going to meet her and have her stay with me tonight until I can find her a place tomorrow."

Chapter Nine

"Is she hurt?" Robert asked, already pulling out his own phone.

"No. He didn't touch her or her mother. Just a lot of yelling and slamming doors and threatening to kick her and her pregnant belly out into the cold."

"She's a minor child. We can call child welfare services."

"We could but they aren't going to do anything. They've got a backlog of cases involving really young children that are going to be higher in the pecking order. The best thing to do is simply get her out of there."

She was probably right. "Don't you think having her stay here is a little bit like waving a red flag in front of Frank Sage? He's already not crazy about you and suddenly you're harboring his wayward daughter."

Carmen shrugged. "I'm not going to have her stay in a hotel by herself, and I'll need at least a day to work out housing in one of our group homes. It will be fine. It's just for tonight, maybe two nights at the most. But I really need to get going if I'm going to be on time to the coffee shop. I wish Raoul was here. I'd feel better if I knew that he was home safe."

"I'll stay and wait for him," Robert said. That way he'd be there when Carmen and Alexa returned. Just in case dear old Dad decided to follow her. "What's his friend Jacob's number just in case I need to track him down?"

Carmen scrolled through her phone and rattled it off. Robert entered it into his own phone.

Robert used Carmen's keys to let himself into the apartment. It seemed longer than five hours since they'd left. The movie had been good. Sitting in the dark, holding hands with Carmen, sharing popcorn laced with chocolate, had been pretty damn fabulous.

That stupid crack about having to get married had just popped out of his mouth. Had no idea where it had come from. Certainly after hearing about the litany of husbands his mother had collected, she'd understand why he wasn't the marrying kind.

He hadn't wanted the afternoon to end. But he could only stretch out a bowl of ice cream for so long. On the walk back to her apartment, he'd found himself thinking about whether she might invite him in and then wondering what he would do if she did.

As though he were a seventeen-year-old boy on a date with the head cheerleader.

Thank God Sawyer wasn't around to witness how pathetic he was. Speaking of which, he should check in. He'd left a message for his partner earlier when Carmen had been in the shower.

"Hi, it's me," Robert said. "Got a minute?"

"Not much more than that," Sawyer said. "It's my turn to cook and I'm making jambalaya. The rice is almost done."

Robert smiled. The image of Sawyer, one of the toughest cops he'd ever worked with, sitting home waiting for rice to boil, was pretty damn amusing. "Were you able to check out the Gottart Studio?"

"Yeah. Good call on your part. Ben Johanson and Henry Wright both took music lessons there."

Victims two and four. "But not the other boys?"

"Not on the customer list. I called Michelle Whitmore just to make sure that Johnnie hadn't taken lessons there and she'd never heard of the place."

That was disappointing. "So we've got one slim link between two of the kids. I guess that's more than we had before."

"Absolutely," Sawyer said. "You can chase it down tomorrow, although I do think a whole lot of middle-school kids play an instrument."

"Yeah, I think it gets them out of a science class or something like that."

"Maybe," Sawyer said. "Got to go. I don't want my rice getting sticky."

RAOUL WAITED IN line for the diving board, his arms wrapped around his naked chest. He didn't like swim parties. He was always the skinniest kid there. Even so, when Mrs. Minelli had called and invited him to Jacob's surprise party, he hadn't been able to say no. After all, Mrs. Minelli cried easily. She used to cry at soccer games and everything. And Jacob was his best friend.

But Jacob was mad at him. Mrs. Minelli didn't know that. Probably not many knew it besides Jacob and Raoul. Carmen couldn't know it. She'd freak out. She'd start asking a bunch of questions and he'd have to lie to her.

It had been a mistake to show Jacob the gun. He'd gotten all freaked out, said that Raoul was going to get arrested. Had gotten so loud that Raoul had needed to tell him to shut up. Jacob had told him that he was going to laugh when Raoul needed bail money. Had told Raoul that he was crazy to take a gun from somebody that he didn't know just because the guy claimed to be a friend of his brother's.

But Jacob never had a brother who'd died. Jacob maybe didn't understand everything.

Now Jacob came up and stood behind him in line. He didn't say a word. Two more people jumped off the board. They moved up. Raoul had his foot on the first step of the ladder.

"I don't know why you came," Jacob whispered.

Raoul didn't turn around.

"I don't know why you want to spend time with a bunch of kids when you could be out shooting people."

Raoul whipped around. "I already told you once. Shut up."

"Hey, maybe you can join a gang, too. That would be cool. Who wears blue?" Jacob pointed at Raoul's swim trunks.

"You don't know what you're talking about," Raoul said.

"You're so stupid," Jacob said. "I'm not even going to feel bad when they find you all shot up."

Raoul could tell his friend was about to cry. "Jacob, look—"

"Hey, you're holding up the line," someone yelled from the back.

Raoul climbed up the remaining eight steps. He turned one last time to his friend. But Jacob was gone. Raoul looked around and saw Jacob and Pete, another kid from class, jump into the shallow end. They were laughing.

Screw it. Screw them. He didn't need any of them. He jumped off the board, not bothering to kick to the surface until his lungs were about to explode. He swam over to the side, picked up his towel and walked over to Mrs. Minelli.

"I'm not feeling so good," Raoul said. "I think I better call my sister."

"I'm sorry to hear that." Mrs. Minelli grabbed his chin and gave him a close look. "Did you eat too much before you swam?"

"Yes, that must have been it," Raoul said.

"You boys," Mrs. Minelli scolded.

"Well, I guess I'll go get dressed."

"Jacob will be so disappointed."

Jacob wouldn't even know Raoul had left. If he did, he sure wouldn't care.

Raoul thought about calling Carmen to pick him up. She was expecting him to get a ride home from Mrs. Minelli. It didn't matter. It was warm enough to walk home.

He'd been walking for less than a minute when an old black car pulled up. The passenger door swung open. Apollo was driving. There was an open beer in the cup holder next to him.

"Hey, Raoul. Want a lift?"

Carmen would kill him if he got in a car with somebody who had been drinking. "No, thanks," he said. "What are you doing here?"

"Last night you mentioned that you had a birthday party here today."

He had. Apollo had asked him if he wanted to learn to shoot the gun on Saturday and he'd had to tell him why he couldn't. But he hadn't expected the guy would be hanging out, waiting for him. What if Carmen had picked him up? What if she somehow found out that he had a gun in his backpack?

"Look, I've got to get home," Raoul said.

"How's your sister?" Apollo asked.

"She's okay, I guess," Raoul said, feeling uncomfortable with the question.

Cars were swerving around Apollo's car and some were honking their horns.

"Get in. We can talk some more."

Raoul slid into the car. The car smelled bad, sort of like the locker room but different. "Does Carmen know you?"

Apollo shook his head. "We met a couple times when Hector was alive. But that was a long time ago. So, do you have the gun?"

Raoul nodded and pointed at his backpack. "It's heavy."

"Yeah. Meet me tomorrow night at ten o'clock and I'll show you how to shoot it."

Ten o'clock. Carmen would never let him leave the apartment at ten o'clock on a Sunday night. "I don't know," he said, not willing to admit that he might not be able to get out of the apartment.

"Speedy's Used Cars. Don't disappoint me, Raoul." Apollo pulled up next to the curb and motioned for Raoul to get out. Once he did, the black car sped away.

Ten minutes later, Raoul was a half a block from his apartment when Beau and JJ came around the corner. They didn't look surprised to see him. What the hell were they doing in his neighborhood? He had no idea where they lived, but he doubted that it was nearby. He'd been living in the area his whole life and he'd never seen them around before.

"Hey there, Raoul," Beau said. "All done with your little friend's birthday party? Did you play pin the tail on the donkey? Oh, never mind. It was at a pool. It would have been pin the tail on the porpoise."

"What are you doing here?" he asked. He felt braver than usual. Maybe it was the gun in his backpack. "How did you know about Jacob's party?"

"Aren't you full of questions?" JJ said.

"I help out in the office," Beau said. "'Cause I'm such a good kid," he said mockingly. "Your friend's mother came in and was telling one of the office bitches all about it. I looked up your address. Thought it might be nice if we knew where you lived."

"Why?"

He shrugged. "Haven't you heard, Raoul? Knowledge is power. We own you. You better bring more money to school next week for lunches."

They walked past him. Beau bumped into his shoulder, sending him sideways. They never looked back.

He walked the rest of the way home, feeling sick to his stomach. He unlocked the door and pushed it open with his foot. Once inside, he stopped. The cop was sitting at his kitchen table.

Could the day get any worse?

"What are you doing here?" Raoul asked.

"Hi. Nice to see you, too." Robert took a drink of coffee that he'd evidently helped himself to. "Your sister had to go help a client. She should be back soon."

"So now I need a babysitter?"

Robert shrugged. "Carmen didn't want you coming home to an empty apartment. She cares, Raoul. That's not really something to be mad about."

"Whatever." He bent down to pick up Lucy, who had suddenly appeared from wherever it was that she'd been hiding. Raoul gently slung her over one shoulder. "I've got things to do in my room."

"No problem," Robert said, as if he couldn't care less what Raoul did. "How was the birthday party?"

Man, was Carmen telling this guy everything? "Fine," he said. He opened his bedroom door, went inside, and slammed it shut behind him.

ROBERT DRUMMED HIS fingers on the table, more agitated than he'd been in some time. It had been a crazy day. Some deep lows. Some big highs. Like Carmen licking her butter pecan ice cream off her spoon—that vision was likely to keep him up a few nights.

And then the call from Alexa. Big downward dip. Not that he didn't appreciate and understand Carmen's commitment to OCM's clients. After all, he was pretty committed to his work, too.

But why the hell did this particular commitment have to involve Frank Sage? Robert had gotten a look at the guy's eyes. They were so angry.

Plus for the past half hour, he'd been wondering just what it could have been that had made Carmen so sad. Sad enough that she'd been crying hard.

Was she worried about money? He'd give her some.

Had someone been mean to her? He could make that stop fast.

Was it simply the stress of trying to raise a fifteen-year-old on her own?

Wasn't sure how to make that better. He'd been a fifteen-year-old boy at one time but he sure as hell didn't know anything about parenting one.

He heard the downstairs door open and then footsteps. Quiet voices. Carmen came in first. She was smiling, and he took that as a good sign.

"Hi," she said. "Raoul get home?"

"Yes. In his room."

She turned to the young girl behind her. "Alexa, you remember Robert Hanson?"

The girl nodded. "I think my dad does, too."

Good. That's the way he wanted it. Robert stood up. "Does your dad know that you're here?"

"I don't know. I told my mom. Not sure if she'll tell him. I don't think he cares," she said.

Robert wasn't so sure. "What's next?" he asked, looking from Carmen to Alexa.

"Alexa will stay here tonight, and then tomorrow we'll visit a couple places where she might stay for the duration of her pregnancy and for a few weeks after delivery."

Well, it sounded as if they had a plan. And it didn't include him.

That was okay. He had his own plans for tomorrow. Another Wednesday loomed. He'd be solo tomorrow. Sawyer had worked his extra shift today because Liz's parents were celebrating their fortieth anniversary and Sawyer and Liz had a command performance for lunch in the suburbs.

Sawyer had said that he might be back in time to join the rest of the department as they helped Wasimole turn fifty on Sunday evening at Bolder's, his favorite neighborhood bar. There'd be beer, darts, pizza and stupid humor.

Just what Robert needed to get his head back on straight. To keep him from thinking about raising teenagers and consoling crying women.

There'd been some discussion about canceling the party but in the end, Lieutenant Fischer had settled that. He was smart enough to realize that what the group needed was a couple hours to blow off steam before they hit it hard again.

Robert put on his coat and buttoned it. "I'll check in with you on Monday." *Check in.* That was lame but it was the best he could come up with.

"Thank you, again," Carmen said. "For today. For waiting for Raoul. For everything." She stepped forward and brushed her lips across his cheek.

He felt his heart flip in his chest. Didn't think it was medically possible but was pretty sure that was what had happened.

"No problem," he lied as he walked out the door.

He had a very big problem.

Carmen Jimenez was getting to him. Big-time.

Chapter Ten

Sunday

Robert was in the office by seven the next morning. He spent a few hours tackling the paperwork that seemed to multiply overnight. He wasn't the only one working, and somebody had tossed a box of doughnuts on the break-room table so the morning wasn't a total loss.

At ten, he dialed the number in Gabe Monroe's file. Victim number three. The only African American in the group. The rest of the kids had been white. Gabe was four-teen and a freshman at Liekert Academy, a charter school that had opened less than ten years earlier. Mom worked in retail and his dad for the park district. Had a much older brother in his third year of a football scholarship at Notre Dame. Had a sister who was just a year older.

The phone rang. No answer.

He waited ten minutes and tried again. Same result.

He looked up the address. It was less than twenty min-utes away. And Carmen's apartment was on the way.

Fifteen minutes later, he was knocking on Carmen's door. She opened the door a foot and peeked around the edge. All he could see was her head and part of her shoul-der. Her silky hair was floating around her face and her skin was bare, with the exception of the narrow straps of her very little blue tank top.

"Hi," she said. "Shhhhh." She put a finger to her lips. She smiled self-consciously. "I know it's almost eleven but Raoul and Alexa are still sleeping. Teenagers," she said, shaking her head.

"Did I wake you?" he asked.

She shook her head. "I've been up for hours. Already drank a pot of coffee. Very quietly. Alexa was wired last night. We watched movies until the wee hours of the morning. I think she was trying to avoid thinking about the real world for a while."

"I just wanted to make sure everything was okay," he said.

She smiled and stepped out into the hallway, almost closing the door behind her. She was wearing blue-and-white-plaid flannel pajama pants that rode low on her hips and the little shirt. He could see a line of bare skin where the pajama pants stopped and the shirt didn't start.

Holy hell. He could feel his body get hot.

"I wanted to thank you again for yesterday," she said. "I'm not comfortable saying much more than this but I want you to know that I'm very grateful for what you did. The movie. The ice cream. It was really just what I needed."

He nodded. More gratitude. It was nice but not what he was interested in. He edged forward just a little, feeling off balance. His coat felt too tight and the muscles in his legs were jumping.

He couldn't move. All he could do was stare, like some adolescent boy at his first girlie magazine.

Her breasts were fuller than he'd imagined and he could see the outline of her nipples. Her waist and hips were slim but so feminine. And her skin was a beautiful mocha color.

"You're beautiful," he said.

Her eyes widened and he knew that he'd surprised her. Well, hell, this was going to shock her, then.

He reached for her and pulled her into his arms. Then he angled his lips over hers and kissed her.

For the briefest of seconds, she was still.

Then she opened her mouth and welcomed his tongue. He felt the jolt, the sharp shock, all the way to his toes.

He kissed her for several long minutes, learning her mouth, nibbling on the corner of her lips. Then, very slowly, he slid one hand underneath her shirt, running his hand up her ribs. When she didn't resist, he angled his hand so that his thumb brushed over her bare breast.

She groaned, and he pulled her in tighter to his body. He regretted his big coat but focused on the feel of her hot skin against his hand. He breathed in, taking in her scent, holding it deep in his lungs.

He shifted his hand, just slightly, to cup the full weight of her breast. He lifted the edge of her shirt, desperately needing to taste her.

She moaned and sagged in his arms. He thought his own knees might give out. He bunched the soft material of her shirt into his hand and raised it, exposing one small, round, beautiful breast.

He bent his head and licked her nipple.

She shook in his arms.

He closed his mouth and sucked her gently.

And a door down the hallway opened.

Robert moved fast, pulling the shirt down, shifting so that Carmen was protected from prying eyes.

The old woman, a big purse on her arm, shuffled by. "Morning, Carmen," she said, amusement in her tone.

"Morning, Mrs. Curtiss," Carmen answered, her voice

muffled by his coat. "Have a nice day," she added, her voice fading at the end.

"Oh, you, too, dear," the woman said. She walked down the steps, leaving a trail of lilac in the air.

Carmen didn't move until the downstairs door opened and closed. Then she couldn't get out of his arms fast enough.

Her cheeks were pink and her lips, her gorgeous lips, were trembling. She put a hand to her forehead. "It's a good thing she has a strong heart."

It wasn't what he'd expected, but then Carmen Jimenez was a constant surprise. He ran a hand across his own jaw. His own heart was still pumping pretty fast. "It's likely she's seen people kiss before."

She gave him a look that probably made pregnant teenage girls sit up straighter in their chairs. "I think we were a little past that," she said.

Yeah. But not nearly far enough. "Look, Carmen, the circumstances might not have been perfect but—"

She held up her hand. "Please. I don't want to talk about this. Not right now. I have to go," she said, edging back toward the apartment door.

"But—"

She shook her head, stepped inside and softly closed the door.

He knew that he was fast enough that he could get it open again before she locked it. He could force his way into the apartment, force her to talk to him.

But he didn't do anything like that. He just took his trembling legs and his tingling fingers back out into the cold.

WHEN ROBERT RANG the doorbell at the Monroe house, he knew somebody was home because he could hear the television right through the walls of the small Cape Cod. This was a section of the city where the houses had all been built in the forties and fifties, mostly of brick, and close together. Garages were all detached and people got to them through the alley that ran behind their houses.

Nobody came to the door. Robert bypassed the bell, took his fist and pounded on the wooden frame. He got someone's attention because the television got turned down and he could hear locks turning on the door. An old African American woman, wearing a bright orange housecoat and no socks, opened the door.

Robert held out his badge. "My name is Detective Robert Hanson, with the Chicago Police. I wanted to talk to Maurice or Carol Monroe."

"Maury and Carol aren't here," the woman said. "I'm Maury's mother. It was my turn to watch the dog."

Robert didn't see or hear any dog.

"Tippy's asleep," the woman said. "She doesn't hear so well anymore."

Right. The television had probably damaged her ears. "When will they be back?"

"Tuesday night."

They could have another dead kid by the following morning. "Would you have a few minutes that I could ask you some questions?"

She waved him into the house. The furniture was leather, the hardwood floor gleamed with polish and the television was a newer flat screen. There was a fat bulldog sleeping in one of the chairs.

"I'm sorry about the death of your grandson," Robert said.

The woman nodded. "Gabe was a good boy. His death has been hard on my son and his wife. His brother, too, of course. But probably the hardest on his sister, Trina. Being so close in age and everything, they've been best friends since they were babies. I told Maury and Carol that they better get her away from all this for a few days. Especially after that last boy got killed."

"I was wondering if Gabe played any musical instruments."

She shook her head, and Robert could hardly contain the disappointment he felt. He'd been so sure that this was the thread that tied the murders together and that somehow, someway, he'd be able to figure it out.

"You're sure?" he asked.

"I'm his grandmother. I think I would know. His sister played the drums for a few years but Gabe was always more interested in soccer."

Robert stood up. "I'm sorry to have bothered you."

"Did all the other boys that died play an instrument?" she asked, proving that she was sharper than he'd given her credit for.

"Yes, ma'am, they did."

"Well, I'm sorry I couldn't be more help. I want you to find this person who is doing all these awful things to these boys. I want you to find them and I hope they resist arrest and you blow their brains out."

She said it calmly, as if she were commenting on the price of lettuce at the store.

"We'll do our best, ma'am." Robert closed the door behind him and went back to his cold car.

JUDY FRANCONI WRIGHT answered the door with a glass of red wine in her hand. The family resemblance to Alderman Franconi was evident, although her features were more feminine, of course. She seemed more relaxed than her brother, who was always wound tight.

Maybe it was the wine.

Hell, if he'd lost a child, he might just stay drunk.

"Mrs. Wright?" he said. "I'm Detective Robert Hanson."

She motioned him in. "Detective Blaze said that you'd be stopping by. My husband isn't here. It's difficult for him, I guess."

He heard the bitterness and was pretty confident that he got the underlying message. *It was difficult for her, too, but she was stepping up, handling it.*

"No problem. I know that you've provided a great deal of information to Detectives Blaze and Wasimole but I have a few more questions."

"Can I get you a glass of wine before we start, Detective?"

"No, ma'am. Maybe a glass of water?"

"Of course." She left the room and returned within minutes with his glass. She'd refilled her own wineglass.

"My son, Henry, was a remarkable young man," she began.

And Robert let her talk. And when he got the chance, he asked all the questions on his list. When it was over, he felt confident that he'd gotten the information he needed, and Judy Franconi Wright seemed almost happy that she'd gotten to talk about her son, that she'd gotten the opportunity to share significant moments of his life, even if it was with a stranger tasked with investigating the details of his death.

Toward the end, he circled back to the Gottart Studio. While they had been able to connect only two of the dead boys to the place, Robert couldn't shake the feeling that there was something more there.

"You mentioned that Henry played the cornet in his middle school band."

"First chair," she said proudly.

"And I understand that he took music lessons at the Gottart Studio."

"For years. The cornet isn't his first instrument. He also plays piano and drums. You know, just a couple weeks before he died, someone from the Stalwart Academy contacted him. They were trying to recruit him. One of their representatives had met with him several times."

While he hadn't ever heard of the Gottart Studio, he had certainly heard of the Academy. It was a private high school for the arts. Both of Lieutenant Fischer's kids went there. He occasionally bitched about the tuition but Robert had always gotten the impression that he was really happy with the education and the opportunities. Lots of their graduates got full scholarships to good colleges.

Robert made a note. *Stalwart Academy. Recruitment.* He looked up. "What was the representative's name?"

She wrinkled her brow in concentration, then shook her head. "I'm sorry but I never got his name." She paused. "I guess I figured there'd be plenty of time for that." She picked up the wineglass that she'd set aside while she reminisced and took a big drink.

Robert stood up and put on his coat. He handed her his card. "If you think of anything else that might be helpful, don't hesitate to contact me. Anytime."

ON SUNDAY NIGHT, at ten minutes after ten, Raoul waited in the shadows near the front entrance of Speedy's Used Cars and prayed that he wouldn't throw up. He tilted his head to the right, then the left, trying to stretch his neck. He switched his gun from his right hand to his left and wiped his sweaty right palm across his black jeans. How the hell could his hand be sweating when it was freezing outside?

An hour ago, he'd gone to bed, making a big deal that he

was really tired. And then when Carmen and Alexa were in the kitchen, he'd slipped out the front door.

But now he'd been outside for at least forty-five minutes. All the time thinking about Carmen and how disappointed she'd be. He had to make sure she never found out.

"Let's go, my friend."

Raoul jumped a stupid foot. His heart pumped so fast he thought he might be having one of those heart attack things that Jacob's mother was always worrying about.

"Did I scare you?" Apollo wrapped an arm around Raoul's shoulder.

"No," Raoul lied, stepping out of the man's grasp.

Apollo laughed. "Let's go. We're going to accomplish two things tonight. You'll get some target practice, and Speedy will learn not to sell cars that stop running in three weeks."

He held out his hand. "Let me see the gun."

Raoul handed it to him, and his heart stopped again when Apollo pointed it at him.

"Bang," the man said, laughing. He turned away from Raoul. "Now here's how you hold it. Use two hands. And when you press the trigger, it's going to give you some kickback. Don't fall on your butt and embarrass yourself."

Raoul did what Apollo told him to do. He liked the feel of the gun in his hand. It made him feel powerful.

"Now, here's what you need to do. Get around that fence and aim at the windshields. Speedy's going to be sweeping up glass for weeks. Now, go."

Raoul slipped out of the shadows and ran toward the chain-link fence. At one end, between the fence and the building, there was just enough space for a skinny kid like him to squeeze through. He stood in the middle of the dark lot and pointed his gun at the first car. He squeezed the trigger and heard the sound of breaking glass. Dang.

It felt like his shoulder popped out of place. He swung his body to the left, more prepared this time. Another pump on the trigger. More glass. Three times more he repeated the routine.

Dogs started barking. Raoul took one quick look over his shoulder. Across the street, lights flashed on in two different houses. He started to run toward the fence. Just as he went through, he heard the sounds of a siren.

He jerked, ramming his chest into the jagged wire. His coat got caught. He pulled, heard the material rip, and then he was free. He grabbed at the piece of material that was stuck in the wire and then ran the opposite direction of the siren, zigzagging through a backyard and around a Dumpster in the alley.

He ran down the dark alley, his arms pumping at his sides, his breath coming in big gulps. He heard a noise and looked behind him. Headlights, harsh and bright, bore down on him. Raoul leaped to the side, his body crashing into the brick wall. The car screeched to a halt next to him. The front door swung open and Apollo sat inside, laughing.

Raoul wanted to lift his gun one more time.

"Get in, my friend."

In the distance Raoul heard the sounds of more sirens. He jumped into the car.

"Good job," Apollo said. "You did good."

"I've got to go home," Raoul said.

"Don't worry, my friend. Cops are stupid."

Raoul didn't say anything. It took ten minutes for the car to pull up outside of Raoul's apartment building. Raoul got out, feeling every pound of the gun as he hoisted his backpack over his shoulder.

Chapter Eleven

Monday

"Hanson, wake up."

Robert lifted his head from his desk. He had either malaria, West Nile virus or the worst hangover of his entire life.

"Go away." He peered at Tasha through very sore eyes.

"Exactly how many shots did you do with the birthday boy? You know Wasimole drinks like a fish."

"The next time he turns fifty, I'm not going to help him celebrate." Robert leaned back in his chair and barely avoided moaning. The room literally spun.

"Get going. Report begins in three minutes."

Robert managed to drag his poor body into the crowded room. It was quieter than usual, no doubt because at least half the department had been at the party. It gave him little comfort that several looked worse than he did.

Robert sank down onto a chair. He hadn't had a hangover for years. Now he remembered why. They made you feel like hell. Not that he didn't like to tip one or two. He knew how to party. A little booze, some cards, a pretty woman. His life. It was a damn good one, too.

All those things had been available last night. But after he'd drunk too much and lost thirty bucks in poker, he'd gone home alone. Not for lack of trying on Tara's part. He'd dated her once or twice before. Nice girl. Wasn't exactly sure how she'd ended up at the party last night but thought he remembered that she was friends with one of the new female recruits who had gotten hired last year.

Tara had been playing dirty last night, rubbing up against him, making sure he knew she was interested in more than the cards in his hand.

It just wouldn't work. He couldn't go home with Tara. Not when all he could think about was Carmen Jimenez. About how her lips tasted, sweeter than any ice cream. About how her skin smelled. About how her eyes looked, shimmering with tears.

So he'd kept drinking until Tara had gotten tired of waiting and moved on.

Now, as he sat up straighter as Lieutenant Fischer walked to the lectern, he'd pay a price for that. He tried to keep his eyes from glazing over as the lieutenant went through the events of the previous twenty-four hours. Two rapes. One murder. Five domestic calls, two to the same residence. Burglary. Assault and battery. Vandalism.

He almost missed it. Speedy's Used Cars. He knew the place. Not much and not in a great neighborhood. He wouldn't normally think twice about it. However, the first-hand witness accounts of a young, thin, dark-haired boy with a slight limp running from the scene had his head clear in about three seconds.

There had to be a lot of kids who matched that description. Robert didn't care. He only knew one. Raoul Jimenez.

And the way Sawyer was looking at him, he was thinking the same thing. Robert shrugged. Sawyer knew him well enough to know that he'd check it out.

Kids make mistakes. Robert kept reminding himself of

that, all the way out of the department, to his car and on the way to Raoul's school.

He parked in the teacher's lot. He went to the office, showed them his ID and asked for Raoul. They gave him a room to wait in and within five minutes, Raoul stood before him, looking confused and scared.

"Sit down." Robert motioned to the chair next to him.

"I don't want to sit down. I want to know what's going on. Has something happened to Carmen?"

It made it more difficult to kick the kid's butt when he so clearly cared about his sister. "This is not about your sister. It's about you. I'm here as a police officer," Robert said.

Raoul dropped down onto the chair. "Okay."

Robert gave him his best hard-ass cop look. "Do you want to tell me what you were doing last night?"

Raoul stood up and started pacing around the small room. "Sleeping."

"No, you weren't."

"Who says?"

"A couple eyewitnesses who live across from Speedy's Used Cars."

"I don't even know where that is."

The kid had evidently rehearsed his lines. "Really?"

Raoul nodded.

"I don't believe you."

"I don't care."

He was keeping up the tough-guy act pretty well. It reminded Robert of many of the conversations he'd had with the *boarders* in his mother's house. "Okay. That's good enough for now. But if I find out differently, you're going to regret ever having lied to me."

"The only thing I regret is that my sister and I had dinner with you."

"Trust me on this. It won't be the last time."

"Are you going to be freakin' spying on me?"

"No. I lo…like your sister." Whoa, had he almost said *love?* Maybe he had really enjoyed kissing her and holding her and he'd been able to think of little else than how she'd looked in her pajama pants and little shirt. Or how she'd tasted when he'd taken her in his mouth.

But love?

Raoul stared at him, like he'd suddenly grown a third eye. It seemed appropriate since he felt as if his head was going to explode.

"Don't you have to read me my rights or something?" Raoul asked.

Robert shook his head and took a deep breath. "You've watched too many episodes of *Law & Order*." He leaned toward the boy. "Look, Raoul. I'm worried about you."

Now Raoul studied the ceiling. "I've got to get back to class. We're having a social studies test."

Robert nodded. "Okay. But watch yourself, Raoul. 'Cause I'm kind of like a bad penny. You just never know where I'm going to turn up."

He left the building and dialed his cell phone on the way to his car. His mom answered on the third ring.

"Hi. How was the bingo?" he asked.

"Pretty good," she said. "Even distribution of men and women. At my age, you don't see that all that often. You know, men are the weaker species and they die off sooner."

"You doing okay?" he asked.

"Oh, sure, honey. Don't worry about me."

"I'll try to stop by later this week," he said.

"I'm free on Thursday," she said.

There might be another dead kid by then. Robert sucked in a breath of cold air. "See you then."

He was halfway back to meet Sawyer when his cell phone rang. It was Sawyer. "Ten minutes," Robert said.

"That's not why I'm calling. I just talked to Liz. She said that Carmen called in, said she'd be late, that somebody had vandalized her car. I made sure a squad went out to get the report but I thought you'd want to know."

Damn straight. Robert did a fast U-turn in the middle of the street, ignoring the horns that blared in response. He was at Carmen's apartment in less than ten minutes. She was standing outside, wrapped in her blue cape. A beat cop he didn't recognize, with his coat collar pulled tight to protect against the cold, stood next to her. He'd parked his squad car in front of her damaged car.

Robert parked and got out. He flashed his badge at the beat cop.

"Officer David Smith," the young man said in response, extending his hand.

Carmen didn't seem as happy to see him. She was frowning at him. "How did you know?" she asked. Then she waved her hand. "Never mind. I just figured it out."

Robert looked the car over. The driver's side had a streak of white paint, starting at the front fender and running down the length of the car. The passenger-side window had a hole in it, as if someone had taken the end of a baseball bat and poked it through.

It was damage that could have been done without anyone even getting out of their car. Which made it unlikely that there would be any physical evidence at the scene.

"Any ideas?" he asked Carmen.

She shook her head. "No. Not even sure when it happened. I parked the car about eight last night. I'd planned to start work later today since I've got evening appointments tonight. I came out around nine and saw this."

"Where's Alexa?"

"She and Raoul left for school around the same time. Raoul wanted me to take him to school but it was Mrs.

Minelli's turn to drive. Alexa took the bus. They must not have seen this or they would have come back inside and told me." She paused. "You look tired," she added.

"I'm okay," he said.

She nibbled on her lower lip. "Late night?" she asked, her voice lower.

Robert glanced at Officer Smith, who was looking down at his report but no doubt listening to every word. "Birthday party for one of my coworkers."

She waved a gloved hand. "It's none of my business."

Maybe not, but they sure as hell had unfinished business between the two of them. If the old lady who lived down the hall hadn't come along, who knows where that business might have taken them. "I went home alone," he said very quietly.

Her cheeks seemed to get a little pinker. "Why?" she whispered, locking eyes with him.

Because I can't think about anybody but you. She wasn't ready for that kind of admission. He decided to play it safe. "I'd worked all day. I was tired."

"Of course."

It was twenty degrees outside but the air suddenly seemed warm, maybe even a little oppressive.

Smith stepped forward. "I'll get you a copy of this report for your insurance company," he said. "At least you can still drive it."

Neither Robert nor Carmen said anything. After several seconds, Carmen spoke up. "Thank you for coming so promptly," she said.

The young officer looked from Carmen to Robert and offered up just a little smile. "No problem." If he'd wondered initially why a detective was showing up at the scene of a car vandalism call, he wasn't wondering anymore.

Robert waited until the man was back in his car. Then

he shook his head to clear it. He needed to get back in the game. He took a step away from Carmen, trying to get away from her scent, something that evoked visions of good brandy and silk sheets. "Sage?" he asked.

She shrugged. "I have no reason to think that."

"Who else is pissed off at you?"

She rolled her pretty brown eyes. "Maybe it was just random violence. Maybe," she said, evidently warming up to the topic, "it was somebody who was angry that I had a parking space. You know how nutty people in Chicago get when it snows."

She was right about that. Street parking was always limited in the city, but when piled-up snow took up several spots, it became somewhat of an Olympic sport to protect one's parking place. People dragged furniture out of their homes to block their neighbors from taking an empty spot. Just last week, in one of the more affluent neighborhoods on the north side, there'd been a hell of a fight when a woman had used her Lexus to push a couch out of the way.

It was possible that Carmen was right. Robert looked up and down the street. Many spaces were open because people were already at work. But for the cars that remained, there was no similar damage. He shook his head. "I don't think so. No other cars were touched. Face it, Carmen. Somebody went after your vehicle. This is personal."

Robert knew where Frank Sage lived. He'd made it a point to look it up that very first day, after the coffee shop incident. Now he drove there, knowing that Carmen would probably be upset if she knew what he was doing.

He didn't expect Sage to be there but based on what Carmen had said, it was likely that Mrs. Sage would be home. And right now, he wanted the woman's perspective on her husband's state of mind.

He knocked on the screen door of the modest home. The

place had white siding and red shutters, and looked to be a two-bedroom or maybe a small three-bedroom. He saw the curtain move on the interior door.

He held out his badge. "My name is Detective Robert Hanson with the Chicago Police. I'd like to talk to you about your daughter."

Well, sort of. Whatever it took to get the door opened.

Mrs. Sage opened the door halfway. She looked briefly at his badge. "Is my daughter okay?"

"Yes. As far as I know. May I come in?" he asked.

She opened the door the whole way in response and turned her back. She walked over to the couch, picked up the remote, and turned off the television. Then she sat.

It was a small room, maybe twelve by fourteen, and one end was open to the kitchen. The appliances were dated and there were ugly placemats on the table.

The only chair in the living room was a worn recliner, and Robert figured that was where Frank Sage settled in every night. Not wanting to sit there and also not wanting to tower over Mrs. Sage, he walked over to the kitchen table and grabbed one of the wooden chairs. He brought it back into the living room and sat.

"Thank you for seeing me," he said. "Did you happen to tell your husband that Alexa is staying with Carmen Jimenez?"

She nodded. "When she didn't come home on Saturday night, he wanted to know where she was."

"It was my understanding that he threatened to kick her out. That there was quite a scene here before she left."

She nodded again. "You have to understand. My husband, well, he says things that he's sorry for later on." She pushed her short brown hair behind one ear, then did it again when the strand wouldn't stay back. "He's a good man. He just works too hard."

Why did she feel that she needed to defend the bully? "Alexa said that he hit you after you dented your car."

Her face lost its color. "She shouldn't have said anything. That's our business."

"You know," Robert said, softening his voice. "There are places that can help you. Places you can go."

The woman said nothing.

Robert felt sick. While Mrs. Sage didn't resemble his mother physically, they were very much the same person. Afraid to be alone. Ready to settle. Too quick to forgive or forget.

Too willing to accept that they had no value without a man.

He wasn't going to be able to convince her, any more than he'd been able to convince his mother. "You're going to have a grandchild," he said, giving it one last try. "Your daughter needs your help."

Again the woman said nothing.

Robert stood up. "Carmen Jimenez's car was vandalized last night or early this morning. I'm going to go see your husband at his work. If I have any reason to believe he's involved, I'm going to arrest him. If I have any reason to believe that he's going to hurt Alexa or Carmen, I'm going to make sure he doesn't have the chance."

Mrs. Sage walked over to the door and opened it. Robert put the chair back where it belonged and walked out. He was halfway down the sidewalk when Mrs. Sage spoke.

"Tell Alexa that I love her," she said. Then she closed the door.

Chapter Twelve

Frank Sage worked at a factory that was fifteen minutes from his house. On the way there, Robert passed the coffee shop where Carmen had met Alexa that morning. Sage had been nearly out of control that day. Robert had hoped he might settle down, but if he wasn't going to, then Robert was just going to settle his ass down for him.

When he got to the factory, they refused to let him see Sage until he showed them his badge. Then they got significantly more cooperative and stuffed him in a small conference room with a round table and four chairs.

Robert didn't sit.

When Sage came in, he didn't, either.

"What the hell are you doing here?" Sage asked, taking the offensive.

Robert rubbed his chin. "I told you I'd be watching you."

Sage didn't answer. He just crossed his arms over his broad chest.

Robert decided to get to it because he was fast losing the battle with his inner self, who wanted to beat the crap out of Sage's smug face. "I want to know where you were between the hours of eight last night and nine this morning."

"I was home the whole night. Watched the nine o'clock news and then I went to bed. My wife can verify that."

Great.

"I got up this morning, stopped for coffee on my way to work at my usual place, and got here at twenty minutes before seven. I punched in and I've been working ever since. My supervisor could verify that. He's a jerk who watches his employees like a hawk. He'd know if I was gone."

Supervisor was probably hoping the guy would make a break for it. "That should be easy enough to verify and trust me, I will."

Sage shrugged. "Why the questions?"

"Carmen Jimenez's car was vandalized either late last night or early this morning."

Sage's face showed no reaction. "I don't care. About her, her car, her anything. She's nothing."

Robert forced himself to breathe deep. "I want you to know that if I find out that you had anything to do with it, I will arrest you so fast that your head will be spinning. Stay away from her and stay away from your daughter."

"I don't have a daughter," Sage said. He opened up the door and left the room.

Before Robert left, he did exactly what he'd promised Sage. He asked the receptionist to get the supervisor.

He was a young guy, maybe thirty. He had a pencil stuck behind one ear and he was carrying his phone in his hand. His name was Hank Riser.

"What can I do for you, Detective?" he asked.

"Mr. Riser, I'm investigating some vandalism that occurred either late last night or early this morning. I'm trying to verify what time Frank Sage arrived at work this morning and whether he's been at work the entire time."

The man pushed a button on his phone. "Frank is usually in before me but I can check his time-card punch." He used his index finger to scroll through a couple screens. "Yes, he was here when his shift began at seven and I saw him probably a half hour later. He's been here all morning." The man looked up from his phone. "What's this about, Detective?"

"Just trying to put some pieces together," Robert said. "What your general impression of Frank Sage?"

"Stays mostly to himself at work. Gets here on time. Leaves the minute he can."

"You ever have any trouble with him getting along with others?"

The man took a deep breath. "Not that's documented. But I've had a couple of the women in the shop tell me that they aren't comfortable working next to him. It's nothing he says or does, it's just a feeling they get. So I move them to another area and we get past it."

It's just a feeling they get. He understood that. Maybe they wanted to push Sage's face into a brick wall, too.

Robert shook the man's hand. "Thank you for your time."

He walked back to his car and kicked his tire for the hell of it. He didn't have enough evidence to bring Sage in.

He got in, started the vehicle, and texted Sawyer. On my way back. Be there in fifteen.

He was five minutes away from his destination when he saw the jewelry store. He'd shopped there a few times over the years. A necklace here. Some earrings there. They did a nice job with wrapping birthday and Christmas gifts.

There was an empty parking spot in front of the store. He took that as a sign.

"Can I help you, sir?" the young woman behind the counter asked.

"Yes," he said. "Yes, you can."

WHEN ROBERT SAT down at his desk, Sawyer looked up.

"I expected you forty-five minutes ago," he said. "I was getting worried."

"I had to make a stop."

Sawyer nodded.

"You going to ask me where?" Robert challenged.

Sawyer cocked his head. "Well, I guess I could. If you'd like me to."

"You don't have to," Robert said.

"Oh, for God's sake, Robert. Talk."

Robert looked over both shoulders. There were other people in the room but nobody was paying them any attention. Tasha was not at her desk.

"I was at the jewelry store."

"You're getting your tongue pierced?" Sawyer asked.

Robert rolled his eyes. "Right. Just as soon as I do yours." He stopped. "I went in thinking I might get a necklace, maybe some matching earrings. Carmen was upset about her car. I thought it might cheer her up."

"Did you find anything?"

Robert tapped his pen on his metal desk. "I got a ring."

"Okay," Sawyer said.

"An engagement ring," Robert clarified. He sat back in his chair and waited for the inquisition to start.

Sawyer didn't say anything, and that made Robert crazy. "Well?" he prompted his friend.

"Congratulations," Sawyer said. "I guess I didn't realize it had gotten to this stage."

"We haven't actually talked about it," Robert admitted.

"What have you talked about?"

"Oh, you know. Favorite ice cream flavors, best movies of the year, spring soaps."

Sawyer raised an eyebrow.

"Never mind. Am I crazy?" Robert asked. "I feel crazy.

I feel crazy and light-headed and totally out of control. I swear to God I wasn't planning on buying a diamond ring. It was just a day ago that I was reflecting upon why I'd never get married."

"Marriage is wonderful," Sawyer said.

Robert shook his head. "You've met my mother."

"Yeah, and I like her. Here's a news flash, Robert. You're not your mother."

Robert cupped his chin in his hand. "I know that. But I've spent my whole life determined not to follow in her footsteps. And then suddenly I was inside that jewelry store and it was as if the diamond rings were calling my name. It sounded sort of like, 'Hey, dumb-ass.'"

"You answer to that?"

Robert frowned at him. "Not usually. You know, I was this close to beating the hell out of Frank Sage this morning. Just because I thought he might have painted a white stripe on Carmen's car."

"So that's why you bought a ring?"

Robert shook his head. "I bought a ring because she was sad the other day and I don't want her to ever be sad again. I don't want her to be cold or hungry or to ever worry about money. I want to wrap her in cotton and keep her safe from idiots like Sage. I want…I want to come home to her at night and talk about our days. I want to hold hands at the movies and eat off each other's ice cream spoons." Robert stopped. "I'm losing my mind, aren't I?"

Sawyer smiled. "I knew something was different last night. Tara was doing everything but stand on her head to get your attention and you just looked uncomfortable. I've never seen that before. Not interested, certainly. But never uncomfortable. I thought to myself, where is the cool, calm and collected Robert Hanson who can manage a string of women?"

Robert rolled his eyes. "He got caught in his own fishing line and he's choking."

This time Sawyer laughed. "If it makes you feel any better, you'll be over this in forty or fifty years," he said. "Don't be too hard on yourself. Happens to the best of us."

"I love her," Robert said. "But here's the thing. I don't know how to be a husband and I sure as hell don't know how to be a father. My mother had a parade of men, but none of them were very good at either job. I don't have any role models other than you. And unfortunately, the techniques you're using on Catherine probably aren't the same ones that will be effective with a surly fifteen-year-old boy."

"You're worrying about nothing. You know everything you need to know."

"I hope you're right," Robert said, shaking his head.

"When are you going to pop the question?"

"I have no idea."

"Good plan."

CARMEN STOOD IN Liz's doorway and buttoned her coat. "Have a good night," she said to her friend. "Are you getting out of here soon?"

"Yes. I just called Catherine's sitter and told her I'd be there in about fifteen minutes. What about you?"

"My late appointment canceled so I'm almost done. Just need to stop by Montgomery High School. There's a counselor there who wants to talk with me. She's got a potential referral. I told her I'd stop by on my way home from work."

"You should try to get home before it gets too late. I'm a little freaked out about your car getting vandalized. I know you told me that you don't think Frank Sage had anything to do with it, but the timing is sort of suspect, isn't it?"

Carmen tied her scarf around her neck. "That's certainly the path that Robert seems intent upon following."

Liz smiled. "Yes, Robert. What started with a little pizza at my house seems to be flourishing into something more. You know every time you say his name, your cheeks get pink and there's this look in your eyes that I've never seen before."

Carmen unwound the scarf that she'd just tied. Just thinking about Robert made her warm. "I don't know what's going on," she said honestly. "I am so out of my league here."

"No, you're not," Liz said, waving her hand. "Just let it go where it's going to go. Relax."

"He kissed me," Carmen said.

"I figured as much," Liz said, her tone guarded.

Carmen knew Liz would never ask for details. She was way too classy for that. But then why did she have an adolescent need to give her some?

"It wasn't like a *hey, good friend, nice to see you again* kiss. It was…something. My neighbor saw us in the hallway and I'm not sure I'm going to be able to look her in the eye again."

"Mrs. Curtiss?"

"Yes. I forgot that you'd met her."

"You probably made her day. She's cool now so she was probably really cool when she was your age."

"Yeah, well, I've never been cool. I'm a twenty-nine-year-old woman with the dating skills of a fourteen-year-old."

Liz got up from her desk and walked over to Carmen. She hugged her. "I am so happy for you," she said. "Robert is a great guy. A wonderful friend. What could be better than two of my best friends getting together?"

Carmen shook her head. "There's no hooking up going

on here," she said, deliberately using the term that their clients used.

"Well, maybe there should be," Liz said. "Multiple, explosive hookups."

"You're no help," Carmen said, shaking her head in mock disgust. "I have to go. I'll see you tomorrow."

Carmen walked out of OCM and across the street to the parking lot where staff parked. While it wasn't yet dark, the streetlights were on, making the white stripe against the dark paint stand out. The backseat window was covered with duct tape. All in all, it looked pretty bad.

She'd tried to convince Robert that it was random. And she hadn't been blowing smoke. It had to be. Because the idea that somebody disliked her so much that they felt the need to publicly proclaim it was too distasteful.

She'd call tomorrow and see if she could get her car in to get the paint job repaired and the window fixed. It would mean relying on public transportation for a few days, but anything was better than driving this. It looked like an injured skunk on wheels.

Carmen unlocked her door and slid into the cold vehicle. She started the car and shivered while the heater struggled to warm the space. After a couple minutes, she put the car in Drive and pulled out of the lot.

Montgomery School was ten minutes away and then her apartment another ten. She was grateful that no fresh snow had fallen during the day. For once, the streets were pretty good and the traffic not too heavy.

She accelerated toward the green light at the bottom of the hill, only to tap her brakes when it turned yellow.

The pedal went to the floor.

Her brakes were gone. And her car was picking up speed. The light turned red.

She saw the large delivery truck coming from the left,

barreling toward the intersection, and knew there was no way they weren't going to collide.

ROBERT WAS PORING through the reports on all the evidence that had been gathered at the scenes where the dead kids had been found, looking for some connection, when his cell phone rang. "Hanson," he answered.

"This is Officer Smith. We met yesterday."

At Carmen's. Good. Maybe they had found some shred of evidence. "What can I help you with?" Robert asked.

"Well, nothing, I guess. I just had some information that I thought you might be interested in."

"Okay."

"The car that was vandalized, well, it was just in an accident. When the responding officer entered the license plate, my name came up. He gave me a call."

Robert shoved back his chair and grabbed his coat. "Where?"

"Corner of Pecan Street and Webster Avenue. Pretty big mess," he added.

"Fatalities?" Robert forced himself to ask.

"No, but the female driver was transported to Mercy Memorial."

Chapter Thirteen

When Robert got to the emergency room, nobody would tell him anything. He pulled his badge and demanded information.

"I'll get a charge nurse," the woman at the desk told him. "I'm not authorized to provide any information."

"Just tell me that she's alive," he said, leaning over the counter.

Either he scared her or she felt sorry for him because she entered a few clicks on her computer. "Alive and stable upon arrival. That's all I can tell you."

It was enough. Carmen was alive. Stable didn't mean that there weren't injuries, even serious ones. But stable was better than all kinds of other potential descriptors that were making his knees weak.

What the hell had happened? He pulled out his cell phone and in minutes had the responding officer on the phone. "This is Detective Hanson. I'm looking for information on the accident that you just processed at the corner of Pecan Street and Webster Avenue. What happened?"

"Female driver, C. Jimenez, driving a dark 2010 Honda blew through the intersection. Back end was clipped by a delivery truck that managed to swerve, or the damage and the injuries would have been significantly worse."

"How badly was she hurt?"

"I don't know. Paramedics were worried about internal injuries. She was conscious, though. Told me that her brakes failed. The lack of skid marks at the scene supports that."

Failed brakes. It happened. But rarely.

Had someone tampered with her car? Deliberately put her at risk? "Where's the vehicle now?"

"It wasn't drivable. We arranged to have it towed to our impound lot so that one of our guys could take a look at it."

"Push it up on the list," Robert instructed. Screw it. Let his boss scream and yell about the importance of not appearing too personally interested in a case.

He wanted blood.

"Will do. Seems like a nice woman, Detective. Kept apologizing for the accident, for causing so many people to have to come out into the cold. Wouldn't get in the ambulance until she'd talked to the driver of the truck, just to make sure he was okay."

Carmen Jimenez was as nice as they came. And she could have easily have been killed today. "Call me the minute you have results."

Robert disconnected and punched Sawyer's number.

"What's up?" Sawyer answered.

"Carmen was in an accident this afternoon. Her brakes failed. She's at Mercy Memorial hospital. Stable condition. I haven't seen her yet."

"Damn," Sawyer hissed.

Robert understood. He knew that Sawyer thought the world of Carmen and that he'd be worried about how Liz would take the news. He also knew that Sawyer wouldn't like the proximity of the danger. If someone was threatening Carmen, then Liz could potentially get caught in the cross fire.

He put his hand into his pocket and ran his fingers

across the flat sterling-silver case that held the diamond ring. "I need your help," Robert said.

"Anything."

"Do you know where Carmen parks her car?"

"Yeah. There's a small lot just east of OCM. That's where they all park."

"Okay. Get out there. See if there's anything to suggest that somebody tampered with her car."

"Done."

"I need you to do something else, too. Go find Frank Sage. If he can't account for every minute of his time, arrest him." Yeah, he didn't even know for sure if Carmen's brakes had been tampered with, but he didn't care. He wasn't going to give Sage time to think of an alibi.

"Anything else?"

"Yeah. Tell Liz that I'll call her with an update on Carmen's condition just as soon as I know something." Robert disconnected.

Robert thought about what he should do next. Should he find Raoul? School was out but the kid was probably at band practice. Robert decided to wait. He'd spent the day being pretty irritated with the kid, but there was no doubt that Raoul thought the world of his sister. There was no need to worry him needlessly.

Oh, God, he hoped it would be needless worry. Hoped that somebody would walk out of those doors right now and tell him that everything was *fine*. Just fine.

He went up to the desk again. "I'm still waiting for information on Carmen Jimenez."

The clerk shook her head. "Hang on," she said. She pushed her chair back and walked away. She was back in about two minutes with another woman, ten years older, in blue scrubs with a white lab coat.

"I'm Chelsea Andrews," the woman said. "I'm in charge

today. I understand that you're interested in an update on Carmen Jimenez. Is she under arrest, Detective?"

Police business generally took precedence over personal business. "Miss Jimenez is a material witness to a very important ongoing investigation," he said. "I need to talk to her. Now."

"Come with me," she said. "But for what it's worth, the woman has had a hell of a day. I would think the cops would cut her a little slack."

She led him past six closed doors. At the seventh, she stopped and knocked briefly before opening the door.

The exam room was small, with a bed taking up most of the space. Carmen was in a faded blue-and-white gown, in a bed, propped up by two or three pillows.

She had airbag burns across the bridge of her nose and her cheeks. Under her eyes, the skin was red and bruised and he suspected she might have a black eye in a day or two.

She'd still be beautiful. "Hi," he said.

She smiled at him. "I'm not even going to ask how you knew I was here."

He shrugged. "How are you?"

"I'm okay. Lucky," she said, looking at the charge nurse who continued to stand in the doorway. "That's what everybody is telling me."

He reached for her hand. Her skin was warm and he felt himself relax for the first time since he'd received the awful phone call. "Do you have to stay here?" he asked.

"At least until they read the results of the abdominal CT scan. Then I'm hoping to go home."

Robert looked over his shoulder. The charge nurse was frowning at him. "Material witness?" she said, letting her gaze rest on their linked hands.

Robert shrugged and the woman shook her head, turned and left. She closed the door behind her.

Robert leaned over the bed and kissed Carmen. Gently. Sweetly. "I'm so sorry that you're hurt."

"I'm going to be okay," she said, her voice a mere whisper. "It was so scary," she added.

"What happened?"

"I don't know. I mean, I know that I was driving and I saw the light turn yellow. I pushed on the brake and the pedal went to the floor. I knew something was terribly wrong but by then, I was so close to the intersection. There are businesses on both sides. I didn't see anywhere to go." She swallowed hard.

"Then I saw the truck and I really, really thought I was going to die. I pulled my emergency brake and my car went sideways. Then the truck hit me, my air bag went off, and I think I might have blacked out for a minute because the next thing I knew, there was somebody at my door, telling me to just sit tight, that help was coming. I kept asking if anyone else had been hurt and nobody would tell me anything."

"Everybody else is okay," he said. "Don't worry about that." He hated seeing the look of despair in her pretty brown eyes.

She shook her head. "I just feel horrible. I always maintain my car. I had no idea my brakes were bad. That poor man driving the truck. I finally got to talk to him and he said he was fine but it could have been so much worse and it would have been all my fault."

"Where was your car today?"

"Where it is every day. We park next to the dry cleaner's."

"Any cameras in the lot?"

"I have no idea. There could be, I suppose, but it's a really small lot. Probably only space for six or eight cars." She pushed herself up in the bed. She winced, and he absolutely hated that she was in pain.

"Should I get a nurse?" he asked.

She shook her head. "I'm just a little sore," she said. "I think I got tossed around a little when my car was spinning. Why the questions about where I park?"

He hated that they had to have this conversation, but she needed to understand that the situation had changed today. Until he knew otherwise, he was going to assume that somebody had deliberately tried to harm Carmen. That meant that she needed to be on high alert, cautious of everything and everybody. "Brakes can fail on a car, Carmen. They can. But when brakes go bad, it's usually more of a gradual loss, they get sort of spongy. What you're describing, where there is a total loss of responsiveness, makes me think that there's something else going on here."

"You think somebody messed with my brakes?" She spoke so fast that her words were almost clipped.

"I don't know," he said honestly. "But we will know. Your car got towed to one of our impound lots. I've already talked to somebody about getting it looked at, to figure out what happened."

"This is crazy," she said.

He couldn't argue that. "Sawyer is going to go talk to Frank Sage."

"But—"

He shook his head, stopping her. "And if we find out that someone messed with your car and he can't account for every damn minute of his day, we're going to arrest him."

She didn't try to protest again. He figured that was as good an indication as anything that the past hour had taken a toll on her.

"Why don't you just rest for a few minutes?" he suggested.

She nodded and closed her eyes. He sat by her bed, continuing to gently hold her hand. After a few minutes, her eyes opened again. "Why didn't you go see Frank Sage?" she asked.

He considered what he should tell her and decided to go with the truth. "Because I need to be here. Close enough to touch you, to feel your warm skin, to see the pulse in your neck beat, to hear your breath, to know that you're really okay."

Her eyes widened. He'd surprised her.

He wanted to say more, to explain that he realized it had been just a few days that they'd been spending time together, but that he knew that *this* was something different. Something that he'd never had or felt before.

He wanted to pull the ring out of his pocket, get down on one knee and beg her to marry him.

But he didn't want to have that conversation with her lying in a hospital bed, in a room that anybody could walk into at any minute.

Fortunately, she didn't press. She simply closed her eyes and within a few minutes, her breathing was such that he was pretty sure she'd drifted off to sleep.

He continued to hold her hand, tracing the shape of the delicate bones with the pad of this thumb. It was forty-five minutes before the door opened again. It was the charge nurse. She ignored Robert and gently roused Carmen.

"Ms. Jimenez," she said. "The results of your CT came back normal. No internal injuries."

Carmen smiled, and Robert felt the relief flood his body. She was okay.

"Your ribs are probably going to be sore for a few days

so I'd suggest you take it easy. Take some ibuprofen. It's best to try to stay ahead of the pain."

"I can go home?" Carmen asked.

"I'll go get your discharge paperwork ready," the nurse said.

"Thank you," Carmen said. "Everyone here has just been wonderful."

"You're welcome," the nurse said. "I'll be back within fifteen minutes." She left the room.

Carmen smiled at Robert. "Good news," she said.

"Great news," he corrected.

"Yeah." With her free hand, she plucked at the thin sheet that covered her legs. "Time marches on," she said.

"I suppose it does," he said, not sure where she was going.

"Where do you live?" she asked.

He hadn't seen that one coming. "I've got an apartment in one of the high-rises on Lake Shore Drive."

She smiled, a little half smile. "Does it face the lake?"

"It does. On a clear day, I can see fifteen miles out onto Lake Michigan."

"I'll bet that's pretty. Even when it's all iced up, I'll bet it's nice. You know, I used to ice-skate when I was younger."

He got nervous. The CT of the abdomen may have been fine, but maybe they'd missed something. She thought that she'd blacked out for a minute. Was it possible that she'd hit her head? He leaned close and looked at her eyes. Both pupils were the same size.

"I used to do a lot of things. And then I stopped. I got cautious. Told myself that Raoul had lost so much already, that he shouldn't have to lose anything else."

"Honey, I'm not sure—"

"But I think I was just kidding myself. You ever do that, Robert? Kid yourself?"

He was still holding her hand and as unobtrusively as possible, he shifted his hold, then rested his thumb on the inside of her wrist, testing for her pulse. He counted and watched the second hand on the clock for fifteen seconds and multiplied by four. Seventy-two and steady. Skin was warm but not hot. Still, he was just about to call for the nurse to come back. "I'm not sure I'm following you."

"I'd like to see it."

"What?"

"Your apartment."

"Okay," he assured her. "We can make that happen sometime."

"Tonight. Now."

He let go of her hand. "I'm not sure I understand."

She smiled at him. "I'd like to get dressed, get out of here, go to your apartment and finish what we started in the hallway yesterday morning."

He gripped the bed rail. Her pulse was fine, but his was bucking and heaving. "You've just been in a car accident," he said. "You need to go home and rest. Have some chicken noodle soup. Take a warm bath."

She shook her head.

"What about Raoul?" he asked. Lord, he wanted what she was offering with a vengeance, but the last thing he wanted to face was morning-after regrets.

"He knows nothing about this. He was already expecting me to be home late tonight because I thought I had late clients. I called him a little while ago and told him that I'd be a little later than I expected. He's home, safe, and expects to see me around ten. I'm not planning on spending the night with you, Robert. I thought a couple hours might do it."

He was wound so tight that a couple minutes might take care of it.

"You've thought of just about everything, haven't you?" His voice cracked at the end.

For the first time since he'd seen her lying in the hospital bed, her smile reached her eyes. "You've heard the extent of my ideas. From here on out, we'll have to wing it."

He'd been told he could wing it with the best of them but it had never mattered more. "You're sure? What about your ribs?"

"Maybe we'll need to be inventive?"

He turned and strode to the door.

"Where are you going?" she asked.

"I'm getting that nurse and we're getting the hell out of here."

Once he was safely in the hallway, he took a minute to compose himself. Then he called Sawyer.

"How's Carmen?" his friend asked.

"She's going to be okay," Robert said.

There was a pause on the other end. "How are you doing?"

He forced himself to chuckle. "I'm okay. You know, if not for the circumstances, I bet you'd be laughing your ass off. Robert Hanson has himself plumb undone over a woman or some other equally nutty Southern saying."

"Plumb undone," Sawyer repeated. "Naw. Smitten. More excited than a hen in a frying pan. Now, that's Southern."

"I'm a little freaked out."

"Of course you are. You're going to be even more freaked out when I tell you that there was a puddle of brake fluid found in the parking lot."

Robert gripped his cell phone. "Sage?"

"I don't think so, buddy. I found him at home, sitting

in his easy chair, drinking a beer. I got in his face pretty good until he produced a receipt from his doctor's office. Guess he had to stop in and have some blood work done after work. I was able to verify the time he left his work and when he arrived and left his doctor's office. He wouldn't have had time to disable Carmen's car. I think it was someone else."

"Maybe he paid someone else to do it?" Robert said, unable to forget the animosity he'd seen in Sage's eyes.

"Maybe. But then he's a pretty good actor. I got the feeling he didn't have a clue why I was so interested in his day. I really think it might have been someone else."

That meant that someone else had deliberately tried to hurt Carmen. Why? Who?

He was going to have to tell her. He would.

After.

Chapter Fourteen

It was forty long minutes before an aide came with a wheelchair to escort her out of the emergency room. When they got to the door, Carmen stood up and felt wonderful. She was taking charge of her life.

"How long will it take to get there?" she asked, once she'd gotten settled in his car.

"Fifteen minutes," he said. His jaw was tight.

"Traffic seems pretty light," she said.

He nodded.

"Looks like it might snow again. The nurses were talking about a possibility of four inches."

He didn't answer.

"Is everything okay, Robert?"

"Yes," he said without looking at her.

He was definitely acting odd. "Are you sorry we're doing this?" she asked.

He turned to look at her. "Hell, no."

She smiled. "You seem preoccupied."

"Thoughtful," he said.

Was it possible that she'd put the sexy, confident Robert Hanson off his stride? That was, quite frankly, rather empowering. Exhilarating, really.

But she was going to need a lot more than that to get

her through the next couple of hours. "There's something you should probably know," she said.

She didn't hear him sigh, but his chest went up and down in silent anticipation or perhaps, apprehension.

Both might be in order.

"I…uh…haven't had sex for some time."

He nodded and kept his eyes on the road.

"Quite some time, actually," she said.

He turned to look at her. "I don't need details, Carmen."

"Yeah, well, maybe they might be helpful. You see, it's been about thirteen years."

The car jumped forward in a burst of speed. "Sorry," he mumbled.

Sorry I'm a bad driver or sorry I ever agreed to this?

"I guess I just wanted you to know in case…in case I'm not very good at this."

He glanced in his rearview mirror, cut across a lane of traffic and made a sharp left. Then he took a quick right into an underground parking structure. It was dark, and Carmen was grateful for that. Could this get any more embarrassing?

"I'll do my best," she said. She was babbling. Knew it. Couldn't seem to stop. She was so nervous.

"Carmen," he said, his tone kind. "Shut up. Please."

He drove to an empty parking space and pulled in. He shut the car off and opened his door. She sat.

"You can still change your mind," he said, his voice sounding hoarse.

She reached out and opened her door. When he got out, she followed him, staying just a half step behind as he strode into the building. He got into the elevator and punched 34.

He hadn't said another word.

His apartment was at the end of the hallway. He opened

the door with a key and motioned her in. The door shut behind him with a final-sounding thud. Across the room, the drapes were open on the big windows and there was a half-moon hanging over the frozen lake. Ice caps sparkled against an expanse of darkness.

She walked across the room and looked down. Lake Shore Drive was lit up and there was still enough evening traffic to make it look interesting.

He walked into the kitchen and flipped on a light above the stove. It was lots of stainless steel and granite counters. There were bar stools with leather seats and lots of art on the walls. There was more leather in the living room and glass tables with nothing on them.

It was beautiful. So different from her apartment with the old furniture, the sagging couch, the sheet music lying everywhere.

What the hell had she been thinking? They couldn't be any more different. He was a handsome, single guy living an upscale kind of life in an upscale kind of place. She was a tired counselor, raising her fifteen-year-old brother and over the years had adopted his attitude that they were cool if they put tomato and bacon on their grilled cheese sandwiches.

"Maybe—"

He put his finger to her lip, silently shushing her. "Would you like something to drink?" he asked. "Some wine, perhaps?"

She shook her head. He wasn't going to get a chance to shush her a third time.

He smiled. "Would you like to see the rest of the apartment?"

This time she nodded.

He motioned for her to precede him down the short hallway. There was a bathroom that looked as if no one had ever used it. The soap was new and the towels were fresh.

Next, there was a room that looked part office, part workout room. There was a treadmill and a rowing machine and some hand weights. There was also a desk and glory be, there were actually a few files on it and a rogue stapler had found its way out of a drawer.

There was only one door left. It was partially closed. He reached over her shoulder to open it. It faced the lake, as the living room had. And here the drapes were also pulled open, letting in moonlight and the reflection of city lights.

It was a large room, yet still the bed took up a great deal of it. It had to be a king, and the padded headboard added to its overall mass. She was pretty sure that if she sat on it, her feet might not touch the ground.

It was a far cry from the little double bed in her twelve-by-twelve bedroom.

The bed was made. It had a thick gray duvet. Several gray and purple pillows were tossed on a big leather chair in the corner of the room. It made her want to smile. He was neat enough to make his bed but he wasn't going to mess with pillows.

They'd probably been a gift from some girlfriend.

And he didn't want to hurt her feelings so he likely tossed them back on the bed every time she visited.

She wasn't going to kid herself that she was the first woman who'd spent a few hours here. She wouldn't even be the last.

But tonight she was the woman who was going to lie on the gray duvet with a man who made her literally crazy with need. That was enough. She was going to celebrate life. Celebrate the ability to touch and feel.

Robert walked across the room to a door in the far corner. He flipped on a light and she could tell that it was another bath. He closed the door most of the way, allowing just a little of the light to come into the room.

"Is this okay?"

She shrugged.

He raised one dark eyebrow but didn't say anything. He took off his coat and gloves and tossed them over the pillows in the chair.

"May I take your coat?" he asked.

She slowly peeled her gloves off and put them in the pockets of her blue cape. Then she took off her scarf, then the cape. She tossed them all to him.

He caught them, walked over to the chair, and more carefully laid them on top of his own outerwear. He walked back to the bed and sat on it. He was facing the window.

She continued to stand near the door.

He patted the bed next to him. "Care to have a seat?"

She walked over to the bed and sat down, making sure there was a good foot between them. She was right. Her feet didn't touch the floor. She clasped her hands together and rested them in her lap.

He didn't say anything for a minute. Finally, he turned to her. "I'm sorry I told you to shut up."

"I was babbling," she said, accepting his apology. She'd wanted to tell herself to shut up.

"You were nervous," he said. He reached out a big hand and covered her clasped hands.

"Am nervous," she clarified.

"I am, too," he said, smiling at her.

She rolled her eyes. "Oh, please. I don't think it's been thirteen years since you had a woman stay over."

With his thumb, he stroked her wrist. "That's true," he said. "And if I tell you that this is different, you're probably not going to believe me." He hesitated. "So I'm not going there. But what I want you to know is that I want you so much that I'm scared to death that I'm going to blow this. That I'm going to move too fast or do something that you don't like and you're going to be sorry that you ever came here."

His voice cracked at the end. That, and the look in his eyes, gave her the courage to reach out, to stroke the side of his face with the palm of her hand. "I want to be here. With you."

"Why?" he asked, staring in her eyes. "You've waited a long time. Why now? Why me?"

Because I think I love you. Maybe ever since you poured the M&M'S in my popcorn and said we had to get married. "I could have died today. I didn't want to die without this."

"I guess I'm glad I could be of assistance," he said, sounding a little irritated.

She let it go. Better he think that he was a convenient hookup. Otherwise, he'd probably be scared enough to take a leap out of the thirty-fourth-floor window.

"Would you kiss me now?" she asked.

He leaned in. His mouth was warm and heavy and she could feel her cold bones start to melt. He pushed his tongue in her mouth and when she sucked on it, he groaned.

And then he wrapped an arm around her shoulders and gently pulled her down onto the pretty gray duvet that covered the big soft bed.

He kissed her for a very long time and she could feel other parts of her body come out of hibernation and begin to beg for attention. Her skin felt warm and extra sensitive. Her breasts, heavy.

She reached up to unbutton his shirt. He stilled her hands. "Not quite yet," he said softly.

He slipped his hand under her shirt and traced her ribs

gently with the pad of his thumb. "You're sure you're not too sore?" he asked.

"Sure," she said and settled back into his kisses.

His hand traveled upward and when he encountered only skin, he lifted his head.

She smiled. "My bra is in my purse. I didn't put it back on at the hospital."

She heard a low growl and reveled in the feel of his broad hand holding her breast, caressing it. He gently pinched her nipple and sparks shot through her.

Her body had moved from anticipation to full-blown engagement. She pressed against him. He was hard. Sinfully hard.

Another growl and this time he lightly bit at her bottom lip. "You're not playing fair," he said.

"I've waited a long time," she said.

"And you'll have to wait just a few minutes longer. You're a fine wine, Carmen. Meant to be sipped, savored, enjoyed."

And he did just that. Her shirt came off, then her slacks and panties, and there wasn't a part of her that wasn't kissed, stroked, sucked or loved. When he spread her legs and touched her with his tongue, she responded with an explosive orgasm that left her panting and a little embarrassed that she might have squeezed his poor head with her thighs.

"Did I hurt you?" she asked.

He lifted his head. "You were perfect," he said.

"Even if that's all there is," she said, "it's the best sex I ever had."

"That's not all there is," he said. Then he rolled her underneath him and proceeded to prove his point not once, but twice.

ROBERT FELT THE mattress shift and in one quick movement, Carmen slipped from the bed. He could have stopped her but he knew it was time for her to go home.

Damn. He wanted her to stay. Had loved having her in his bed, in his arms, under his body.

Loved.

He loved Carmen Jimenez. But was she ready to hear that?

He watched her pull on her clothes. She'd turned, giving him her back. He was grateful for the moon. It gave enough light that he could see the delicate ridge of her spine, the sexy muscles in her upper back, her gently rounded shoulders.

Her skin had been so soft, smelled so good.

Now her pants, shirt.

"I'll drive you," he said, throwing off the covers.

"I can catch a cab," she said, pulling on her sweater.

He moved behind her and wrapped his arms around her. Her long hair brushed against his chest. He gathered it up in his fist and pulled it to the side. He kissed the back of her neck. She stilled.

"Don't be ridiculous," he murmured, moving his lips close to her ear. "Thank you," he added. He could feel his body reacting to their closeness, wanting her again.

"You're welcome," she said, amusement in her tone. She moved away. "I really do need to get home."

Resigned, he started pulling on his own clothes. When he got to his pants, the ring in his pocket felt heavy against his thigh.

Should he ask her?

What if she said no? The night had been perfect. One that he would remember forever. Could he take the chance of ruining it?

It wasn't a conversation he wanted to have when she was

hurrying to get home. Maybe this weekend. That might be nice. He pulled on his coat and less than five minutes later, they were in his cold car, driving toward her apartment. It had started to snow and the streets were slick. She was quiet and spent the time looking out her window.

Did she regret the past two hours?

That caused a sharp pain to slice across his chest. "What are you thinking?" he asked, even though he wasn't sure he was strong enough to hear the answer.

"I wish I knew more about cars."

Well, that wasn't what he'd expected. "Why?"

"I'm going to need to buy a new one. It would save me some time if I had some idea of what I wanted. Or what I could afford," she added.

"Don't worry about it," he said.

"I've got a little money saved," she said. "I guess I'll just have to wait until I hear from the insurance company."

He could hear the worry in her voice and it made him so angry. This was a woman who already had her share of worries. She didn't need another one. "Carmen, it doesn't matter what your insurance pays. Whatever extra you need, I'll give it to you."

She didn't say anything for two long blocks. Finally, she turned in her seat. "As payment?" she asked, her tone hard.

He almost wrecked his damn car. "I don't even know how you could suggest that."

"I'm sorry," she said, looking down at her gloved hands. "I don't know where that came from. I guess I'm still not sure why a guy like you would want to be with a woman like me. I'm not your type, Robert."

There was no place to pull over the car but there was no traffic either, so he simply slowed down. Moving at a snail's pace, he drove with one hand and reached for her with his other. He wrapped an arm around her shoulder and pulled her close.

"The past two hours of my life have been the best two hours that I've ever had," he said. "And based on those two hours, I'd say you're exactly my type."

Her face was sort of muffled by his coat but he could feel her nod her head. Five minutes later he pulled up to her apartment.

"I think it might be better if I go in alone," she said. "Less questions from Raoul and all."

"Just tell me that we're okay, Carmen."

She leaned across the car and kissed his cheek. "It's all good, Robert. Thank you so much."

"Okay. Then I have one more thing to tell you. When I talked to Sawyer earlier, he confirmed that there was a puddle of brake fluid in your parking lot. Then, while we were at the apartment, I got a text. Your brake lines were definitely tampered with. Looks like somebody took a hacksaw and cut through both the front and back lines." He stopped, letting her absorb the information.

"So, it was deliberate?" she said, her tone flat. "Someone deliberately tried to harm me, maybe even kill me."

"Looks that way."

She turned to him, her dark eyes big. "Who would do something like that?"

"I don't know. We don't think it was Sage. He's got an alibi." He waited for her to throw out an *I told you so* but she said nothing. "We're going to need a list of all your clients."

"Jamison won't go for that," she said.

"Your boss almost lost OCM last year to a bomber. I think he's developed a healthy respect for working with the law. Besides, he cares about you."

She nodded. "He still won't be happy. I'm not happy.

I just can't see it being any of them. I help them. They know it."

"Family members then?"

She shrugged. "Maybe." She looked at her watch. "Speaking of family, I better get inside." She looked up. "What if Raoul had been with me today? What if he'd been injured because someone has a grudge against me? I couldn't bear it, Robert."

He started to pull her close again, but she resisted.

"I have to go," she said. "I need to talk to Raoul. He needs to understand what's going on. We both need to be watching."

"How are you going to get to work in the morning? I could swing by and give you a lift."

She shook her head. "Thank you, but no. A cab will work just fine." She opened her door.

He opened his. When she started to object, he held up a hand. "Give me a break here, Carmen. At least let me walk you to your door."

She smiled. "I'm not used to having someone do things for me."

"Yeah, well, I hope you're the type that adjusts to change quickly."

RAOUL WAS ALREADY in bed when he heard the apartment door open. He glanced at his clock. Carmen had worked really late.

He heard footsteps in the hallway and then a knock on his door. "Hi, sis," he said.

She came in and kissed him on the forehead, like she used to do when he was a little kid. "How was your day?" she asked.

He didn't think the cop had told her about his visit to the school and the conversation about Speedy's. He knew his sister. She would not have waited until ten o'clock to have a conversation with him. "Pretty good," he said. "Band practice went better," he added, because she was always interested in that.

"Just a few more days until the concert," she said.

"Yeah. Thursday at seven. I have to wear black pants and a white shirt."

"No problem. Hey, do you have a minute?"

He was in bed. "I guess."

"I had some bad luck today," she said. "This morning, when I was leaving for work, I discovered that somebody had vandalized my car. They painted a white strip along the side of it and broke out the backseat window."

Oh, man. It was going to be embarrassing riding around in something like that.

"Can we get it fixed?"

"Of course. But that's not all. This afternoon, when I was driving to an appointment, my brakes went out. I couldn't stop for a red light and another vehicle hit me."

He sat up and jammed pillows behind his back. "Are you okay?"

"I am. Got checked out at the hospital and everything is just fine. But here's the thing, Raoul. The police think that somebody cut my brake lines. Somebody wanted me to get in an accident."

That didn't make any sense. Everybody loved Carmen.

Raoul felt a pain in his stomach. Everybody didn't love him. JJ and Beau hated him. They also knew where he lived and the kind of car his sister drove. Were they crazy enough that they would have spray painted her car and then messed with the brakes?

The pain became sharper when he realized that he'd just recently had a conversation about Carmen with somebody. With Apollo.

If the guy was crazy enough to shoot up a car lot, then he was probably crazy enough to cut some brake lines. It didn't make sense because Apollo had said that he was a friend of Hector's. But maybe he'd been lying. Maybe he'd been nice to Raoul just so that he could get close to Carmen? He seemed to be about Carmen's age. Maybe they'd gone to school together? Maybe she'd turned him down for a date or something and he'd been pissed for a long time and was finally getting his revenge?

Raoul's head was spinning. Maybe his sister had almost died because of him. He wanted to tell her about JJ and Beau and about Apollo but he knew how disappointed she'd be that he hadn't told her the truth before. And when she found out about Speedy's, she would be crazy mad.

"What are you going to do?" he whispered.

"Keep living my life. And that's what you're going to do, too. But we're going to be a little more careful, a little more watchful, until we figure this out. Okay?"

He nodded and reached his arms out to hug her. She looked surprised and he realized that it had been a long time since he'd hugged his sister.

She grabbed him tight and hung on. "It will be okay, Raoul. I promise."

It would. He was going to make sure of that.

Chapter Fifteen

Tuesday

Robert was at his desk by six. He made fresh coffee because the guys who had worked overnight evidently liked drinking mud. He was standing in the break area, waiting for the toaster to pop up his bagel, when Lieutenant Fischer came in. He nodded at Robert.

"You're in early," his boss said.

Robert nodded and reached for the cream cheese packet. "You, too."

"Yeah. My wife said she could take the kids to school this morning."

That reminded Robert of his conversation with Judy Franconi Wright. "Henry Wright was getting recruited by Stalwart Academy. That's what his mom told me when I saw her on Sunday."

His boss cocked his head. "Recruited? That school never recruits. It's a competitive application process with pretty good transparency."

Robert's stomach felt weird and he was pretty sure it wasn't because his bagel was still on the counter. "You're sure?"

The man nodded.

Robert pulled his notebook out of his shirt pocket and

started flipping through pages. "Here it is. Stalwart Academy. Said that some representative had been talking to Henry for the last couple of weeks. He was very excited—evidently music was his life. But she didn't know the guy's name. Wanted Henry to get his business card but he never brought it home. She felt bad because she was wondering if the man knew Henry was dead."

He met his boss's eyes. "Maybe this is it. Maybe this is the thread that we've been looking for. I'm going to that school."

"If they give you any trouble, drop my name. In addition to the tuition, I just made a nice donation to their new music room."

Robert was anxious but still he drove carefully. The snow that had started falling last night when he'd been making love to Carmen had continued on through the middle of the night and there had to be at least five fresh inches. Fortunately, it had stopped in time for the plows to clear most of the main roads, although the side streets probably wouldn't all get plowed until much later in the day.

When he got to the school, it was not quite seven. He pressed the buzzer on the outside door and waited.

"Yes?" It was a woman but she was hard to hear over the static.

He looked up at the camera that was pointed toward him. "Detective Robert Hanson of the Chicago Police. I need to speak with somebody in charge."

He heard a buzz and pulled open the door. There was an arrow on the wall, indicating that the office was to his right. He walked into the small administrative area and could smell flavored coffee. There were two women sitting at desks. One had a phone to her ear, and he heard enough to figure out that she was talking to somebody about a kid being ill and missing school. The other woman smiled at him.

"It's pretty early, Detective," she said.

"I wanted to catch someone before the day started." There was no need to tell this woman that time was running out. Tomorrow was Wednesday. "I need to talk to someone about one of your recruitment representatives."

She cocked her head to the left. "I've only been here a month. I'm filling in for someone who is on maternity leave. But I guess I didn't realize that we had recruitment representatives." She looked at the other woman, but she was still on the phone. "I suppose you could talk to Assistant Principal Bryant. She's the only administrator who has arrived. I'll go get her."

"Perfect," he said. In less than three minutes, the woman was back, this time followed by another woman.

Assistant Principal Bryant was mid-thirties, and had blond hair that fell straight to her shoulders and a knockout figure. She wore a classy white wool suit with boots that came up to her knee.

He was reminded of what Carmen had said. *I'm not your type.* Well, if he had a type, this woman was it.

And he felt nothing when she shook his hand.

"What can I do for you, Detective?" Her tone was friendly.

"I am investigating the murder of Henry Wright. He was the young man who was killed last week."

"Of course," she said. "I read about it in the newspaper."

"I understand that someone from your school had made contact with Henry in the last couple of weeks to discuss his possible attendance here next year."

She tapped her index finger against her bottom lip in thought. Her polished fingernails were nicely shaped. There was no wedding ring. "I suppose it's possible that he knew one of our teachers outside of school and they had some conversation about what it's like to attend Stalwart Academy."

"No," Robert said. "That wasn't the way it was explained to me. Someone from Stalwart Academy had made contact with him specifically to discuss the possibility of a freshman scholarship."

She smiled. "I can guarantee you that didn't happen. Stalwart Academy doesn't have to recruit," she said somewhat smugly. "We have a waiting list of candidates every year. And we certainly don't offer any scholarships."

It was exactly what Lieutenant Fischer had thought. He stood up. "Thank you for your time."

She had a stack of business cards on her desk and she reached for one. She flipped it over and wrote a number on the back. "My pleasure, Detective Hanson. Here's my card and my personal cell phone on the back, in the event that you'd want to follow up. On anything."

The message was clear. She was interested.

He put the card in his pocket. He wasn't.

THE BUS WAS ten minutes late and by the time it dropped him off at his corner, Raoul had to run the last two blocks to make it to band practice on time. He didn't want to be late. With the winter concert only two days away, his teacher was acting crazy about that kind of stuff. He was practically on school grounds when Apollo stepped out of the bushes.

"Hey," Raoul said, stopping fast. For the past twenty-four hours, ever since Robert Hanson had shown up at his school, demanding to know about Speedy's, he'd been worried sick about what he'd done. Every time he heard a siren in the distance, he'd envisioned that it was the cops coming to get him.

All the trouble had started with this guy. "I'm late," Raoul said.

"No worries," Apollo said. "I remembered that I had one more thing of Hector's that he wanted you to have."

"What?" Raoul asked.

Apollo held up both gloved hands. "Can't say, can't say. But it's a big deal. What time does your band practice start tomorrow?"

"There's no practice tomorrow morning. Our band teacher has a meeting."

Apollo smiled. "Good. Then meet me here this time tomorrow. That will give me plenty of time to show you and you can still get to school on time like a good boy."

Raoul didn't like Apollo's attitude. "Hey, my sister was in a car accident yesterday. You don't happen to know anything about that, do you?"

Apollo frowned at him. "No. Why should I?"

Because you're a creep. "I don't know. I just had to ask."

"Raoul, I only want what Hector wanted for you. Now, meet me tomorrow. You'll be glad you did."

He would meet him but that was the last he was going to have anything to do with him. He might have been Hector's friend at one time but there was something Raoul didn't like about him.

"I'll think about it," he said.

"On Wednesday," Apollo said before he disappeared back into the snow-covered bushes.

CARMEN HAD BEEN at her desk for less than ten minutes when her office phone rang. "Carmen Jimenez," she answered.

"Hey, just checking to make sure you made it to work okay."

Robert. Just thinking about him made her warm. She

hadn't showered before bed. Hadn't wanted to wash away his scent. Instead, she'd gone to bed naked, something she never did, especially not on a cold winter night. But she'd lain naked in her double bed and imagined what it would be like if Robert was next to her with his warm skin, his strong muscles, his talented fingers and mouth.

It was almost embarrassing and certainly not something she intended to share with Robert. "Yes, got here just a little while ago. I asked Raoul to text me when he got to school and he's also safe and sound."

"Good." He paused. "Can I see you tonight?"

"I don't want to leave Raoul home alone," she said.

"Of course. I could stop by. It would probably be late anyway. He goes to sleep at some point, right?"

Was she ready to have a man in the apartment? Raoul was a heavy sleeper, but what if he somehow overheard them? What if he knocked on the door?

She needed to talk to him first. Maybe she could do that at dinner?

"I'm not sure, Robert. I want to. But I have to handle this carefully."

"I know. I can respect that. But there's something that I want to ask you."

"About?"

"Let's just wait until tonight."

He clearly didn't want to talk about it now. "I'll call you later and let you know if it's okay to come over," she said.

WHEN ROBERT GOT back to the station, he made fast tracks to where Blaze, Wasimole and Sawyer were having a heated discussion. He could see the frustration on their faces.

"I think I've got something," he said.

All three of them looked up. Blaze and Wasimole looked exhausted; Sawyer looked interested.

He filled them in on his conversation with Judy Franconi Wright and his more recent conversation with Assistant Principal Bryant. When he finished, he rubbed his cold hands together. "Somebody made contact with Henry Wright just weeks before he died. Somebody that we know now wasn't legit. We need to go back to the families of the other three victims and see if we can find a similar thread."

Wasimole and Blaze nodded. "We can take Johnnie Whitmore and Ben Johanson, victims one and two."

"Okay. We'll take Gabe Monroe. I never did get to talk to his parents, just the grandmother. Hopefully they will be back from vacation."

Blaze was walking away when she turned. "Let's try to circle back together early afternoon." She didn't need to say anything else. Time was getting the best of them. Wednesday was now less than eighteen hours away.

"Okay," Robert said.

On the way out of the building, Sawyer eyed him. "Anything you want to tell me?" he said.

"No," Robert answered.

Sawyer rolled his eyes. "I'm not looking for details, idiot. I know you planned on taking Carmen home from the hospital. How is she?"

Fabulous. Sexy as hell. Inexperienced in a wonderful way. "She said her ribs are a little sore but she got lucky. Real lucky."

"Lieutenant Fischer assigned it to Vance. He's a good cop. He'll figure it out if there's anything there."

"I know. I sent him a text last night asking who he was going to assign it to. Vance is a good choice. I'd have been a better one."

"You'd have been the worse one. Plenty of motivation

but not a lot of credibility when it came time for a trial. *Yes, Judge, I am sleeping with the victim.* That never goes over well."

Sawyer was right. It still didn't make him happy.

"So, did you ask her?" Sawyer asked.

"No. Yesterday was absolutely crazy. Maybe tonight. I told her I wanted to talk to her about something."

"You'll know when it's the right time. Come on, let's go talk to Maury and Carol Monroe."

WHEN THEY GOT to the Monroe home, there was no grandmother this time. Maury answered the door. He was wearing dress slacks and a nice shirt, and he had a cell phone in his hand.

"Detectives Montgomery and Hanson," Robert said as they flashed identification. "I stopped by last week and spoke with your mother. She said you were out of town. I know we didn't have an appointment but we were hoping we could spend a little time with you and your wife today."

"My wife isn't here. She ran to the grocery store," he said.

"Do you have a few minutes?" Robert asked.

"Sure. We just got home a little while ago." He led them into the living room. There was a young woman on the couch holding the ugly dog. Robert guessed her age at about sixteen.

"This is my daughter, Trina," Maury said.

He and Sawyer took chairs. Maury sat on the couch next to his daughter.

Robert remembered that the grandmother had indicated that the sister was having a hard time. "Maybe your daughter would want to do something else for a little while," he suggested.

Maury looked at his daughter, and she shook her head

violently. He patted her leg. "She stays. She feels that she's been left out of discussions about her brother and that makes her angry."

Information was a funny thing. Everybody wanted it until they heard something they wished they hadn't. But it wasn't his decision.

"We are wondering if during the weeks prior to his death, if Gabe had mentioned meeting anyone new? Maybe someone from a school or something like that?"

Maury shook his head. "He talked about kids sometimes that I didn't know, but I don't think anybody was really new. Just his classmates. I think you guys already looked at his computer and his Facebook page."

Blaze and Wasimole had secured that immediately after the killing. There was nothing on there that made them believe that he had met up with someone. "Where did Gabe hang out after school?" Sawyer asked.

"He usually came home, watched some television, played video games." Maury looked at his daughter. "Right?"

She nodded. "Sometimes he came to band practice with me. Mr. Reynolds didn't care if he watched."

Robert looked up from his notepad. "You play the drums, right?"

"Yeah. Gabe used to screw around with them all the time," she said. "It used to make me so mad."

And now, Robert could tell, she felt bad about that.

"Have you ever heard of the Gottart Studio?"

She shook her head. "I'm not sure. When I was at band camp last year, a couple other kids were talking about taking lessons somewhere. That might have been the place."

"Band camp?" Robert asked. "What's that?"

"It's the citywide camp at Grant Park. It's huge. Gabe went with me a couple days. He hung out in the park while

I was practicing. I remember I came back from lunch one day and I caught him sitting behind my drums pretending that they were his. I told him to get lost." Her eyes filled with tears. "I told him that a lot."

Maury patted his daughter's leg again.

Robert pulled out his cell phone and sent a quick text to Blaze. *See if either of the victims attended the citywide band camp at Grant Park last summer.*

"Do you recall anything unusual happening at band camp?" Robert asked, hating that he had to push the girl. "Did Gabe get to know any of the other attendees when he was hanging around?"

"I don't know," she said. "It's just a bunch of kids and you get paired up with people that you don't even know. The teachers are usually okay. Most of them are music teachers from either middle school or high school. There was one guy that was sort of a dork and he may have talked to Gabe. I wasn't paying attention."

"That's fine," Robert assured her. "You've been extraordinarily helpful. Really."

They left the Monroes and immediately headed toward Henry Wright's house. They knocked and when Judy answered, Robert was relieved to see a cup of coffee in her hand. He introduced Sawyer, and they sat.

"We'll only take a minute of your time. I know you told me that your son played the cornet. Do you recall if he attended band camp last summer at Grant Park? The citywide camp?"

She nodded. "Of course. That was his third year. I told you. He was very talented."

"Of course. Did he ever talk about anybody that he met at camp?"

She shook her head. "Not that I recall. I used to pick him up and there were kids everywhere."

WITHIN THE HOUR, Blaze had confirmed that both Johnnie Whitmore and Ben Johanson had attended the citywide band camp. The air in the station fairly hummed with energy. It was the first solid link among all four victims.

They'd discovered that while it was generally referred to as a citywide band camp, it was really hosted by a corporation out of Dallas, Texas, that put on similar events across the country. Schools helped distribute the information to students, payment was made directly to the company, and it subsequently secured space and staff to run the program. The company employed very few staff members on a full-time basis. Most were simply contracted locally for the three weeks that the camp lasted. It was good extra money for teachers who didn't work in the summers.

When they'd spoken to the senior administrator whose office was in Dallas, he'd assured them they would drop everything to prepare a list of attendees, teachers and all other staff.

"Come on, come on." Robert drummed his fingers on the desk and waited for Blaze to tell them that the list had come in her email.

It was two o'clock before they had anything of substance. The first list had over four hundred kids' names. The second list had the names of sixteen teachers. The detectives set aside the first list. The person who had contacted Henry Wright had posed as a representative of Stalwart Academy. He had to have appeared to be an adult or it wouldn't have been believable. There were ten men and six women on the list.

They didn't worry about the women.

These crimes had been brutal and would have required some strength to move the bodies. There were women who had that kind of strength but when time was short, you played the odds. Plus Judy Franconi Wright had said that her son referred to the recruitment representative as *he*.

"You and Sawyer take these five," Blaze said, handing Robert a list. "Wasimole and I'll take the rest."

The list had included the home address. They probably had that for tax forms. That was helpful. However, it did not have the school where the teacher worked.

Robert drove to the first address, that of a Mr. Burt Willow, while Sawyer worked the phone, trying to get all the information he could about the people on the list.

Everyone was working as fast as they could. Robert only hoped it would be fast enough.

Chapter Sixteen

"Hey look, it's Limpy."

Raoul didn't turn around. Damn. All he wanted was to get to band practice. One more hallway and he'd have been safe.

He was sick of these jerks. And he wasn't taking it anymore. Plus, he wanted some answers about Carmen's car.

He veered to his left, pushed hard on the crash bar of the exterior door, and was outside. He didn't stop to put his coat on. Instead, he carried it, stuffed under his arm. He had his backpack slung over that same shoulder and he carried his trombone case in his other hand.

The sidewalks were empty. He started walking faster. Footsteps, harsh against the concrete sidewalk, chased him. He smiled. These guys were in for the surprise of their lives.

He turned, holding his trombone in front of him.

"We been looking for you," JJ said.

"You're not avoiding us, are you?" Beau asked.

Raoul shook his head.

"How's your trumpet?"

"It's a trombone," Raoul said. "There's a difference. But you guys are probably too stupid to know that."

"Trombone. Ooh, la la." JJ pushed him on the shoulder and he fell back a couple steps.

"Stop it," he said.

JJ pushed again. And again. And Raoul let himself get propelled into the long alley that separated the block.

Beau pointed to a Dumpster about twenty feet away. "Last time he crawled down the hall like a dog. And don't dogs get their dinner out of the Dumpster?" He grabbed Raoul's right arm.

Raoul let his coat fall to the ground but he kept his backpack on his shoulder.

JJ opened the lid and pulled out three white garbage sacks. He ripped open the top of all three, dumping the contents on the ground.

Raoul thought he might get sick just from smelling it. Dirty diapers and food and wet newspapers. All kinds of other stuff he couldn't even identify.

Beau put both hands on Raoul's shoulders and pushed him down to his knees. "Get down, dog. Eat your dinner." Again he shoved Raoul, causing him to lose his balance. His shoulder hit the ground. Icy gravel surrounded the garbage container and it hurt.

The boys laughed, pushing each other around. "You know what my dog does?" said JJ. "He likes to roll around. Start rolling, doggy." He kicked Raoul in the stomach so hard it took Raoul's breath away.

Another kick. "Roll."

Raoul rolled in the garbage. He rolled back. Over and over again. Until the boys tired of the game.

Beau grabbed the back of his collar and lifted him up. "Don't make us come looking for you," he said. "Now give us your money."

"It's in my backpack," Raoul said.

"Then get it out. We don't have all day."

Raoul unzipped his backpack and pulled out the ten-dollar bill that Carmen had given to him that morning. "Here," he said.

"That's better," JJ said. He put the money in his pocket and started to walk away. Beau fell into step next to him.

Raoul reached into his backpack again and pulled out his gun. He stood up. The boys paid no attention to him. After all, he was just a little kid.

He held his arms out, both hands around the gun, just as Apollo had taught him. "Hey," he yelled.

Both boys turned, laughing. They stopped when they saw the gun.

"It's never going to stop, is it?" Raoul said, walking toward them. Wet newspaper clung to his pants. His arms, cut by the sharp rocks, bled. He didn't care.

"Come on, man. We were just having some fun. Put your gun away," JJ said, edging back a step.

"You're both just stupid jerks," Raoul yelled, waving his gun from one to the other.

They didn't move.

Raoul took another step toward them. His arms started to shake. They had to pay. The sons of bitches had to pay.

BURT WILLOW LOOKED about seventy. His apartment was at the end of a long, narrow hallway. He answered the door with the newspaper in his hand. He was probably five-two and a hundred and twenty pounds.

"May I help you?"

"Detectives Hanson and Montgomery," Robert said. They showed him their badges. "We understand that you were an instructor at the citywide band camp last year."

He smiled and his teeth were in better shape than the rest of his body. "For the past eight years. Ever since my wife died. Love those kids."

Sawyer and Robert made eye contact. Willow wasn't

physically strong enough to be their guy. But maybe he could help.

"We're trying to identify a couple people who were there," Sawyer said.

The man shook his head. "There are hundreds of kids. It would be hard to remember a couple."

"We're more interested in the staff," Sawyer clarified. "Did you know the other instructors?"

The man nodded. "Most of us had been teaching at the camp for years. Of course, every year there were a couple new folks. Most were real nice."

"Most?" Robert asked.

The man appeared uncomfortable. "Well, I don't like to talk bad about people. Never know when the good maker is going to call me up and I don't want my last deed to be something like that."

"Mr. Willow, this is important," Robert said. He nodded toward the newspaper that the man had folded under this arm. "Have you been following the story of the suspected serial killer?"

He nodded. "Of course. Terrible thing."

"We have reason to believe that all four of the victims were at last year's citywide band camp. Three played instruments and one was there visiting his sister who played."

He didn't respond, but Robert could tell that the news startled him. Robert didn't waste time. He reached into his shirt pocket and pulled out the list of instructor names. "Can you take a look at this list and identify the individuals who were new?"

Mr. Willow studied it. He pointed to a name. "This guy."

Barry Taylor. Excellent. Robert rubbed his hands together. "Anybody else?"

Mr. Willow ran a long finger down the list, then he did

it a second time. It took everything Robert had not to grab
the list and run out the door.

Time wasn't their friend.

It was already almost four.

"I think this was the other new guy."

Douglass Sparrow.

"You'd have thought the two of them might forge a
friendship but they were both loners. Just odd ducks."

They were almost back to their car when Robert's cell
phone rang. He saw the number and his heart did some
kind of funny spin in his chest.

"Hi, Carmen," he said.

"Are you busy?" she asked.

He could hear the tension in her voice. "What's wrong?"
he asked.

"I just got a call from Raoul's school. He's not at band
practice. Their winter concert is Thursday night and if a
kid misses this week, they don't get to play in the concert.
He's first chair and the band director really wants him at
the concert. I think that's why he made the extra effort to
call my cell phone."

"And you know that he went to school today?"

"We left at the same time. And remember, he sent me
a text telling me he'd arrived."

"Okay. Are you still at work?"

"No. I was in a cab on my way back to the office when
the call came in. I tried a couple times to reach Raoul on
his cell phone. When that didn't work, I couldn't go back
to the office. Plus, I was less than ten minutes from my
house. I was so sure that he'd be here."

"Were there any signs that he'd returned to the apartment at some point during the day?"

"No."

"Kids skip school stuff all the time," Robert said. "It's probably not a big deal."

There was a pause on the other line.

"Carmen?" he prompted.

"I searched his room. I found a box of bullets in his bottom drawer."

Speedy's Used Cars. He was surer than ever that the kid had been lying. What the hell else had he been lying about? "He has a gun?"

"Not that I know about," she said, her voice cracking. "It's not in his room. It's not in this apartment. I've looked everywhere."

He could tell she was close to tears. "Okay, honey. Don't worry. I'll go find him," Robert said.

"Just bring him home safe, Robert. That's all I ask."

Robert hung up, hoping like hell he wouldn't have to disappoint her.

"What's up?" Sawyer asked.

Robert explained the situation.

"Go," said Sawyer. "I've got this. You should probably start looking near his school. On the way there, you can drop me off and I'll grab my own car. I'll go check out Barry Taylor. We'll reconnect once you've found Raoul."

"I'm going to find him, right?" Robert asked. He could show his friend the fear that he'd had to hide from Carmen.

"You will. You're the best damn cop I know, Robert. If you can't find him, nobody can."

AFTER ROBERT DROPPED off Sawyer, he sped toward Mahoney High. School had been out for about twenty minutes. If Raoul had decided to duck out of band practice, then he could be several blocks away. Of course, if he'd gotten on a bus, then all bets were off. He could be anywhere.

Robert debated whether he should broadcast Raoul's description. Certainly more eyes looking for the kid was better, but the whole thing about Speedy's Used Cars stopped him from doing that. He didn't want any of his fellow cops looking too closely at Raoul right now.

He drove up and down the streets that would have been the logical ones for Raoul to have taken if he'd decided to walk home, all too aware that there was less than an hour of good daylight left. Once it got darker, it would be so much harder to find him.

Damn kid.

It was another ten minutes before he heard something come across the car radio that sparked his interest. He turned up the volume. Report of kids fighting in an alley. Between Parker Street and Venture Avenue.

Less than two blocks away.

Robert flipped on his lights but no siren.

When he got to the entrance of the alley, his heart almost stopped.

Raoul was standing in the middle of the icy alley and he had a gun pointed at two other boys who had their hands up and their backs against the alley wall.

If Raoul pulled the trigger, it would be cold-blooded murder.

Silently, Robert got out of his car. He was far enough away that nobody was paying him any attention. The boys with their hands in the air were staring at the gun. Raoul was staring at them.

"Come on, man. We were just kidding around." That was from the tallest boy. The shorter boy said nothing. It looked like he was about to fall down.

"Shut up," Raoul said. "Just shut the hell up."

Damn. He couldn't let Raoul shoot these other kids. His hand inched toward his own gun.

Carmen would hate him. She would never forgive him if he shot her brother.

He edged around his car and took a few steps into the alley. He had his hands in the air, his gun still in his side holster.

"Hey, Raoul," he said softly. "It's Robert. Put your gun down."

Raoul's head swirled toward Robert. "No," he yelled. "I'll kill you, too, if I have to."

"You're not going to kill anybody, Raoul."

"Stay away," Raoul yelled. "Don't come near me."

Robert stopped. "Fine. Just calm down. We can work this out."

"They made me roll around in the garbage like a dog."

Robert could see the boy's shoulders heaving and knew that he was close to breaking down. "They're the animals, then. Not you. Now put your gun away. You don't want to spend the rest of your life paying for this moment, Raoul. It's not worth it."

"They'll get away," Raoul cried. "And tomorrow it will be worse."

"They're not going anywhere. There are about six cops right behind me. The lady who lives upstairs saw everything. She's the one who called it in. Come on, Raoul, you're a good kid. Don't screw up your life."

Chapter Seventeen

The kid didn't put down the gun.

Robert knew he had one last shot. "Don't do this to Carmen, Raoul. Don't let her lose another brother. She won't be able to take it. She's given up everything for you. Don't make her regret it."

Raoul's arms were shaking so badly that Robert was scared the gun was going to go off accidentally.

"I think they might have messed with Carmen's car. They said stuff about her."

Now that got his attention.

"What kind of stuff?" he asked.

"We were just kidding," the taller one said. "We meant no disrespect, man."

Based on that comment, Robert could pretty much figure out what they'd said. That pissed him off. But if they were responsible for Carmen's car, Raoul was going to have to pull him off them.

"Carmen Jimenez's brake lines were cut. I want to know what you know about that." He watched their faces closely and he could tell that he'd surprised them.

"We sprayed the car with paint and JJ broke the window," one of them said. "We didn't do anything with any brake lines. I wouldn't even know how to cut a brake line."

"They might be lying," Raoul yelled.

He didn't think so. "If they're responsible," he said, "then they'll be prosecuted. Trust me on this, Raoul. They won't get away with it. It's not your job to take the law into your own hands."

It took another thirty seconds of painful silence before Raoul lowered his arms. Robert's heart started to beat again when the boy dropped to his knees and laid the gun on the ground. He pointed his finger at the boys. "Stay right where you are," he said. He got close enough to kick Raoul's gun far out of reach. Then he reached out his arm and grabbed the boy and pulled him tight into his body.

"It's going to be okay," Robert said, his voice close to Raoul's ear. "It's all going to be okay."

AN HOUR LATER, Raoul and Robert walked into the apartment. Carmen met them at the door. She wrapped her arms around her brother and held him.

Robert stepped back. He'd called her as soon as he could, but then it had taken another hour to get things straightened out. Beat cops had arrived within minutes of Raoul putting down his weapon. It still made Robert queasy to think how differently things might have turned out if another cop had arrived before he had.

Raoul might have been shot, might have been killed. Carmen might be mourning the loss of another brother.

"I'm sorry," Raoul said, wiping his nose with his sleeve.

"I know, honey. Tell me what happened." She led him over to the couch, where they sat, side by side. Robert took the chair and listened while Raoul told his sister about the bullying that he'd been enduring and how it had all culminated in the alley.

Robert had already heard the explanation once at the police station. Raoul's account of what happened in the alley matched what the eyewitness had called in. The other boys had started it. Raoul had attempted to finish it, once and for all.

"You should have told me," Carmen said, her voice soft.

"I couldn't. I knew you'd want to help but it would only get worse."

Carmen nodded. She was wise to the world of teenagers and probably realized that what he was saying was true.

"Then the stuff with your car happened and I knew they knew where we lived. They had to be stopped."

"I understand," she said. She turned to him. "Any reason to believe that they're responsible for the damage to my car?"

"They admitted to the spray paint and breaking the window. Flatly denied messing with the brakes. I think they were telling the truth. Plus, they were both in school on Monday. Every teacher takes attendance and they didn't miss any classes. I don't think they had an opportunity."

"So they are just a bunch of cowardly bullies," she said.

"Yeah. They won't bother him again," Robert said before she could ask. "I spoke with them and their parents. They're already lawyering up to make a plea bargain on the vandalism charge. I guess they're worried about football scholarships. Anyway, I made it very clear that if one hair on Raoul's head is harmed, that the police are going to be looking in their direction. I think both the kids and their parents got it."

She smiled at him. "Thank you," she whispered. Then she turned back to Raoul.

"Where did you ever get a gun?" Carmen asked.

Robert sat forward in his chair. This was the only part of Raoul's story that hadn't made sense.

"Some guy gave it to me," he said.

"Some guy?" Carmen questioned.

Raoul nodded.

"Some stranger just gave you a gun and you took it?" Carmen asked, her voice heavy with suspicion.

This time Raoul shrugged. "I gave him twenty bucks."

Robert forced himself to keep quiet. The gun had been registered to a Martin Olsen from Oak Park who had reported the gun being stolen from his car over a year ago. There were no prints on it besides Raoul's.

Was it possible that some guy had stolen it and resold it? Sure. Stolen goods got converted into money for drugs every day. It was the banking system that lots of people were familiar with.

But something just didn't seem right. And Raoul had not copped to being involved with the shooting at Speedy's Used Cars even though Robert had once again asked him about it.

Robert had called in a few favors with the state's attorney's office, and Raoul would not be prosecuted for possessing the stolen gun. JJ's and Beau's parents, likely wanting similar leniency for their sons, hadn't pushed in the opposite direction.

"I'm sorry, Carmen," Raoul said. "I never meant to worry you. Can I go to my room now?"

Carmen kissed his cheek and nodded. "We'll eat something in a little bit," she said.

Robert looked at the clock on the wall. Half past six. He'd left Sawyer a little more than two hours earlier.

He waited until he heard Raoul's door close. "I'd like to stay but I have to go," he said.

"Of course. Robert, I don't know how to thank you. I don't know exactly what happened in that alley but what I think is that I have my brother because of you."

He shook his head. "I didn't do that much. He really didn't want to kill those boys. He'd just boxed himself into a corner."

Carmen's eyes filled with tears. "A gun. In my wildest dreams, I'd never have considered that he'd have a gun. I'd like to get my hands on that person," she added.

"Nobody forced him to buy it," Robert said, keeping his tone neutral.

She frowned at him, then shook her head. "You're right. The responsibility lies with him. I know I'm too quick to cut him some slack. It's just that when I think of how close I came to losing him, I just can't stand it."

He wanted to tell her his suspicions about Speedy's Used Cars but he just couldn't. Not tonight. She'd been through enough. Robert reached for her hand. "It's over. Forget it."

"No. I need to say something. I lost one brother and today, I almost lost another one. I would have. Whether he'd killed those boys or they'd killed him. Either way, I'd have lost him."

"He's lucky to have you. In lots of families, this would have caused a huge blowout. But you listened. You gave him a chance to explain."

She sighed. "I wanted him to know that he could tell me anything. You know, it's a terrible burden to have to hide things from those who love you. I know, better than most."

Was she hiding something from him? Robert rubbed his chin. "I'm not sure I understand."

Carmen got up and started to pace around the room. "I made a mistake when I was not much older than Raoul. A big mistake."

She looked miserable. "Honey, that's in the past. You don't need to tell me."

She stopped. "I have to tell someone. I have to. It's killing me."

She was scaring him. "Okay. I'm listening. Please, just sit down. Talk to me."

She sat in the chair across from him. "My junior year of high school, I fell in love with a boy who loved football more than he loved me. When I got pregnant, all he could see was his hopes and dreams ending. He didn't want me or the baby."

The bastard. "What happened?"

"I couldn't tell my parents. I just couldn't. They'd worked so hard. Hector had already split off from the family, had gone his own way with the gang. That had almost killed them. I couldn't disappoint them again." She clasped her hands together. "My mother barely spoke English and my father worked at a minimum wage job. But still, they had dreams that their children would have a better life."

"What happened?"

"I hid my pregnancy. And every day, I tried to do something so that I'd lose the baby. I jumped off chairs. I turned cartwheels in gym class. I ran miles on the track at school. And eleven weeks into my pregnancy, my wish came true. I miscarried. I never told anybody."

His heart broke for the young girl she'd been. "I'm sorry there was nobody there for you," he said.

"It was almost exactly thirteen years ago. On January 18."

Robert did the calculation and realized that the day he'd knocked on Carmen's door, the day she'd been crying, had been the eighteenth. "You were just a kid, Carmen. A kid faced with an adult circumstance. And everything you did probably had nothing to do with you losing the baby. It probably just happened."

"I guess we'll never know. And that haunts me. I was a kid trying to handle an adult situation. Raoul had to make an adult decision today. I'm just thankful to you that he didn't have to do it on his own."

Neither of them would ever have to be on their own if he had his way. But now wasn't the time to tell her that.

"What I've learned over the years is that none of us can go back," Carmen continued. "Raoul can't go back to being the kid he was before he threatened to kill two boys. He can't go back. A person can only go forward. Thanks to you, he's got a future to look forward to."

She stood up. "I have a future to look forward to," she added. "Now maybe you understand a little better why I waited thirteen years to be with another man. In some sick way, I was punishing myself, repentance for my sins, if you will. I had done something very wrong. I denied myself pleasure or love because I didn't think I deserved it."

He felt his soul rip for the youth she'd lost. "You so deserve it," he said.

She rubbed the back of her hand across his cheek. "I know. It's amazing. I know it now. You helped me see it."

He wished he didn't have to go. But now that they had a lead on the serial killer, everybody would work all night if necessary. He stood up and put his coat on. "I'm sorry, but I really do have to go. I'm needed back at work. I want to talk to you about something but now isn't the right time. I just can't do it right now."

"I understand," she said and wrapped her arms around his neck. She pulled his face toward her and soundly kissed him.

And he let himself drink in all the goodness that was Carmen Jimenez.

When they stopped kissing, he rested his forehead against hers. "Now I really wish I didn't have to go to work."

"We could go out in the hallway and make out again," she said, humor in her tone.

"Don't tempt me," he said. He lifted his head. "I don't

want to put a damper on things but you know, we still don't know who messed with your brakes. You and Raoul need to continue to be vigilant about your safety."

"We will. We aren't going anywhere tonight. No need to worry about us. Mrs. Minelli is taking Raoul to school. I'll catch a cab to work."

He kissed her again. "Okay. Good night."

BY THE TIME Robert caught up with Sawyer, he'd interviewed Barry Taylor and two other staff members who lived in the same general vicinity. "What do you think?" Robert asked.

"I think Mr. Willow was right," Sawyer said. "Barry Taylor is an odd duck. Well, he was more right than you might imagine."

"I don't get it."

"We got his permission to look around his house, and I think maybe the only thing he takes vengeance on *is* ducks. He carves them, paints them, mosaic-tiles them, you get the picture. Every room of his house, there are ducks. The artwork in his house, all ducks."

"So maybe that's why he didn't play well with the other instructors? They were human?"

Sawyer smiled. "It's a possibility. I have to admit, when I saw the carving tools, I got a little excited, given that our guy likes to take home body parts for trophies. That's why I asked permission to search. The guy didn't even hesitate."

"Could he be doing the killing somewhere else?"

"Of course. But here's the kicker. He doesn't have a car. He said he didn't, that he didn't even have a driver's license. I was able to verify that with the State. I also took the time to talk to a few of his neighbors after I left, and they have never seen him in a car. He rides his bike everywhere."

"Our guy has a car or use of a car," Robert said, shaking his head. "He's spreading bodies out all over the city. Not doing that on a bike."

"I think we can scratch odd guy number one off the list. Anyway, the other two staff members that I spoke to seemed pretty normal. One has a teenage boy and I could tell the killings had been especially upsetting for him. The other had been traveling recently and was happy to show us his passport, which verified that he wasn't even in the country when the killings started. What was interesting was that when I asked both of them if there was somebody on staff who had stood out as odd or different, they both said Douglass Sparrow. That he was a real loner."

"Maybe he was afraid that Barry Taylor was going to start carving him. You know, ducks today, sparrows tomorrow," Robert suggested.

Sawyer rolled his eyes. "Keep your day job," he said. "Come on. Let's go. It's going to be a long night."

DOUGLASS SPARROW LIVED three blocks from where victim number three had been found. That didn't necessarily mean anything since all the other victims had been found miles away.

They knocked on the door of the small brick home and waited. They both had flashlights out and on. It had been dark for hours, and Sparrow evidently didn't believe in porch lights. The temperature had once again dropped and was now hovering around zero.

"I'm going to go check the back," Robert said. He walked between the houses, which had been built so damn close together that if neighbors both leaned out their windows, they could pass the proverbial cup of sugar.

The back door was locked. Robert pounded on the door and waited a couple minutes. The night was quiet otherwise and he didn't hear or see anything that gave him any indication that somebody was home.

Maybe Sparrow was at the grocery store or a movie?

Or maybe he was scouting for his next victim?

Robert circled back to Sawyer. "Let's talk to some neighbors."

The neighbor on the right was a woman in her sixties. In her living room, there was an ironing board and a treadmill, both set up in front of the flat-screen television. She was obviously a multitasker.

They did introductions. Olivia Borsk was her name, and she was a widow.

When they asked about Douglass Sparrow, she looked satisfied. It wasn't the reaction they'd expected.

"It's about time you got here," she said.

"Time?" Robert asked.

"I've called three times. That's twice more than I should have needed to."

"What did you call about, Mrs. Borsk?" Sawyer asked.

"His sidewalk, for goodness' sake. He never shovels it. Only house between here and the grocery store that doesn't do what he's supposed to. Forces me to walk out into the street and that's wrong."

Robert and Sawyer shared a look. "Have you ever spoken to Mr. Sparrow about your concerns?"

The woman huffed. "Two *s*s and two *r*s."

"What?" Sawyer asked.

"Douglass Sparrow. Two *s*s and two *r*s. When he introduces himself, that's what he says to everybody. Pompous ass."

"Does Mr. Sparrow have much company?" Robert asked.

"No. But then again, he's rarely here."

"What do you mean?" Robert asked.

"What I mean is that the man is only here about half the time. I know because his car is old and loud and I have to turn up my television to hear the news when he pulls up. Maybe if he was here more often, he could do the sidewalk. Or maybe, if you people talked to him, he would do the sidewalk."

You people. Robert could not look at Sawyer. Otherwise, he would bust a gut and the woman would have a whole other reason to be calling the police department.

"Yes, of course," Robert said. "What kind of car does Mr. Sparrow drive?"

"Black and noisy. Two doors. Mildred and Ben, his folks, bought it for him when he was in high school."

"Does Mr. Sparrow work out of town? Is that why he's gone?" Sawyer asked.

The woman shook her head. "I don't even think he works. He inherited this house from his parents last year. The Sparrows died in a car accident, poor things. At least they went together. Anyway, they were always saying that he was going to be a famous musician someday. I felt sorry for them. They couldn't even see the fact that their son was as odd as a three-dollar bill."

"You don't think he's been successful as a musician?"

The woman shrugged. "He was bagging groceries at the supermarket down the street up until his parents' deaths. That doesn't seem all that successful to me."

Robert stood up. "Thank you. You've been very helpful."

They were halfway out the door when Mrs. Borsk called after them. "What about the sidewalk?"

"If we see Mr. Sparrow, we'll make sure we mention it," said Robert.

Once they were back in the car, Sawyer rubbed his hands together. "I think this could be our guy. The music fits. And lots of times, something sets these idiots off. Maybe that was his parents' deaths? Maybe there wasn't anybody left who believed in him? The only thing I don't get is that he's rarely home. Where the hell do you think he is?"

Robert shook his head as he pulled away from the curb. "That's the weird part. Let's figure out what he's driving," he said. He picked up his cell phone and when the call was answered, he gave them the pertinent details.

"I need information on a car owned by either Douglass Sparrow or Mildred or Ben Sparrow." He rattled off the home address and hung up.

It didn't take long for him to get a return call. Robert listened and nodded. "Okay, thanks. Put out a BOLO for that vehicle with instructions to not apprehend or approach. I just want to know where it is."

Robert turned to Sawyer. "Black Mercury Cougar, 1995."

Chapter Eighteen

They got a judge to order a search warrant for Douglass Sparrow's home.

It didn't take long to search. There was lots of old furniture that his parents had probably had for years. He had a few clothes in the closet and dresser drawers. Some toiletries in the bathroom and a jar each of mustard and pickle relish in his refrigerator.

"Sparrow must eat out all the time," Robert said. He opened cupboards and found a few plates and two cups.

Sawyer stood in the middle of the kitchen with his hands on his hips. "It's almost as if…"

"He doesn't really live here," Robert said, finishing the sentence. "Which matches what Mrs. Borsk said that he's hardly ever around."

"So why do you keep a house but you don't live in it?" Sawyer asked.

"Because where you're really living is a secret," Robert said.

"Gay?" Sawyer asked.

Robert shook his head. "Parents both dead. No high-profile job. Little risk if the secret gets out."

"Into something illegal?" was Sawyer's next guess.

Robert met his partner's eyes. "Like luring young boys to your place and then killing them?"

"Bingo," Sawyer said.

Robert rubbed his hand across his face. They were running out of time. "We need this guy's bank account. Maybe he's writing out rent checks. And his IRS records, too. Maybe there are earnings from another employer."

"It's late," Sawyer said.

"Looks as if we're going to have to get a few people out of bed," Robert answered, already pulling out his phone.

WHEN CARMEN GOT up on Wednesday morning, she carefully opened Raoul's bedroom door. He was still asleep. Had pushed off his covers at some point and he lay sprawled in the single bed, dressed in an old T-shirt and sweats.

He looked very young and vulnerable.

And he'd threatened to kill two people yesterday.

The two images were so jarringly different that it still made her head hurt.

Thank God Robert had been there. In his calm way, he'd been able to intervene and he had saved lives. He'd certainly given Raoul his life back.

Robert had wanted to ask her something but had said that he'd wait for a better time. What the heck?

Maybe he wanted her to go away with him? That day after the movie they'd had that ridiculous conversation about tropical vacations. Aruba? Bermuda? The Cayman Islands?

If he asked, would she go?

Could she leave Raoul?

Two weeks ago, she'd have said no. But now, she'd had a taste of living, a taste of feeling whole as she shattered in a man's arms.

She'd had a taste of loving Robert. So if he asked, she'd

make sure that Raoul was in Liz and Sawyer's capable hands and she'd go.

She opened a cupboard and pulled coffee out. Got a pot started and walked back to the bathroom for her shower. By the time she'd finished and dried her hair, she could hear Raoul moving around in the apartment.

She got dressed, pulled her hair back into a low ponytail and put on a little makeup. She'd just finished with mascara when her phone rang.

It was Robert. She smiled at herself in the mirror.

"Hi," she said.

"Good morning," he said. "I just wanted to check in and make sure everything was okay."

She'd been taking care of herself and Raoul for a long time. Had been pretty proud of that fact. Was it wrong that it felt so good to finally have someone who cared about them, maybe even worried about them? "We're fine," she said. "Uneventful night. Mrs. Minelli should be here any minute."

"Look, I wish I knew what the day was going to bring. Maybe we could catch a late dinner together?"

He sounded wistful. And tired. "Did you work late?" she asked.

"All night," he admitted. "I caught a catnap this morning in my chair."

"Oh, Robert." If anyone thought police work was glamorous, they didn't understand it.

"We're getting close," he said. "Can't say much more than that but I think we're on the right track."

"Good luck," she said.

"Just be careful today, Carmen. Frank Sage is a wild card. We can't prove that he messed with your brakes but my gut tells me that he's a bad guy. I've got somebody keeping an eye on him, and he's already been to his coffee shop and he's on his way to work. I think you'll be okay."

She felt very warm inside. Robert Hanson was watching out for her.

"Call me later," she said. "Even if it's really late."

She heard his breath catch and it made her feel pretty powerful. "I will."

By the time she got to the kitchen, Raoul was at the table with a bowl of cereal in front of him.

But he wasn't eating. He was just staring at his hands, which were cupped around his bowl.

"Morning," she said. She poured herself a cup of coffee.

"Morning," he answered.

He looked tired, and she suspected that he hadn't slept well. Was he worried about school? About the two boys who were no doubt going to be there that morning?

"I don't think those boys will bother you," she said. "Remember what Robert said?"

Raoul nodded. "I'm not worried about that."

But he was clearly worried about something. She sat down at the table and sipped her coffee. After about two minutes, Raoul looked up from his cupped hands.

"I wasn't honest with you last night," he said. "You were great about everything and I couldn't even tell you the truth."

Her heart sped up. There was more?

"Then maybe you better take another stab at it," she said, hoping that she sounded more confident than she was.

He looked her in the eyes. "I didn't pay somebody twenty dollars for the gun," he said. "Someone gave it to me."

"Who?"

"This guy. He's about your age, I guess. He says his name is Apollo. He was a friend of Hector's."

Hector's. She felt her heart start to beat even faster. All of Hector's friends had been bad news. She'd known many of them because he was just two years older. She'd never heard of anyone named Apollo.

"How long have you known this man?"

"Not long. He said that Hector had asked him to watch out for me. He wanted me to have Hector's gun."

Hector had had a gun. She'd seen it in the waistband of his shorts just days before he'd died. The people he hung with all had guns. But Hector's had been recovered from his body, confiscated by the police.

Was it possible that he'd had another gun?

Perhaps. But after all these years for it to surface with some lame story about Hector asking for his baby brother to be watched over seemed preposterous.

No way.

"Apollo said that he met you a couple times. He knew your name."

He was going to know more than her name by the time she got through with him. What kind of trash gave a gun to a fifteen-year-old?

"There's something else," he said. He looked even more miserable. "You're going to be so mad at me."

He was scaring her. "I may be angry," she admitted. "But you need to tell me everything or I can't help."

"The other night, I used the gun to shoot out some windshields at a used car place. Speedy's. I'm not exactly sure how many cars."

Her heart sank. Shooting out car windows.

He'd committed a crime. Her brother was a criminal. "When? How?"

"On Sunday night. I snuck out while you and Alexa were busy in the kitchen. I met Apollo there. He wanted to teach me how to shoot."

She was going to rip this guy's head off.

"We're going to have to tell the police," she said. The idea of Raoul having a police record made her want to throw up, but they had to do what was right.

"I think they know," Raoul said, tears in his eyes. "At least I think Robert does."

What? How could that be? "Why would you think that?"

"He's asked me about it a couple times."

Robert had reason to believe that her brother had a gun and had used that gun to commit a crime and yet he'd said nothing. She felt sick and hollow and terribly betrayed.

He knew that Raoul was her life.

She was such an idiot. She'd gotten blinded by the attention and she'd lost track of what was important.

Raoul. He was important. And he'd gotten himself into a bunch of trouble.

And now he needed her help.

"Do you know how to contact Apollo?" she asked.

"I'm supposed to meet him at eight o'clock this morning, outside my school."

"I'm going with you," she said. She got up and carefully pushed her chair in. Her bones felt very brittle. "I don't believe that he was a friend of Hector's. He certainly wasn't looking out for you when he gave you a gun so that you could vandalize someone's property. What you did was wrong," she said.

"I know. It's all I can think about. I'm so sorry, Carmen."

She could forgive Raoul. He was a teenager who had gotten caught up in something that was bigger than him. It was harder to forgive Robert. He was an adult and he hadn't been honest with her.

"What about Mrs. Minelli?" Raoul asked. "She's driving this morning."

"I'll call her," Carmen said. "I'll let her know that I'm taking you to school. Once I tell Apollo that he is never to contact you again, then we're going to the police. You're going to tell them everything. There's going to be consequences to your actions, Raoul. You understand that, don't you?"

He nodded. "I just want this to be over with."

"Me, too," she said. "Finish getting ready," she added, as she walked back to her bedroom. Once inside the door, she pressed her hands to her eyes.

She would not cry. She would not.

She and Raoul would get through this.

The same way they'd gotten through everything else. Together.

She picked up her cell phone, which she always kept on her nightstand during the night. She punched in Robert's number. She was relieved when it went right to voice mail.

"It's Carmen," she said. "You...you should have told me, Robert. You should have told me about Speedy's and your suspicions about Raoul. I deserved to know that my brother had a gun. I deserved the truth from you." She took a big breath. "Don't call me again."

WHEN THE CAB pulled to the corner, Carmen tossed a ten at the driver and opened her door. The cab had been late picking them up, plus they'd hit some slow traffic. She'd been impatient to get here, to meet the man who claimed to be Hector's friend who had lured her fifteen-year-old brother into being a criminal.

She wrapped her scarf tight around her neck. Raoul slid out of the cab and slammed the door shut. "Do you see him?" Carmen asked. The sidewalk was heavy with human traffic, people all bundled up, walking with their heads down to avoid the wind.

She looked at her watch. Seven minutes after eight. He should be here.

For the first time, Carmen got nervous. It was broad daylight and there were lots of people around but still her gut was telling her that something was wrong. She heard Raoul's cell phone buzz. He pulled it out. It was a text.

"It's him," he said.

"He has your cell phone number?" she asked. Then she waved her hand. "Never mind. That's not important. What does it say?"

"Be there soon."

They weren't waiting. They were going to the police and telling them everything. Then they could find Apollo and deal with him. "Come on," she said. "Let's go."

Damn, she wished she had her car. There were no cabs. She walked toward Mahoney High, feeling that she'd be safe there.

They'd walked less than thirty feet before a man emerged from the bushes that lined the street. He fell into step next to them. They were three abreast on the wide sidewalk, her, then Raoul, then the man. She pulled on Raoul's sleeve, wanting to get him away from the man.

"Not so fast, pretty sister," he said.

She stopped and looked at the man. He had dark hair pulled back into a ponytail. His skin was very pale. She did not recognize him. If he'd been a friend of Hector's, he was one that she'd never met.

He was probably five-eight and a hundred and sixty pounds. Not an overly big guy. But she realized that didn't matter when she saw that he had a very deadly looking gun in his hand and it was pointed at Raoul.

"We want nothing to do with you," she said, hating that her voice was shaking. "You just go your way and we'll go ours and we'll forget that we ever saw each other."

"And spoil the fun?" he asked. "I don't think so. You're an unexpected complication but certainly not one that I can't deal with." He motioned with his index finger. "Step through the bushes. There's a black car. Get in the driver's side. If you make one wrong move, you're going to have another dead brother."

It was crazy. There were people on the sidewalks, on both sides of the street. Mostly kids. Some adults. But nobody was paying attention to them. They were just hurrying to school or to work.

She looked in the man's eyes. They were completely devoid of emotion. She wanted to refuse, to tell him to go to hell.

Raoul could be dead before she finished her sentence.

She turned and started walking, and she could hear Raoul and the man behind her.

Chapter Nineteen

With the exception of the short nap, Robert had been awake for more than thirty hours. They had pored through Sparrow's banking records. He had over two hundred thousand dollars in the bank. It had all come from one deposit that occurred about thirty days after his parents' deaths.

Life insurance proceeds, most likely.

He wrote out a few checks, for utilities and property taxes, for the property they had searched. Each month he also withdrew a thousand dollars in cash. Maybe he spent that on gas and food and all the other things that ate up dollars, but there was no way to know.

During the night, teams of detectives had spoken to every one of Douglass Sparrow's former coworkers and his neighbors, trying to glean any kernel of information. That hadn't made them very popular. And in normal circumstances, they would have never woken people up in the middle of the night to ask questions.

But these were not normal circumstances.

They were waiting to hear that another dead boy had been found.

"We need to start on the students," Sawyer said.

There were over four hundred names on the list. It was like looking for a needle in a haystack. "We need to separate the boys from the girls."

Tasha, three desks away, held up a sheet of paper. "Done."

Robert smiled. "You need a raise."

"Got that right. One hundred and ninety boys. Sorted alphabetically."

Robert scanned the list. About halfway down, a name jumped off the page.

Raoul Jimenez.

Holy hell.

He needed to call Carmen, tell her what was going on. He picked up his phone, which was charging on his desk. He saw that he had a voice mail message and realized that his phone was on vibrate.

He listened to the message.

And his heart sank.

I deserved to know that my brother had a gun. I deserved the truth from you.

He'd talked to her just thirty minutes earlier. Everything had been fine. Now she was so angry her words were clipped. *Don't call me again.*

That wasn't going to happen. He punched in her number. It rang four times before it went to voice mail. "Carmen, it's Robert. I got your message. Listen, I don't know what happened but we need to talk. Before you or Raoul do anything, you need to call me. Please." He hung up.

He dialed Carmen's office phone and left a similar message.

By now, Sawyer had scanned the list, seen Raoul's name, and was dialing Liz's number. From the side of the conversation that Robert could hear, he knew that Liz had not yet seen Carmen.

Both last night and this morning, Carmen had said that Raoul was getting a ride to school with Jacob's mother. He had that kid's phone number. Carmen had given it to him.

He scrolled through his phone and pushed the number. It rang three times before it was answered.

"Hello."

"Is this Jacob Minelli?"

"Yeah."

"My name is Detective Robert Hanson. I'm a friend of Carmen and Raoul Jimenez. Is Raoul with you?"

"No. Why would he be?"

"Your mother drove you both to school."

"Nope. Carmen called this morning and said that she was taking Raoul to school. I've got to go. Class starts in a minute and if you get caught with a phone, they take it away from you."

Robert hung up and shoved back his desk chair. He started running for the door. He stopped halfway through the station and yelled back at Tasha. "Every car in the vicinity of Mahoney High needs to be on the lookout for a woman, Hispanic, five-three, a hundred and ten pounds, likely wearing a blue cape. Also, a Hispanic fifteen-year-old boy, five feet, ninety pounds, likely wearing a red jacket."

"You want them picked up?" Tasha asked.

"Hell, yes." He wanted them safe, in his arms.

CARMEN GRIPPED THE steering wheel of the old car, unwilling to let the man see that she was shaking. He'd made Raoul climb in back and he sat in front, twisted in his seat, his gun aimed at Raoul.

Carmen didn't intend for them to be in the car long. The first cop she saw, she was going to run into the squad car. Hard enough that the guy would get spooked and run but not so hard that either she or Raoul were seriously hurt.

"Turn here," he said.

They'd gone less than two blocks. She didn't have a choice. She turned.

Halfway down the alley, he motioned for her to make a quick right. She did and found herself in a small space, just big enough for the car. It looked as if many years ago it had been a small courtyard. There were scraggly, bare branches curving upward on the brick walls. She could see patches of dirt underneath the mostly snow-covered ground.

There was a back door on the bottom level. Above it, there was a sign. Augusta Custom Framing. It didn't look as if anybody had used the back door in some time.

There was a set of wooden stairs that rose from the ground up to the second level. He pointed at them. "Let's go."

She waited for Raoul to get out of the car. She grabbed his hand and squeezed it.

"Sweet," said the man. Then he pushed her forward.

At the top of the landing, he handed her a key and made her unlock the door. It opened into a kitchen that had an old tile floor, a small sink and an avocado-green stove. It smelled like bacon and she could see a dirty plate in the sink that was smeared with egg yolk.

The bastard had had breakfast before he'd come to the school. That, more than anything that had happened so far, told her that they were dealing with someone who had no conscience.

"In there," he said.

She walked into the living room. There was a couch and one chair. There was a table in the corner.

On it was a stack of red handkerchiefs.

And she remembered the conversation that night at Liz and Sawyer's house. *The victims have all been found with red handkerchiefs in their mouths. Shows an arrogance*

*on his part—that he's so confident that he won't be caught
that he can afford to leave clues at the scene.*

She looked at her brother. He looked scared to death.
Oh, Raoul, what have we done?

THERE WAS NO sign of Carmen or Raoul. He hadn't really
expected to see any. School had already started. If they
were on time, the cab would have already dropped Raoul
off and Carmen would be on her way to work.

Robert tried her cell phone again. It went straight to
voice mail. He didn't leave one.

Answer your damn phone, Carmen.

He parked in a no-parking zone and pushed the buzzer
on the school door. It felt as if it had been a lifetime since
he'd been at the school but it was really just forty-eight
hours ago. Then he'd been here to bust Raoul's chops about
Speedy's Used Cars. Now, he just wanted to hug the kid
and celebrate that he and his sister were okay.

But he wasn't going to get that chance, he realized,
when the school secretary confirmed that Raoul's homeroom teacher had already reported him as absent from
class.

Now what?

Robert walked out of the office and leaned against the
gray metal lockers. Now what?

He looked up. Three boys were walking down the hall.
One was looking at his phone, and the other one was laughing at something his friend was saying.

Friend.

What was it that Carmen had said? Jacob Minelli and
Raoul had been best friends since third grade.

Robert strode back into the office. "I need to see Jacob
Minelli. Right now."

The woman didn't hesitate. "I'll have to look up his first

period," she said. She typed a few letters into her computer. Then she pressed a button. "Mrs. Black, can you please send Jacob Minelli to the office."

"Yes," came the static-filled response.

Robert waited impatiently, watching out the windows of the office. He saw a kid come down the steps at the far end of the hallway and recognized him from the photos in Carmen's apartment.

He met him halfway.

"I'm Detective Robert Hanson," he said.

"Are you still looking for Raoul?" the kid asked.

Robert nodded. "Neither Carmen nor Raoul are answering their phones. Raoul never made it to school."

"Look, I'd like to help but Raoul and I are sort of not talking to one another right now. I don't think he's going to call me."

That didn't match what Carmen had said. "Why?"

The kid didn't say anything.

"Listen, Jacob. Raoul may in trouble. Carmen, too. I need the truth and I need it now."

"He's been doing some crazy stuff lately."

"Like what?"

"Like carrying a gun. He showed it to me."

"Did he tell you where he got the gun?" Robert asked.

Jacob nodded. "Some guy named Apollo gave it to him. What kind of name is that?"

Apollo. The God of Music.

Robert pressed a hand against his stomach. His coffee was about to make a return appearance. "Did you ever meet Apollo?"

The kid shook his head.

Robert wanted to slam his fist into the locker. "Okay, thanks," he said.

Jacob stared at him. "I may have seen his car," he said.

"I had a birthday party. And Raoul got mad and left before everybody else. I saw him going and ran out to stop him. He's been my best friend for a long time and I didn't want to fight with him. He was about a block ahead of me when I saw a car pull up and offer him a ride."

"What kind of car?"

"An old black one like my uncle used to drive."

"You get a license plate?" Robert asked, hoping like hell his luck was about to change.

The kid shook his head.

"Make or model?" Robert asked.

"I'm pretty sure it was an old Mercury Cougar. They have a real distinct style."

ROBERT'S HANDS WERE shaking when he pulled out his cell phone and punched up his boss. When Lieutenant Fischer answered, Robert didn't waste any time.

"I need all the street camera video from around Mahoney High School this morning. We're looking for Douglass Sparrow's black Mercury Cougar and—" Robert stopped and drew in a deep breath "—I think it's possible that he has Raoul and Carmen Jimenez."

Lieutenant Fischer was silent for a long minute. Then he asked, "Are you okay?"

Hell, no. He was a wreck. So scared that his mind seemed to have stopped working.

"Don't worry about me," he said.

"Be careful," his boss said. "Keep your head in the game."

His head, his heart. Everything was in the game. Because Carmen was everything, meant everything.

She'd sounded so angry.

He'd been wrong to hide his suspicions from her. Realized that now. Maybe that whole horrible scene in the alley with Raoul and those two boys would have never happened if he'd been more forthcoming.

No wonder she didn't want him to call her again.

The diamond ring felt heavy in his pocket. What the hell had he done?

"Have you talked to Sawyer?" Robert asked.

"Just got off the phone with him. He tracked down a former coworker of Sparrow's from his grocery store bagging days. Said that the guy was always talking about going to some fancy music school and that he was going to be famous someday."

But something had derailed those plans and he'd found himself bagging groceries and teaching music in the summer to a bunch of sweaty middle-schoolers.

And somewhere along the way, he'd decided to start killing them.

"WHO ARE YOU?" Carmen asked.

"Didn't Raoul tell you? I'm Apollo."

"You weren't a friend of Hector's," she accused.

The man smiled. He was sprawled in the chair, his butt halfway down, his legs extended. She'd have thought he was relaxed if he didn't have the gun pointed straight at Raoul.

"Ah, so he did tell you about me." The man looked satisfied. "Brilliant, don't you think? The internet makes everything so easy. Birth records, death records, addresses. After I met Raoul at band camp last year, it was easy to find out more about the Jimenez family. Hector's stabbing didn't make front-page news of the paper but there was a nice little article in the archives."

She remembered that article. Remembered how her mother had carefully cut it out and put it in the Bible that she kept on her nightstand. And Carmen suspected that every night until her mother died just two years later, the woman had prayed over it.

It made her furious to think that this man had used it to target Raoul, to make him think that he was somehow closer to the brother that he'd never had the chance to know.

"You bastard," she said. "You won't get away with this."

He laughed. "Of course I will. It's perfect. The police will never find me here. There's no record of me here. I give the man who owns the frame shop cash every month. He's happy because his wife doesn't know he has the money and I'm happy because everything is in his name. I don't exist."

"The police know more than what was reported in the paper. They're very close."

The corner of his mouth raised up in a sneer. "I'm not the bad person here," he said. "I'm saving them. From a lifetime of disappointment. From a lifetime of never realizing the dream. Because the dream is an illusion. A damn illusion."

He stood up and started pacing around the room. "They fill your head with all kinds of lies. And you start making plans. And then one day, they say, ha-ha, we were only kidding. You're not that talented. You're nothing."

He took two big steps toward her, leaned into her face, and yelled. "I am not nothing."

"Of course you aren't," she said. She needed to calm him down. "What instrument did you play?"

He cocked his head. "The piano, the oboe, the drums. The music just came to me. I heard it in my sleep."

"I bet you were very good," she said.

"My parents were proud of me," he said, sounding like a little boy. "But then they gave up, too. Said that I needed to do something with my life. That was wrong of them. You should never give up on your child."

She didn't know what to say to that. It didn't seem to matter because he was on a roll.

He smiled at her. "You know they died in a car accident. Their brakes failed, just like yours. But you didn't die. That was really too bad."

She heard Raoul's gasp but she didn't look at him. "So you tampered with my brakes. Why?"

"It was Raoul's fault. He was pulling away. He was going to choose you over me. I couldn't have that. I'd worked too hard on him. He was tougher than the other boys."

She licked her lips.

"Do you want to hear about them?" he asked.

She needed to buy time. To figure a way out of this mess. "Yes. Yes, I would."

Raoul was looking at her as if she were crazy.

Apollo smiled. "Johnnie Whitmore was the first one. Actually, I thought he would be the only one. But then it was so nice that I had to do it again."

She was going to throw up. Swallowing hard, she nodded, as if she was really interested in what he was saying.

"Johnnie wasn't very respectful to me. I was his teacher. The expert. He was lucky to have me at that crappy little camp. You know, he was the only one of the boys who remembered me. Of course, my hair was different and I didn't have these contact lenses then. But he knew me right away. I told him that I was making a CD. He wanted to be part of that. Suddenly, I had value."

She risked a glance at Raoul. He hadn't known about the red handkerchiefs, but he'd figured out who Apollo was. She could see it on his face. She wanted to reach out to assure him that she was going to get them out of there.

"But you decided to do it again?" she said.

He nodded. "Ben Johanson was the easiest of them all. I told him that I was his father. I told him that I had always loved his mother and that once I got to know him a little better, I was going to be back in his mother's life, in his life. The poor kid just wanted a dad. He hung out here several times before it had to end."

"Of course," Carmen said.

"Gabe Monroe needed to be taught a lesson. He had no respect for the music. He came to camp like he had a right to be there. I saw him sitting behind his sister's drums, bragging that he was going to be at band camp the next year. He had no idea the work that it takes, no idea of the sacrifice a musician makes. Let's just say he had stopped boasting by the time I finished him off."

Carmen glanced at her watch. It had been almost twenty minutes since Apollo had stepped out of the bushes.

"Henry Wright was almost as gullible as Ben Johanson. On the camp enrollment sheet, there was a question about musical aspirations. Henry had answered that he wanted to go to Stalwart Academy. I never forgot that because I, too, wanted to go to Stalwart. Once he believed I was trying to recruit him, he was more than willing to visit my home. I don't think he was very impressed, however." He motioned with his hand, as if he were showing off a prize property. "I guess we'll never know, will we?"

"I guess not," she said.

Apollo walked over and put his hand on Raoul's head. Raoul flinched and it took everything Carmen had to stay in her chair. "You haven't asked why I picked Raoul."

Could she bear this? "Why?"

"Because he reminds me of myself. He works hard, does all the right things. It won't be enough. Just like it wasn't enough for me. And of course, I've already told you how I got to know him. It was my most brilliant effort to date."

"If Raoul reminds you of yourself then you must care about him. You can still let us go. It's not too late for you to do the right thing."

He stood up. "I am doing the right thing," he yelled. Then he grabbed her arm and pulled her up from the couch.

FROM THE TRAFFIC command center, they fed images from the street surveillance cameras into the computer screen in his car. Lieutenant Fischer was back at the station watching the same images. Sawyer was en route to join Robert.

The blocks near Mahoney High were highly traveled business districts. Fortunately, with the fresh snow, traffic was light and moving slower than usual. In this particular area, they had cameras at every intersection. So, while there were portions of the street where activity could not be viewed, they could easily track movement in and out of the area.

Because they had the approximate time and location, it took them just minutes to find the car. A black '95 Mercury Cougar. It cruised through one intersection but not the next. There were no side streets between the two intersections.

"He parked somewhere in this area," Robert said, pointing to the map on the side of his screen. "Keep the tape going," he said.

They kept watching, fast-forwarding when they could. "Stop," Robert said. "I think that's him. Get closer," he said.

The technician running the tape zoomed in.

Oh, no. Robert was grateful he was sitting or his legs might have given out. The camera angle was good and they could see Carmen driving. She looked terrified. Apollo was sitting next to her, half-turned in his seat.

They could not see Raoul in the backseat but Robert was confident that he was there.

They tracked the car through the next two intersections. The equipment was sophisticated enough that they could calculate that Carmen was driving twenty-eight miles per hour.

Then suddenly, the car disappeared.

Robert put his finger on the screen. "I'm less than a block from there."

"Wait for backup," Lieutenant Fischer instructed.

Like hell. Robert started driving.

When he saw the alley, he knew that was where they had disappeared to. He drove down, stopping when he saw the black car pulled into the small area that might once have been a delivery area but now was home to garbage containers and just enough space for one car.

He got out of his car. He took off his winter coat and replaced it with a bulletproof vest. Street level, there was a back door to a custom framing shop. There were no tracks leading up to it. The steep steps up to the second floor were a different story. Several people had walked them.

He clicked on his radio, gave the dispatcher his position and said, "I'm going in." He clicked off before anyone could tell him not to.

He put his hand in his pocket and touched the ring case. It felt warm and solid. He took that as a good sign.

He started up the steps and was at the landing when he heard Carmen scream.

He kicked the door open and went in low.

Apollo was across the room, a knife in one hand, a gun in the other. Raoul had his hands spread on the coffee table. He was crying. Carmen, tied to a chair, watched in terror.

"Police," he yelled. "Put down your—"

The bullet hit him in the shoulder, knocking him back. Searing, white-hot pain spread through his arm. He stayed upright and returned fire. Three shots.

And he saw the man go down.

Raoul ran to his sister. They were both alive.

"Robert?" Carmen said.

"I'm going to be okay," he said, right before he blacked out.

ROBERT WOKE UP in a hospital bed. His arm hurt like hell and he felt sick to his stomach. He tried to move but stopped quickly when pain rocketed through him.

"Good afternoon, Mr. Hanson." A young man dressed in dark blue scrubs was five feet away, his fingers clicking on a keyboard. "I'm Keith, your nurse. How do you feel?"

"Where's Carmen?" he asked. His throat was so dry.

The young man smiled. "You have some visitors outside. You can see them in a few minutes. You were shot. Do you remember that?"

Robert nodded. "How bad?" he asked.

"You're going to be fine. You were brought in an ambulance to the hospital and you had emergency surgery for a severed brachial artery. You almost bled out, sir. You're a lucky guy. Surgeon said you probably won't even have much residual shoulder damage."

Robert lifted up the sheet. He was in a hospital gown but that was it. "Where are my pants?" he asked.

"I imagine they took them off you before surgery," the nurse said. "You didn't become my patient until you came to the recovery room. I can check for you."

"I need my pants," Robert said.

"They're not going to do you any good," the nurse said. "You're not going anywhere for a few days."

"Please. Can you just go look? I had a ring in my pocket. I was going to ask someone to marry me."

The young man smiled. "I got married last summer," he said. "I'll go look. Just don't try to get out of bed on me, okay?"

He wasn't going anywhere. He wiggled his fingers, grateful that he still could.

Severed brachial artery. That explained it. One minute he'd been standing, then his vision had grayed, and he'd realized he was going down for the count.

He needed to talk to Carmen. She might never be able to forgive him but he had to know for sure that she and Raoul were okay.

The door opened a few minutes later and he expected to see the nurse. But it was Carmen with her silky-shiny hair and her beautiful face peeking around the corner. "Hi," she said.

He tried to sit up in bed.

"No," she said gently. "Be still. I just talked to the doctor. You've lost a lot of blood. By the way, your mother is here. She's been entertaining everyone in the waiting room."

He shook his head.

"She's lovely," Carmen said.

"Are you okay? Raoul?"

She leaned down and brushed a kiss across his cheek. "We are both fine. We wouldn't be, you know, if you'd been even a minute later. That man was about to cut Raoul's fingers off. I've never been so frightened in my life. He said that I had to watch, that that was my punishment."

"Oh, honey," he said. He swallowed hard. "I'm so sorry you had to go through that."

"You saved our lives, Robert. You're making a habit of that." She rubbed her hand across the blankets. "Raoul told me about Speedy's Used Cars. He shot those car windshields out. That monster was with him."

He licked his dry lips. "I should have said something. I didn't have any proof but I did have my suspicions. I guess I didn't want to burn Raoul. Subconsciously, I think I didn't push as hard as I might have because I wanted Raoul to trust me, to like me." He hesitated. "I knew his opinion about me would matter to you."

"I was so angry," she said softly. "So hurt."

"I'm sorry," he said. It was inadequate but the best he could do. "I screwed up." Robert used his good arm and rubbed the back of his palm against his forehead. He had a bitch of a headache.

"There's something I need to tell you," she said.

Could he bear it? He nodded.

"I had some time to think," she said, "while you were fighting for your life. It's amazing what something like that does for perspective. I love you, Robert. I want you to know that."

He could feel his heart start to beat fast and figured he was ten seconds away from the alarm on some machine starting to wail. "But—"

The door opened. The nurse stuck his head around the corner. "Sorry, sir. Pants weren't where I thought they'd be. It's possible your personal belongings were already sent up to a room. I'm checking now," he said. He pulled back and the door closed.

His ring was MIA. That wasn't stopping him.

"Carmen, this is totally the wrong place and the wrong time but I waited once before to ask you this question and I'm not going to make that mistake again. I love you, too. I want to help you raise Raoul. I want us to be a family." He took a breath. "I can't promise that I won't make any more mistakes, but I can promise that every day I'll be thankful that you and Raoul are in my life and I'll work hard to always earn your trust and your love."

She didn't say anything, but her dark brown eyes were big.

"I had a ring in my pants pocket that I've been carrying around for days but apparently I've managed to lose it," he said. "And I'm afraid getting down on one knee is out of the question. So I'm doing this all wrong."

She shook her head. Her eyes were shimmering with tears.

"You're doing it perfectly. Yes, yes. I will marry you." She raised her arm that had been at her side. In her hand was a plastic bag. He could see his shoes sticking out the end.

He grabbed the bag from her. With one arm, he pulled everything out of the bag. When he got to the pants, he stuck his hand into the pocket.

It was there.

He pulled it out and flipped open the hinge of the silver box. "Be my wife, Carmen. I love you."

She slipped the ring onto her finger. It fit perfectly. His heart soared.

"I love you, Robert."

It was amazing. A minute ago, a cannon going off couldn't have gotten him out of the bed. Now he felt as if he could run down the damn hallway. Carmen was going to be his wife. "Is Raoul here?"

She nodded. "Right outside."

"Can you get him? I want to tell him."

They were back within seconds. Carmen had her arm wrapped around the boy's shoulder.

"Raoul," Robert said, "I've got a question for you."

The boy nodded.

"Do you have any sheet music for the 'Wedding March'?"

The boy's dark eyes, the eyes that were so like his sister's, blinked fast. A grin broke across his face. "You guys are getting married?"

"Yes," Robert and Carmen spoke at the same time.

"How do you feel about that?" Carmen added.

"I think it's great. Really great." Raoul pulled his cell phone from his pocket. "I've got to call Jacob. He's going to bust a gut."

Epilogue

Carmen Jimenez and Robert Hanson were married three weeks later, on a sunny, yet chilly, February day. The bride wore a long white dress and the groom wore a black suit with his arm in a sling.

Raoul Jimenez played the trombone, accompanied by Jacob Minelli on the drums.

At the reception, the bride and groom danced the first dance, the second dance and the third dance together. At the end of the night, they took a limo to the airport, where they caught a flight to Jamaica. In his carry-on, the groom packed a travel-size container of spring soap. In her carry-on, the bride packed M&M'S and microwave popcorn.

While they were on their honeymoon, Raoul stayed with Liz and Sawyer Montgomery and worked at Speedy's Used Cars, making restitution for broken windshields.

* * * * *

A sneaky peek at next month...

INTRIGUE...

BREATHTAKING ROMANTIC SUSPENSE

My wish list for next month's titles...

In stores from 17th January 2014:

- ❑ Undercover Captor – Cynthia Eden
- & Rocky Mountain Revenge – Cindi Myers
- ❑ Blood on Copperhead Trail – Paula Graves
- & Rancher Rescue – Barb Han
- ❑ Tennessee Takedown – Lena Diaz
- & Raven's Hollow – Jenna Ryan

Romantic Suspense

- ❑ Cavanaugh Hero – Marie Ferrarella

Available at WHSmith, Tesco, Asda, Eason, Amazon and Apple

Just can't wait?

0114/46

Special Offers

Every month we put together collections and longer reads written by your favourite authors.

Here are some of next month's highlights— and don't miss our fabulous discount online!

On sale 7th February   On sale 17th January   On sale 7th February

Save 20%
on all Special Releases

Find out more at
www.millsandboon.co.uk/specialreleases

Visit us Online

0214/ST/MB456

Join the Mills & Boon Book Club

Subscribe to **Intrigue** today for 3, 6 or 12 months and you could **save over £40!**

We'll also treat you to these fabulous extras:

- 🌹 **FREE L'Occitane gift set worth £10**
- 🌹 **FREE home delivery**
- 🌹 **Rewards scheme, exclusive offers…and much more!**

Subscribe now and save over £40
www.millsandboon.co.uk/subscribeme

SUBS/OFFER/I1

Discover more romance at

www.millsandboon.co.uk

- ❤ WIN great prizes in our exclusive competitions
- ❤ BUY new titles before they hit the shops
- ❤ BROWSE new books and REVIEW your favourites
- ❤ SAVE on new books with the Mills & Boon® Bookclub™
- ❤ DISCOVER new authors

PLUS, to chat about your favourite reads, get the latest news and find special offers:

- 🅵 Find us on facebook.com/millsandboon
- 🐦 Follow us on twitter.com/millsandboonuk
- ❤ Sign up to our newsletter at millsandboon.co.uk

EB_SD